Mothering Psyc

MOTHERING PSYCHOANALYSIS

HELENE DEUTSCH, KAREN HORNEY, ANNA FREUD AND MELANIE KLEIN

Janet Sayers

HAMISH HAMILTON
LONDON

HAMISH HAMILTON LTD

Published by the Penguin Group
27 Wrights Lane, London W8 5TZ, England
Viking Penguin, a division of Penguin Books USA Inc.,
375 Hudson Street, New York, New York 10014, USA
Penguin Books Australia Ltd, Ringwood, Victoria, Australia
Penguin Books Canada Ltd, 2801 John Street, Markham, Ontario, Canada L3R 1B4
Penguin Books (NZ) Ltd, 182–190 Wairau Road, Auckland 10, New Zealand

Penguin Books Ltd, Registered Offices: Harmondsworth, Middlesex, England

First published 1991
1 3 5 7 9 10 8 6 4 2

Filmset in Monophoto Melior
Printed in England by Clays Ltd, St Ives plc

A CIP catalogue record for this book is available from the British Library

ISBN 0-241-129451

For my mother,
Shirley Toulson

Everything in the sphere of this first attachment to the mother seemed to me so difficult to grasp in analysis – so grey with age and shadowy and almost impossible to revivify – that it was as if it had succumbed to an especially inexorable repression. But perhaps I gained this impression because the women who were in analysis with me were able to cling to the very attachment to the father in which they had taken refuge from the early phase that was in question. It does indeed appear that women analysts . . . have been able to perceive these facts more easily and clearly because they were helped in dealing with those under their treatment by the transference to a suitable mother-substitute.

(Sigmund Freud, 1931)

Contents

IV. ANNA FREUD

V. MELANIE KLEIN

VI. CONCLUSION

List of illustrations

Pitlochry
SCOTLAND
Edinburgh
NORTH SEA
IRELAND
WALES
ENGLAND
LONDON
THE NETHERLAN
AMSTERDAM
The Hague
BRUSSELS
BELGIU
ATLANTIC OCEAN
PARIS
LUXEMBOURG
FRANCE
Lyons
MONACO
ANDORRA
Marseilles
PORTUGAL
MADRID
LISBON
SPAIN
BALEARIC ISLANDS
MEDITERRANEAN SEA

NORWAY
OSLO
SWEDEN
STOCKHOLM
BALTIC SEA
RUSSIA
DENMARK
COPENHAGEN
Danzig
Hamburg
Bremen
BERLIN
GERMANY
WARSAW
POLAND
Göttingen
Dresden
Freiburg
Frankfurt
Silesia
Krappitz
PRAGUE
Würzburg
Przemyśl
Lwów
Bohemia
Galicia
Rosenberg
Moravia
Lucerne
Munich
VIENNA
TATRA MOUNTAINS
Berchtesgaden
LIECHTENSTEIN
Salzburg
Semmering
Zürich
Innsbruck
BUDAPEST
Austria
VITZERLAND
Tirol
Graz
Hungary
Siebenbürgen
Krain
AUSTRO-HUNGARY
ROMANIA
Abbazia
Croatia
BELGRADE
BUCHAREST
noa
ITALY
Bosnia-Herzegovina
Sarajevo
SERBIA
Dalmatia
SOFIA
BULGARIA
CORSICA
ROME
MONTE-NEGRO
ALBANIA
SARDINIA
GREECE

Acknowledgements

First and foremost my thanks to the following for reading parts or all of the manuscript in draft: Maggie Cartridge, Diane Cunningham, Martin Deutsch, Elspeth Earle, Mary Evans, Andrew Franklin, Sanford Gifford, Bob Hinshelwood, Douglas Ingram, Annie Lee, Caroline New, and Kate Osborne. Whether or not they agree with the final result, their detailed comments, criticisms, encouragement, and support have been invaluable.

Many thanks also to my sons and husband, patients and colleagues, students and teachers in Canterbury and at the Tavistock Clinic and the British Association of Psychotherapists in London, from whom I have learnt so much; to the Ferguson-Colyer Award for funding my visit to Boston and New York and to those there who shared with me their first-hand knowledge of the life and work of Helene Deutsch and Karen Horney; to the Schlesinger Library, Cambridge, Massachusetts, and the Wellcome Institute for the History of Medicine, London; and to fellow-lecturers at the University of Kent for giving me study leave to complete this book.

J.S.

The author and publishers would like to thank the Institute of Psycho-Analysis and The Hogarth Press for permission to quote from *The Standard Edition of the Complete Works of Sigmund Freud*, translated and edited by James Strachey; and to Basic Books for permission to quote from *The Adolescent Diaries of Karen Horney*.

I

INTRODUCTION
From patriarchy to mothering

Psychoanalysis has been turned upside down. Once patriarchal and phallocentric, it is now almost entirely mother-centred. Its focus has shifted from the past and individual issues concerning patriarchal power, repression, resistance, knowledge, sex and castration, to the present and interpersonal issues concerning maternal care and its vicissitudes – identification, idealization and envy, deprivation and loss, love and hate, introjection and projection.

Mothering Psychoanalysis tells the story of this revolution through the biographies of its first women architects – Helene Deutsch, Karen Horney, Anna Freud and Melanie Klein – all of whom lived and worked first in German-speaking and Eastern Europe before it was divided by today's now opening up frontiers (see map on p. x), and then in England and the USA where they were scattered by war and its precursors both within and outside psychoanalysis.

All four were major figures in the early institutions of psychoanalysis. Deutsch was instrumental in founding and was the first director of the Vienna Psychoanalytic Training Institute. Horney was the first woman member of the Berlin Psychoanalytic Clinic when it began in 1920. Anna Freud established Vienna as the first centre of child analysis. And Klein was the first to start England's distinctive British school of psychoanalysis.

But their importance to psychoanalysis is not only to its institutions. Far, far more important and long-lasting was their work in pioneering the expansion of the scope of psychoanalysis to include narcissistic personality disorders, character analysis, ego psychology, and the treatment of depressive and schizoid as well as neurotic conditions in children and adults. In the process they drew attention to the interpersonal and maternal determinants of our psychology so scandalously overlooked by Freud. In this, I shall argue, all four used their own mothering experience and that of their patients, which they elicited and to which they were sensitized by the social equation of women with mothering, whether or not they have children. They thereby initiated the psychoanalytic focus on mothering, now unfortunately often rather one-dimensional, of today's women and men analysts and psychotherapists alike.

Before detailing the mothering aspects of each woman's work in the following chapters, what of psychoanalysis's patriarchal beginnings? Why was Freud's work so father-centred? What does it mean to say that modern psychoanalysis is mother-centred? And why is its current gynocentrism so widely adopted by feminists, often to the neglect of the variations of women's mothering so well illustrated by the lives of psychoanalysis's four 'founding mothers' and their child and adult patients?

First, and by way of introduction to the theoretical and clinical foundations of this quartet's development of psychoanalysis,[1] what of its father-centred origins? It is usually dated as beginning with the forty-year-old Freud's discovery of the unconscious and infantile sexuality – the twin hallmarks of psychoanalysis – in the course of his self-analysis around the time of his father's death in October 1896. Certainly Freud then abandoned his previous view that hysteria is the effect of childhood sexual abuse by a nurse or governess, or by an older sibling themselves a victim of such abuse.

Analysis of his own dreams and the childhood memories they revived persuaded Freud that hysteria and neurosis stem not so much from any actual abuse as from unconscious fantasies first constructed in infancy out of the child's own incestuous wishes – oral, anal, and phallic – and their patriarchal repression into the unconscious. Writing almost exactly a year after his father's death to his Berlin confidant Wilhelm Fliess, Freud announced: 'I have found love of the mother and jealousy of the father in my own case too, and now believe it to be a general phenomenon of early childhood.'[2] Hence, he went on, the gripping power of *Oedipus Rex* and *Hamlet*, with their evocation of this childhood complex and its repression.

Again and again Freud's personal preoccupations, at least as recounted in his first book of psychoanalysis, *The Interpretation of Dreams*, involved rivalry with patriarchal figures represented by his professional colleagues. Other dreams revealed his desire as a father for his older daughter Mathilde, and his 'wish to catch a father as the originator of neurosis'.[3]

This wish seemed likely to come true. Again and again his patients dwelt on their fathers in association to their symptoms. Indeed all Freud's major case histories – Dora, Little Hans, the Rat Man, Schreber, the Wolf Man, and a case of female homosexuality – centre on the father. Eighteen-year-old Dora, for instance, dwelt on her continuing desire to have her father to herself, and on childhood memories of him getting her up at night as a child to prevent her wetting the bed. The Rat Man, a soldier in his late twenties, recalled in his very first sessions with Freud his childhood fear lest were he to indulge his sexual wish to see a woman naked his father would die. The worries that now brought him for treatment included an obsessive fear lest, were he not to discharge a debt for having his glasses mended, his father would be subjected to an Eastern torture whereby a basin of rats is inverted on the victim's buttocks so as to bore into his anus.

Only by interpreting the patient's free associations to such ideas, Freud maintained, is it possible to make conscious and thus free their sexuality from being held back – through regression and fixation – to past wishes and fears, dreams and nightmares both for, and of, the father. But, he found, patients resisted this process of free association not least because they transferred on to him the full force of their childhood love and resistance to the father. Indeed Dora dismissed Freud, as her father might have dismissed a servant, when he thwarted her wishes as her father had before him. Similarly the Rat Man heaped the grossest abuse on Freud as on his father, albeit only in imagination, not directly, lest Freud, like his father, beat him.

Generalizing from such cases, Freud described how patients regularly feared and rebelled against him, or fell in love with him as they had with their fathers as children. Either way these negative and positive 'transference' feelings prevented them following his fundamental rule of freely telling him whatever came into their mind. Indeed, Dora's negative transference was so powerful that she prematurely quit therapy, her embitterment against her father and men generally thus remaining intact, to stalk her to the end of her days.

Only by interpreting and putting into words such feelings as transferred on to the analyst, argued Freud, is it possible to forestall their being acted out as in Dora's case. Thereby contained by the analyst's interpretations, the transference then has the inestimable advantage of bringing the past into present consciousness, emotionally as well as intellectually. Attending increasingly to patients' transference feelings about him, Freud maintained that these feelings regularly centred on childhood rivalry with the father for love of the mother or, in the case of women, rivalry with the mother for love of the father. Indeed, he claimed that this Oedipal constellation constitutes the heart of all neurosis. He attributed, for instance, his eighteen-year-old female homosexual patient's lesbianism to her flaunting it to embarrass and thereby avenge herself on her father (just as she rebelled against Freud in therapy) for preferring her mother, as indicated by his making her pregnant yet again just three years previously.

In his 1905 book, *Three Essays on the Theory of Sexuality*, Freud attributed our general unawareness of such Oedipal rivalry and desire to its repression into the unconscious because of the conscious ego's recognition of society's taboo on incest. Later, drawing on the analysis of Little Hans by his father, and on the Rat and Wolf Men's patriarchal transference on to him, Freud concluded that the Oedipus complex is brought to an end by the castration complex.

The little boy, he suggested, fears lest the father punish his sexual desire with castration. All the more so because his masturbation is punished in the name of patriarchal authority. Hans's mother, for instance, threatened: 'If you do that, I shall send for Dr A to cut off your widdler.'[4] No wonder Hans interpreted his younger sister Hanna's lack of a penis as the effect of castration. The boy's resulting fear for his masculine identity and individuality – his castration complex – is only overcome, Freud wrote, through superego identification with the father's authority in the hope of later acquiring his status. Five-year-old Hans, for instance, consoled himself with the thought that one day he too would have as big a penis as his father.

Many years later Freud described the interminability of therapy in cases where patients unconsciously equate submission to cure by the analyst with castration by the father. He referred in his account of this 'negative therapeutic reaction' to his treatment of the Wolf Man, whom he had previously described at length, particularly the analytic reconstruction, via a childhood dream of being watched by wolves, of the patient as a baby himself watching his parents' sexual intercourse, his father penetrating his mother from behind so he could see she had no penis.

If the boy fears a similar fate befalling him through castration by the father, the reverse, claimed Freud, is true of girls. He concluded from his women patients' experience of him as father-figure that girls respond to the discovery of genital sex difference by wanting to become like boys – to gain a penis from the father. Indeed, he suggested that such penis envy was allied to feminism at least in the case of his lesbian patient whom he described as:

> A spirited girl ... not at all prepared to be second to her slightly older brother; after inspecting his genital organs she had developed a pronounced envy for the penis ... She was in fact a feminist ... and rebelled against the lot of women in general.[5]

Blaming the mother for their phallic lack, Freud hazarded, girls turn from her to the father in the hope of getting from him a penis – or its unconscious equivalent, a baby. The girl's penis envy or castration complex, Freud maintained, thus initiates rather than ends the Oedipus complex, as in boys. Girls, he said, therefore do not have the same reason to abandon the latter complex or to identify with the father and the social authority and morality he represents. Hence, Freud tendentiously concluded, women's weaker superego, deficient sense of justice, greater subjectivity, and lack of submission 'to the great exigencies of life'.[6]

Freud's sexism as much as his sex shaped the patriarchal and phallocentric bias of his theory and therapy. Not only did his sex, indeed his status with time as grand old man of psychoanalysis, elicit his patients' memories of their fathers. In a sense, and unlike subsequent male analysts, Freud also courted such reminiscences through his patriarchal stance in therapy. Certainly he wanted authority over his patients. Indeed one of the reasons he abandoned the use of hypnosis in treatment was because his patients resisted his authority in trying to hypnotize them. Even after he gave up hypnosis for free association he still felt, as he acknowledged to his analysand Abram Kardiner, that he was too much the father with his patients. 'I do not like to be the mother in the transference,' he told another patient, the symbolist poet HD, 'it always surprises and shocks me a little. I feel so very masculine.'[7]

But his patriarchal bias was not only due to his sex and personal predilection. It also spoke to the centrality – in male-dominated society – of the father as first representative in the child's mind of power, sexual repression, and knowledge, however much the father deviates or demurs from this attribution in reality. Not for nothing children still describe the father as 'boss', even though, as in the case of Little Hans, women often exercise more immediate authority over their day-to-day lives, so much more are they involved in childcare.

Children continue to experience the father as lawgiver – as arbiter of truth and justice, crime and punishment – even when this is quite inappropriate. Melanie Klein's analysand, the analyst Wilfred Bion, recounts just such an instance in his autobiography. Recalling church services at school – 'Sermons, the Headmaster, God, The Father Almighty, Arf Arfer Oo Arf in Mphm, please make me a good boy' – Bion goes on to describe an occasion when, at his wits' end after repeatedly pleading with his father to admire a vase of flowers he had arranged, he finally added:

> 'I'm not lying Daddy. I did it all myself.'
>
> That stopped him in his tracks. He was upset. 'Why did you say that?'
>
> 'What Daddy?'
>
> 'I never expected you to be lying.'
>
> 'Well, I wasn't,' I replied becoming afraid that Arf Arfer would appear. Arf Arfer was very frightening.[8]

Doubtless children too readily fear the father and his seeming power. Nevertheless the social dominance of men eliciting such images of the father as powerful and punitive patriarch live on. Yet it is Bion's emphasis on the analyst 'containing' the analysand's anxieties, as he says the mother takes in and digests her baby's fears and worries, that is now much more widely known and adopted by analysts and psychotherapists. Indeed, although couched in very obscure terms, Bion's later work comparing psychoanalysis to early mothering and 'maternal reverie' is now enjoying increasing vogue among therapists and feminists alike.

Much more generally adopted – and this for many years now – is the mother-centred work of other British and US psychoanalysts such as Donald Winnicott, W. R. D. Fairbairn, Margaret Mahler, and Heinz Kohut, and their account of the way patients sometimes treat the analyst as no different from themselves, just as the baby apparently has no sense of itself as separate from the mother.

Also influential is Fairbairn's account of patients' experience of the therapist as tantalizing or forbidding mother – a bifurcated image first internalized, Fairbairn maintained, as a means of mastering maternal frustration in infancy. Similarly Melanie Klein's sometime student, Donald Winnicott, wrote of babies faced with abandonment by a depressed or self-absorbed mother developing a compliant 'false-self' façade behind which their 'true self' goes into hiding. And Anna Freud's colleague, Heinz Kohut, described the phoney grandiosity that develops when the mother fails empathically to mirror and laud the baby's nascent narcissism through celebrating him as 'His Majesty the baby'. Indeed Kohut re-analysed one of his patients in these maternal terms, having first understood his problems in the light of Freud's father-centred, Oedipal theory of neurosis.

Something of the flavour and variety of this post-Freudian, mothering approach to therapy can be gleaned from therapist Harry Guntrip's account of his own analysis, first with Fairbairn and then with Winnicott. He recounts Fairbairn's formal, somewhat austere, precise, and distant manner – exacerbated by the death of his first wife – and the way it elicited Guntrip's memories of battles for his mother's warmth and attention following the death of his two-year-old brother Percy when Harry himself was only three. By contrast, Winnicott's more relaxed approach to therapy enabled Harry to retrieve memories of a much earlier period when his mother had been more responsive. It also enabled him to bear recalling his feelings on first being abandoned by her subsequent emotional withdrawal both from Percy and himself as a toddler, so drained was she by mothering her numerous brothers and sisters as a child.

This mothering approach to therapy has proved immensely appealing – not least to feminists. How much more attractive than Freud's masculine and apparently aloof, rationalistic and patriarchal stance in therapy, it has seemed to many, the empathic, warm, and maternal approach of Winnicott. It is even argued that mother-centred therapy is preferable because mothering is inherently egalitarian and thus dissolves the usual hierarchies of society – of father and child, therapist and patient.

Not only that. The mothering approach to therapy of Winnicott and others is also often preferred because it attends so much more than Freud to the importance of mother-love, and to the all too real effects of its deprivation, loss, and abuse – realities of which Freud seemingly lost sight with his abandonment of his early seduction theory of neurosis. Mother-oriented therapy, unlike Freud's theory and therapy, recognizes the very real importance of women in shaping our psychology –

not least because of the continuing social assignment to them of childcare, of overseeing the earliest and seemingly most psychologically formative phase of our life. Indeed, women's childcare, often justified in terms of their childbearing, is a far more real aspect of sexual difference and inequality and the complaints and disorders to which it gives rise than the phallic difference so emphasized by Freud.

Most of all, feminists have been attracted to mother-centred psychoanalysis because it apparently valorizes women's work, at least as mothers. The therapist as mother, recommends feminist counsellor Jocelyn Chaplin, strengthens women by enabling them to journey back to reconnect with their power in childbearing and childrearing. Furthermore, this return seems to promise women the means of recapturing the earliest psychological unity, described by Winnicott, of mother and infant. And this in turn seems to some to offer the foundation on which to build the identification and solidarity between women necessary to their challenging the oppression they collectively suffer as a sex.

Paradoxically, however, in adopting psychoanalysis's current attention to mothering because of its woman-centredness, feminists and others are often unaware of its origins in women's work – in that of Helene Deutsch, Karen Horney, Anna Freud and Melanie Klein. Yet their work is vital. This is not least because, in drawing attention to mothering, they seldom lost sight of the patriarchal determinants of our psychology as is so often the case in today's psychoanalysis and feminism, as though it were not possible to keep in mind both patriarchal and maternal factors – without subsuming one within the other – as independent but related in our biological and psychological genesis.

Not that feminists entirely overlook our psychology's patriarchal determinants. Quite the reverse. The women's movement of the 1970s spent much time and energy exposing in order to undo the wrongs done women by patriarchy. As part of this process Juliet Mitchell, in her book *Psychoanalysis and Feminism*, showed the relevance of Freud for understanding the way we situate ourselves, via the Oedipus and castration complex, as male or female in relation to patriarchal authority as signified by the phallus. Since then others have also used Freud's account of sexed identity to emphasize its shifting and precarious character, and the differences between women not least in mothering.

Many more, however, now pursue the opposite tack of stressing the essential sameness of women as a sex. They often join those who reject Freudian psychoanalysis altogether because of the harm it does women in reducing their every interest – feminism, work, sexuality, and so on – to an effect of phallic lack and Oedipal desire for the father. It was as though, for Freud, women had no other stirring independent of the father and his penis, no desire arising from their own biological and social being including that involved in mothering. He entirely neglected the way desire is transmitted to the daughter, among other things, by the mother's desire, or its lack, as described today by French psychoanalysts Luce Irigaray and Christiane Olivier in the wake of Helene Deutsch – one of the first analysts to attend to the mother's as well as to the child's desire.

The job of exposing patriarchy's ills seemingly done, however, Irigaray and others have begun to develop an alternative mother-centred theory and practice as if attention to mothering of itself guaranteed this project's service to feminism. US feminist Elaine Showalter, for instance, after charting the abuses done women by the paternalism of nineteenth- and twentieth-century psychiatry and psychoanalysis, concludes without further explanation: 'The best hope for the future is the feminist therapy movement [and its] analysis of the mother-daughter relation'.[9]

Just such a switch of attention from patriarchy to mothering characterizes feminist critiques of Freud's treatment of Dora. Many have pointed out Freud's phallocentrism in this case – his focus on Dora's supposed unconscious wish to suck at her father's penis as she recalled sucking her thumb as a child. Freud, it has been demonstrated, colluded despite himself with the wish of Dora's father to have her submit sexually to his friend Herr K so that he could continue his own liaison with Herr K's wife. Others, by contrast, have taken Freud to task less for his patriarchalism than for his neglect of mothering in Dora's case – for writing off her mother as an obsessional housewife without reference (except in footnotes) to Dora's desire for her or for Frau K, also a mother. As if to bolster his own male ego, Freud seemed more intent on persuading Dora of her desire for her father and Herr K. Certainly he insisted on the latter's 'prepossessing' masculine good looks.

Generalizing from such cases, Luise Eichenbaum and Susie Orbach, co-founders in 1976 of the London Women's Therapy Centre, characterize Freudian therapy as seeking to coerce women into Oedipal and heterosexual desire through disqualifying their early desire for the mother as unrealizable pre-Oedipal longing. Rather than subject women in therapy to the prevalent male narcissism, authority, and abuse of our society, they urge therapists to validate and meet their women patients' otherwise repressed and unacknowledged craving for the mothering of which they were often starved in infancy. This, they say, means undoing the defences resulting from mothers, having learned in our currently sexually unequal society to sacrifice themselves to others, losing sight of their own needs both in themselves and as seemingly reflected in their daughters. Denied legitimizing recognition, Eichenbaum and Orbach argue, the daughter's needs retreat behind an outward, mother-directed, 'false self' façade – as Winnicott might have put it. The business of feminist therapy thus becomes one of undoing this mother–daughter defence as relived in the therapist–patient dyad.

Feminist therapist Mira Dana likewise understands women's eating disorders as effect of the mother's failure to validate her daughter's need. This, she suggests, is the cause of anorexic refusal of need, compulsive eating as an attempt to staunch it in ignorance of what is really wanted, and bulimia as the obsession with no sooner indulging than expelling all need, so repellent does it become on being fed.

Dana's colleague Sheila Ernst also attributes many of women's psychological ills to maternal factors – to the initial identification of mother and child whereby, as Winnicott puts it, the child identifies with the mother just as the latter, through a process of 'primary maternal preoccupation', identifies with the child. Ernst also points out, however, that such identification often persists because our society provides women with so little opportunity to realize themselves outside mothering and the identification it involves. As a therapist she seeks to undo the harm done women in remaining identified with, and wedded to, their mother's image of them since infancy. Examples include three patients: Angela, still imprisoned within her mother's early image of her as there to satisfy her; Mary, who remains identified with the distressed and occasionally mad mother of her childhood; and Evelyn, still held in check by her mother's picture of her as a sick baby, this being the only way she felt able to mother Evelyn.

Feminist theory, as well as feminist therapy, also adopts post-Freudian accounts of the baby's initial identification and fusion with the mother. US sociologist Nancy Chodorow, for instance, explains sexual inequality and its reproduction in these terms. She argues that the infant's initial psychological oneness with the mother, as described by Winnicott, is particularly long-lasting in girls because they are biologically the same as the mother. Girls accordingly grow up, she says, ready to identify in turn with their babies just as Winnicott deems necessary, to 'good enough' mothering. Not so boys. Chodorow maintains that they quickly negate their initial sense of oneness with the mother in the interests of forging a separate, masculine identity. In the process, she says, they grow up with the individuated and more impersonal traits necessary to occupational work. In sum, she claims, women's mothering reproduces the existing division of labour whereby men work while women mother.

Others have adopted this mothering perspective to characterize sex differences in science. Physicist Evelyn Fox Keller, for instance, argues that women remain more psychically merged and interdependent with the mother and are therefore more attuned as scientists to interdependence in nature. Men scientists, by contrast, she maintains, because of their earlier individuation from the mother, tend to have a more in dividuated, atomistic approach, relatively blind to the interplay and interaction of the things they study.

Certainly – whatever may be claimed to the contrary – science reflects the social, biological, and psychological being and interests of its practitioners. And this is doubtless shaped, among other things, by their mothering. Scientists are arguably no different in this from psychoanalysts and feminists, although to the glee of their detractors the latter have always been much more candid about the personal and parental roots of their theory and practice.

But there are major problems with the current celebration of mothering – both in feminist theories of science and society and in feminist therapy – whereby women are paraded as more empathic and at one with others simply by virtue of the mothering of their sex. Mothering is thereby falsely idealized as though – but for those who become alienated from their needs by existing sex inequalities, or who are too wrapped up in their own concerns or malaise – women generally identify with and thereby meet their children's every need, at least initially. But, as both Karen Horney and Melanie Klein long ago pointed out, this idea is more a product of infant fantasy than actually realizable in reality.

Women have too long been held hostage to ideals of mothering they cannot possibly fulfil. Indeed, Klein herself has often been vilified as a monster for drawing attention – through her life and work – to the negative as well as the positive aspects of mothering. For too long women have been pilloried for falling short of our ideals of mothering as though this alone were the cause of children's and society's ills – including, it now seems, the reproduction of existing social inequalities between the sexes. Such mother-blaming, however much it is dressed up as feminism, hardly serves women's interests, not least because it loses sight of the patriarchal and wider social factors that also condition our lives, mothering included. In this it works against the feminist project of drawing attention to the latter factors, and of exploding the myths about women and their mothering that otherwise stand in the way of women's needs being recognized and met, actually and in fact.

A corollary of the idealization of mothering – underlying much post-Freudian psychoanalysis and its feminist appropriation – is failure adequately to attend to its variations, good as well as bad. It is, of course, all too easy to be mesmerized by the uniformity of the biology and social oppression of women and mothers into overlooking the changing character of mothering cross-culturally, historically, and over the course of each woman's lifetime. And indeed the constants and similarities in women's mothering experience – both biologically and social – have been a major source of the solidarity of women's movements across the world, both now and in the past.

But if this solidarity is to be based on something more substantial than the apparent sameness of women as a sex – including the illusory psychological identity of mothers and children – it also has to take on board the differences between women (and indeed between men, as Guntrip's example illustrates) in their social and maternal being. This brings me back to this book's principal characters. In a sense the following chapters adopt the recent feminist view that women draw on their mothering experience in advancing science in a more inter-relational direction. However, whereas Keller and others assume the essential uniformity of women's mothering experience – as regards identification and empathy with children and the world in general – I shall be emphasizing the way Helene Deutsch, Karen Horney, Anna Freud and Melanie Klein drew on quite different mothering experience in advancing psychoanalysis.

True, they all grew up in turn-of-the-century, German-speaking Europe, and all four emigrated westwards. But, within the commonalities of their shared white middle-class upbringing in imperial Austro-Hungary and Germany followed by not dissimilar wartime and post-war eventualities, they differed considerably from each other in their mothering experience. This, of course, raises questions regarding the validity of the conclusions each drew from her own particular version of this experience about psychology in general. Indeed, an overwhelming impression gained from reading their biographies and work is that there may well be as many psychologies as there are psychologists. Nevertheless there is an important and common interpersonal and maternal core to their development of psychoanalysis, albeit each attended to different aspects of mothering – whether that of identification, idealization and envy, deprivation and loss, or introjection and projection.

The book starts with Helene Deutsch's focus on identification arising out of her hatred of her mother, her consequent flight from self-demeaning identity with her, and consequent difficulties in becoming a mother herself. Nor was Deutsch alone in this. The social devaluation of women and mothering she so much suffered persists. And with it the problems thereby posed women's sexuality and self-esteem – both in sanity and madness – as described by Deutsch in the first ever psychoanalytic book devoted to women's psychology. Often dismissed by feminists and others as nothing but a dreary exponent of Freudian phallocentrism, Deutsch turns out to have been very alive to political and social questions and to have taken issue with Freud. She went well beyond him in drawing attention to and illustrating the vagaries of maternal and parental identification – now taken up by followers of Heinz Kohut and others – in a host of detailed case histories of both mothers and children, women and men.

Not so Karen Horney. Certainly her celebration of mothering and femininity is a refreshing antidote to Deutsch's focus on its repudiation. Not for nothing Horney's work remains much more popular, especially with feminists, than that of Deutsch. Yet it lacks any of the latter's clinical detail. Instead it veers from complacent biologism, through bland sociological generality, to a plea for complete self-sufficient individualism. Perhaps Horney's childhood identification with her mother against her father led her to take for granted the feminine identity and self-realizing individuality that Deutsch recognized from her own case to be so problematic. On the other hand, Horney's adoration of her mother and pleasure in becoming a mother herself alerted her, unlike Deutsch, to men's idealization, envy, and defensive denigration of mothering, and to this as a cause of women's flight from femininity. As her own children became older, Horney dwelt increasingly on the way her mother incited her childhood admiration. And this informed her later work on the character disorders – particularly the compulsive striving for love and power – resulting from the childhood hurts bred of parental narcissism and abuse. She thus heralded today's work in this area by Alice Miller and others. Horney herself, however, eventually focused on present character trends almost to the total neglect of their past determinants, including those involved in early mothering.

After thus telling the story of Deutsch and Horney and the way they used their differing mothering experience to initiate current interest in narcissistic personality disorders and character analysis in adults, the second half of the book recounts the biographies of Anna Freud and Melanie Klein, to show how they drew on quite different experiences of being mothered and mothering to pioneer child analysis, ego psychology, and object relations theory.

Alone of all four women Anna seems almost totally to have ignored her mother, so captivated was she with seeking to gain the affection of her father, to whom she remained arguably the most faithful disciple to the end of her days. Not only did she seemingly seek to efface her mother from her mind. She was also most self-effacing and self-abnegating towards her father and his favourite daughter Sophie. This experience in turn informed her early work on adolescent girls' beating fantasies and her description, for the first time in psychoanalysis, of the ego's defence of 'altruistic surrender' and its obverse – 'identification with the aggressor'. In many ways her work was guilty of rather mechanical repetition of her father's later theory of the ego's control over the id – in which she lost sight of the sexual verve and imagination that so enlivened his early account of the unconscious. On the other hand, as I shall explain, Anna also went much further than him once she became involved in mothering – at least in helping bring up the children of her life-long companion Dorothy Burlingham, and later children from London's badly bombed and impoverished East End. Her vicarious involvement in, and matter-of-fact approach to mothering which she so rejected for herself, and her grief at her own mother's death in 1951, informed her pioneering work in child analysis, in which she movingly drew the attention of psychoanalysts and others – through a mine of examples – to the maternal environment necessary to children's emotional, social, and language development. In this she emphasized the ill-effects of maternal anxiety, separation, and loss suffered by children in war, sickness, and family breakdown – as also later recounted by Winnicott, Bowlby, and others.

If Anna Freud attended to the externals of mothering, Melanie Klein attended more to its internal effects. While Anna's case histories are a model of clarity and light, Klein's are filled with dark foreboding. In this they arguably reflect Klein's enmeshed relation with her mother and her own children, and the depression therein involved. This led to her own analysis and to her analysing children, beginning with her own. She thereby discovered the child's very early Oedipal rivalry with, and envy of, the mother's sexual relation with the father. In turn both her own and her patients' intensely ambivalent mothering experience alerted her to the admixture of love and hate, incorporation and expulsion, destruction and reparation, triumph and control, envious spoiling and gratitude for early mothering that lives on in the images peopling the inner world of child and adult creativity, depression, and schizoid states of mind. Klein thereby immensely extended the account of the contents of the unconscious first put forward by Freud in *The Interpretation of Dreams*.

Her work marks the culmination of all four women's use of their mothering experience – whether that of loathing, adoration, rejection, or ambivalence – in transforming the psychoanalytic theory and practice bequeathed by Freud. Their work has in turn been developed into today's mother-centred psychoanalysis often to the neglect of the father – a point to which the last chapter returns. It also deals with the problem of the individuation of self from other, initially of self from mother, raised by today's mother-centred, interpersonal alternative to Freud's patriarchal individualism. Now, however, without more ado, to this book's main purpose – the details of the work and lives of Deutsch, Horney, Anna Freud, Klein, and their patients, all too long eclipsed by the life and case histories of psychoanalysis's founding father, and by today's mothering psychoanalysis that these women began.

Helene Deutsch with her son Martin, 1934

II

HELENE DEUTSCH

1

Socialist rebel

To begin at the beginning. Helene Deutsch was the first leading woman member of Freud's Vienna Society. She was also one of the first to use her mothering experience – and its personal conflicts in her own case, to which she attributed her youthful socialism – to pioneer today's psychoanalytic attention to the place of identification with others, beginning with the mother, in personality formation and disorders of narcissistic self-esteem.

Born Helene Rosenbach on 9 October 1884 in Przemyśl – an old, medium-sized garrison town in Polish-speaking Galicia, on the Ukrainian border of the Austro-Hungarian Empire – she said in old age that she always hated her mother, Regina: 'She was a mean woman, and I did not want to be like her.'[1] No wonder. Regina beat her

> not to punish me, but as an outlet for her own pent-up aggressions. She let me feel the full force of the grudge she bore me for not being the boy she had wanted and expected.[2]

But although she felt her mother regarded her as 'poison', she also longed to be loved by her. Regina was thirty when Helene was born the youngest of four children. Her sisters Malvina and Gizela were then eleven and seven, and her brother Emil ten years old.

They lived in a 'grandiose' second-floor flat above their paternal grandmother and her daughters – Sonja and Frania – who, together with the apartment block's other residents, later peopled Helene's clinical writing. The mysterious Mrs Nawska, for example – the made-up 'pale countess' – who dressed her illegitimate daughter in ornate clothes and supported her by fortune-telling and teaching French. Helene remembered her as mothering her and the other neighbourhood children much more tenderly and interestingly than their own mothers.

In the first place, however, Helene recalled being mothered by 'nine different nurses'. As for her own mother, she so hated feeling dependent on her that she daydreamed that someone else was her real mother. She felt most truly mothered by her older sister Malvina, whom she later idealized as being known for her good works throughout Przemyśl as 'holy Malvina'.

Malvina, like Helene, was also a victim of their mother's pressure on her daughters to marry well. Forced by their maternal grandfather to give up the Christian army officer she loved, Malvina instead married someone more in keeping with her family's taste, a Jewish lawyer from Rzeszów, near Krakow. For Helene it was a bitter tragedy: 'There is a Polish saying . . . "When a girl becomes a wife, she is buried alive." I certainly felt that way, and so (I believe) did Malvina.'[3]

Helene was ten. Without Malvina and her beloved Aunt Frania, who married three years later, Helene felt bereft of all mothering. Her other sister Gizela – 'unquestionably my mother's favourite' – was more involved with other girls her own age, and when Helene was eleven she too became engaged – to a young doctor, Michael Oller.

Their brother Emil was no solace. He had sexually abused Helene when she was a toddler. In a later, thinly disguised autobiographical account of the affair,[4] Helene described how Emil continued to torment her through her childhood. As a teenager, she said, she relived the pleasurable aspect of this illicit and masochistic relationship through telling everyone of a torrid love affair in which she was very much the sufferer, and of the rendezvous, impassioned letters, and presents she invented receiving from her supposed student lover, thereby earning herself the dubious distinction of 'fallen woman'.

Meanwhile, she said, Emil's poor schoolwork disappointed his parents' wish to have 'a great man for a son'. Instead he became a gambler and profiteer, abandoned the family's Jewish faith to become a Christian, adopted a Polish name, and married into an aristocratic, anti-semitic family.

Helene felt she never successfully made up for Emil's failure in her mother's eyes. But she did apparently replace him as favourite of her father, Wilhelm Rosenbach, whom she idealized as a widely admired and respected lawyer, judge and district magistrate, and Galicia's representative to the Federal Court in Vienna. She accompanied him on visits to his village clients, thereby learning of the social problems that informed her later political and clinical work. Ashamed of the defeatism of her fellow-Jews, she identified more with her father's Polish patriotism, and with his legal work. Later she joined others in a sit-in protest to secure women's admission to Vienna University's Law School.

But she also experienced her father as much weaker than her mother. As a child she sat up late at night worrying lest he be murdered on the way home from playing cards. And she complained that even though her mother was nine or ten years his junior, her father nevertheless let her rule the roost. All too often, it seemed, he sided against Helene with her mother's 'reactionary counterattacks on my efforts to liberate myself'.[5]

Unlike her father, Helene's mother seemed uncultured, intellectually insecure, and above all a slave to bourgeois propriety. Perhaps, Helene speculated, this was in reaction to the scandal caused by her own mother's desertion of her father to live with the clerk who worked in her draper's shop. Regina herself never worked. She only gave orders, said Helene, as 'beneficiary of an economic system that exploited domestic help'.[6]

Regina seems to have expected Helene to live a life of similar domestic idleness when she left school at fourteen. But Helene rebelled. She started writing for the *Przemyśl Voice*. And then she ran away, pioneering the way – in her eyes – for six other Przemysl girls to follow suit. She herself agreed to stop running away only provided her parents sign a contract guaranteeing to help her gain university entrance.

Her studies took her to Zürich, where she met Russian refugees from Tsarism. Apart from their intellectual mentor Plekhanov, their most revered member in Helene's eyes was Vera Figner, a Russian physician and revolutionary, of whom she later wrote in *The Psychology of Women*. Helene herself was inspired more by the romantic aspects of socialism – 'the danger, the heroic self-sacrifice' – than by the mundane detail of party politics and workers' movements. But most of all she felt she became 'a young revolutionary' out of hatred of her mother's 'bourgeois materialism'.

She took her revenge on Regina even further by having an affair, beginning when she was sixteen, with a much older married man, the prominent socialist leader Herman Lieberman, a lawyer acquaintance of her father, whom she met through Gizela. Helene later wrote of the affair

> My hate of my mother and horror of identification with her, my dangerous love for my father and the difficulties of identifying with him, and my separation from Malvina – all these problems could be resolved in only one way: I needed a stronger relationship with a person outside my family yet endowed with qualities that would make a transition from my father-identification possible.[7]

Helene kept the affair secret from the outside world in obedience to Lieberman's fear lest it damage the socialist cause. Later, however, he pettishly complained of her 'absolutely undemanding submission to him' – so different from the rebellion against her mother that seemingly motivated it. For it meant she never made him get the divorce he wanted.

She might have been publicly secret about the affair in obedience to his apparent wishes. But she was open in her political rebellion to shame her mother. This included courting arrest by throwing herself under police horses on demonstrations, taking forbidden propaganda to the frontier, and organizing the first ever strike of Przemyśl women – an ill-timed action which she later attributed to her own need to gain the women's affection in face of their lack of organizational readiness effectively to protest against their working conditions.

All this took place during the revolutionary ferment in Poland at the time of the 1905 St Petersburg uprising. The crushing of this revolt coincided with the dashing of Helene's more personal hopes. In 1905 Lieberman's one-year-old son died. Previously he had hoped to bring him up with Helene, leaving the care of his daughter to his wife. The boy's death, however, cemented the Liebermans' marriage. They now went abroad together in their grief.

This galvanized Helene into becoming more independent. Since local high schools still did not admit girls, she left to study for university entrance in Lwów (Lemberg). But with the Liebermans' return, and Herman's involvement in Poland's first general election, Helene became depressed. Her father consulted a doctor in Vienna, and on his advice she was sent for treatment to a sanatorium in Graz.

Meanwhile her mother pressurized Herman to end his affair with her daughter. But it continued. He visited Helene in Graz and took her to the opera – *Carmen*. And they went together to Vienna in 1907 – Lieberman as a Member of Parliament, Helene as one of the first women medical students at its University. She now learnt of psychoanalysis for the first time through reading Wilhelm Jensen's recently published novel *Gradiva* (about an archaeologist's obsession with a classical sculpture of a young girl) and Freud's dream analysis interpretation of it. Most of all, she later recalled, she was attracted to Freud's work by his 'theory of infantile sexuality and the unconscious, but also his protest against society'.[8]

Not only did she share her life in Vienna with Lieberman: they also holidayed together, and in 1910 attended an International Socialist Congress in Stockholm and Copenhagen. Here Helene met leading socialists Jaurès, Bebel and Kautsky. But it was the women socialist leaders, apart from Clara Zetkin whom she distrusted, who most impressed her, particularly Angelika Balabanoff and Rosa Luxemburg, of whose motherliness she wrote with mixed feelings:

> She [Rosa] took a sporadic interest in me because I was good-looking and obviously burning with adolescent devotion to the Party . . . in her attitude to me I felt something soft and perhaps motherly. This was not what I wanted . . . I often wished to be like her, but I was realistic enough to know that this was impossible.[9]

Like Helene, Luxemburg was also a Polish Jew. She was now leader with her lover, Leo Jogiches, of an internationalist splinter group of Lieberman's nationalist Polish Social Democratic Party. Her example inspired Helene to ask herself why she too was not a 'leading woman', and to end her affair with Lieberman, which, begun out of rebellion against her mother, now seemed to embroil her in hopeless self-defeating subservience, both personally and politically. Although Lieberman self-pityingly felt himself the more tormented, masochistic victim of the two, Helene experienced her self-esteem as destroyed by her submission to him and by socialist 'self-sacrifice on behalf of society'.

In a bid for independence she left him to study in Munich. Here a Polish philosopher friend, Joseph Reinhold, gave her Freud's *Interpretation of Dreams*. Here too she had an abortion, of Lieberman's child. This prompted her final break with him: 'I was ripe for motherhood, and the nature of our relationship made it out of the question.'[10] In any case, she had now fallen in love with a quite different man – a Vienna-born Zionist, a fellow-doctor the same age as herself, Felix Deutsch. She sought to mother him. But for all that, and despite being less ambitious than her, he was already an outstanding physician and became an analyst and one of the pioneers of psychosomatic medicine. He was also a musician – a pastime Helene had abandoned early on after her piano teacher gave her up, as she saw it, because he was so appalled when one day she burst into hysterical laughter at her mother's falling down on the shiny music-room floor and being too fat to get up.

2

Madness and mothering

In old age Helene relished the image of herself as a rebel. But from 1911 on her life was a model of respectability. That autumn she and Felix returned to Vienna, where they married on 14 April 1912. The next year she graduated as a doctor and took a job in a hospital for mentally handicapped children. She had at first wanted to be a paediatrician, which Lieberman had linked with the illness and death of his son, to whom he had hoped she would become stepmother. But she did not like the work. Instead she went to work in Vienna University's Psychiatric Clinic under the direction of Krafft-Ebing's successor, Wagner-Jauregg (later to win the Nobel Prize for his discoveries in treating syphilis). Here she now adopted something of a mother role as a psychiatrist, recalling particularly vividly a severely withdrawn patient she treated by whispering in her ear, 'I love you.'

Frustrated, however, by the embargo on women becoming Medical Assistants, and by Vienna's relatively low standing in psychiatry, Helene spent the early months of 1914 studying in Munich under the then internationally renowned psychiatrist Emil Kraepelin. Her work included word association tests by which Kraepelin sought to discredit Freud's theory of the link between thought and feeling. Of her own feelings, she wrote of her continuing conflicts about mothering. She likened her then pregnancy – which ended in the first of several miscarriages – to being 'corroded and heavy as a fattened pig, a well into which all cares and slaveries are swept'.[1]

She also toyed with the idea of starting a woman-run psychiatric clinic for teenage girls. But the plan came to nothing. In a sense, however, she realized it on her return to Vienna where, in the absence of men psychiatrists at the war, she was put in charge of the women's section of Wagner-Jauregg's Clinic. While her home town, Przemyśl, heroically withstood siege by the Russians, the Austrian forces were decimated by cholera. Some ended up in Vienna's old mental hospital, where Helene felt her mothering capacity overwhelmed by their wounded masculinity:

> . . . reminded by their surroundings that they were expected to die a hero's death in battle for the fatherland instead of having to wallow in their own stinking excrement, these dying soldiers were beyond my help and indeed beyond what I could bear.[2]

Meanwhile her psychiatric work furnished her first psychoanalytic case material. In 1916 she had had to comment on Lou Andréas-Salomé's paper, 'Vaginal and anal', as a condition of her acceptance at Freud's Wednesday night meetings. She herself, however, was much more interested in her women patients' mothering experience, particularly the deception and self-deception it involved.

An example was a middle-aged war widow whose sixteen-year-old son induced her to believe that his father was still alive and that a very wealthy family had taken them under its wing and was even now planning to marry their son to the widow's seventeen-year-old daughter.[3] Another case was a thirty-four-year-old woman blinded and bereft of all family since infancy. How nice, she said to Helene, to have a brother and a child by him. At other times she believed this wish had come true, that she had a brother by whom she had had a baby when she was still a child. Indeed, she protested, 'all the birds on the roof are twittering about it'.[4]

Like this patient, Helene was also still childless. She had had many miscarriages, which she blamed on pregnancy seemingly embodying identification with her hated mother – a nice corrective to the implication of recent feminist theory, mentioned above (p. 14), that identification with the mother smoothly socializes daughters into becoming mothers themselves.[5]

Deutsch described her own difficulties in this sphere as though they were those of a patient, Mrs Smith:

> As a little girl she had reacted to her mother's rejection with conscious hatred and devaluation. The idea of identification with her aggressive mother had filled her with almost conscious horror . . . Her identification with her older sister, her childhood substitute mother, was also disturbed. During her early puberty Mrs Smith had discovered that her sister, like herself, was engaged in a hate-filled conflict with her mother, and perhaps unconsciously sensed that this sister had many children not because she was motherly but because she was sexually subjected to her husband. With whom, then, could she identify herself, in order to become a mother?

The solution came through identifying with a pregnant friend, particularly with the friend's mother:

> While her own mother was tall, domineering, cold, and aggressive, her friend's mother was very small and full to the brim with maternal warmth. She spread her motherly wings both over her own loving daughter and Mrs Smith, who was thus able to achieve motherhood by sharing in this benign mother-daughter harmony.[6]

Only six hours after her friend gave birth (a month late), Helene gave birth on 29 January 1917 to her first and only child Martin (perhaps called after Freud's oldest son). Labour, she later recalled, started when she was in the middle of 'demonstrating at the clinic how you force-feed an insane patient'.[7] Feeding her own child proved more difficult. She felt drained by breast-feeding. Felix acquired substitutes – two goats who grazed in the Clinic courtyard while Helene worked.

The next year she left the Clinic to work in Karplus's neurological department. Paul Schilder's return from the front had put Wagner-Jauregg in an awkward position. He wanted to appoint Schilder as Clinical Assistant but could not do so out of loyalty to Helene. By leaving she eased the situation. She also felt that Wagner-Jauregg's hostility to psychoanalysis made it impossible for her to continue working at the Clinic now that she had decided to become a psychoanalyst.

In 1918 she became one of the first women to join Freud's Vienna Psychoanalytic Society. She started seeing patients analytically, beginning in January 1919 with Victor Tausk – one-time lover of Lou Andréas-Salomé – whose treatment Helene terminated, at Freud's suggestion, after just three months. Freud not only supervised her treatment of Tausk and others, he also analysed her. Her analysis began on the very day her father returned to Przemyśl from Vienna after the war. She took Mrs Rado's hour, and in turn most unhappily gave it up the next year, again at Freud's request, to his patient the Wolf Man on the latter's return to Vienna from Russia.

Of her own analysis, Helene reported quickly falling in love with Freud. Perhaps to mollify Mrs Freud – recently recovered from pneumonia – she brought her some of her goat's milk when she came to see Freud. Of her treatment itself, she complained that Freud – in keeping with the already discussed patriarchalism of his work – focused too much on her identification with her father (who died the same year her treatment ended) and her affair with Lieberman, to the neglect of her mothering difficulties. Indeed, Freud even fell asleep when she talked of her difficulty in getting a wet nurse.

She now described these difficulties in a brief essay[8] about the temporary regression to soiling and bed-wetting and eating disturbance of two-year-old Martin following the loss of his nurse Paula, for whom he had first learnt to control these functions. Perhaps Paula left because Helene balked at her stipulation that Helene abdicate Martin's mothering entirely to her. Certainly Helene had repeated difficulties with servants, which Martin, giving her some of her own psychoanalytic medicine, later attributed to sibling rivalry.

Whatever her analysis of Martin, Helene never became a professional child analyst, just as in 1913 she quickly tired of child psychiatry. Child analysis, she later ruefully wrote of Anna Freud's pioneering work in this field, depends on understanding normal children – something Helene felt she had proved singularly inept at doing as a mother.

Nevertheless, and like other analysts, she dwelt on child psychology through its reconstruction in adult analysis. In autumn 1920,[9] for instance, describing the disappointment of children like Martin at the loss of their first maternal love object, she drew attention to the anger to which this can lead. Through projection, she said, it becomes converted into suspicion of others, this being exacerbated by the recent war. She also described a patient, possibly based on herself, torn 'between her strong masculine aspirations and the feminine role she had assumed as housewife and mother'.[10]

This was the subject of her first International Psychoanalytic Congress talk – in The Hague. The same conference saw the first bringing together by Karl Abraham of Freud's otherwise scattered references to penis envy in women. Deutsch was impressed – all the more so because it detailed the castration complex which she felt Freud had wrongly neglected in her analysis.

She herself, however, was not yet particularly interested in women's psychology. She was more interested in inauthenticity. It was to become a major theme in her later work on narcissism in both men and women. In 1921, describing her own experience of getting back at her mother by passing herself off as a 'fallen woman', she also recounted examples of others who likewise sought falsely to inflate their self-esteem, as in the case of a Polish woman who told tall stories of her supposed heroic war deeds even after their truth had been exploded.[11]

Later that same year Helene again drew on her family experience to illustrate the theme of phoney identity. Again disguising the case, she described to the Vienna Society[12] how her nephew, to win his mother Malvina's love, became increasingly like his older brother, both physically and mentally, after the latter's death (which Helene witnessed and long mourned) from tetanus-infected war wounds. His mother, who before the war had already lost one of her four children as a baby, became quite mad with grief and spent all day at his grave.

Deutsch, whom her friend Kardiner recalled as 'Freud's darling' and one of the great beauties of Vienna,[13] was also reminded of her sisters by her new 1922 colleagues, Jeanne de Groot and Anna Freud. She identified with the latter as also 'the youngest of three sisters and her father's chosen heir'.[14] That year also saw the beginning of the Vienna Society's Clinic. This, together perhaps with a crisis in Deutsch's work and marriage, but most of all her wish to be analysed by Abraham, led her to leave Vienna for Berlin in January 1923 to learn about the work of analysts there in founding the first ever psychoanalytic training centre. Possibly she had an affair here with the Hungarian analyst Sandor Rado, also in analysis with Abraham. Certainly her son regards the whole Berlin episode as a 'deep infidelity', which disrupted his routine not least because, when they returned to Vienna, it was to a new and larger flat that put his parents under some financial strain.

Freud himself had written to Abraham that on no account was his analysis of Helene to disrupt her marriage. Nor did it free her from her father identification, which so inhibited her using her mothering experience to go beyond Freud's work. Indeed, it has been suggested that Freud sought 'to indoctrinate her and to influence Abraham to the same'.[15]

In Berlin Helene lived in the same boarding house as another of Abraham's analysands, Melanie Klein, whom Helene dismissed as 'a housewife with fantasies'. Abraham, she wrote,

> achieved therapeutic success in treating Mrs Klein's neurotic problems, but her analysis did not have a lasting influence on her extremely speculative thinking in child analysis.[16]

Martin, who had come with Helene to Berlin, was now six. That summer he returned to Vienna where Felix looked after him, for which Helene not altogether flatteringly equated Felix with her mother. At her suggestion Felix also went into analysis – with Siegfried Bernfeld. Felix's own patients now included Freud, and Freud's former analysand, Dora. Meanwhile, in Berlin, Helene cautiously began taking issue with the patriarchally minded approach that informed Freud's analysis of Dora and others.

3

Female sexuality

At first, especially while Martin was with her in Berlin, Helene felt depressed and inhibited in her work. Yet she also lectured and gave talks: about fantasies of castration by biting, and about a man who, like Klein's older son Hans, she said sought to sublimate his fear of castration through sports.[1] But she was now more interested in women's psychology. This culminated in an April 1924 talk in Salzburg.[2] The problems posed women by the first onset of menstruation, the menstrual cycle, defloration, sexual intercourse, pregnancy, childbirth, and the menopause, she now suggested, are due not so much, as Freud had argued, to these functions signifying castration. Rather, she said, they are the effect of these reproductive events triggering conflicts between narcissistic self-love and motherly love of others.

This talk formed the basis of her 1925 monograph, *The Psychology of Women's Sexual Functions*, the first book ever devoted by a psychoanalyst to women's psychology. Of it Deutsch later wrote:

> My intense interest in women stemmed from ... my own narcissism ... the fact that research until then had been chiefly concerned with men ... [and from] Freud's interest in feminine psychology.[3]

Subservient as ever to Freud, however, she like him characterized the first stage of the girl's genital – or clitoral – sexuality as 'phallic'. Like him, she also went on to argue that the girl abandons the phallic or active phase of her sexuality as a result of recognizing her lack of a penis. Mortified by this comparison with boys, she wrote, echoing Freud, the girl abandons her previous phallic activity in favour of the complementary passive trends of her bisexual constitution.

Puberty, she said, likewise starts with a wave of activity which again succumbs to passivity, this time because the girl construes menstruation not only as castration, as Freud characterized it, but also as signifying the lack of a baby. Both disappointments, she claimed, motivate the desire for sexual intercourse as a means of gaining both a penis and a baby. The latter enables women to recreate the relation they first enjoyed with their mothers.

In this last respect Deutsch went beyond Freud in emphasizing the maternal, as well as the patriarchal, roots of women's sexuality. She described the female reproductive cycle as moving essentially full circle, via men, from mothering to mothering. Sexual intercourse, she said, recapitulates early mothering – the vagina sucking the penis revives the early memory of sucking at the mother's breast. At the same time, she added, women identify in sexual intercourse with a childhood image of the mother as masochistic victim of the father.

Women's experience of pregnancy, she maintained, is likewise informed by early infantile oral and anal fantasies of incorporation and expulsion, the latter expressed in morning sickness and miscarriage. Overlooking, perhaps because of her hostility towards her own mother, the way women draw on their positive as well as their negative feelings towards their mothers in pregnancy, Deutsch instead implied that positive feelings about the expected baby come solely from identifying it with the father they idealized as infants. But since women vary in their childhood experience of their parents, she said, so too do they vary in the extent to which pregnancy enhances or depletes their own self-esteem.

Anticipating recent feminist criticism of modern obstetrics,[4] Deutsch berated it for so drugging up women in childbirth that they lose all sense of connection with the baby. Instead they experience it as alien to themselves, as thus depleting rather than enhancing their self-esteem. She also decried the use of narcotics in childbirth. For they numb the intense feelings of life and death, external gain and internal loss, evoked by giving birth – feelings she described as 'an orgy of masochistic pleasure',[5] a phrase for which she was immediately ridiculed by Karen Horney.[6]

While Deutsch regarded childbirth as the acme of feminine sexual achievement, she regarded maternal femininity as only finally achieved through breast-feeding whereby, she said, women regain once more the unity of self and other they first experienced at their own mother's breast. This state of early union with the mother, she later wrote,[7] is idealized in fantasy as one of blissful union to which we seek to return in the brief respites afforded by sex to the self-division resulting from the hostility of self and others.

Deutsch's focus on mothering and her account of pregnancy and breast-feeding from the mother's rather than the child's standpoint is a major advance on Freud's father-centred account of female sexuality. But so much did she couch her theory in his terms that the differences between them are often overlooked. She herself recognized being still too much under Freud's influence in her Salzburg paper. But she was nevertheless disappointed that he neither recognized the independence of her contribution, nor cited it in his first major account of female sexuality – an oversight she blamed less on him than on the supposed jealousy of his daughter Anna, who read his paper on the subject to the 1925 Homburg Congress.

The previous autumn, a few months after Helene's return to Vienna, when she promised Felix she would be more 'motherly' both to him and to Martin, mothering psychoanalysis suffered a severe blow. On 9 September 1924 the first woman member of the Vienna Society and supervisor of the Child Guidance Centre it established in 1922, Hermine von Hug-Hellmuth, was murdered by the nephew she had brought up and analysed. It was precisely her making him 'merely a guinea pig for her psychological experiments', he said, that drove him to kill his aunt.[8] After his release he asked to be treated by Helene. But, fearful lest she suffer the same fate as his *ersatz* mother, she refused. Instead he took to stalking her in the streets, where Felix had her protected by a private detective.

Meanwhile Helene cited Hug-Hellmuth's work in a talk in

Würzburg about the menopause – a talk on which Lieberman, who met up with her in Venice the next year, congratulated her. So did Klein's English translator, Alix Strachey, who pronounced it 'a great success, only capped by her evening gown (from Paris, they all said)'.[9]

In her talk she again dwelt on mothering, this time on the loss of maternal function and self-esteem involved in menopause. At first, Deutsch said, perhaps thinking of herself, women react to ageing by becoming increasingly sexually active. They then return to earlier sexual attachments – to their children, for instance. As illustration she cited von Hug-Hellmuth's case of a fifty-year-old woman, obsessed with looking after her son, who disguised her incestuous desire from herself in a dream of being ready 'in fulfilment of a patriotic duty to offer herself for the satisfaction of the erotogenic needs of the military, officers and men' – not unlike her son, who was also in the army.[10]

Post-menopausally, maintained Deutsch, women return to even earlier, pre-Oedipal stages of development, and to the associated ills of obsessionality and paranoia to which, like Freud, she believed these stages prone. But, whereas Freud was to characterize middle-aged women as showing 'psychical rigidity and unchangeability' with 'no paths open to further development',[11] Deutsch suggested that this would not so often befall women were they socially enabled to realize their motherliness in work outside the home.

She herself was now forty. Her work was going from strength to strength. In 1925 she became, for the next decade, the first President (with Anna Freud as Secretary) of the Vienna Society's Training Institute which she had been instrumental in founding, although, in keeping with her general deference to Freud, she later said she would not have instigated it had she known of his distaste for the scheme.

She was now working twelve hours a day, seeing eleven or twelve cases six times a week, as well as being heavily committed to administration and teaching. No wonder Martin experienced his mother as 'inaccessible'. Her teaching included courses on feminine psychology, later taught by Jeanne Lampl-de Groot and

Grete Bibring, fellow-members with Helene and Felix of an informal group of analysts who met together to discuss psychoanalysis and play Hearts. This replaced an earlier card-playing circle in which, to her son's resentment, Helene played poker with her Polish friends to the exclusion of Felix.

Having earlier dwelt on the female reproductive cycle, Helene now attended to the genesis of masculinity as well as femininity in women. Freud had attributed the former to defensive denial of penis envy. Perhaps drawing on her own experience of identifying with her father out of hatred for her mother, Deutsch now emphasized the maternal as well as the patriarchal roots of women's so-called 'masculinity complex', in a lecture about George Sand given first in Vienna and then in the USA.

Like Helene, Sand (born Aurore Dupin) was also of Polish descent. Indeed, Helene suggested, therein lay the tragedy of her femininity. For the little Aurore's grandmother wanted her, like her father Maurice, to live up to the name of her ancestor, a King of Poland. Nor was it only her grandmother who turned Aurore against femininity. So too did her mother, whose jealousy drove her while pregnant with Aurore's brother to ride to Spain to join her husband, who was fighting in the Napoleonic wars. Sand attributed her brother's early death to this cause. Furthermore, Deutsch claimed, Sand flaunted her masculinity as a means of embarrassing and revenging herself on her aristocratic-minded grandmother for bad-mouthing the lowly Sophie after Maurice's death. Indeed, anticipating current feminist literary opinion, Deutsch[12] saw in this championing of her mother the source of Sand's feminism.

Deutsch also drew attention to the way Sand invented for herself an ideal God in place of her father (who died, when she was four, from falling off his horse). She likewise described a seventeen-year-old patient who imagined ideal parents for herself,[13] just as Helene as a child invented a nice mother in place of her own. Whereas Freud dwelt on the patriarchal roots of such 'family romances', Deutsch also drew attention to their maternal sources which, in her teenage patient's case, included her mother's death when she was ten, disappointment at her father's remarriage, and regret at her stepmother not loving her.

Having attended in the case of George Sand to the maternal roots of women's masculinity, Deutsch now drew attention to the maternal as well as the patriarchal roots of women's femininity – something all too long overlooked, she complained, so much had analysts focused instead on these traits in men, not women.

At first she adopted Freud's patriarchal account of women's femininity. Abandoning active, 'phallic', clitoral masturbation because of the narcissistic humiliation involved in recognizing her lack of a penis, Deutsch said, the little girl converts this disappointment into the Oedipal but masochistic wish: 'I want to be castrated by my father.'[14] Hence, claimed Deutsch, the frequent rape fantasies of little girls that inaugurate their femininity. As illustration she cited a patient's dream of being forcibly penetrated by a male doctor with obstetric forceps while Deutsch stood by and reprimanded her for struggling.

Drawing on such maternal transference data, Deutsch suggested that the roots of femininity also lie in the girl's identification with the mother, understood as masochistic victim of the father's sexual penetration. This in turn, said Deutsch, colours children's 'birth-fantasies' with 'a bloody, painful character'.[15]

Not that she condoned the feminine masochism supposedly resulting from identification with this image of the mother. Quite the reverse. As Barbara Webster points out, Deutsch drew attention to the conflicts posed for women's self-esteem by the equation of mothering with masochism. So fearful, Deutsch observed, are women of losing their self-esteem through identification with a debased image of the sexual mother that they often lose all pleasure in sex by either fleeing their femininity or becoming frigid. But she also attributed frigidity, which she discussed at the 1929 Oxford Congress, to the social pressure on women to be sexually passive. Indeed, it seemed, her uncle abandoned her maternal aunt for no other reason than that she was too active in sex.

Others, Deutsch wrote, give up all hope of self-esteem by abandoning themselves to masochistic femininity. Either they subject themselves to men through prostitution and non-orgasmic, maternal giving in sex. Or they submit themselves, *mater dolorosa* style, to their children. Still others stave off the threat to their self-esteem, seemingly involved in sexual submission to men through fantasies of immaculate conception – of becoming a mother without male intervention.[16]

In the absence of psychoanalytic accounts of the conflicts posed women's self-esteem by sex and mothering, Deutsch drew on literary sources. She recounts, for instance, Balzac's 1841 novel, *Two Women*, in which he locates sex and mothering in two different characters. Louise lives in Paris and devotes herself to being loved and being in love with first one husband and then another. All three, however, fall victim to the jealousy which, like Tolstoy in *Anna Karenina*, Balzac says such single-minded sexual passion breeds. Meanwhile Louise's friend, Renée, devotes herself in Provence just as single-mindedly to mothering her husband and children.

Deutsch also recounted her own patients' divorce of sex and mothering. She described, for instance, a German midwife who came for treatment because she felt compelled to be present at every one of her patients' deliveries, and because she was so obsessed with looking after babies and their mothers. These symptoms, it seemed, stemmed from attacks she wanted to make as a child on her mother's sexuality and babies. Fearing lest her own sexuality and childbearing be similarly attacked, she left sex and mothering to others. Instead she vicariously enjoyed these functions, the attacks she wanted to make on them, and the guilt thereby evoked, by simultaneously enjoying and punishing herself by always having to witness other women's labours.

Another patient, by contrast, had a constant succession of lovers. Through them she sought to recreate the mothering – the mother–infant unity – that she jealously supposed as a child her younger brothers enjoyed. She also sought to mother her lovers to atone for this jealousy and resulting hatred and guilt toward her brothers. But so divided in her mind were motherhood and sex that the one precluded the other. In mothering her lovers she became frigid.

While Deutsch dwelt increasingly on the conflicts posed women's sexuality and self-esteem by maternity – evident in her analysis of US as well as European patients – her own narcissism and self-esteem were enormously enhanced by being invited, with several other leading European psychiatrists, to the May 1930 International Congress of Mental Hygiene in Washington. New York papers lauded her as 'Lady-in-Waiting at the Freudian Court', as 'the master's foremost feminine disciple'.[17] Hungarian analyst Franz Alexander offered her a job in Chicago. But she declined. Karen Horney accepted instead. Meanwhile, with plans to visit her mother in Poland, Helene returned to Vienna and the publication of her second book, *Psychoanalysis of the Neuroses*.

4

Mothering and neurosis

Freud's patients' transference to him as father-figure convinced him that the 'kernel' of neurosis is the Oedipus complex, namely rivalry with the father for sexual possession of the mother. By contrast Deutsch's *Psychoanalysis of the Neuroses*, based on her lectures to the Vienna Training Institute, provides a wealth of cases illustrating the roots of various neuroses not only in patriarchal but also in maternal factors as transferred on to Deutsch in therapy.

First she reiterated Freud's two-stage account of neurosis as resulting from a present event triggering return to the past. In Dora's case, for instance, Freud said her recent seduction by her father's friend had provoked regression to early oral and Oedipal desire for her father. Deutsch, on the other hand, illustrated this two-stage theory by reference to adult events also evoking early mothering experience.

She described, for example, a woman whose husband fell in love with her niece. The patient thereupon retreated to the childhood means by which she had dealt with Oedipal rivalry with her mother for love of her father – namely through exaggerated love of her mother. Fixation to her earlier Oedipal desire prevented her leaving her husband or being angry with him. Instead she courted her niece, as in childhood she had courted her mother, and as she now courted Deutsch. Her present neurosis, it seemed, was due to the failure of this mother-oriented defence because her niece rejected her advances.

Another example of a current event triggering early mothering conflicts was a woman, not unlike Deutsch, whom she termed a case of 'fate neurosis'. She recounted the story in a series of fortnightly seminars in the winter of 1928–9, thereby introducing a method of 'continuous case' presentation that has become a standard part of psychoanalytic training. Deutsch herself initiated this teaching format as a means of dealing with controversies surrounding the seminar's previous leader, Wilhelm Reich's, character analysis technique.

The case has all the makings of tragic romance:

> The patient was twenty-five years of age and had made the long journey from overseas to Vienna . . . She was beautiful, cultured, and of wealthy family. Shortly before her departure she had made an unsuccessful attempt at suicide; a scarcely visible scar on her temple was all that remained of the revolver shot. She had made the attempt in a small hotel in her native town.[1]

She had no idea why she had tried to kill herself – it seemed to be the working of fate, not of conscious intent.

Analysis revealed the following story. She had been engaged to a cousin who, while he loved the 'woman' in her, left her intellectually unsatisfied. Much more engaging was her friendship with an elderly widowed diplomat. At length he confessed to loving her just as he had his now dead wife. But, when he was called away to his present wife's sickbed, Deutsch's patient immediately had an affair with a casual acquaintance, became pregnant, and planned to marry him. All this, however, was gradually put to an end. She returned to the diplomat, who separated from his wife and planned to marry her. It was on the eve of their wedding that she attempted suicide, in despair lest were the marriage to fail she would 'be forced to continue in dependence on her tyrannical father', like her mother whom she dismissed as 'stupid and uneducated and above all so slavishly devoted to her father'.[2]

She now transferred on to Deutsch her Oedipal image of her mother as a 'loathsome, tactless woman who had come between her and her father to upset their relationship'.[3] Therapy seemingly enabled her to overcome her dread of becoming like her apparently worthless mother. She married the diplomat and studied for university entrance. Over ten years later, after becoming established in a career, she had a child. Not that the old mothering conflict had entirely disappeared. At follow-up she was still contemptuous of motherhood. She dismissed Deutsch's treatment, as she had earlier dismissed her mother, as 'a hoax – all bunk – purely constructions of your own mind . . . Analysis gave me nothing.'[4]

From the beginning Deutsch's practice consisted mainly of women – both patients and trainees. But her sensitivity to maternal issues also informed her work with men. She described, for instance, a man who suffered from bed-wetting and impotence. These symptoms seemed to be due both to fear of patriarchal prohibition of sex and to fear of being raped and murdered by an old woman, like the victim of Dostoevsky's novel *Crime and Punishment* – a character Deutsch associated with her mother's rich sister, Leika, who made a big pretence of being poor. Underneath her patient also wanted to be the object – like his mother – of his father's desire. This in turn gave rise to hatred of Deutsch – expressed in eating binges following therapy sessions with her – so humiliated did he feel at being made to feel feminine in front of her. Similar anger towards his mother, whom he had wanted to oust from sexual relations with his father, had previously given rise to hypochondriacal self-punishment out of guilt at her death when he was twenty.

While Freud traced psychosomatic symptoms – Dora's nervous cough and anorexia, for instance – to Oedipal desire for the father, Deutsch thus also attended to the maternal roots of such symptoms, as in the case of the above hypochondriac. Another example was a fifteen-year-old girl whose symptoms included eating difficulties following severe tonsillitis, due, as it emerged from her treatment with Deutsch, to her illness reviving early oral longing for her mother and consequent jealousy of her sister and father. This now took the form of revenging herself on him, his brutality towards her mother, and her repeated pregnancies, by using her illness to flout the Jewish law of the father forbidding the taking of milk after meals.

So much did Freud's women patients transfer on to him their Oedipal desire for the father that, as already indicated in

Dora's case, he at first overlooked the 'complete Oedipus complex', the fact that as well as desiring the father, the girl also desires the mother. The latter lesbian, or 'negative' (as Freud termed it), form of the Oedipus complex was first revealed by the erotic maternal transference elicited by women analysts like Deutsch and Lampl-de Groot.

This in turn informed Deutsch's development of Freud's account of phobias. He had attributed the phobia of horses and resulting agoraphobia of five-year-old Hans to displacement on to horses of the hatred Hans felt towards his otherwise loved father for stopping him getting into bed with his mother.

Using her mothering experience, Deutsch paid more attention to the maternal determinants of phobias. An example was a widow who, after her husband's death, moved in with her friend, with whose husband she had an affair in defence against her desire for the friend, just as in therapy she fended off her Oedipal desire for Deutsch. Her phobia began with the birth of her friend's first child. She now displaced on to cats her hatred of her friend's pregnancy and child – cats, as witch's familiar, seeming a particularly appropriate repository for such anti-mother feelings.

Deutsch likewise recounted in maternal terms a young man's hen phobia. It began when he was eight and his brother jumped on him from behind, shouting, 'I'm the cock and you're the hen.' This in turn elicited a yet earlier wish – to be like the hens his mother put her finger up to see if they had any eggs. But this also made him fearful lest in becoming the passive sexual object of his mother or brother he thereby become castrated like women seemed to him to be. Hence his avoidance both of hens and homosexual encounters unless he could be the active partner – the 'cock of the roost'.[5] For this reason, Deutsch claimed, he chose as lovers feminine-seeming men with whom he could identify and thereby vicariously enjoy his passive desire.

Deutsch extended her mothering account of phobias to include agoraphobia. She attributed its roots not only to ambivalence towards the father, as Freud had, but also to ambivalence towards the mother. An example was a twenty-seven-year-old woman whose agoraphobia began after she broke off her intimacy with a childhood boyfriend to marry another man. In thereby disposing of one man to have sex with another, she revived the childhood guilt and anger she felt when her mother left home out of grief at her brother's death when she was four. At the time she derided her mother as a prostitute, and took her place in bed with her father. Her present agoraphobia, Deutsch claimed, was due to her feeling that without her mother she had no protection against sex and its dangers – the death of her brother in the first instance, and now the possible death of her friend at being rejected by her. The mixed feelings that fuelled her agoraphobia – her sense of her mother's absence as sexual abandonment, and her presence as moral damper on her desire – was revealed in her experiencing Deutsch both as sexually incontinent (as even masturbating through sessions) and as 'hypermoral and self-castigating'.[6]

Another case involved similar transference of the patient's mother fixation on to Deutsch. The patient was eighteen and still slept with her mother, who had long ago taken her into bed with her out of disappointment at her husband's indifference. Her daughter's agoraphobia, it seemed, stemmed from fear lest were she to go out without her mother the latter would leave her for her father, while she was also obsessed with the thought that if she went out with her she might 'throw her mother under a tram or a motor car'.[7]

Deutsch described other obsessions from a similarly maternal angle. Freud, as shown, had attributed obsessions – the Rat Man's obsessive rumination, for instance, about an unpaid debt – to sexual guilt towards the father. Deutsch now focused on such obsessions' maternal origins, as in the case of a patient whose obsessional avoidance of being touched she linked to the patient's mother early stopping her masturbating. At the time the patient reacted by becoming dirty and tormenting her siblings. This included seducing her younger brother, who later committed suicide after contracting syphilis. This, it seems, precipitated her obsession with touching. Her symptom expressed both her masturbation wish, and her identification with her mother's strictures against it. In her late teens, and to atone for her previous hatred of her mother, she devoted herself to looking after her mother in her final illness. Following her father's death, she likewise devoted herself 'masochistically' – as Deutsch put it – to the care of her siblings. Her compulsive self-sacrifice led her finally to enter a convent, where she fell into hopeless obsessionality and catatonic stupor.

Another patient was obsessed with a dream that her fiancé had died. It was triggered by his mother's disapproval of their marriage, and by the patient's resulting jealousy of his relations with other women. Extending, on the basis of her mothering experience, Freud's account of male jealousy as involving homosexual as well as heterosexual identification and rivalry, Deutsch traced this patient's jealousy to infantile desire for her now dead mother as transformed into preoccupation with Deutsch's death.

Deutsch concluded her 1930 book with an account of depression in which she again used her mothering experience to go beyond Freud. He attributed depression to fixation to narcissistic falling in love with others only in so far as they reflect oneself. The narcissist, he said, responds to loss of those he loves not by transferring his affections elsewhere but by instead withdrawing them into their original source, himself. He thereby also withdraws the image of those he has lost whom he now berates within himself. This identification with and hatred of the lost other, he maintained, constitutes the stuff of the depressive's self-loathing.

Deutsch traced such identification to early mothering. She described, for instance, a patient – a noted writer – who as a child hated her younger sister, in whose name she performed a number of obsessional rituals lest something awful befall her. After their mother died the patient had become more genuinely motherly towards her sister and, when their father died, postponed realizing her ambition by instead working as a secretary to support them both, only to be thanklessly deserted, as it seemed, by her sister getting married. It was the death of a dog she bought to replace her lost sister that precipitated her depression. Its loss unleashed her previously pent-up anger at her sister's loss. Now she scarcely knew whether it was herself or her sister she most desired and dreaded being punished by being 'thrown out into the street'[8] so much had her depression revived the early mother–child identification she had earlier enacted in relation to her sister.

Deutsch again took up this early mothering theme in her next major work – an account of lesbianism prepared initially for the 1931 Psychoanalytic Congress, but instead first given to the Vienna Society early the next year, after the 1931 Congress was cancelled because of Germany's economic collapse.

5

Lesbianism, loss, and 'as if' identity

It is perhaps a measure of Deutsch's caution in using her mothering experience to go beyond Freud that her paper on lesbianism was first mistakenly published under the title of Freud's 1931 paper, 'Female sexuality'. As indicated before, he attributed the lesbianism of an eighteen-year-old patient to her sense of betrayal by her father when, at sixteen, her mother once more fell pregnant by him. The girl sought to take revenge by embarrassing him through publicly courting a society lady well known to be bisexual.

For her part Deutsch argued that lesbian desire is not so much due as Freud (and Ferenczi) claimed to disappointed Oedipal desire for the father. Rather it stems from pre-Oedipal mothering. An example was a woman she analysed at about the same time that Freud reported the above case. Deutsch's patient came for treatment for suicidal depression and difficulties in asserting herself with her female servants. Her husband, it seemed, was too passive to help. This recalled her childhood hatred of her mother punishing her masturbation with binding, at which her father simply looked on – just as Deutsch felt her own father passively gave way to her mother's torment of her as a child. Though repressed, Deutsch's patient's hatred and fear of her mother's attacks persisted. This seemed to be the cause of her difficulties with female servants, and of her inability to have anything but platonic relations with women even though she felt sexually attracted to them as warm maternal figures. Her transference of this attraction on to Deutsch, however, seemingly enabled her to work through her hatred of her mother. As a result she was no longer inhibited by fear of women's hatred from realizing her lesbian desire, actually and in fact. This outcome was quite different from that aimed for by Freud. Although he insisted that homosexuality no more needs treating than heterosexuality, he in fact treated his eighteen-year-old patient's lesbianism as neurotic rebellion against her father and himself that needed undoing rather than gratifying.

Deutsch, by contrast, associated lesbianism, as do many feminists today, with the woman-to-woman attachment involved in early mothering. Just as Deutsch characterized heterosexual intercourse as recapitulating early mother-child mutuality of sucking and giving suck, so too she characterized one of her lesbian patient's sexuality in these terms. But for this patient sex also involved denying her childhood hatred of her mother and sister by instead desiring them in her lovers. So guilty did she feel as a child for hating her mother's pregnancy, especially since it ended in miscarriage when the patient was two, that she was unable to sustain any desire for her father lest it destroy her mother. Instead this desire was repressed, as was her wish to be treated by Freud or his daughter, Anna. She could only realize this desire in illusory form – in a dream of 'herself in analysis with Miss Anna Freud, who was dressed as a man', followed by a dream of Deutsch 'sitting opposite her, instead of behind her as I always did . . . [with] a cigar in my hand [like Freud]'. [1]

Just as Deutsch emphasized threatened loss of the mother to others, including siblings, as source of the hatred and guilt fuelling lesbianism, so too she drew attention to maternal loss as source of mania in depression. Freud had attributed manic excitement to the energy released once sexual energy is withdrawn from those whose loss first causes depression. Drawing on her mothering experience, Deutsch argued the reverse – that mania is due not to acknowledging and working through loss but to its denial.

An example was a woman who envied the attention her mother gave her siblings just as she now envied the oral gratification she dreamt Deutsch gave her son Martin. This led her both to attack Deutsch as apparent source of all her frustration, and to ward off her resulting guilt and fear of Deutsch's loss by manically denying it. She excitedly embarked on a series of affairs, showered Deutsch with flowers, and stressed how much everyone – including Deutsch – loved and admired her.

Another patient, faced with Deutsch's actual loss when she went away, also responded with manic denial. She negated any separation between them by identifying with Deutsch and going away herself.

> She went abroad ... traveled under an assumed name ('French'), and related an entirely imaginary life story to the many acquaintances that she readily acquired. When she returned, it appeared in analysis that all the details she had related were compatible with my life, and that the name 'French' actually represented a variant of 'Deutsch'.[2]

The loss suffered by this patient, however, was nothing compared to the mass loss of psychoanalysts from Germany following Hitler's rise to power in January 1933. That year saw the temporary ending of the German Psychoanalytic Society and Institute. For Deutsch it also saw the exile of Lieberman from Poland and, within psychoanalysis, the exile of Wilhelm Reich from the Vienna Society in 1934. Deutsch took over his seminar and ran it with her usual zeal, even calling for fresh cases in the early hours of the morning.

Meanwhile, in April 1933, Felix had given lectures in New York, from where he saw the growing Nazi menace more clearly than those actually in Austria, where Helene gave a further talk about manic states to the Vienna Society that March. She then briefly went on holiday with Martin in Switzerland, before returning to Vienna where she gave a talk in May about femininity, stressing that the roots of women's desire for motherhood lie not in envy of the father's penis but in identification with the mother.

Deutsch's long interest in maternal identification stemming from her own mothering now culminated in the development of psychoanalysis for which she is best remembered by analysts

– her January 1934 account of 'as if' identity, or 'narcissistic personality disorder' as it is now termed in the USA.

The source of personal identity in identification with others was something of an afterthought for Freud. Preoccupied during the First World War with the problem of narcissism, he suggested that this is the source of the depressive's identification with, and berating within himself, those he has lost. Following the war, Freud suggested that such identification occurs not only in depression but also in childhood – that the boy identifies with the father in the process of resolving his Oedipal rivalry with him for love of the mother. By contrast, Deutsch's mothering led her to stress the importance in personality formation generally of identification with the mother as well as with the father.

Taking issue with Freud's and orthodox psychiatry's division of adult psychiatric disorders into neurosis and psychotic madness, she now described people who fall into neither category, who appear entirely normal save for the superficial and merely formal character of their emotions and morality. This, she suggested, stems from lack of any close Oedipal attachment to parental figures in early childhood, such that no stable superego identification with them is formed. In the absence of such identification the 'as if' personality is formed through unstable, outward rather than inward, identification with others.

An example was an aristocratic patient who, as a child, was brought up 'in accordance with ceremonial tradition' by three nurses who were frequently changed[3]–just as Deutsch's were in her infancy. Initially, and also in common with Deutsch, the patient bolstered her self-esteem by idealizing her parents and developing a 'family romance' about them. But in the absence of any close relation with her parents this romance collapsed. Instead she devalued them and passively identified with the succession of different religious and sexual *personae* with which her convent school peers experimented.

Another case was a pretty, thirty-five-year-old woman who had also been unable to form any secure sense of self or inner morality through identification with her parents. She despised her father because of his alcoholism and brutality towards her mother. She also looked down on her mother on discovering that she 'was not merely a passive victim of her husband but took pleasure in being brutalized'. In analysis she seemed '"tired" after a long series of adventures' involving 'concurrent identifications' with a number of different people. Having broken with them, however, she was now completely penniless. She had come for treatment, it transpired, to identify with Deutsch and thereby gain work as an analyst. Only the thwarting of this ambition brought her in touch with the emptiness of any real sense of self and feeling behind her superficial, normal-seeming façade.

Yet another example was a twenty-two-year-old girl of whose shifting identifications Deutsch wrote:

> ... she changed her place of residence, her studies, and her interests in an almost manic fashion. Her last identification had led her from the home of a well-established American family to a Communistic cell in Berlin.[4]

From there she went to Paris and on to Vienna. But with the sudden termination of her treatment by Deutsch at her parents' instigation – the young woman being too passive to protest – her 'as if' identification collapsed into madness: 'One day she bought a dog and told me that now everything would be all right; she would imitate the dog and then she would know how she should act.'[5]

The sincerity of Deutsch's own identification was now itself brought into question. On 12 February 1934 her son, Martin, was involved in a General Strike, provoked and brutally crushed by Dollfuss's regime. He regarded his mother's socialism by contrast as a charade, 'a joke – an ornament of her love affair with Lieberman'.[6] She herself now illustrated an extreme form of the phoniness of which he accused her in a talk to the 1934 Lucerne Congress about Don Quixote's empty identification with an idealized, heroic image of the father, thereby fleeing reality and the base maternal instinct as represented by Sancho Panza.[7]

Meanwhile Martin – a teacher friend of Felix having suggested he might not be accepted back in school in Vienna because of his part in the February uprising – went to Tschulok's crammers in Zürich where he was looked after by Mira Oberholzer, one of the very first women analysts, and from where he remained active, along with Dorothy Burlingham's daughter Tinky among others, in Vienna's underground socialist movement.

His parents now decided to emigrate. Perhaps this was partly motivated by Helene's 1930 US triumph. Certainly she 'loved to be the diva, the star',[8] and the move benefited her more than Felix, who in going to the US left his birthplace, many lifelong friends, his university title, and the very successful medical practice he had established in Vienna.

Helene herself never got over Freud's disapproval of her departure. She agonized over it and remembered to the end his telling her he remained 'loving but unforgiving'. All too ready to be lulled into a false sense of security by the Schuschnigg regime which replaced that of Dollfuss, Freud was at one with most others in seeing no reason to quit Vienna. Only one analyst, Robert Waelder, supported the Deutschs' decision to leave.

Undeterred, Felix visited Boston in early 1935 to negotiate work for himself and Helene with Stanley Cobb who, in 1934, had founded the first full-time psychiatric unit in a US general hospital. At first, though, negotiations broke down because Cobb's colleagues opposed hiring a woman to train their students.

Coincidentally Deutsch now illustrated her 'as if' thesis in a talk about training and trainee analysts' identification with their patients and analysts.[9] Meanwhile things seemed to have been sorted out in Boston. Certainly Cobb was charmed. He might be sceptical about psychoanalysis, he said, but, he added, 'You have to believe in a woman with such magnificent eyes.'[10]

After a visit to her childhood home in Przemyśl – later to become a transit station for the concentration camps – Helene left Europe with Martin in September 1935 for Boston where she at last felt free of Freud's patriarchalism:

> ... here [in Boston] is life, and there [in Vienna] is dull, narcissistic brooding round about people's own intellectual fog. What is good for Freud's genius and his age, and for Anna's yielding herself up to the paternal idea, is becoming for others a mass neurosis.[11]

Not that mothering did not also continue to have its problems. Without Felix, who had returned to Vienna, Helene got on abysmally with her eighteen-year-old son. She now described him as full of 'murderous, hate-filled aggression against me',[12] not dissimilar to the anger she had felt towards her own mother. Like her, Martin also wanted to become more like his father, only to find himself too like his mother for his own liking. Convinced by Mussolini's 1935 Abyssinian adventure that this move to the US would not be the fleeting trip he had hoped, he kept his distance by getting a separate flat, from which he studied at MIT where he later became a nuclear physics professor.

Meanwhile Helene and Felix, who after some hesitation joined her in early 1936, stayed in a hotel while buying their very first house, in which Helene had her office, in Cambridge. In her writing and lecturing Helene continued with the theme of maternal identification that had so long been a central motif of her life and work. In a December 1935 talk[13] she described a thirty-year-old man, unable to express his sadness at his mother's death lest in acknowledging her loss he lose himself, so much was his identity bound up with hers. She went on to describe a middle-aged woman who could only experience grief at her own losses through identifying with her friends' sadness. Again Deutsch[14] returned to the issue of identification in the 1936 Marienbad Congress, where she talked about a woman analyst whose over-intellectualization with her patients seemed to stem from the insecurity of her identification with her father's intellect since he was the opposite sex.

Deutsch herself now received Freud's patriarchal affirmation. In a letter stamped 'Der Führer in Wien', he at last approved her decision to stay in America. He himself moved to London, where he died the following year. Deutsch honoured his memory with an essay which again dwelt on identification. Specifically she criticized those in Vienna who had sought to boost their self-esteem through identifying with Freud's greatness, and who, in insisting that no one depart from his ideas, laid a dead hand on their further development by 'revolutionists of the spirit' like herself.[15]

In 1935 she and Felix had started a farm in New Hampshire in imitation of Hochroterd, established by Anna Freud and Dorothy Burlingham outside Vienna. The Deutschs' farm was called Babayaga, Polish for a good witch – a magical image with which Helene sought to identify as a mother. She and her former analysand Molly Putnam immersed themselves in a 'back to the soil'[16] life while Felix took up a professorship in psychosomatic medicine in St Louis, from where he complained to Helene:

> . . .you told me I need a mother. Now that's utterly wrong! What I need is to live with you again like man and wife – the mother has been overcome.

She retorted:

> . . .you are wrong in saying that you don't need a caring mother. From birth until death, hated or loved, feared or blessed, a man (as boy and father) needs his mother. Only . . . the wanderings and confusions make it necessary to flee or liberate the self from the mother in the woman.[17]

In her work she also dwelt on flight from mothering and its identifications – specifically in relation to anorexia. Felix[18] attributed this condition to regression, in the name of patriarchal authority, from adolescent sexuality to infantile preoccupation with food. Anticipating today's mother-centred psychoanalytic and feminist understanding and treatment of anorexia, Helene suggested it was related to maternal identification. Drawing on a twenty-two-year-old anorexic's experience of her as mother, she attributed her condition to fear lest were she to get fat she would become the same as her hated, pregnant stepmother. Food for the anorexic, she wrote, is 'like a paranoid enemy in the stomach. The hated and dangerous mother.'[19]

Following Felix's return from St Louis in early 1941 – the same year she and Horney were lauded as America's 'outstanding women psychiatrists' – Helene again dwelt on maternal identification, this time in a talk about surgery. Freud had implied that operations evoke fear of patriarchal castration. This might be true for men, Deutsch wrote, but in women surgery evokes fear lest destructive impulses once felt towards the mother get turned against the self. This anxiety in turn hides a deeper longing – to be reunited with the mother as in death or life before birth. The negative aspect of this double-edged identification was illustrated by a fifteen-year-old patient's fear that Deutsch would try to make her a mother like herself. After surgery she dreamt

> that a woman would tie her up and force her to become pregnant by introducing a fluid into her body through her mouth. The analyst who sent her to me had told her that I had recently had a child myself and would know how to make her into a real woman.[20]

Such patients, however, belonged to Deutsch's life in Vienna. With the German invasion of Poland she lost all contact with her family. 'This,' she wrote, 'and Professor's death make it seem as if the whole past lay in ruins.'[21] She and Felix were now taken up with trying to secure the escape from Europe of their friends and relations. Meanwhile in America they were prevented from seeing their son Martin and their adored daughter-in-law Suzanne Zeitlin, whom Martin had married in 1939, by Martin's war work at the Los Alamos testing centre.

1944 also brought news of Lieberman's death while serving in London as Minister of Culture in the Polish Government-in-Exile. Later still, as Helene sourly observed, she learnt that her mother had taken with her into hiding from the Nazis her big diamond earrings – Jewish 'symbol of success and prosperity . . . usually left to the oldest daughter'.[22]

For Deutsch herself the war at first drained her work of all meaning: 'Sitting for hours on end behind someone whose talk is so empty and barren because one has heard it so many times before . . . [Instead] I stare incessantly at the clock.' Soon, however, her zest returned. With a vengeance – 'eleven analyses and one-three consultations a day'[23] and work on an enormous project, a two-volume account of women's psychology based on her own and her Vienna patients' mothering experience, as recounted above, and on that of social work cases from the Judge Baker Clinic and the Massachusetts General Hospital, where she was now an Associate Psychiatrist.

6

Women's psychology – youth

Freud had described women's psychology from the perspective of men and children. In the process he variously idealized or repudiated woman as mother or castrate. Now more than ever Deutsch described women's psychology from their own viewpoint, starting not with childhood but with adolescence, and focusing particularly on mothering.

Her own conflicts in this sphere informed the book's inception, of which she wrote to her anticipated grandchildren, perhaps out of desire to win Suzanne's love as recompense for not wholeheartedly gaining that of her son:

> It would be much nicer for you both – whoever you are – to have a knitting type of grand mother. She is very, very sad that she is not – but for her work your Mommi may buy for you plenty of things.[1]

Freud, Deutsch reminded her readers in beginning *The Psychology of Women*, assumed that the girl early turns away from the mother and adopts her father as main object of her affection. In fact, she insisted, drawing on von Hug-Hellmuth's self-portrayal in *A Young Girl's Diary*, this changeover is 'never completely achieved'. The main influence on the pre-teenage girl, she insisted, is the mother. It is this relationship, not the girl's attachment to the father as Freud implied, that constitutes the main danger to the teenage girl, failure to separate from the mother resulting among other things in eating disorders. Better by far, she advocated, tomboyish and active masculinity than 'withdrawal into domesticity'.

Puberty, she went on, revives early sexual and bisexual

feelings towards the parents. Girls are more conflicted about this than boys, who repudiate femininity much more readily than girls resist masculinity. Particularly important in resolving this conflict, Deutsch emphasized, is the girl's friendship with another girl. But this leads to problems if the friend leaves for someone else. For then she has to look elsewhere if she is not to be thrown back on the mother.

An example of such 'trauma', wrote Deutsch, describing a case not unlike her own sense of being abandoned to her mother's clutches when Malvina married, was a Boston welfare case, Evelyn, who at fourteen persistently ran away from home. This was apparently triggered by her best friend – her older sister – deserting Evelyn for a boyfriend, and by the consequent break-up of her four sisters' gang. This led Evelyn to look for another close friend and gang outside home – a solution fraught with danger, said Deutsch, given the soldiers then on the rampage because of the war. Despite this, however, Evelyn felt compelled repeatedly to leave home, not least to protect her mother against the rage she felt at her being so against her, this feeling of rejection being exacerbated by her mother again being pregnant.

Continuing with the theme of adolescent girls' friendships and identifications, Deutsch detailed the importance of fantasy in this process. Describing the way she as a teenager indulged the fantasy of being a 'fallen woman', she went on to describe the problems posed for girls by being pressured to embody and identify with the mother's fantasies. An example was fifteen-year-old Dorothy, whose mother was beaten as a child by her drunken father and who now got Dorothy to realize her own adolescent ambition to go on stage. But Dorothy gained no pleasure from this achievement, so bound up was it with her struggle with her mother, now transferred on to Deutsch.

Girls, wrote Deutsch, are more susceptible to such fantasy. Whereas boys engage with the external world, girls are more prone to inward-turning dreams. Both tendencies, however, are pathological if taken to excess, girls losing all contact with inner feeling if they become too masculine.

Deutsch then turned to the topic of menstruation and girls'

frequent complaint of not being warned of it by their mothers. Behind this complaint, she said, lies that against the mother for keeping other 'secrets' from them. Menstruation also poses problems because of associated cultural taboos. These are fuelled, Deutsch added, by childhood guilt about masturbation and by the simultaneous dread and wish for childbirth and mothering, expressed for instance in fourteen-year-old Molly's ambivalent exclamation, when she began menstruating: 'Anything might happen to me now.'

Deutsch also dwelt on the seeming masochism involved in mothering and femininity and the problems this poses women's sexuality. It gives rise, she maintained, to three distinct 'feminine types'. The first is easily 'conquered' but the man soon finds himself excluded from the woman's innermost self by the narcissistic shield she builds around it. Nevertheless she remains vulnerable to being masochistically overpowered by men's aggression. A second type protects herself with a more external shell. She is, accordingly, more difficult to conquer and much more prone to narcissism. Lastly, Deutsch described the guilt-ridden 'moral masochist' who chooses her lover on the model of her father, or of a child to be mothered. Either way her sexual enjoyment is inhibited. Such women, Deutsch argued, easily fall prey (as her sister Malvina did) to obsessional neurosis, whereas the former two types are more liable to hysteria.

Taking issue more explicitly than she had in Vienna with Freud's penis envy account of women's sexuality, Deutsch claimed that where such envy occurs it is secondary to bitterness against the mother and her other children. Feminine passivity, she now maintained while still adopting an essentially biologistic thesis, stems not from envy of the penis but from the little girl's lack of an organ whereby to realize her active and aggressive strivings. Nor is the vagina an active organ. Against Horney's and Klein's claims to the contrary, Deutsch insisted:

> The awakening of the vagina to full sexual functioning is entirely dependent upon the man's activity; and this absence of

> spontaneous vaginal activity constitutes the physiologic background of feminine passivity.[2]

But, she added, women's passivity is also an effect of the social restrictions on their sexuality, as in the case of her maternal aunt (see p. 42 above).

The social inhibition of women's activity and aggression, along with the biological and psychological inhibition of these impulses, Deutsch wrote, result in their being turned back on themselves into passivity and masochism. She instanced various ways women realize masochistic aims in sex. Taking issue with Freud's claim that lesbianism is rooted in a father-based 'masculinity complex', she argued as she had before that it is much more often an expression, usually platonic, of passivity and masochism related to early mothering. These impulses are also expressed in fantasies of being raped – fantasies she claimed to be less often realized in women than in men.

Prostitution fantasies, she said, likewise involve masochistic 'subjection of woman to man'. Again, however, she drew attention to the maternal as well as the patriarchal origin of such images. An example was Anna, whose prostitution seemingly expressed unconscious identification with her mother as masochistic victim of her father. She also sought to prove herself, in Deutsch's eyes, as object of her father's and boyfriend's desire by asking Deutsch to retrieve jewels her lover had supposedly given her. Deutsch went on to argue that the prostitute's relation to her pimp also expresses unconscious reproach against the father for not rescuing her from the mother, now identified as madam or brothel-keeper, as 'wicked woman', just as Deutsch reproached her father for not defending her against her own 'evil' mother.

On the other hand, she also stressed that the mother's subjection to the father and the daughter's self-protection against identifying with this fate is a major source of women's rebellion. The latter, she wrote, is

> unconsciously directed against those who oppressed their mothers and limited their own freedom . . . the revolutionary woman leaders of the anti-tsarist movement, for example, were

> often daughters of authoritarian generals or – and this only an apparent contradiction – oppressed minor officials.[3]

Horney, she insisted, was wrong to read her as saying women want to be humiliated. Quite the contrary. One of woman's main tasks, Deutsch stressed, is to preserve herself from the injuries to her self-esteem threatened by the masochism associated with mothering and woman's 'normal' social lot.

Such self-preservation, she said, is helped by women identifying with an image of the mother as active and forceful. *Carmen*, she wrote, represents just such a type of assertive femininity. So too George Sand, in so far as she identified with her powerful grandmother rather than with her downtrodden, prostitute mother. Such women's masculinity, she again insisted against Freud, and the lesbianism to which it can lead, stem not from penis envy but from fear, which Deutsch herself shared, of becoming one with a debased image of the mother's femininity.

But, she emphasized in concluding the first volume of *The Psychology of Women*, women's psychology is not static. It changes with time. Here she cited Alexandra Kollontai's 1923 novel, *Love of Worker Bees*, in which a grandmother resolves the conflict between sex and mothering by appeal to the Revolution's ideals of monogamy. Her daughter rationalizes her affair with a younger party-worker in terms of a later generation's philosophy of free love. In turn her daughter defends her own promiscuity by reference to socialist ideals of sex equality and Marxist opposition to private property.

Meanwhile women in the west were increasingly being drawn by war into the workforce – the new site, in Deutsch's view, of their age-old conflict between active masculinity and masochistic femininity. And, of course, women still went on having babies as living proof of being loved, said Deutsch, and as means of gratifying men's more than ever intense desire – against the odds of war – to secure some semblance of immortality. It was to women's resulting problems as mothers that Deutsch now turned.

7

Women's psychology – motherhood

Stressing the historical and social as well as the biological and psychological determinants of mothering, Deutsch also drew in the second volume of *The Psychology of Women* on her analyst friend Kardiner's anthropological interest in the Marquesas cult of the witch-like Vehini-hai. She began by describing the way fears of similarly vengeful maternal figures feed women's anxiety in our society lest their sexuality be destroyed by mothering, as depicted in Tolstoy's *Anna Karenina*.

Rejecting Freud's penis envy account of women's motive in having babies, Deutsch attributed it instead to the attempt to counter feminine passivity through identifying, in fantasy, with an active image of the mother. Teenage girls, she wrote, sometimes prematurely act out this fantasy. But it collapses in the absence of any actual motherly person with whom to identify. Sixteen-year-old Lydia, for instance, became a model mother's help to her employer, Mrs K. But her motherliness failed when Mrs K, who had previously served as role model to Lydia's mothering, became ill. Similarly, social work client Mrs Baron, who first became pregnant when she was fifteen, became extremely nervous about looking after her child when her husband, whom she relied on to mother their child, went out to work.

Perhaps drawing on her experience of looking to Felix to mother Martin, Deutsch emphasized the importance of men's as well as women's motherliness. An example was Mrs Booth, so frightened of being swamped by mothering that she left it to her husband. In attending to such cases Deutsch anticipated today's feminist and psychoanalytic stress on men's motherliness. But in doing so she underestimated the problems posed men by mothering, or at least reproduction. Women, she maintained, suffer more because of the divorce of sex from childbirth, whereas for men sex involves reproduction at one and the same moment.

An illustration of women's conflict in this sphere was twenty-nine-year-old Mrs Andrews. She was obsessed and fearful of pregnancy and sex seemingly because she dreaded becoming like her mother, whom she hated for her numerous pregnancies and affairs with men who beat her, and because of her mother's supposed Vehini-hai-like curse that she would die in childbirth.

Fear of such maternal retribution against the daughter's hatred of her mother's sexuality, claimed Deutsch, often contributes to infertility. She recalled how Polish women traditionally protected themselves against witch-like images of the mother to which this fear gives rise by calling on the Black Madonna to help them conceive. Surgery, she suggested, sometimes helps, not least because it seems to assuage the guilt and hatred towards the mother that can otherwise impede conception.

In this she tendentiously forwarded the not entirely sympathetic view that sterility can be caused as much by psychogenic as by organic factors. She went on, perhaps thinking of her daughter-in-law's miscarriages, that psychological causes of infertility can include child-like dependence on the mother – or husband – such that the woman feels unconfident of becoming a mother herself. Alternatively women do not conceive because they intuitively recognize that their husbands need to be mothered by them, without any other drain on their attention. Others, she said, remain sterile because their masculinity causes them to reject motherliness. Still others realize their masculinity precisely through the activity of mothering. Lastly, there is the woman who feels too emotionally drained and empty to withstand the rigours of pregnancy and motherhood.

As for pregnancy itself, Deutsch claimed that this too revives in women memories of their own early mothering. Some feel fortified by this, like Alice, whose fourth pregnancy was threatened with miscarriage. Feeling angry at her husband going away to war, she revived her old affection for her mother and thereby, hypothesized Deutsch, carried this pregnancy to term.

For others, pregnancy evokes childhood feelings of guilt and fear of the mother, against which women seek to defend themselves by appeal to the patriarchal protection of the doctor. Yet others look to pregnancy to free them from dependence on the mother, only to find it thereby exacerbated. Alternatively, pregnancy is disrupted by identification with a hated image of the mother, as in Deutsch's own case. But, in addition to backward-looking identification with the mother, there is also forward-looking, narcissistic identification with the child. Nor did Deutsch neglect the social factors that also affect women's experience of pregnancy, sterility, and abortion – all of which she had experienced herself.

After attributing miscarriage, such as her own, to rejection of self-injuring identification with a hated mother, Deutsch discussed pseudo-pregnancy. An example was a twenty-five-year-old unmarried woman who, fearful lest she impetuously flee her work as cook and household drudge to her brothers and sisters through precipitate pregnancy, refused to have sex with her boyfriend till he married her. She then felt guilty at thus blackmailing him. A month after they broke up she became convinced she was pregnant. She thereby put pressure on him to marry her, but only in fantasy, thus saving herself as it were from real blackmail.

Imagined pregnancy, wrote Deutsch, regularly involves such 'disavowal', the women both knowing and not knowing she is pregnant. It involves the same kind of triumph in deceiving others as Deutsch herself enjoyed in taking revenge on her mother by falsely passing herself off as a 'fallen woman'.

The contradictory desire both to be and not to be a mother likewise characterizes childbirth. Again drawing on anthropological data, Deutsch suggested that women in all societies fear being attacked by primitive demons in labour. This fear, she wrote, is related to unconscious guilt towards the mother. The midwife helps allay this fear, albeit her traditional role has been increasingly appropriated by doctors to whom the labouring woman transfers feelings more about her husband than about her mother.

Women's fears of childbirth, she said, are also related to the fear of separation the baby first feels, according to Rank and Freud, in being expelled from the mother's womb. But childbirth also involves euphoria. Yet this is often dulled and labour protracted, as in the case of a woman who told herself, 'I cannot give birth to a living child.' Another's labour was interrupted by fear of femininity and anger with Deutsch on this score. Still another was able to be active in childbirth only through identifying with Deutsch, who had had her baby in the same hospital.

Doctors, wrote Deutsch, undermine rather than increase women's confidence in childbirth in preventing their active participation in labour through the use of anaesthetics. Their administration, she suggested, is often motivated less by pain than by fear. Anticipating today's feminist observation that it is as though obstetricians wanted to wrest control from women of the mothering they otherwise fear, Deutsch argued that, by depriving women of active involvement in childbirth, men risk pushing them into competition in the same spheres of activity as themselves.

Presaging today's psychoanalytic claims regarding the initial psychological oneness of mother and infant, Deutsch drew attention to the mother's initial experience of her baby as one with herself. Only later, she wrote, does the mother come to experience the baby as separate. This entails resolving the tension between backward- and forward-looking, regressive and progressive tendencies towards dependence and independence, identification and separation from her own mother.

Some, Deutsch noted, only gradually become independent. This sometimes involves transferring dependence on the mother on to the husband. Such women often turned to social services for help in the absence of their husbands at the war. Others, like Deutsch herself, escape self-mortifying identification with a negative image of the mother through 'as if' identification with a more positive image. Yet others fear lest the mother take the baby away. Alternatively, another mother, cited by Deutsch, was so afraid of harming her baby that she gave it to her mother-in-law.

In discussing the conflict posed women's self-esteem by mothering, Deutsch indicated how this conflict is exacerbated by the simultaneous encouragement of US women both to realize their own individuality and to sacrifice it to their children. She contrasted this with the heroine of a Russian novel, *Verinea*, who, far from being torn between individual self-love and maternal self-sacrifice, is devoted both to her child and to the Revolution. Problems only arise, Deutsch suggested, where women lack the sense of self necessary to such shifting of self-interest on to others.

Similar problems also beset breast-feeding – some enjoying, others, like Deutsch, feeling drained by it. This variously stimulates love and hate of the baby. The latter is another source of Moses-like myths, previously interpreted by Freud in patriarchal terms, now seen by Deutsch – at least in the bulrushes incident – as depicting protection of the child from the mother's hostility resulting from her feeling depleted by its care.

Others, she pointed out, find their narcissism enriched by mothering. Their sense of unity with the child also enables them to anticipate its needs. But, perhaps because of her own mothering experience and her psychiatric work, Deutsch focused more on the pathological aspects of women's self-realization through mothering. An example was social work client Mrs Manzetti, who had always wanted to raise herself above her Italian working-class origins. Having made an unsatisfactory marriage, she now looked to her children to realize this ambition. She berated them for not doing so – a failure Deutsch attributed to Mrs Manzetti's lofty ideals replacing the warm motherliness her children needed.

Deutsch then went on to describe the mother's fear of self-loss in being separated from her child as akin to fear of being separated as a baby from her own mother. This, she claimed, can result in mothers seeking to keep their children identified with them, as described in D. H. Lawrence's *Sons and Lovers*, Ibsen's *Peer Gynt*, and Gorky's *The Mother*. By contrast, Deutsch observed, others have a more negative identification with their children, wish their own masochism on them, and predict the worst for them as for themselves.

Here she foreshadowed what has now become a central issue in psychoanalysis, namely unconscious communication between mother and child, psychoanalyst and patient. Deutsch had previously illustrated the latter process in developing Freud's interest in telepathy. She showed how patients sometimes seem to intuit what is in the analyst's mind as a result of the latter's seeming similarity to the patient's mother.[1] Now she described how she used to tell Martin stories of three imaginary grown-up sons of hers – giants – whom she had left in Poland. They had enormous appetites, she told him, and could 'eat a whole ox and a pot of spinach as big as this room for every meal'.[2] Far from reassuring him that she loved him best of all, this tale took away Martin's appetite so much did it unconsciously convey his mother's continuing rivalry with her three older siblings and her seeming wish to leave him for Poland.

Returning to her observation that some women seek to separate and become independent of their mothers through becoming mothers themselves, only to find themselves even more dependent if they feel unmotherly towards their children, Deutsch went on to describe women who believe in themselves as mother only as long as they are pregnant. Such women sometimes have one baby after another in an endless quest for the motherly self-esteem that constantly eludes them. Still others feel motherly only through 'as if' identification with others. An example, said Deutsch, was a German socialist of the 1890s who, in mothering her son, imitated the famous agitator Lily Braun's mothering – an example earlier cited by Melanie Klein in her account of child development.

Deutsch herself also drew attention to the social causes of the problems posed for women's self-esteem by mothering – conflicts she felt would be helped by society providing women with the means of realizing themselves outside mothering. And she pointed out how social stigma exacerbates the plight of unmarried mothers.

This causes some to have their illegitimate children adopted, only to feel guilty of abandoning them. Others keep the child and fend off social ostracism as best they can, like the unmarried 'Mrs Nawska' (see p. 25 above). For others, wrote Deutsch, the social stigma of illegitimacy is a means of getting back at the mother, as perhaps she herself had sought to do in becoming pregnant by Lieberman. On the other hand, the single mother's resulting guilt towards her mother can also lead her to feel she should have her baby adopted. In other cases, Deutsch maintained, adoption or fostering is motivated by the wish to flee conflict-ridden identification with the mother.

Illegitimate pregnancy, she added, is also fuelled by feelings of maternal deprivation or abandonment. Daughters may have children on whom to lavish the motherly care of which they felt deprived themselves. Seventeen-year-old Louise, for instance, sought in her boyfriends and baby the tenderness she lost with her mother's death when she was ten. Similarly, twenty-three-year-old Elise, starved of affection by her emotionally inhibited family, sought external and objective proof of being loved through having a child.

For others, paradoxically, and despite the social stigma of illegitimacy, single motherhood flatters their narcissism in seemingly realizing the self-sufficient, parthenogenetic fantasy: 'I have a child born of me alone, I am its mother and father. I do not need or want a man for the begetting of a child.'[3] Some even go so far as not to accept the father's support, so much does it wound their self-esteem. An example was a peasant woman Deutsch recalled from her youth. Seduced and abandoned by a member of the European court, she refused to demean herself by asking him for any financial help to raise their child.

Just as psychoanalysts and psychologists have focused on the psychology of children to the neglect of that of mothers, said Deutsch, so too they have focused on the psychology of the adopted child to the neglect of that of its adoptive mother. Seeking to right this balance, she pointed out that adoption, like natural motherhood, gratifies both self-sacrificing and narcissistic impulses. The outcome in both cases depends on the woman's capacity for motherliness. Adoption also offers the mother a means of displacing on to the child, and its supposed tainted heredity, feelings that might otherwise injure her self-esteem. Social work client Mrs Slutsky, for example, unable to bear her adopted niece Rose's unhappiness and resulting unruliness after Mrs Slutsky married and had a baby, blamed Rose's biological father for her bad behaviour.

Adoption, Deutsch observed, can either weaken or bolster the mother's self-esteem depending on whether she experiences it, in fantasy, as robbery or rescue of the child from the natural mother. Telling the child of its adoption can also wound the adoptive mother's narcissism. It threatens to displace her as 'first lady' in the child's affection. One might also add that adoptive mothers sometimes displace on to the child the fall from grace thereby involved. The child then becomes the damaged goods the adoptive mother otherwise feels herself to be in not being its natural mother.

Unlike adoptive mothers, stepmothers much more readily experience themselves as flawed, so much does folklore depict them as such. Again, however, Deutsch, who nearly became stepmother to Lieberman's children, was more concerned with the psychology of the mother than of the child, and with the way fairy-tales of wicked stepmothers fuel negative feelings evoked in the stepmother by rivalry with stepchildren for their father's affection, by guilt at not having gone through the same suffering as the natural mother, and by her stepchildren's simultaneous desire for and hatred of her as stepmother.

Deutsch then described, as she had years before, the psychology of menopause. Now, however, she also drew on her experience as mother-in-law and prospective grandmother. Freud had described the psychology of the former only from the viewpoint of the son-in-law's patriarchally understood Oedipal desire. By contrast Deutsch now described the rivalry over mothering of grandmother and daughter-in-law. The former may even put pressure on the latter to have the child she would unconsciously have liked to have had by her son. Perhaps this feeling was elicited in Deutsch by her own daughter-in-law Suzanne's frequent letters to her from Santa Fe about her difficulties in conceiving.

Grandmotherhood itself, concluded Deutsch, encompasses a number of different responses. Some treat their grandchildren as though they were their own children. Others relive their mothering through vicarious identification with their daughter-in-law's mothering. The ideal, however, is the grandmother who seeks no such repetition of her own mothering, nor any identification with the mothering of others, but is instead free of all such competition.

It was on this note that she ended. Lauded by some and lambasted by others,[4] her resulting book was pronounced by British psychoanalyst Marjorie Brierley to be 'the most important contribution to feminine psychology that has yet appeared'.[5] But Brierley would have liked another volume, not on mothering but on spinsterhood. And she also took exception to Deutsch's rejection of Klein's ideas about early vaginal eroticism, and to her neglect of the contradictions of love and hate in early mothering. Nevertheless she valued Deutsch's emphasis on the importance of identification with a 'good mother' in the development of narcissistic self-esteem. This was the subject of Deutsch's final work.

8

Narcissism – male and maternal

Within a decade of the 1945 publication of *The Psychology of Women* Helene's two sisters died – Malvina in Przemyśl in 1950, and Gizela in Australia in 1954. 1954 also saw the celebration of Helene and Felix's seventieth birthday, and the establishment by the Boston Institute of a prize in their honour.

Although she still dwelt on women's psychology – in talks about gynaecology, the follow-up of two women patients, frigidity, and examples of women patients' acting out in the transference[1] – Helene regretted that this was the topic for which she was best known. Increasingly she focused on men's psychology, particularly on the vicissitudes of their narcissism and self-esteem, in which she again drew on the problems posed her own self-esteem by identification with her hated mother.

Echoing the solipsism of the myth of Narcissus, who fell in love with his reflected image, Freud had described narcissism in essentially intrapsychic rather than interpersonal terms, as stemming from childhood fusion of the individual's supposed oral, anal, and phallic instincts such that the child comes to love itself as a whole rather than in oral, anal, and phallic bits and pieces. He went on tendentiously to claim that for women, unlike men, such self-love only gives way to true other-directed 'object love' with the birth of their first child.

Analysts today adopt a more interpersonal account of narcissism, thanks largely to Deutsch's attention to its dependence on identification with others. In 1934 she had illustrated this theme by reference to women and mothering, and the unstable self-esteem involved in 'as if' identification with others. Now she described similar cases in men, beginning with a patient, Jimmy, whom she first treated in 1935 when he was fourteen. She described his mother as doting and masochistic and his father as tyrannical. His older brothers left home early and were disowned by their father on this account. But Jimmy idealized him until he became a chronic invalid when Jimmy was seven. This shattered Jimmy's previous idealization of his father and, with it, the self-esteem he had established through identifying with this ideal. Losing all sense of inner worth, he now depended instead on the admiration of others outside himself. As a grown-up he passed himself off variously as a gentleman farmer, great writer, movie producer, and inventor. He rejected his wife as soon as she doubted his genius, and likewise dismissed Deutsch when she punctured his cocksure arrogance – 'Are you a Freudian? . . . The old man [Freud] isn't even a doctor' – by pointing out his ignorance.[2] In general, she wrote, the narcissism of such 'impostors' – and here she included Thomas Mann's *Felix Krull* – depends entirely on others crediting their inflated self-esteem.

Deutsch returned to this theme after attending the 1956 Freud centenary celebrations in London and visiting Spain – home of the narcissistic *Carmen* and *Don Quixote*. This time she dwelt[3] on the depression resulting from wounded self-esteem described in *Lord Jim* by fellow-Pole Joseph Conrad, a distant relative of her Aunt Frania. In the novel Conrad tells of a sailor so injured in his ideal of masculine duty after jumping an apparently sinking ship with its cargo of Indian pilgrims that he keeps changing jobs lest this, his now spoilt identity, be revealed. Ending up in thrall to the admiration of another Asian people, Jim gives himself up to being shot by their leader as soon as he seems to them to have betrayed their trust. Conrad attributed his tragedy to being so dominated by 'exalted egoism' that he left the living, including his lover, for 'pitiless wedding with a shadowy ideal of conduct'.[4]

Increasingly Deutsch devoted herself to trying to understand such overweening egoism. In the process she abandoned the topic of femininity, as she had wanted to with the publication of *The Psychology of Women*. Her own narcissism was flattered by receiving the Menninger Award in 1962. Felix, however, suffered the blow that year of being forcibly retired as a training analyst because of arteriosclerotic confusion and memory loss. Helene retired out of sympathy with him. But she was out of the country – holidaying in Greece – on the occasion of their last wedding anniversary.

In January 1964 Felix died. Helene now fell to idealizing him. She recalled the help he had given her as a mother, and felt terribly lonely at his loss. Meanwhile in her writing, and almost for the first time, she turned to the way mothering bolsters rather than detracts from women's self-esteem. Freud had argued that such esteem – the 'ego ideal' – is formed through identification with the father. By contrast, and drawing on the way patients inflated their self-esteem through identifying with an idealized image of her in therapy, Deutsch now described a particular form of mother–son identification in which the son, in collaboration with the mother, resolves the Oedipal conflict between them by seeking to live up to a non-sexual, ascetic ideal. This can take the form in Catholic families, she said, of dreaming of the son becoming a saint through being a priest – a fantasy involving 'idealistic union between mother and son' in which the mother idolizes her son in seeking to realize herself.[5]

In a 1966 essay[6] in honour of ego psychologist Heinz Hartmann, she again dwelt on narcissism, of which she herself was accused as always 'wanting to be the centre of attention' while sarcastically putting others down. In particular she described two cases of post-traumatic amnesia – one a Mr Jones, the youngest of four children and the only boy, whose father had left home when he was four. He had completely forgotten a row he had had with his much older mistress who, like his mother, already had three daughters. The row happened when his lover told him her son, whom he had fathered, was a genius. This was too much. For he had decided to leave her and would thereby lose the son with whose genius he might otherwise identify to boost his self-esteem. He only recalled the row when his self-regard was buoyed up by marrying and having another son who he felt was also a genius.

A second case, Mr Smith, had amnesia for his second brother's birth when he was ten, although he remembered his first brother's birth quite clearly. His amnesia for the later event, it seemed, was due to the second brother's birth proving his mother wrong in predicting she would have a girl. It thereby punctured his idealization of his mother, and thus threatened his own self-esteem in so far as it was based on identification with her – an identification he now transferred on to Deutsch. He wanted to give up his profession and become an analyst like her. This alternated with a debased image of her as of his mother.

By now Deutsch's grandsons – born in 1946 and 1949 – were both in college. To gain a sense of what their generation was about she interviewed, on an informal basis, several Cambridge students, drawing on their 'grandmother transference' to her.[7] On this basis she concluded that the central conflicts of adolescence involve those between fantasy and reality, and between inward-directed narcissistic self-absorption and outward-directed relations with others. In the process she described cases of boys – perhaps thinking of her one-time patient, Norbert Wiener, and also of her own ambitiousness for her son and her older grandson Peter – driven to be 'brilliant' through early symbiosis with their mothers' ambitions. She bemoaned the way fathers seemed to be increasingly taking a back-seat in childrearing, and the way they have become devalued along with the society they represent. This, she said, leads to loneliness, like her own – teenagers seeking to escape it through identification with peers. This was the source, in her view, of Beatlemania, sexual libertarianism, and student protest. Although she supported the Berkeley student demonstrations, she decried this activism as not nearly so politically engaged as the political movements of her youth. She went on to add that today's mothers want their daughters not only to stay home but also to realize their own unfulfilled ambitions through work outside the home. How different from Deutsch's own mother.

In her own role as mother and grandmother, however, Deutsch was less interested in mother–daughter than mother–son relations. Inspired by her younger grandson Nicholas's performance in *The Bacchae*, she dwelt on the Greek myth's account of Dionysus's quest for eternal glory through destroying his mother Semele's mortal family so as to make both her and himself immortal through their reunion in Hades.[8]

She took issue with Freud's idealization of mother–son relations as initially conflict-free, and then went on to describe another version of the Semele myth. In this version Apollo retaliates against the threat to his narcissism posed by Semele's life-giving powers by destroying her when she becomes pregnant by him. Subsequently he inspires Orestes likewise to kill his mother as though, suggests Deutsch, to prove reproduction the work of men, just as Freud also implied, in attributing the penis's 'extraordinarily high narcissistic cathexis' to 'its organic significance for the propagation of the species'.[9]

The next year, in a paper for an international symposium held in Israel on the Freud–Einstein correspondence 'Why War?',[10] and drawing on her own attempt as an adolescent to secure her self-esteem through rebellion against her mother, Deutsch[11] attributed to adolescent revolt the origin of Rosa Luxemburg's and Angelika Balabanoff's opposition to the First World War, in the case of Balabanoff to revolt against her aristocratic Russian mother. She also recalled Luxemburg's longing for motherhood. Deutsch herself now appealed to mothering in deploring Nixon and the Vietnam War. 'Women are mothers,' she said. 'They would not allow this killing.'[12]

In her last book, her 1973 autobiography, which she regarded as a supplement to her *Psychology of Women*, Deutsch described Balabanoff and Luxemburg as her 'ego-ideal'. Although she identified with women – an etching of Virginia Woolf (also seduced by her brother) adorned her walls, as did a picture of the Black Madonna of Czestochova – and although she contributed to Nancy Friday's research for her 1979 book, *My Mother, Myself*, it was the men in her life she most recalled in her last days. Just before her death on 29 March 1982 she muddled up her father, Felix, and Lieberman. Previously she had written to her doctor that she had just seen and spoken with 'the Professor'.[13]

In her autobiography she had written:

> I see three distinct upheavals in my life: liberation from the tyranny of my mother; the revelation of socialism; and my release from the chains of the unconscious . . . In each of these revolutions I was inspired and aided by a man – my father, Herman Lieberman, and lastly Freud.[14]

Deutsch's seeming need to preserve her narcissism through fleeing identification with her mother for her father, Lieberman and Freud led her to be very cautious in using her mothering experience to go beyond the latter's work. Indeed, there was a split in her 'between her political attitudes and her super-conservative adulation of Freud'.[15] In a sense she used her mothering experience simply to spell out the effects on women's psychology of the repudiation of femininity Freud had described – a repudiation now recognized to be an effect of women's social subordination. Her abhorrence of her mother also led to a rather one-sided, negative, and static equation of mothering and femininity with passivity and masochism. Nor, unlike Horney and Klein, did she produce a comprehensive theoretical development of Freud's work. Nevertheless, as I have sought to show, she used her own and her patients' mothering experience to go well beyond his ideas. In doing so she provided a wealth of detailed clinical illustration of the maternal as well as the patriarchal determinants of women's and men's psychology. The result was the foundation of today's psychoanalytic concern with understanding and treating the injuries to self-esteem – the narcissistic personality disorders – suffered by men as well as women as a result of the often fractured maternal and parental identification Deutsch knew so well from her own case.

Karen Horney with her daughter Brigitte, born 1911

III

KAREN HORNEY

1

Adored mother

Unlike Helene Deutsch, Karen Horney adored her mother. She used this experience forcibly to oppose Freud's phallocentric account of women's and men's psychology; to emphasize the social and parental as opposed to the instinctual determinants of neurosis; and finally to abandon Freud's theory of the unconscious and infantile sexuality altogether. The result was a body of work that remains tremendously popular, especially in the USA – much more so than that of Helene Deutsch. Horney's work has proved particularly inspiring to feminists both because of its gynocentric rejection of Freudian phallocentrism, and because of its attention to the psychological causes and effects of sexual inequality

Karen's father, Berndt Henrik Wackels Danielsen, was Norwegian by birth. He was twenty years older than her mother Sonni, and was already an established sea-captain with four nearly grown-up children by his first marriage, and a three-year-old son, Berndt, by Sonni, when Karen was born on 15 September 1885 in Eilbek, just outside Hamburg.

Sonni was the daughter of an Amsterdam-born architect and as such felt socially superior to Wackels. She had met and married him in Bremen in 1881 – not out of love, she told Karen, but out of fear of being left on the shelf. As a child Karen went on sea voyages with him. And in her later work she often cited the writing of his fellow-Scandinavians – Ibsen and Kierkegaard. But in her teens Karen mostly sided with her mother and brother against Wackels. And when that failed she took refuge in adventure stories, 'eternal crushes', and doing well at school. By thirteen she had also decided to become a doctor.

This meant leaving her local church school for a Gymnasium in Hamburg, where classes had recently been opened to prepare girls for university entrance. Persuaded by Berndt, her mother gave in, as she did to Karen's every other wish. She pressurized Wackels to support this change of school, even though he was more interested, in Karen's eyes, in financing her stepbrother's career. He seemed to have no other goal for her than having her stay home to help with the housework so that they could dispense with the maid.

Backed by her mother, however, Karen had her way. Benefiting from this, as from an earlier generation's struggle to secure women's university entrance, she started high school in early 1901. Meanwhile, at home, she continued to take the part of her mother – her 'dearest in the whole world' – against her father and his stepchildren. Imitating her mother's snobbish contempt for Wackels, she dismissed his rigid version of Lutheranism thus:

> . . . he [Wackels] delivers conversion sermons, says endless, rather stupid, prayers every morning . . . I cannot listen to his sensuous, materialistic, illogical, intolerant views of everything high and holy. He is simply a low, ordinary, stupid character, who cannot rise to higher things.[1]

Sonni made no secret of wanting Wackels dead. Karen let him know she also wanted him away: 'We are so unspeakably happy when you are not here,' she told him. 'Mother is our greatest happiness.'[2]

Fleeing the sight of her mother's distress, Karen sought refuge in obsession with one man after another – first with an actor, then a whirlwind Christmas 1903 romance with a friend of Berndt's. This was followed by longer affairs with Rolf, a Jewish music student, and with Ernst, a lodger whom Sonni took in after she left Wackels to settle with the children in Hamburg. Being in love, Karen wrote, displaced all other worries: 'For if "he is my thought day and night," how then should other thoughts have room?'[3]

Following her parents' separation in August 1904, Karen became more ambivalent about her mother. She complained of

Sonni's and Berndt's snobbery and anti-semitism against Rolf. And she felt at a loss at home when first he and then Ernst left. Her desolation persisted through her first term, in spring 1906, at Freiburg University where, again benefiting from earlier feminist campaigns, she began studying medicine.

That July, however, she began yet another affair, this time with fellow medical student Louis Grote (Losch), with whom, as with Rolf before him, she listened to Wagner. But, unlike Rolf, Sonni liked Losch. That autumn she moved to Freiburg to be with Karen and took in both him and Karen's schoolfriend Ida Behrman as lodgers. Meanwhile Karen had also begun an affair with Losch's friend Oskar Horney, who was now studying political economy in Braunschweig. To him she wrote warmly of Sonni's Freiburg 'doll's house':

> . . . she knows not only how to cook well, but above all how to spread about her a fluid atmosphere of cosiness . . . she seems to me a truly perfect, exemplary mother.[4]

But she also berated Sonni's closeness to Berndt despite his 'meannesses', her duplicity in getting both her and Berndt to lie to their father, and her smothering affection. It left Karen feeling 'as though I would suffocate under all the love and care surrounding me'.[5] This grated on her still more when Oskar returned to Freiburg in autumn 1907. For her part Sonni complained to Berndt, then a law student in Hamburg, of Karen's self-centredness:

> I have been too considerate, too modest and generous, and I misled others into a healthy selfishness by being that way . . . but their egoism has something very hurting, especially from Karen who is my own very beloved child and who should have more heart and sense and understanding for me . . . does she have to run over to his [Oskar's] place so often and every evening . . . couldn't they stay once or so with me?[6]

But although Sonni confided in Berndt, he was unwilling to have her live with him when Karen passed her preclinical exams the next year and moved to Göttingen to begin her clinical training. Instead Sonni went to live with her stepdaughter in Stockholm. But she was unable to get work there, and Karen soon found herself having to invite Sonni to live near her.

Lacking Wackels's financial support, Sonni and Karen had long had to support themselves – the one through landladying, the other through tutoring. Now their money troubles were at an end. In 1909 Oskar got a job with the industrial tycoon Stinnes, who to further his wealth had backed the brutal suppression that year of workers in one of his coal mines. The plight of miners was the subject of one of Deutsch's first medical papers.[7] Not so Karen. Although liberal-minded, she never became politically involved. And Oskar was positively right-wing. Both did well by Stinnes in Berlin, where they moved and married in October 1909. First they lived in a boarding-house and then, after Oskar's promotion, in their own flat in middle-class Lankwitz.

Meanwhile Karen studied at the Berlin medical school and its neuropsychiatric clinic, where she met Hamburg-born Karl Abraham, established since 1907 as Berlin's first psychoanalyst. Together with her friends Ida Behrman and Carl Mueller Braunschweig, she went into analysis with him in early 1909 for depression and sexual difficulties.

Abraham attributed the latter to Karen's attraction to 'forceful men', dating from

> the time when I loved my father with all the strength of my passion . . . In Oskar I found everything I consciously wished for – and behold: my instinctual life rebels. It feels itself drawn to a Karl U. [another of Abraham's patients] because it scents the beast of prey in him.[8]

Her readiness to abandon herself to such patriarchal figures, said Abraham, was betrayed by her leaving her handbag in his office on her very first visit.

Soon afterwards her actual father died – in May 1910. Karen now became increasingly depressed, but gave up her analysis that summer. To judge from her diary, she became increasingly preoccupied by identification with her mother. Feeling herself in 'no position to shine through beauty', Karen now wrote, she sought to attract attention through being 'uncommonly intelligent', just as Sonni likewise constantly sought attention:

> She has to be first everywhere . . . hence her craze for giving presents, her grand bearing, her desire to command in the house; hence her having managed to make me, even up to my eighteenth or nineteenth year, look upon her as perfection itself.[9]

Karen was also about to become a mother herself. Too bad, she felt, that pregnancy interfered with her affairs and 'vagabonding'. Too bad that it made her more than ever like her mother, with whom she felt increasingly irritated not least because of Sonni's husband-hunting and endless demands:

> . . . all her arguments take on a kind of rigid monotony: that she is always putting herself aside, sacrificing herself, and yet people owed her some consideration . . . [She] is now morbidly seeking for expressions of affection from those nearest to her – insatiably . . . [thus becoming] an almost intolerable burden to everybody.

But Karen also relished mothering:

> It is just the expectation and the joy in it that are now so indescribably beautiful. And the feeling of carrying in me a small, becoming human being invests one with higher dignity and importance that makes me very happy and proud.[10]

Then suddenly, Sonni died of a stroke on 2 February 1911. Karen felt guiltily relieved: 'For Sonni was my great childhood love.' She thought of going back into analysis, especially after the birth the next month of her first daughter, Brigitte. Instead, fearful of her 'readiness for transference', she decided to go it alone through self-analysis.

This included luxuriating in mothering:

> In nursing, such an intimate union of mother and child as never occurs later. Mutual sensual satisfaction; hence perhaps strengthening of the longing for one's own mother . . . what I value most just now in a woman is motherliness.[11]

Breast-feeding came first. Around it were fitted her final medical exams that summer.

These were followed by psychiatric work in Berlin and Lankwitz, where Karen and Oskar enjoyed the sexual licence and social whirl of pre-war Berlin. From 1911 Karen also attended evening meetings of the Berlin Psychoanalytic Society where, in February 1912, she presented a paper about children's sex education which Abraham commended to Freud as showing 'real understanding'. By 1915, with the absence of men at the war, she became the Society's secretary. And in February 1917, having seen patients analytically since 1912, she gave her first lecture about psychoanalytic therapy to fellow-doctors, in which she followed Freud in stressing the patient's transference as main vehicle of cure.

Thanks to 'super-profiteer' Stinnes, her own life was becoming increasingly comfortable. Following the birth of two more daughters – Marianne and Renate, in 1913 and 1916 – the Horneys moved to wealthy Zehlendorf. From here Karen vacationed on the Baltic and in Berchtesgaden. When not on holiday she saw private patients both in the city and at home, while also continuing a psychiatric practice in Lankwitz.

Not surprisingly her daughters – especially her middle daughter Marianne – experienced her as distant and unavailable. She wanted them to be prematurely independent. In 1917, for instance, she sent the still very young Brigitte and Marianne for several months to Switzerland because of Brigitte's TB. Back home their father played with them more, but he was also a harsh disciplinarian. Karen's childrearing, by contrast, was more a mixture of benign neglect and whimsical impulsiveness. This included sending the children to a variety of experimental schools, and for analysis (starting in 1923) with Melanie Klein, against which all three variously rebelled. Marianne refused to see her, and Renate hid under the couch with her hands over her ears so as not to hear Klein's interpretations, albeit she learnt enough rude words to write them everywhere and send obscene letters to the neighbours. Even Marianne, who stayed the course the longest, dismisses Klein's treatment:

> It had nothing to do with real problems I may have had. My

> parents didn't talk to Melanie. Melanie wasn't interested in talking to my parents ... I was put on the couch and went through this meaningless procedure, which doesn't seem to have hurt, and which couldn't possibly help.[12]

Meanwhile the war had enormously increased the fortunes both of Stinnes and of psychoanalysis. In 1914 Karen had written her qualifying psychiatry thesis on physical trauma as cause of psychosis in a fifty-seven-year-old private patient, an underwear factory owner. The success of psychoanalysis in treating such psychological effects of trauma, particularly of shell-shock, won it many adherents during and after the war. As a result plans were soon afoot to make psychoanalysis more generally available, through founding a clinic where people could be treated virtually free.

In face of Berlin's post-war demoralization and political chaos (including Rosa Luxemburg's assassination), the first such clinic was opened on Potsdamerstrasse, East Berlin, in February 1920, with Max Eitingon as director. Horney was its first woman member, and the first woman teacher in the subsequently founded Berlin Psychoanalytic Institute where she again went briefly into analysis – this time with the Institute's Vienna-born senior training analyst Hans Sachs. Shortly afterwards, drawing on both her own and her patient's mothering experience, she initiated the first psychoanalytically-based critique of Freudian patriarchalism.

2

Innate femininity

Horney particularly opposed the seeming insult to women's self-esteem of Freud's penis envy account of their psychology. In this she used her maternal experience essentially to invert his theory: first to argue that women's psychology is determined by innate identification with the mother, not by disappointed identification with the father; second to draw attention to men's envy of women's mothering.

The ground for battle was set for her by her first analyst, Karl Abraham's, 1920 Hague Congress claim, on the basis of his patients' transference to him as father-figure, that women unconsciously want to be men. Some, he argued, attribute this desire to women's social subordination. But the true cause, he insisted, is childhood envy of the penis. Just as with other things the child wants, he continued, the little girl looks to her father to provide her with one. And when this wish is disappointed, she looks to him to give her a baby instead.

Having analysed his own daughter, Abraham went on to record that little girls have the idea: 'I had a penis once as boys have, but it has been taken from me.'[1] This is the source, he claimed, of women's sense of having a wound in place of a penis – an image revived by menstruation, sexual intercourse, and childbirth. Hence women's sense of vengeance against men, in the first place against the father, for not giving them a penis. This, Abraham argued, is one determinant of female frigidity. Alternatively it leads to defensive belittling of men through having a succession of lovers (as Horney herself did). Still others, he claimed, consciously or unconsciously go on wanting to have a penis. This was a major cause, in his view, of women's homosexuality, masculine ambition, and feminism.

Horney was not particularly offended by the anti-feminist tenor of his talk. Indeed, as her daughter observes,[2] Horney was never a feminist. Her rejection of Freud's work in the name of women's self-esteem has certainly inspired many feminists, both then and now. But she herself was far too much of an individualist ever to engage in collective political struggle – feminist or otherwise. It was precisely Abraham's seeming attack on her self-worth as an individual – as woman and mother – that she found most offensive. On this score she expostulated:

> . . . that one half of the human race is discontented with the sex assigned to it . . . is decidedly unsatisfying, not only to feminine narcissism but also to biological science.[3]

In a November 1921 response to Abraham, later expanded into her first ever Psychoanalytic Congress paper (chaired by Freud) in 1922, Horney acknowledged that women may envy men their penises, as she earlier privately acknowledged envying Berndt as a child. But, she maintained, this stems from envy of the advantages the penis affords boys in enabling them to piss standing up. It thereby maximizes their urinary, voyeuristic, exhibitionist, and masturbatory pleasure. Reiterating this account of penis envy years later, Simone de Beauvoir added that girls also envy boys' ability to project their pee, thereby realizing themselves through seemingly transcending gravity.

Following Horney, de Beauvoir dismissed Freud's theory that femininity is rooted in penis envy. Horney herself claimed that femininity is innate, as is the daughter's sexual identity with her mother. In this she arguably drew on her immediate sense of identification with her own mother. She thereby overlooked the factors leading Deutsch and Klein to demonstrate the fraught and precarious character of such identification.

Neglectful of such factors, and drawing on her clinical experience, Horney argued that identification with the mother can sometimes be so intense that the daughter acts as though, like her mother, she had also had sex with her father. A case in point was a woman who imagined being raped. According to Horney this fantasy expressed the unconscious idea of having 'experienced with her [mother] the father's act of complete sexual appropriation'.[4] Another patient, whose mother had to eat salt because of a lung haemorrhage, which the patient ascribed to her parents' intercourse, felt she too had to eat salt as though she had also been damaged by sexual intercourse with her father. Some women, Horney went on, even become preoccupied with supposed internal injury to convince themselves of being one with the mother as victim of sexual violation as if by the father. This, not penis envy, she insisted against Abraham, is the source of women's image of themselves as genitally wounded.

She derided his and Freud's penis envy account of femininity as due to misplaced 'masculine narcissism'. Such narcissism, however, had little to boast of in 1923. Runaway inflation had led to general economic collapse and, with it, the ruin of Stinnes. Oskar lost his job, and fell ill with meningitis from which he never fully recovered. He now became involved in one losing business venture after another. The same winter Karen's brother Berndt died of pneumonia. He was only forty-two.

Karen herself, however, went from strength to strength, at least in her work. Her 1922 critique of Abraham had drawn the largest audience at that year's Berlin Congress. Her subsequent lectures to social workers and teachers, Institute courses on female sexuality, and 1925 Humboldt University lecture on women's psychology were all very popular. Some even attracted newspaper coverage. Her urge to be the centre of attention, like her mother before her, was crowned with success even though to her surprise it alienated her colleagues.

Yet she also increasingly went against them in adopting the mother-centred views of the self-styled 'wild analyst' Georg Groddeck, to whom she now wrote:

> I consider it rather one-sided that the [Freudian] emphasis is always on the attitude towards the father, with a footnote always explaining that for simplicity's sake only the attitude towards the father is mentioned but that it would also apply to the attitude towards the mother. But it does not also apply to the attitude to the mother. In fact some fundamental differences between men and women must be attributed to this fact.[5]

In Berlin as in Vienna, however, orthodox psychoanalysis

continued to focus on the father. In 1925, partly provoked by Horney's paper, Freud reasserted his penis envy account of women's psychology. He insisted against Horney that women's heterosexuality is not an effect of innate identification with the mother. Neither can be assumed. Rather they need explaining, particularly the girl's move from attachment to the mother and to heterosexual desire for the father. Discovering rather than assuming herself to be the same as her mother in not having a penis and blaming her phallic lack on the mother, Freud argued as indicated above, the girl looks to the father instead to provide her with a penis, or its unconscious equivalent – a baby. Contrary to Horney, he claimed that the girl's sense of lack, of being wounded or castrated, is cause not effect of her Oedipal desire for the father.

In this context he also cited Deutsch's work, which Horney now began to criticize. Taking for granted women's identification with their mothers' femininity, Horney rejected Deutsch's claim that such identification is mediated through a phase of phallic or masculine activity and identification with the father. Instead Horney insisted that femininity develops in girls independent of boys' and men's masculinity. Furthermore, and identifying much more readily than Deutsch with mothering, she was also more willing to acknowledge its pains as well as its pleasures. It was patently absurd, she scoffed,[6] for Deutsch to describe childbirth as involving orgasm and phallic loss.

In 1926 Horney also launched her most vehement attack on Freud – though she felt she pulled her punches – in an essay written for a volume in honour of his seventieth birthday. No wonder he once characterized her as 'malicious-mean'.

Not that she did not begin by lauding his discovery of penis envy. But then, in keeping with the interdisciplinarity that was to distinguish her work from psychoanalytic orthodoxy, she cited sociologist Georg Simmel's observations on the way men in male-dominated society falsely but successfully pass off their subjective experience as objective truth. Although seemingly objective, she claimed, Freud's ideas about women's psychology were no different from the subjective response of the little boy on first discovering that girls do not have a penis.

She also scorned Hungarian psychoanalyst Sandor Ferenczi's claim that, while men enjoy sex because it involves symbolic return to the womb, women achieve this pleasure only in childbirth. As mother of three, she assured her readers that childbirth is not the unalloyed orgasmic pleasure Ferenczi implied. Nor could she accept Ferenczi's claim that pregnancy and childbirth are merely compensations for the disadvantages women suffer relative to men:

> At this point I, as a woman, ask in amazement, and what about motherhood? And the blissful consciousness of bearing a new life within oneself? And the ineffable happiness of the increasing expectation of the appearance of this new being? And the joy when it finally makes its appearnce and one holds it for the first time in one's arms? And the deep pleasurable feeling of satisfaction in suckling it and the happiness of the whole period when the infant needs her care?

Far from being secondary to envy of the father's penis, she continued, desire for motherhood is instinctual, as is the wish to be the same as the mother in having sex with the father:

> . . . we must resist the temptation to interpret in the light of penis envy the manifestations of so elementary a principle of nature as that of the mutual attraction of the sexes.[7]

But the girl also intuitively knows, Horney claimed, that her vagina is not large enough for her father. Hence, she asserted, the girl's early fantasy that 'an excessively large penis is effecting forcible penetration, producing pain and haemorrhage, and threatening to destroy something'.[8] Hence too her fear of being wounded were her desire to take her mother's place in sex with her father realized. Nor, because of the internal character of her genitals, can the girl easily reassure herself that such damage has not taken place. Fear of such damage, Horney maintained, can lead to frigidity, avoidance of motherhood, or flight from femininity into masculinity. Above all, and quite unlike Freud, she stressed that women's flight from femininity is reinforced by their social subordination.

Her argument was reiterated the next year by the President

of the British Psycho-Analytical Society, Ernest Jones. Freud replied by insisting that femininity is acquired, not innate. Meanwhile Horney[9] persisted in assuming as pre-given the daughter's feminine identification with the mother. It is the fear, disappointment and guilt to which this identification gives rise – in so far as it includes the wish to supplant the mother in sex with her father – Horney maintained, that cause women to turn from femininity to masculinity.

She thus used her own and her women patients' sense of oneness with their mothers, and the anxieties and masculinity to which she claimed this gives rise, to reject Freud's claim that masculinity in women is an effect of penis envy. She also used this experience to take issue with his support of non-medical, lay analysis. In a contribution to a special January 1927 meeting of senior analysts she insisted on the need for medical training, not least because it alerts analysts to the possibility that their women patients' complaints of internal damage may reflect actual organic disturbance, not merely fantasies of being injured in sex with the father.[10]

The disappointment and guilt attaching to this incestuous wish, she elsewhere observed,[11] often continues into marriage. Or women seek to assuage their guilt by enjoying sex only on condition of marital suffering. Alternatively, and like Horney herself, women seek sexual gratification outside marriage.

Returning to this theme in a November 1930 talk to the German Women's Medical Association,[12] she suggested that disappointment of women's innate feminine desire to become the sexual partner, like the mother, of the father can also give rise to vengeful feelings against men. Or it can lead to avoidance of sex for fear of being experienced as vengeful. Alternatively this feeling is projected into men, who are then experienced as the source of vengeance and exploitation of which the woman feels herself to be the hapless victim.

But what about actual exploitation and abuse? Nor is Horney's evidence for the biological determination of women's identification with the mother convincing. In this context she cited a patient whose pre-menstrual dreams were sensuous and red, with a feeling of wickedness and sin, her body meanwhile feeling heavy and full. Subsequently the patient was relieved to discover – on menstruating – that she was not pregnant, so much had she hated her mother as a child and felt guilty towards her for supplanting her in her father's affections. The evocation of such mother-related thoughts and images by menstruation, Horney concluded without further ado, is proof that mothering is 'instinctually anchored deeply in the biological sphere'.[13]

As further evidence of the girl's supposed biologically based identification with the mother – specifically in sex with the father – Horney cited the early occurrence of rape-like images in girls, of

> criminals who break in through windows or doors; men with guns who threaten to shoot; animals that creep, fly, or run inside some place (e.g., snakes, mice, moths); animals or women stabbed with knives; or trains running into a station or tunnel.

Furthermore, she claimed, girls early experience instinctively given vaginal sensations and associated fears of masturbation as indicated by dreams of

> doing a piece of needlework and all at once a hole appears, of which she feels ashamed; or she is crossing above a river or a chasm on a bridge that suddenly breaks off in the middle; or she is walking along a slippery incline and all at once begins to slide and is in danger of falling over a precipice.[14]

Girls, Horney added, often flee such fears by repressing all knowledge of the vagina. Analysts, she claimed, had wrongly mistaken this for absence of vaginal eroticism in infancy.[15]

She thereby launched a pattern for subsequent feminist critiques of Freud. Like Horney, for instance, French psychoanalyst Luce Irigaray argues today that patriarchal psychoanalysis wrongly overlooks women's inherent femininity as though it came into being only as effect of men. In fact, she argues, feminine sexuality begins through pre-Oedipal unity and sameness with the mother, an identity homologous to that of the lips of the labia and their embrace. Far from being initiated into femininity by the father, Irigaray maintains, women are alienated from their innate feminine identification with the mother by patriarchal intervention and phallic penetration.

Horney likewise counterposed father-based images of 'overwhelming forces that can vanquish, penetrate, and destroy' with 'early instinctive premonition of motherhood'.[16] Its counterpart, she maintained, is men's envy of women's power in mothering.

3

Womb envy

Horney's claim that women innately want to be raped can hardly endear her to feminists. For it excuses men's sexual abuse of women as something the latter supposedly want. It also turns a blind eye to the reality, as opposed to fantasy, of such abuse. By contrast her celebration of women's mothering, and her account of men's desire for it – their 'womb envy' – has won her considerable feminist following.

In describing such envy she drew on Groddeck's account of his and men's general resentment – 'I am not myself a woman and cannot be a mother.'[1] But she particularly stressed her men patients' envy of her as mother:

> When one begins, as I did, to analyse men only after a fairly long experience of analysing women, one receives a most surprising impression of the intensity of this envy of pregnancy, childbirth, and motherhood, as well as of the breasts and of the act of suckling.[2]

Overlooking the possibility that men analysts had ignored this envy because their sex did not readily elicit it, Horney suggested in 1926 that psychoanalytic neglect of men's womb envy is due to it being more readily sublimated and repressed in male-dominated society than women's penis envy.

The next year saw the break-up of her marriage. The bankruptcy of Oskar, whom she had married perhaps partly for his money, forced them to sell their Zehlendorf home in 1926. From there they moved to a flat in the city. But within a year Karen moved out with her daughters to a nearby apartment where, like her mother before her, she took in lodgers. Meanwhile Oskar had started an affair with his secretary, whom he eventually married.

Karen attributed such infidelity to disappointment at the spouse's failure to live up to ideals first entertained by children towards their parents. In so far as marriage realizes such ideals it can feel tantamount to incest. The guilt resulting from this, she said, can also result in women as well as men seeking extramarital affairs. But these are less well tolerated by men. Marxists have attributed this sexual double standard to men's concern to ensure the legitimacy of their heirs. Horney, by contrast, explained men's jealousy in maternal terms – as stemming from men's oral desire in infancy to have sole possession of the mother, unlike women who she claimed have no analogously exclusive desire for the father.

She elaborated this theme further in a September 1930 Dresden meeting of the German Psychoanalytic Society devoted to the social determinants of human psychology. Her own talk dwelt specifically on the psychology of men's social dominance.

From infancy onwards, she argued, man entertains the image of a 'nurturing, selfless, self-sacrificing mother ... the ideal embodiment of the woman who could fulfil all his expectations and longings'.[3] This in turn gives rise to bitterness at not being able to become a mother himself. To compensate, Horney maintained, men have instead given birth to culture from which they exclude women in the name of their supposed inferiority. Men also stave off envy of mothering by devaluing it and overvaluing male genitality. An example was Freud's theory of female penis envy. Moreover, she observed, because men's theories enjoy cultural hegemony in male-dominated society, women including Deutsch subscribe to these ideologies even though they denigrate women and conceal the conflict of their interests with those of men.

To all of this, and Jones's support of Horney, Freud retorted:

> It is to be anticipated that men analysts with feminist views, as well as our women analysts, will ... object that such notions [of female penis envy] spring from the 'masculinity complex' of the male and are designed to justify on theoretical grounds his innate inclination to disparage and suppress women. But

> this sort of psychoanalytic argumentation reminds us here, as it so often does, of Dostoevsky's famous 'knife that cuts both ways'. The opponents of those who argue in this way will on their side think it quite natural that the female sex should refuse to accept a view which appears to contradict their eagerly coveted equality with men. The use of analysis as a weapon of controversy can clearly lead to no decision.[4]

Undeterred, Horney optimistically used her mothering and analytic experience to insist that women are indeed men's equals. Just as girls fear the father, she emphasized, so boys equally fear the mother. As well as resenting women's mothering, she wrote, men fear entrusting their penis to the vagina given its weakening power in bringing about detumescence following intercourse. This anxiety, she added, is also fuelled by the thought that the sex which, as mother, gives life can also take it away. Lastly, she suggested, men fear women both because they sexually need them more than women need men, and because the female often rejects the male once she has been fertilized and become a mother.

In 1967 this and Horney's other essays on mothering were published together as a readily available paperback, *Feminine Psychology*, which was then taken up by many feminists, among them US poet and feminist Adrienne Rich who, citing Horney's 1930 Dresden talk, attributed male-dominated obstetrics' expropriation of women's traditional control over childbirth to men's envy and wish to divest women of their power in mothering.

Anthropologists[5] likewise adopted Horney's thesis that men fear women's mothering – a fear she also discussed in two 1932 essays on 'Problems of marriage', and 'The dread of woman'. They were among the last she wrote in Germany, and the last to be published in the *International Journal of Psycho-Analysis*.

As regards marriage, she argued that man's attitude is conditioned by infantile desire to escape a forbidding mother, guilt at desiring his wife in so far as he equates her with his mother (this being exacerbated by her actually becoming a mother), and fear lest he not satisfy his wife and hence be ridiculed by her, as he felt his mother ridiculed his nascent masculinity as a child. This, or a somewhat similar point, has in turn been recently developed by the French psychoanalyst, Janine Chasseguet-Smirgel, as a cause of male perversion and fetishism. To defend themselves against such humiliation, Horney wrote, men variously retaliate by over-emphasizing their 'masculinity as a value in and of itself',[6] or by attempting to demean and undermine women. Freud, by contrast, had argued that men seek to do down their lovers to make them as different as possible from the mother with whom sex threatens to invite patriarchal retaliation.

Not that men do not fear the father. Indeed they do. But, Horney pointed out, this fear is double-edged. For it also bolsters men's narcissism in so far as it involves identification with a powerful image of the father. No wonder it is more available to consciousness – and was more obvious to Freud – than men's fear of women, which has no such narcissistic pay-off. Nonetheless Horney reiterated Klein's observation, the general psychoanalytic neglect of which she deplored, that underneath men's fear of the father is a much more deep-seated fear of the mother. Symbolically it is expressed, she said, in dreams such as:

> . . . a motorcar is rushing along and suddenly falls into a pit and is dashed to pieces; a boat is sailing in a narrow channel and is suddenly sucked into a whirlpool; there is a cellar with uncanny, blood-stained plants and animals; one is climbing a chimney and is in danger of falling and being killed.[7]

Dread of mother as vagina expressed in such images, Horney suggested, is fuelled by the boy's early genital sensations. These, she claimed, give rise to awareness of the existence of a complementary female organ to be penetrated. But, she said, the boy 'instinctively judges that his penis is much too small for his mother's genital'.[8] Hence his fear of it – in the first place of being ridiculed as too little.

Though often concealed behind fear of the father, she observed, men's more profound fear of the mother readily emerges in treatment with a woman:

> According to my experience, the dread of being rejected and derided is a typical ingredient in the analysis of every man, no matter what his mentality or the structure of his neurosis. The analytic situation and the constant reserve of the woman analyst bring out this anxiety and sensitiveness more clearly than they appear in ordinary life, which gives men plenty of opportunity to escape from these feelings either by avoiding situations calculated to evoke them or by a process of overcompensation.[9]

Such overcompensation, she wrote, includes men's attempt to prove their manhood over and over again; the stereotype of masculine 'doing' as opposed to feminine 'being'; and male-dominated society's widespread disparagement of women.

Whatever the fears of her sex of which Horney thus wrote, her students warmed to her as a sympathetic matriarchal figure – 'an all-understanding Mother Earth . . . a place of rest in the turmoil of those times'.[10] Her immediate analytic colleagues, however, were less readily charmed and were often suspicious of her attempt to combine psychoanalysis with sociology. Not that she did not have like-minded analyst friends –including Ernst Simmel, Siegfried Bernfeld, Erich Fromm, and Wilhelm Reich. But she was virtually the only analyst to support the eclectic Medical Society for Psychotherapy (founded in 1926), to which, at her suggestion, Fromm talked in March 1928 about psychoanalysis and social class. Later talks included one by Jung in which he took issue with Freud's interpretation of dreams in terms of unconscious sexuality. The German Psychoanalytic Society could not tolerate such dissidence. In January 1930 it formally dissociated itself from the Medical Society for Psychotherapy. Horney nevertheless continued to give talks to both societies and to hold meetings at her home of colleagues of different theoretical persuasions – Freudian, Adlerian, and existentialist.

At the same time she felt snubbed by her Freudian colleagues regarding a number of key positions in the Berlin Institute. But she continued to teach there, and gave a number of talks through 1929–31 to the German Psychoanalytic Society. These included one 'On special difficulties in handling young girls' that paralleled her own experience mothering three teenage daughters. In other lectures she discussed Freud's concepts of the negative therapeutic reaction, death instinct, and phallic phase in which she increasingly took issue with instinct theory, which, through her sense of innate identification with mothering, she had previously insisted on much more vehemently than Freud. She also contributed to discussion of other lectures, including one by Klein's daughter Melitta Schmideberg.

Her position in the Society, however, was becoming increasingly uncomfortable, as was her life outside. The 1929 Wall Street crash, subsequent economic hardship, rising unemployment, and growth of Nazism put paid to the social and cultural life she had enjoyed in the 1920s Weimar Republic. She was therefore not entirely averse to accepting an offer from her ex-student, Hungarian analyst Franz Alexander, of a job as Assistant Director of his newly established Psychoanalytic Institute in Chicago. Two of her daughters were virtually independent: Marianne had begun medical training, and Brigitte, who won the Max Reinhardt acting prize in 1930, was well on the way to becoming a film star. She seemed to Karen to have inherited much of her own mother's dominating character – her experience of which increasingly informed Karen's own work following her move to the USA, where she arrived with Renate on 22 September 1932.

4

Transition

Hitherto Horney had regarded women's identification with mothering and men's envy of it as essentially innate. Now, having brought up her children virtually single-handed, like her mother before her, she increasingly emphasized the influence of social factors in determining psychological development. In particular she drew attention to social stress on parents and its ill-effects in warping their children's individuality.

She herself attributed her transition from attention to internal to external determinants of personality to her move to the USA.[1] This, she said, had first alerted her to cultural variation and its impact on human psychology. But, in fact, this transition began before she left Germany – in, for instance, a 1931 seminar she gave at Leipzig University.[2] Criticizing Freud's recently published *Civilization and Its Discontents*, she argued that there is no necessary conflict between society and individual instincts of sex and aggression. Indeed these impulses are not instinctive as Freud claimed. Rather, she asserted, they result from parental mistreatment, from parents slighting the child's inherent 'life-affirming' drive. It is this, not any innate death instinct as Freud had hypothesized, that is the source of our drive to mastery. Without it therapy would be impossible. Analysis, Horney now implied, aims to undo the damming up of our otherwise forward-looking individuality by untoward parenting due to social hardship, including the emotional and economic insecurity suffered by mothers like her own.

But Horney did not entirely abandon Freud's instinct theory. Not yet. She defended it in reviewing Otto Rank's *Modern Education*.[3] After moving to Chicago, however, she increasingly focused on the social and maternal as opposed to the instinctual forces determining individual character.

She and Renate now lived in an elegant apartment, from which the latter went to yet another progressive school. But Renate felt alienated from her peers' obsession with boyfriends. Instead she went to the cinema, where she recalls feeling lonely and desolate. Meanwhile her mother was helping plan Chicago's first analytic training programme, teaching analytic technique and feminine psychology, seeing patients five hours a day, and studying for the exams necessary to qualify as a US doctor.

As in Germany, she also gave public talks which again attracted large audiences. Increasingly, however, in discussing women's problems, she focused not on disappointment of presumed innate mother-based desire for the father, but on mothering itself. For instance, in her first major US lecture – a November talk to the Chicago Gynecology Society – she traced a patient's frigidity to childhood hatred and fear of her mother as transferred in therapy on to her. Only when she – 'the forbidding mother' – went away, it seemed, could the patient enjoy orgasm.[4] She likewise traced another patient's vaginismus to negative feelings about her mother that now surfaced in fury with Horney, whom she blamed for the failure of her relations with men. Indeed, she even accused Horney of keeping men away from her.

Horney herself soon passed her US medical exams, and in January 1933 she also applied for US citizenship. The next month – now involved in a quasi-maternal affair with a much younger man, an analytic supervisee, Leon Saul – she returned to the theme of mothering in a talk in Boston.[5]

In it she described a woman teacher who, like herself, was also sexually involved with younger men. The patient had first come for treatment full of anger at her husband's infidelity and worries about her adolescent son's obsessionality. Five years later she returned to therapy, this time with fear of having elicited her pupils' desire, for which she felt condemned by Horney as by a mother. She was now in love with a twenty-year-old youth. She visited on him, as it turned out she had previously visited on her son, the desire she had once felt for her father, against whom she had turned as a teenager just as Horney herself had turned against her father in imitation of her mother. When her father died, however, the patient wanted to put him to her breast as a mother does a baby. Yet alongside this longing was also hatred, against which she reacted with oversolicitous care of her son as substitute for her father. It was to this – the ill-effects on her mothering of her own childhood experience – that Horney attributed her son's neurosis. In general, she argued, mothering is not so much an effect of 'maternal instinct' (as she had once believed) but of the mother's experience of her own parents.

The next year Horney again drew on her patients' experience of her as mother – and also perhaps on her teenage obsession with getting a man, and her daughter's present alienation from such obsession – to argue that women's craving for love is not due to innate identification with the mother's heterosexuality. Rather, she now said, this obsession is not innate but a reaction to being bettered in childhood by the mother or an older sister. This rivalry is then repeated in the transference. Patients often experience Horney's interpretations as trying to do them down in relation to men.

Women's compulsive pursuit of men, Horney now argued, both stems from competition with the mother and is stymied by it. The very hostility to the mother that mobilizes relentless pursuit of men also evokes guilt and anxiety. And this thwarts the success of such a quest, so much does getting a man seem to involve triumph over the mother and the risk of her retaliation. Again this mother-centred fear is transferred into therapy, as in the case of a patient whose dreams

> contained the idea of a girl's sexual organs being injured or operated upon by a woman, so that they bled. Once this happened to a girl in a reformatory at the hands of one of the teachers – the opposite of what she would have liked to do to the analyst or to her greatly hated mother.[6]

Nevertheless the girl's 'overvaluation of love', which Horney likened to Marlene Dietrich's song 'I know only love and nothing else', often persists to the exclusion of all other interests. Nor does she want to work, so much is she set on getting a man and economic dependence on him, as was Horney's own mother. Indeed, Horney noted, in therapy such women often translate into maternal terms the analyst's encouragement of their working as an attempt to frustrate their femininity. Yet without work they become more desperate than ever for a man.

Horney soon integrated these observations into the beginnings of what later became a fully-fledged alternative to Freud's instinct theory, in which she attributed neurosis to lack of parental or maternal warmth crippling the self-realizing potential she believed to be innate. First, however, just as her own daughter Renate was in her late teens, she sketched out the adolescent character defences – boy-craziness, ascetism, emotional detachment, and lesbianism – which she believed to be due to parental failure.[7]

The previous summer she and Renate had been to Germany, where the Nazi attack on Freudianism as 'Jewish science' was in full swing. Agreeing with this epithet, Jung had been put in charge of the Medical Society for Psychotherapy. Meanwhile, as fascism bit deeper, Horney's second daughter Marianne decided to leave for Chicago.

She, Renate, and their mother now settled into a cosy flat. Renate described it in much the same terms Karen had used many years earlier to describe her mother's Freiburg ménage:

> . . . with the three of us and a nice German housekeeper we had, again, a real home, a family life with fun and warmth. It now felt good to come home, for someone would be there. We had many guests, good, witty conversational dinners.[8]

Karen's guests and acquaintances now included not only analysts Karl Menninger, Franz Alexander, and Lionel Blitzsten but also sociologists Harold Lasswell, Margaret Mead, and Erich Fromm, who now became Karen's lover.

Her relentless quest for one affair after another, dating as she later explained from reaction to her mother's dominance over her childhood home, now informed yet another talk – this time about feminine masochism.[9] In it she lampooned Sandor

Rado, Director of the Berlin and now of the New York Psychoanalytic Institute. He had argued that girls give up masturbating because they recognize the penis to be superior to the clitoris. They then turn this disappointment into masochistic pleasure in suffering. But this, Horney retorted, is as absurd as suggesting that men can no longer enjoy sex once they have seen Greta Garbo because no other woman is as beautiful.

Rado, she insisted, was wrong to imply that masochism is biologically determined and universal in women. Rather, she maintained, it occurs only in women who feel compelled – not least by social and economic dependence on men – to seek reassurance through love and sex. This makes them ready prey to exploitation and abuse. Not only Rado, she argued, but also Deutsch had wrongly concluded that masochism is determined by women's biology. In fact this only lends itself to masochistic construction given social factors that already lead women neurotically to pursue love and subordinate themselves to others.

In thus lambasting fellow-analysts Horney hardly endeared herself to her immediate colleagues, including Alexander, especially since she ridiculed him for describing mountain-climbing as masochistic. He replied by attributing her critique of Freudianism to resentment, and by dismissing her work as failing to provide anything 'substantially new and valid for what she tried to destroy'.[10]

In fact, however, Horney continued to adopt Freud's ideas – at least about free association, transference, countertransference, and so on. At the same time she supplemented them with attention to character defences – including masochistic craving for love – which she had first discovered through her own and her patients' experience of mothering. She now insisted on starting in therapy with these character traits, not with their putative unconscious infantile causes.

An example was a patient who

> is very eager to bring everything to my attention which he considers important. After some time it strikes me that his attitude towards me is utterly impersonal, he has no affection,

> no antagonism, no fear – just a complete blank. He has told me in the meantime about his deep antagonism against his mother, mostly disguised by a fine understanding between them but sometimes coming out in unexpected outbreaks of hatred which could not be accounted for by the given situation. He also has told me that his opinion about himself vacillates between considering himself unusually gifted and feeling exceedingly stupid.

Horney focused on the most immediate aspects of what he brought to therapy, on

> showing him the connection between his attempts to be rational and impersonal and his fear of being ridiculed and disliked. I leave aside all interpretations which would imply a similarity between his attitude to his mother and me for the simple reason that I do not know enough about the implications of his relation to his mother.[11]

Anyway, she points out, such interpretation in terms of early mothering takes no account of the effects of intervening experience.

Ironically, however, although Horney thus argued the need to modify Freud's technique, she fell out with Alexander because he also tried to modify it – by making therapy shorter. Perhaps she also could not bear being second in command to him. Certainly, starting with her early 1930s papers on mother–daughter rivalry and its transference manifestations, Horney increasingly dwelt on the difficulties involved in such subordination.

As in Germany, she was attracted away from the strait-jacketing of Freudian orthodoxy towards a more free-wheeling, eclectic approach – this time as developed by Harry Stack Sullivan, Clara Thompson, and others in the Washington–Baltimore Society for whom she agreed to teach in late 1934. With this in mind, and perhaps to join Fromm, who was now working in the International Institute of Social Research, recently transferred from Frankfurt to Columbia (an Institute that also included Horkheimer, Benjamin and Adorno), Horney left the Chicago Institute at the end of her first two-year contract in summer 1934. Despite Rado's attempt to get Brill to dissuade her from joining the New York Institute, which later censured her involvement with the revisionist Washington-Baltimore Society, she applied for admission in spring 1934. That August she moved to New York, where she set up home in the Surrey Hotel on the wealthy Upper East Side. Meanwhile her daughters in Chicago moved to a smaller and cheaper apartment.

Fromm continued to be their mother's close companion. Her other friends now included the theologian Paul Tillich and the Washington–Baltimore group, with whom she enjoyed weekly, sometimes uproarious, dinners in New York. Workwise she went on seeing private patients including analytic trainees, supervised and gave clinical seminars for the New York Institute, acted as consultant to social workers at the Jewish Family Service, and commuted regularly to teach in Washington and Baltimore.

In May 1935 she was elected a member of the New York Psychoanalytic Society. But she departed still further from its Freudian ethos in an American Psychoanalytic Association talk that month.[12] In it she argued that neurosis is not fundamentally due to any father-centred Oedipus or castration complex conflict between masculinity and femininity. Rather, she claimed, it stems from conflict between sadistic and masochistic character trends. Their origin, she elsewhere indicated, lies in the hostility and craving for love resulting from lack of maternal warmth in infancy.

By now her own children had gone their separate ways. Marianne had completed her medical training and was doing an internship in Chicago. Meanwhile Renate dropped out of school in the summer of 1935 to marry her childhood boyfriend in Germany, where Brigitte was a film star.

Back in New York, the New School for Social Research had set up a University of Exile for German academics endangered by Hitler's 1933 rise to power. Its members included Paul Tillich, Hannah Arendt and Gestalt psychologist Max Wertheimer, as well as others more sympathetic to psychoanalysis. The School had already invited a number of visiting psy- choanalytic speakers – Adler, Rank and Ferenczi. Now Horney was also invited to teach there.

Her lectures were immensely popular. They were free of psychoanalytic jargon. And they flattered her listeners' narcissism, so readily did they feel themselves mirrored in the characters she described. Nor did she trouble them with any descent into the alien-seeming, conflict-ridden, bitty sexual world of the Freudian unconscious. Her style was also very attractive. Although her flow was interrupted by endless smoking, and although she was felt to be no beauty, she easily won her students' adoration as her mother had won hers as a child: 'She was a little coy, she had a little of the actress in her . . . And everybody was just hanging on what she had to say.'[13]

But it was not just her lecturing that attracted attention. So too did her first book, *The Neurotic Personality of Our Time.* Within a decade of its 1937 publication it was reprinted over a dozen times. Perhaps its success was due to its going beyond Freud and her own previous instinct-based account of mothering and neurosis towards a more interpersonal account. In turn it paved the way for a subsequent generation of analysts to become less distantly patriarchal and more warmly maternal and empathic towards their patients.

5

Maternal culturalism

In a sense *The Neurotic Personality of Our Time* continues Horney's 1931 critique of Freud's *Civilization and Its Discontents*. Freud's starting point was nothing less than patriarchal society. Horney's by contrast was the smaller-scale domestic competition of mothers and daughters, from which she arrived at a much more optimistic conclusion than Freud, namely that conflict between individual and society can be avoided simply through parents fostering rather than thwarting their children's individuality.

She gave preliminary versions of this, her 1937 book's main thesis, in talks in New York and Berlin through 1934 to 1936, beginning with a talk to Jewish social workers[1] in which she argued that neurosis stems not from social repression of instinct but from the parents' attitudes in socializing the child. If this lacks warmth the child may well feel frustrated, intimidated, and angry. If its anger is then greeted with yet more intimidation, feelings of rage may well then be suppressed. Anger can then emerge only in fantasy – now no longer checked by reality – including archaic images of eating up, crushing, and tearing to pieces. These in turn cause children to fear being likewise attacked by animals, burglars, ghosts, and so on. To protect themselves they avoid situations evoking anger. They also develop a variety of character defences to keep their hostility and resulting fears at bay. But these defences restrict and impoverish the child's life, albeit they stave off neurosis provided they are not breached. An example was the schoolteacher Horney had already described in a previous article.[2] Now she attributed the original outbreak of this patient's neurosis to her husband's infidelity exploding the defence whereby she had long kept in check the hostility and resentment she felt against him for coming between herself and her son.

Horney further developed the main themes of *The Neurotic Personality of Our Time* in late 1935 talks[3] to both the New York and Berlin Psychoanalytic Societies, notwithstanding the latter's having been boycotted by many analysts because of its capitulation to Nazi pressure not to have Jewish members. In these talks she dwelt on the negative therapeutic reaction – the re-emergence of symptoms following helpful interpretation – which Freud, as already mentioned (p. 7 above), had attributed to unconscious fear of submission to cure by the analyst as though it were tantamount to submission to castration by the father. Mindful of her patients' competition with her as mother, Horney instead attributed negative reactions to helpful interpretations to patients experiencing them as a blow to their self-esteem. This then mobilizes their competitiveness. Furthermore, whereas Freud attributed patients' clinging to their symptoms to self-punishment in obedience to superego internalization of patriarchal authority, Horney attributed the persistence of symptoms to patients' fear lest were they to get better they might thereby evoke the envy and hostility of others, just as these feelings were evoked in them by lack of maternal warmth in childhood.

Moreover, and here Horney again used her mothering experience to go beyond Freud, the patient's negative reaction to interpretation also stems from patients being torn between seeking power and affection. Interpretations are accordingly experienced as variously dominating and rejecting. And this in turn is rooted in, albeit it is not a direct repetition of, childhood fear of maternal dominance and rejection.

These and related themes also informed Horney's 1935–6 New School lectures. She finished writing them up in book form during a summer 1936 holiday in Mexico, after a visit to Renate in Berlin to celebrate the May birth of her first grandchild, Kaya, whom Karen showered with presents just as her mother had showered her as a child.

Meanwhile Marianne, now a psychiatrist, moved to New York, where she began a four-year analysis with Fromm. Far from being deterred by his intimacy with her mother, she felt that his first-hand knowledge of Karen's 'erratic relatedness or unrelatedness' helpfully affirmed a reality she had had difficulty grasping.

Her mother also moved – to Essex House, 160 Central Park South – and that December, while again in Berlin, she started divorce proceedings against Oskar. She was also mistaken for a Nazi party official while attending one of Brigitte's plays. Her own performances included a talk to the Berlin Institute, then popularly known as the Goering Institute after the cousin of the Deputy Führer who was now running it. He himself enjoyed her talk, which evidently obeyed the Nazi veto on Freudian terminology. At his request she sent him a copy of the book on which it was based, as though her pursuit of others' admiration knew no bounds.

She attributed such craving for love and admiration to 'persistent longing for the love of a mother which was not freely given in early life'.[4] Neurosis, she wrote in her book, stems not from any sexual or aggressive instinct, or castration anxiety in relation to the father, as Freud claimed. Rather it stems from lack of genuine parental warmth. In this she in a sense returned to Freud's pre-psychoanalytic account of neurosis as effect not of anything internal to the child but of external abuse of the child by its caregivers. Not that Horney sought to blame parents. Rather she attributed their failure to pressures from which they too suffered. Nevertheless, she criticized the way parental failure to recognize and meet the child's needs is rationalized in terms of educational theory and the child's supposed 'best interest' not to be spoilt, or masked by maternal over-solicitousness.

At root, she claimed, neurosis stems from parents favouring one child over another, from their injustice or lack of consideration, their interference with the child's wishes and friendships, or their ridiculing of its nascent bids for independence. All this has the effect of breaking its will. So much does the child need and fear its parents, so much does it dread losing their love through being bad, that it dare not express the anger bred of their mistreatment. This causes 'basic anxiety' against which the child defends itself through endless search for affection, submission, power, or withdrawal on the assumption: 'If you love me you will not hurt me,' 'If I give in, I shall not be hurt,' 'If I have power, no one can hurt me,' and 'If I withdraw, nothing can hurt me.'[5]

Not that these defences themselves cause neurosis. Indeed, as Horney pointed out, the defence of submission is often adaptive for women, so well does it accord with society's injunction on them to submit to family and husband. In this her book paralleled Anna Freud's 1936 insistence on the adaptive aspects of the ego's defences. But, unlike Anna's reiteration of her father's claim that such defences stem from conflict between individual and society as represented by the unconscious id and conscious ego, Horney argued that it is conflict between different character trends within the individual that causes neurosis.

In particular she focused on the conflict between craving for affection and power. As before, she pointed out how obsessive pursuit of love often fails through being poisoned by the hostility that first evokes it. All too often the result is not genuine love but search for reassurance to the neglect of the needs of others.

Alternatively, she wrote, underlying hostility causes people to fear the dependence and affection they crave. One patient, for instance, felt positively humiliated when Horney offered her a weekend session because she was upset. Neurotic striving for the affection of others, including that of the analyst, is also thwarted, Horney added, by its accompanying jealousy and overweening demand for unconditional love, as in the case of mothers

> who rather naïvely feel justified in expecting blind devotion and sacrifices of all sorts from their children because they have 'borne them in pain'... [or the mother who] derives no satisfaction from the relationship to her children because she feels ... that the children love her only because they receive so much from her, and thus secretly begrudges them whatever she gives them.[6]

Women, she went on, are particularly prone to seek affection through love since they are brought up to believe this to be their only means of achieving 'happiness, security, and prestige'. Alternatively they seek affection through evoking the pity of others; through threats of suicide; or through claims to justice, as Horney's mother did in demanding her children's affection in return for all she had done for them.

Sex is another way people seek to secure affection. It is then an effect, not a cause, of neurosis as Freud claimed. Furthermore, Horney argued, neurotic dependence on the analyst is not the result of any universal infantile Oedipus complex. Rather, she suggested, incestuous Oedipal clinging occurs only where parental coldness elicits neurotic need of affection and reassurance.

Having detailed this character trait, Horney turned to its obverse – compulsive striving for power, prestige, and possessions. Here she drew not so much on examples like her mother but on her own reaction to such mothering. In a thinly veiled autobiographical piece she described how as a child she enjoyed a tender, sexually tinged relation with Berndt until he suddenly put an end to such intimacy. They were too old for that kind of play, he said. Karen felt terribly humiliated, especially since she felt rejected by her mother who had 'not wanted her in the first place'. Indeed, Karen 'was made to feel insignificant because the mother, a beautiful woman, was much admired by everyone'.[7] At eight Karen reacted by throwing herself into a love affair and, when that failed, into frenetically competitive schoolwork.

Generalizing from this experience, Horney argued that such competition includes always wanting to be right, having one's own way, never giving in, and the wish to control, humiliate, deprive, or exploit others. The latter traits, she maintained, originate not from any anal-sadistic instinct, as Freud implied, but from anxiety due to early parental failure.

The conflict in neurotics between the desire both to shine and to be loved, she wrote, leads to their rationalizing or masking the competitiveness our culture so much reinforces. In Horney's case this involved telling herself she was stupid in face of being 'regarded by everyone as a brilliant student'.[8]

Such guilt-ridden self-belittlement, she maintained, is not the effect of superego identification with the father's moral censure, as Freud implied, but an attempt to ward off others discovering one's underlying hostility. In just the same way the child dreads betraying this feeling, not least because of 'the cultural attitude that it is a sin to criticize parents'.[9]

It was on this point – the cultural reinforcement of character trends initiated by parental mistreatment – that Horney concluded her 1937 book. A couple of years later she related its themes to fascism. Previously she had prided herself on her tolerance of it and its opponents. Now she attributed such failure to take a political stand to a childhood sense of not being acceptable unless one 'uncritically adores one parent or fulfils their ambitions for her or becomes subservient to the demands of a self-sacrificing mother'. Such childhood history, she claimed, makes people willing dupes of fascism with its 'promises to fulfil all their needs' and demands for unquestioning subservience. The answer, she concluded, is for people to become stronger in their self-resolve and 'individual capacity for forming judgements and making decisions'.[10]

A couple of years earlier, British psychoanalyst Marion Milner had developed this theme in a somewhat different maternal vein. Welcoming rather than deploring indecisiveness, she suggested that our acquiescence in the certainties of authoritarian ideology is an effect of flight from inner emptiness and muddle. Later she traced this to fear of loss of the all-encompassing care and support first provided in infancy by the mother.

Much more attention, however, has been given to the politically and patriarchally minded psychoanalytic accounts of fascism developed by Reich and Fromm. The former argued in *The Mass Psychology of Fascism* that the support of the German lower middle classes for Hitler stemmed from their sexual instincts having been repressed in the name of the father's authority, in order to secure their work and allegiance to his farm or business. This in turn groomed them for submission to any other figure, like the Führer, who masqueraded as patriarch.

Unlike Reich, Fromm adopted Horney's anti-instinct psychology. In his book *The Fear of Freedom*, which Horney had envisaged would parallel her own, he argued that German support of fascism was the effect of it promising to provide the patriarchal leadership and strong state Germany lost with the First World War and subsequent economic collapse. Fascism, he went on, trades on the means whereby, instead of realizing their inner freedom, authoritarian individuals seek to bolster their self-esteem through identifying with and submitting to those who pass themselves off as powerful father-figures while also sadistically dominating those perceived as weaker than themselves.

Polish-born psychoanalyst Alice Miller has recently returned to the more even-handed attention, developed by Horney in the 1930s, to the maternal as well as the patriarchal roots of fascism. She suggests that the character traits of masochism and sadism – of neurotic craving for affection and power, as Horney termed them – stem not from innate instinct but from parents using the child for their own ends. Parents, she says, seek to justify this abuse by appeal to what Miller calls 'poisonous pedagogy' – the educational philosophy that assumes the existence of inborn instincts needing training for the child's own good through subjection to the parents' will. Fearful of expressing its resulting pain and hostility, writes Miller, the child represses these feelings. Instead it later compulsively re-enacts its parents' abuse either as masochistic victim or sadistic parent. It is in these terms that she explains both Hitler's and the German people's sadism – as effect of poisonous pedagogy. She attributes Hitler's pathology – his sado-masochistic perversions and nightmares – to his mother being too cowed by her husband to ward off his violence towards her son, and to her being so wrapped up in idealizing her older children who were dead that she never loved him for himself.

Miller rightly draws attention to such untoward mothering and parenting generally. And she rightly emphasizes the need for both analyst and patient to recognize the reality of parental abuse. But she overlooks the way its psychological effect is mediated by the child's own needs, desires, and fantasies. In this respect Melanie Klein's account of the child's internal world, which I will describe at length in later chapters, represents an advance on the purely external, reality-oriented perspective of Miller and Horney before her.

Horney herself, and the 'culturalist' school of psychoanalysis she founded with Fromm, have been criticized for losing sight of Freud's observations on the conflict of individual and society in the very process of drawing attention to the latter's effect in shaping individual psychology.[11] Horney thereby in effect replaced Freud's recognition of social conflict – albeit highly schematic and ahistorical – with the complacent nostrum that individuals and society would be in essential harmony were it not for selfish parents.

More immediately she was taken to task for abandoning Freud's theory of infantile sexuality. This, and the further conclusions she drew from her mothering experience, soon resulted in her being exiled from Freudian psychoanalysis.

6

Psychoanalytic exile

Horney's relations with the New York Psychoanalytic Institute had never been easy. Her offers to teach its main courses were turned down. Instead she was invited to give subsidiary courses. Her development of psychoanalysis accordingly occurred primarily outside the Institute in her New School teaching, occasional lectures, and writing.

Things became harder still with the 1938 influx of orthodox-minded analysts from Freud's Vienna. Perhaps this was why she refused to join the New York Psychoanalytic Society's immigrant relief committee. She was more willing to help people on an individual basis, like Rita Honroth, with whose father she had had an affair years earlier just after Brigitte's birth. She also did everything she could to help Renate and her family in Germany – including taking them butter and pints of cream.

By contrast her own life in New York was increasingly luxurious – roulette parties and Hassidic singing led by Fromm, summer holidays in 1938 to France and Switzerland, and plans for an office apartment at 240 Central Park South and a summer cottage in Croton-on-Hudson. Renate's family joined her after Hitler's October 1938 invasion of Czechoslovakia, but they soon had to leave (for Mexico in early 1939) because Horney was unable to secure them US residency.

Early 1939 also saw the publication of her second book, *New Ways in Psychoanalysis*. In it she used her mothering experience to take issue with most of Freud's fundamental concepts. She also suggested major revisions in psychoanalytic theory and therapy which were generally rejected by analysts at the time. Ironically, however, many have since adopted her suggestions, particularly her insistence on attending to the present rather than the past in interpreting the patient's transference to the analyst.

It is on this point she began. Rejecting Freud's focus on childhood and instinct, she instead focused on here-and-now character and social context. But she still retained Freud's insistence on the psychological determinants of neurosis, its roots in unconscious repression, and on accessing the unconscious through the patient's free associations and relation with the analyst.

But the source of repression and neurosis, she now argued, is not any instinct – of sex or aggression. Rather it is the effect of a hostile environment against which the child feels unable effectively to rail, so dependent is it on those who most provoke its anger. Faced with such hostility, she maintained, the child adopts wholesale character defences, not the piecemeal defences against component sexual instincts described by Freud.

She went on to reject even more forcibly than before Freud's claims regarding the universality of infantile Oedipal rivalry with the father for sexual possession of the mother as 'nucleus' of the neuroses. Instead, she insisted, neurosis is the effect of basic anxiety due to parental abuse. Unable to express the hostility to which this gives rise, she wrote, the child instead represses it. The resulting insecurity this breeds then leads the child to cling, Oedipal fashion, to the seemingly most powerful parent. Often this is the mother – at least in the case of Horney and the patients she described. She thereby anticipated later US and British psychoanalysts' accounts of neurosis – those of John Bowlby and Donald Winnicott, for instance – as effect not of any biologically given Oedipus complex but of insecure and clinging attachment bred of maternal deprivation, and failure of early maternal holding, both physical and psychological. Like Horney, however, these analysts tend to neglect the fact that the child's sense of deprivation by the mother is also coloured by the inordinate character of its desire whatever her behaviour.

Again anticipating subsequent developments in psychoanalysis, Horney went on to argue that narcissism is not rooted in instinctual love of the self nor, by implication, in identification with others as Deutsch and Klein argued. Instead, she wrote, narcissistic self-love depends on the degree to which others acknowledge one's 'real self' – or 'true' or 'integrated' self as Winnicott and Kohut respectively describe it. Where such acknowledgement is lacking, she claimed, an alienated 'social self' develops – akin to the 'false self' described by Winnicott. Defending against not feeling loved for himself, maintained Horney, the narcissist seeks to inflate himself – his 'social self' – in his own and others' eyes. This is also reinforced by society's adulation of image and appearance over reality.

Horney now explained women's penis envy in these terms – as socially acceptable cover for otherwise unacceptable neurotically destructive ambition. Similarly, and again taking issue with Deutsch, she attributed feminine masochism to search for reassurance from others towards whom there is also underlying hostility. Masochistic submission, she claimed, suits women because it is socially expected of them.

Not content with criticizing Deutsch, Horney went on for the first time in print to criticize Klein. The latter located the source of children's destructive fantasies towards the mother in the death instinct. Not so Horney. In her clinical experience, she maintained, such fantasies are a reaction to feeling abused, humiliated, or rejected. An example was a patient who

> grew up in the shadow of a beautiful, egocentric mother and a greatly preferred sister. She could not give vent to any resentment directly, because her mother was self-righteous and could not stand anything but blind adoration.

But why did the patient continue to feel 'unfairly treated . . . pushed aside, cheated, taken advantage of, treated with ingratitude or with disrespect'? Not because of any compulsion to repeat the past to master childhood conflict with the father, as Freud might have argued. Rather, Horney claimed, the above patient's preoccupation with her mother's past unfair treatment of her was an aspect of her present preoccupation with being unfairly treated. It served as defence against recognizing her own selfishness and lack of consideration for others, betrayed by the following:

> ... first, anxiety appeared when she wished something for herself which she could not justify on the grounds of needing it for education, health, and the like; second, she was subject to frequent attacks of fatigue which covered up an impotent rage, the latter occurring whenever certain secret demands were not fulfilled, when things were not done for her, when she was not first in any competition, when she had complied with the wishes of others or when others had not complied with her own unexpressed wishes.[1]

The unpacking of such character trends, Horney insisted, is the nub of therapy. Unearthing and reconstructing the past is relevant but not crucial. True, she acknowledged, character is partly determined 'by the relation to the mother'. But more than mothering is involved in childhood, intervening history, and the neurotic's present situation.

Turning against the theory that led her to this position – namely her patients' transference on to her of early mothering experience – Horney now argued that the central issue in seeking to understand and treat upsets to the patient's equilibrium concerns not the past but the present character trends whereby the patient now seeks to achieve stability. This involves noting the effects of these trends on the patient's relation to the analyst and the latter's counter-transference reaction. But it is no good tracing the patient's present character structure to early mothering, not least because this fosters dependence without touching the patient's current conflicts.

Not only had Freud attended to the past and the supposed sexual instincts of childhood to the neglect of the present, Horney continued. He also wrongly neglected the cultural determinants of neurosis: the conditioning of penis envy by our society's patriarchal organization; the undermining of self-confidence by economic insecurity, individualism, and competition; and the social stereotypes determining choice of defence against basic anxiety.

All too often, she wrote, such defence is mistaken for health because it accords with prevailing social norms. An example was a patient

> more gifted than her husband ... [one of whose] deepest problems was her total incapacity to do anything for herself. But because it was hidden behind a 'normal' feminine attitude [of passivity] this problem had always been overlooked.[2]

Paradoxically Horney ended up urging such people to realize themselves as individuals while at the same time criticizing individualism. Increasingly she insisted on the self-realizing potential of the individual ego independent of the id – a theme later taken up by New York analysts Hartmann, Loewenstein, and Kris. Rejecting Freud's account of the conflicts of individual and society, and ignoring the fissures thereby introduced into individuality between conscious allegiance and unconscious resistance to social pressure, Horney replaced Freud's focus on dreams and the unconscious with attention to conscious anxiety as means of accessing, and thereby treating, neurotic character.

Often, she maintained, such anxiety involves simultaneous resentment and fear of going against the wishes of others – in the first place those of the parents. This results in a compliant, other-directed morality as substitute for sincerity to the real self. It is in these terms, she insisted, that neurotic self-recrimination should be analysed – as an attempt to ward off criticism by others, not as effect of any patriarchally based superego nor, as Anna Freud implied, as effect of identification with the aggressor.

The aim of therapy, Horney concluded, is to free patients from the anxiety causing their present character defences so that they can at last be true to themselves. This in turn requires a morally committed stance of 'constructive friendliness' on the part of the analyst – a quasi-maternal, caring attitude that she contrasted with Freud's more scientifically neutral approach of probing the present for knowledge of a presumed infantile sexual past.

This was hardly likely to please his followers. Although an *International Journal of Psycho-Analysis* reviewer acknowledged the compatibility of Horney's arguments with Freudianism – and indeed her emphasis on maternal empathy and attention to the present has been adopted by many psychoanalysts today – most analysts dismissed her book at the time for sociologizing psychoanalysis.

Non-analytic reviewers, however, enthusiastically welcomed both its critique of Freud and its advocacy of caring 'friendliness' on the part of the analyst. But the popularity of both her writing and her teaching – her students now petitioned the New York Institute in June 1939 to include her work in its curriculum – only served further to alienate her fellow-teachers in the Institute. Freud's death that September did not help. Her colleagues more than ever felt the need to defend his work against its detractors. They still did not hire Horney as a main course teacher. Instead she was offered a senior year elective course and a few occasional lectures. These included an October 1939 talk in which she criticized Freud's emphasis on the childhood determinants of neurosis. It was so ill-received that Horney wept, perplexed 'why we can't have different opinions and still be friends'.[3] Friendship in the face of disagreement seemed impossible. The Institute's President, Lawrence Kubie, ruled: 'I am dead against . . . one group of students . . [hearing] nothing but Horney, another group nothing but orthodoxy, and a third group little but Rado, etc.'[4]

How different from the London Psychoanalytic Society's later agreement to disagree (see pp. 243–4 below). On the other hand, just as in London Klein's dissent from Freudian patriarchal orthodoxy was attributed to personal neuroticism and subjectivity, so too was Horney's in New York. Like Horney, Klein was accused of seeking to make disciples of her trainees through not adequately analysing their positive and idealizing maternal transference to her. And just as Klein's situation was aggravated by her analyst daughter's hostility to her, so too Horney's analyst daughter, Marianne, now asserted herself against the slights she felt she had suffered in the past at her mother's hands.

For Horney the major crisis came after a number of her trainees' final papers were referred for revision in 1940. The students felt discriminated against. Indeed they were – at least, to judge from a specially conducted February 1941 questionnaire. Instead of righting matters, however, the Institute decided on 29 April 1941 to reduce Horney's status to that of occasional lecturer. In response, and having previously failed to gain alliance with Rado's dissident faction, Horney's group resigned to form an independent Association for the Advancement of Psychoanalysis (AAP). It was soon joined by the fourteen trainees whom the original fuss had been about. As AAP members they were formally excluded from the American Psychoanalytic Association – just months before the US entered the Second World War in December 1941. Undaunted, Horney now used her mothering experience to further her ideas about self-analysis and self-realization.

7

Self-analysis

Balked by patriarchalism, Horney had at least twice previously retreated into self-analysis: once after she had been excluded because of her sex from dissection classes; another time, after the birth of her first child, when she decided against renewing her analysis with Abraham because of her fear of patriarchal transference. Now, exiled from official Freudian psychoanalysis, and following a summer 1941 holiday with Fromm and others in Monhegan, she got down to writing a book about self-analysis. In it she provided a sustained account – albeit disguised – of her childhood experience of her mother that laid the basis of the systematic alternative to Freudianism that she developed in her final years.

Perhaps she was enthused by the initial energy of the AAP. It set up its own training institute and journal within months of its first formation in 1941, had many prestigious members – including Fromm, Sullivan, Thompson and Silverberg – and attracted prominent guest speakers – including Margaret Mead, Franz Alexander, Abram Kardiner and Abe Maslow.

Meanwhile, in Berlin, Horney's daughter Brigitte, who like Marianne married that year, was increasingly suffering as a result of the war. This came to a head with Nazi persecution of her close friend Joachim Gottschalk and his Jewish wife. In late 1941, to save being taken by the Gestapo, the Gottschalks killed themselves and their son. Soon afterwards Brigitte suffered a recurrence of her childhood TB, and she spent the next three years recovering in Switzerland.

Back in New York her sister Marianne joined the thriving AAP. That spring it held its first conference, where it became a ritual to toast 'luxurious and lecherous living'.[1] Not that Horney, as its founding member, entirely ignored the war. She drew attention, in a 1942 New School seminar, to its stressful impact on women and mothering. But her own life remained very comfortable, even running to indulging one housebuying whim after another. In spring 1942 she gave up her Croton house for one she found with Marianne's mother-in-law, Gertrude Lederer-Eckardt. Gertrude had now become her constant companion, secretary, nurse, and partner at cards – at which, it seems, Horney was an inveterate cheat.

Self-Analysis was published that June. It echoed the ebullient self-confidence of Karen's adolescent diaries – a self-confidence she now took for granted as innate. This was her book's starting point, in which she argued that Freud had underrated the potential of self-analysis – despite analysing himself – because he failed to recognize the individual ego's capacity for its own self-development irrespective of any social or instinctual input.

For Horney self-analysis was a means of undoing the character trends she believed prevent such individual self-realization. As before, she located the source of these trends in the failure of parents to love the child for itself. They thereby fail to foster its supposedly inherent tendency towards self-realization.

A case in point was Clare, who Horney later acknowledged to be an amalgam of her own and her patients' experience:

> Clare . . . has a self-righteous mother who expects the child's admiration and exclusive devotion . . . She was an unwanted child. The marriage was unhappy. After having one child, a boy, the mother did not want any more children. Clare was born after several unsuccessful attempts at an abortion . . . There was a strong, though for a child intangible, community between the mother and brother from which she was excluded. The father was no help. He was absent most of the time, being a country doctor. Clare made some pathetic attempts to get close to him but he was not interested in either of the children. His affection was entirely focused on the mother in a kind of helpless admiration. Finally, he was no help because he was openly despised by the mother, who was sophisticated and

> attractive and beyond doubt the dominating spirit in the family. The undisguised hatred and contempt the mother felt for the father, including open death wishes against him, contributed much to Clare's feeling that it was much safer to be on the powerful side.[2]

Since neither her mother nor her brother recognized any ground for complaint, Clare began to feel that her discontent was her own fault. She thereby lost sight of her mother's faults. Instead she joined the others in adoring her. This did not win Clare the affection she craved, but it did win her mother's admiration: she became 'the wonderful daughter of a wonderful mother'. But this at the cost of becoming alienated from her true feelings. Instead she depended for her self-esteem on her mother and others admiring qualities she actually despised in herself. This led to compulsive modesty as to her own wishes and demands; inordinate need of someone else on whom to depend; and an over-riding need to excel and triumph over others to restore her own self-regard and get back at others for her accumulated hurts and humiliations.

Analysis, Horney wrote, involves recognizing and uncovering the causes, manifestations, and effects of such character trends. For Clare, separated from her husband in her twenties, this involved examining the way these trends manifested themselves in her professional work and dependence on her present lover.

Like Freud, Horney emphasized the need to undo the patient's resistance to such self-knowledge through analysing its transference manifestations. An example was a man who, following a productive session that revealed his fear of taking responsibility, arrived next time feeling tired and uneasy. He then went on with a recollection of 'his mother dragging him through museums and of boredom and annoyance at the experience', just as he now felt irritated at Horney pushing him from one problem to the next.[3]

Herein, as Horney pointed out, lies a major drawback of self-analysis. It totally lacks the maternal caring – or friendly support and respect, as she put it – necessary to overcome the resistance of individuals to getting to know themselves. Nevertheless, she claimed, some gains in this direction can be achieved through self-analysis including the mother-related conflicts it uncovers. An example was a businessman who discovered for himself a link between his headaches and his irritation at his mother and others for not meeting his wishes. Another man, a doctor, associated his panic attacks with anger at his girlfriend speaking favourably of his colleagues just as he likewise felt angry at his mother favouring his brother. A third man, a barrister, linked his 'stage fright' in court to the way he used charm rather than real achievement to win over the judges, just as he had won over his mother in childhood.

Horney went on to give practical hints for doing self-analysis –using dreams, starting with minor not major difficulties, and not being bound by a regular hour as in orthodox analysis. She also advised against using diaries – such as she kept – because, she revealingly claimed, they are intended for an audience and are therefore written in narrative rather than free association form.

Returning to Clare, specifically to Clare's inability to ask her estranged lover to return, Horney showed how self-analysis enabled Clare to trace this difficulty to childhood inhibition against asking her mother for anything lest this lead to yet further rejection. Hence Clare's obsession with getting a man who would protect her and shower her with presents without her having to ask for them. Hence too her idealization of her lover as of her mother. She thereby concealed from herself the way they both trampled on her feelings and made her feel guilty for her resulting resentment, which she expressed in misery and martyrdom aimed at securing their attention and consolation.

Repeating her objection to Freud's neglect of the individual's inherent resources for overcoming resistance to self-knowledge, Horney went on to argue that such resistance becomes a major obstacle to self-analysis only where there is excessive alienation from the 'real self'. Examples included the resignation, cynicism, and destructiveness of self and others depicted in Ibsen's *Hedda Gabler*. Dispensing with such difficulties,

Horney concluded by stressing the need to examine present difficulties in relation both to early mothering and to the factors causing their continuing repetition. This process, she maintained, is helped by self-analysis being preceded by therapy with an analyst who adopts a cooperative rather than an authoritarian stance.

Some dismissed Horney's resulting book as simple-minded cultural determinism. Most ignored it. Perhaps this contributed to the cooling of her relationship with Fromm. Certainly his recently published *Fear of Freedom* was much more widely acclaimed, and she seemed to feel bereft and in search of someone else close.

Her bitterness at his abandonment of her – she even called him Freud by mistake – made it difficult to bear his continued presence in the AAP. Nor could she bear his popularity with students. Not that her own was in doubt: like her daughter Renate, several of her AAP colleagues called their children after her. She was also very sought after as an analyst. Indeed, she could not accommodate all the people who wanted analysis with her. Yet she seemed unwilling to refer patients to Thompson or Fromm. The crunch came, however, with her Institute's January 1943 refusal of a student request that Fromm teach clinical as well as theoretical issues. The Institute also revoked his teaching privileges, ostensibly because his lack of medical training made him unacceptable to the New York Medical College with which the AAP was then seeking affiliation. In April 1943 he resigned, taking with him Thompson, Sullivan, Blitzsten, Janet Rioch and others. Torn between Fromm and her mother, and much to the latter's embitterment, Marianne also increasingly withdrew from the AAP. The rivalries her mother provoked there, she said, were much the same as those she provoked between her and Brigitte. Others likewise speak of her 'imperiousness' and seductiveness exciting dissension among her followers.[4]

Horney's reaction was to move house, just as she had pressed her mother to do when she was faced with difficulties as a teenager. Having purchased a property on Fire Island in 1942, Horney now sold it and bought a place in Wildwood Hills on

Long Island. Seemingly undaunted by the battles of her Institute and outside – indeed, unlike Deutsch, Anna Freud and Klein, she hardly referred at all to the war in her 1940s writing – Horney continued her usual round of dinners and parties. Her friends now included bathroom manufacturer Cornelius Crane, through whom she later met the Zen Buddhist scholar Suzuki, and various European artists and existentialists around whom she spread an atmosphere of cosy '*Gemütlichkeit*' like her mother before her. That Christmas she holidayed in Florida, only to return to yet further trouble in the AAP. Silverberg and five others now resigned to teach psychiatry with the New York Medical College after negotiations with the AAP had broken down, largely, it seems, because Horney seemed more committed to promoting her own work than that of psychiatry generally.

The loss of Silverberg ended all hope of the AAP securing official psychoanalytic recognition. Horney instead looked increasingly for support to a very much younger colleague – previously her analysand and trainee – Harold Kelman. He, it seems, now provided the unquestioning admiration that she, like her mother, demanded. Also like her mother, and in keeping with her desperation since adolescence to stave off any feeling of emptiness, Karen was very demanding of her children. Renate, for instance recalls:

> I had three kids and a complicated household and a very difficult husband. So when she [mother] said, 'Do nothing,' I knew it meant that she would keep me busy shopping, picnicking, touring, playing cards, you name it, but . . . something all the time.[5]

Karen also made time – on holiday with Renate in Cuernavaca in summer 1944 – to work on her fourth book, *Our Inner Conflicts*. It was published the next year when, as a result of misleading newspaper reports, she thought Brigitte was dead. In fact she was alive and well in Switzerland.

8

From mothering to self-realization

Our Inner Conflicts, and its 1950 sequel, *Neurosis and Human Growth*, mark the culmination of Horney's alternative to Freudianism. In their insistence on the essential self-sufficiency of the individual, Horney's last books are also poles apart from Deutsch and Klein with their recognition that, far from being self-sufficient, the individual psyche is dependent for its very formation on identification with others, in the first place with the mother.

Horney began *Our Inner Conflicts* by reiterating her then established view that neurosis is due to uncaring parenting and the conflicting character trends it sets in motion. She now described these trends as involving variously moving towards, against, and away from others. These movements eventuate in three distinct character types. The 'compliant type' seeks to resolve conflict between movement towards and against others by emphasizing the first trend. The 'aggressive type' emphasizes the second trend. And the 'detached type' – to whom Horney likened Fromm – seeks to stave off all conflict through retreat from others.

Common to all three types, Horney continued, is a tendency to generate an idealized self-image – or 'grandiose self' as Kohut calls it – to overcome the factors that otherwise undermine individual self-esteem. It provides a sense of purpose and conceals the neurotic's conflicting character trends. But it is a precarious formation. For it is at odds with the 'real self'.

One way of attempting to resolve this conflict, Horney wrote, is through externalization. This can involve foisting on to others the idealized self's contempt for the real self. An example was a patient who criticized her husband's indecisiveness rather than her own. Alternatively the ideal self's criticism of the real self is projected into others, as in the case of a woman who expected others to judge her by the standards of her ideal of being as good as the priest in Victor Hugo's *Les Misérables*. She was accordingly bewildered when people liked her more, not less, when she deviated from this ideal by assertively taking a stand and even being angry.

With her account of externalization Horney altogether turned her back on the mothering experience that first led her to this theory. She now rejected the attribution of neurosis to having a dominating mother as an instance of falsely externalizing the conflict between ideal and real self, which she believed to be essentially self-generating rather than formed through identification with others. This neurotic conflict, she concluded as she had her 1939 book, rules out Freud's stance of scientific and moral neutrality towards neurosis. For the division of neurotics from their real self by the ideal self makes them morally culpable of insincerity; of pretending love, suffering, interest, and so on; of arrogance; of failing wholeheartedly to take responsibility for their own actions; of lack of inner freedom; and of concealing inner conflict. She therefore urged people to become aware of this conflict so as to become true to themselves. This project, she believed, is eminently realizable, so much did she assume, unlike Freud, that true individuality is essentially self-realizing and at one with society.

Many, including her old friend Harold Lasswell, welcomed her book's integration of her previously somewhat fragmentary alternative to Freudian theory. In particular they welcomed her optimism, in contrast to Freud's pessimistic conclusion that the best that can be hoped from therapy, given the conflict of individual and society, is conversion of 'hysterical misery into common unhappiness'.[1]

Optimistic hedonism also characterized Horney's post-war life of long weekends and holidays. Even her waiting-room was adorned with copies of *Gourmet* magazine. Not that she did not work hard. She saw patients from very early morning till evening, with only a brief lunch. But she also socialized hard. Her friends now included Harold Kelman's AAP rivals

– Alexander Martin, Frederick Weiss, and Kelman's nephew Norman. Marianne's mother-in-law continued to be her main companion and amanuensis. And she took yet another lover, a young AAP candidate who had been her analysand.

She now divided her summers between Brigitte in Switzerland and Renate in Mexico. Here, in informal discussions with friends of the existentialist and essentially individualistic philosophy of Kierkegaard and Husserl, and in her New School and AAP lectures, she began collecting material for her sixth book, *Neurosis and Human Growth*, published in autumn 1950.

From its very inception it broke with her earlier insistence on the maternal and social origins of neurosis. She briefly alluded to her earlier claims on this score before going on to focus entirely on present character defences without reference to their possible past causes. An example was her description of a girl much like herself:

> At the age of eight she placed some of her toys in the street for some poorer child to find, without telling anybody about it. At the age of eleven she tried in her childish way for a kind of mystic surrender in prayer. There were fantasies of being punished by teachers on whom she had a crush. But, up to the age of nineteen, she also could easily fall in with plans evolved by others to take revenge on some teacher; while mostly being like a little lamb, she did occasionally take the lead in rebellious activities at school. And, when disappointed in the minister of her church, she switched from a seeming religious devotion to a temporary cynicism.[2]

Horney went on to focus again on the divorce of real and idealized self which she believed to be self-generated in defence against an also internally generated conflict between movement towards, against, and away from others. She then illustrated the idealized self's compulsive striving by reference to Ibsen's *John Gabriel Borkman* and Flaubert's *Madame Bovary*.

Far from attending to the origins of neurosis in maternal and social failure to meet individual need, Horney now criticized dependence on others meeting our needs as in itself neurotic.

Neurosis, she argued, is not the effect of social frustration of need. The very idea that it is, she said, is part and parcel of a neurotic tendency to assume we have the right to have others meet our needs. It is precisely this sense of entitlement, she continued, that give rise to the indignation and vindictive triumph portrayed in Shakespeare's *Merchant of Venice*, Ibsen's *Hedda Gabler*, and Nietzsche's concept of '*lebensneid*' (or 'envy of life'). Then, in a passage reminiscent of her description forty years earlier of her mother, she characterized neurotics as seeking to legitimate their claims on others through appeals such as 'Because I am a woman – because I am a man – because I am your mother – because I am your employer.'[3] Not, she added, that neurotics do not also make huge anxiety-making demands of themselves in seeking to live up to impossible ideals, such as that of being a perfect wife and mother.

The neurotic, she wrote, also seeks external affirmation of the idealized attributes they illusorily appropriate to themselves. An example is *Peer Gynt*, or the mother who is a paragon of virtue only in imagination. The obverse is the shame, humiliation, and hurt pride the neurotic feels at inevitably failing to live up to such inflated images. Hence the self-loathing and self-destructiveness of the drug addict and suicide. All too often, she pointed out, the individual is in thrall to an ideal, like Raskolnikov in *Crime and Punishment*, mesmerized by Napoleon. Again Horney described the externalization of the 'central inner conflict' of real and ideal self, this time as depicted in Kafka's *The Trial*, or as occurs in women who judge their appearance in terms of an outward ideal of feminine beauty.

Neurotic alienation from the real self, she continued, results in uncertainty as to who one really is. To resolve this uncertainty some opt for an expansive, others for a self-effacing, identity. The former expansive solution can involve identification with the ideal self – as in Ibsen's *John Gabriel Borkman* – or arrogant vindictiveness – as in *Wuthering Heights*'s Heathcliff, or *Scarlet and Black*'s Julien Sorel. By contrast, and here Horney harked back to *Self-Analysis*, the self-effacing solution stems from growing up in the shadow of an adored parent – a 'long-suffering mother who made the child feel guilty at any failure to give her exclusive care and attention'.[4] A third resigned and withdrawn solution, Horney added, involves stifling the aims of both the real and the ideal self. While the goal of the expansive solution is mastery and of the self-effacing solution love, the resigned solution's goal is freedom from coercive or intrusive involvement with others. Its aim is thereby to safeguard the genuine self. But this becomes increasingly empty the less it is realized in practice.

Again abandoning the means by which she originally arrived at this personality theory – specifically her patients' experience of her as mother – Horney now criticized orthodox psychoanalysis for setting too much store by the transference. Therapy's main method, she now insisted, should not be analysis of the individual's relation to the therapist. Instead it should lay bare the patient's character trends, central inner conflict, and its externalization:

> A patient may for instance become aware of both hating his mother and being devoted to her . . . on the one hand he feels sorry for his mother because, being the martyr type, she is always unhappy; on the other hand he is furious at her on account of her stifling demands for exclusive devotion . . . Next, what he has conceived as love or sympathy becomes clearer. He should be the ideal son and should be able to make her happy and contented. Since this is impossible he feels 'guilty' and makes up with redoubled attention. This should (as next appears) is not restricted to this one situation; there is no situation in life where he should not be the absolute of perfection. Then the other component of his conflict emerges. He is also quite a detached person, harbouring claims to have nobody bother him or expect things of him and hating everybody who does so. The progress here is from attributing his contradictory feelings to the external situation (the character of the mother), to realizing his own conflict in the particular relationship, finally to recognizing a major conflict within himself.[5]

Once the tendency towards self-realization is thus set in motion through therapy, she argued, patients can work on their remaining conflicts for themselves.

Horney concluded by contrasting her optimistic belief that neurosis can be overcome through the individual's inherent potential for self-realization with Freud's pessimistic belief that some degree of neurosis is inevitable given the conflict of inner and outer, individual and society. In this she appealed to our culture's ideology – today celebrated as enterprise culture – which holds individuals capable of fending for themselves and meeting their needs on their own without recourse to others.

But this overlooks the fact that, far from being essentially independent and whole, the ego or self is dependent and divided at its very inception by the division of self and other.[6] Even Horney's own daughter Marianne, perhaps voicing her long-standing distaste for her mother's self-serving individualism, now insists, 'I have not been very much in favour of the concept of self-realization divorced from the idea that self-realization also means an improvement in interpersonal relationships.'[7]

Horney, however, implied in her later work that neurosis calls for individual not social change. She thereby appealed to the narcissistic and omnipotent illusion, fostered by individualism, that we can do everything off our own bat without any help from others. No wonder her 1950 book, with its celebration of such self-sufficiency, was much praised.

She herself, however, seemed increasingly lonely. She took to reading detective stories and relied on the Weisses for her social life. Troubled by abdominal pains, she gave up teaching at the New School in 1951. Earlier that year she had met Suzuki, who was now teaching at Columbia. Believing that there was an affinity between Zen and her philosophy – albeit the former belief in transcending individuality is quite contrary to her own insistence on realizing it – she embarked on a last desperate fling, a summer 1952 trip to Japan. With her went Brigitte, now divorced, who had arrived in New York the previous December.

Within weeks of their return Horney was diagnosed as having cancer. In keeping with the individualism that characterized her life and work, she read *The Egoist* in hospital. On 4

December 1952 she died there, leaving a legacy of work drawing attention to men's envy of mothering, and to the psychological effects of sexual inequality, mothering, and parenting, that has been immensely appealing to many feminists. Ironically, however, and perhaps because it chimes in better with US individualism, it is her later work – in which she turned her back on its mothering roots – that has been particularly taken up by non-analytic psychologists like Maslow, US psychology textbooks, the AAP's continuing *American Journal of Psychoanalysis* which she founded, and by therapists working in today's Karen Horney Psychoanalytic Institute and Center in New York. Above all, however, they value the active, friendly, and optimistic stance she introduced into therapy, and her emphasis on the constructive forces of the personality against the tyranny of the 'should' of the Freudian patriarchal superego.

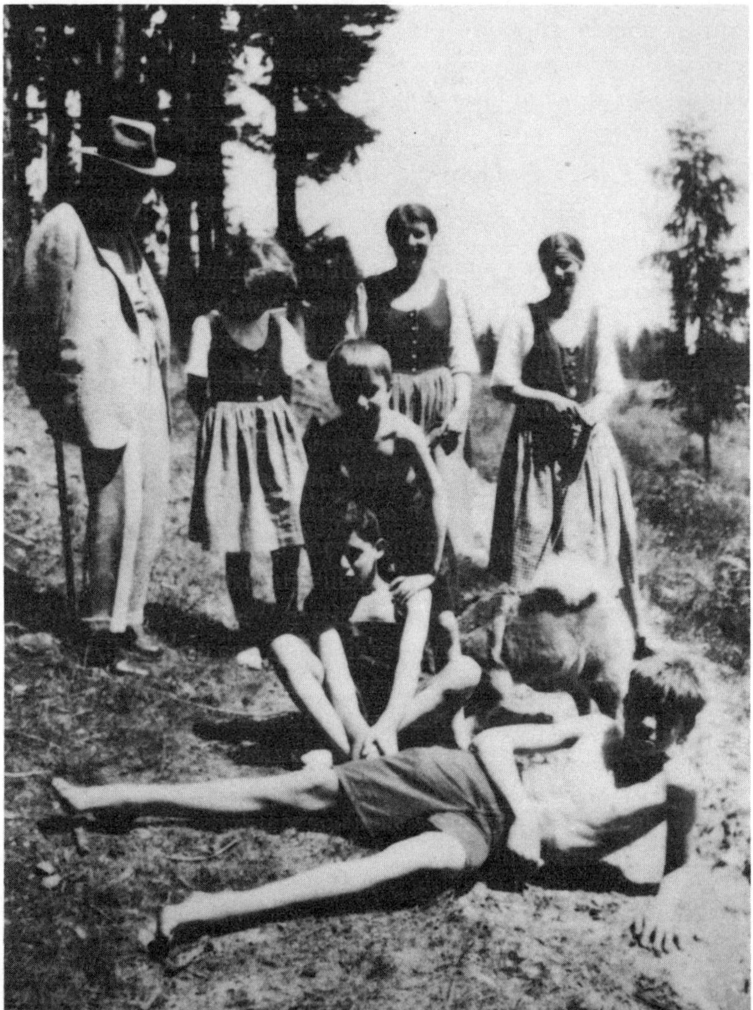

Anna Freud (centre) with Freud,
the Burlinghams (Tinky, Dorothy, Mikey, and Bob)
and Anna's nephew, Ernst Halberstadt Freud, c. 1928.

IV

ANNA FREUD

1

Father's child

Anna Freud's life and work hardly involved Horney's mother-centred rejection of Freudian patriarchalism. Quite the reverse. Although she lived with her mother for over half a century, Anna seems almost totally to have ignored her while taking her place as her father's secretary, nurse, and main exponent of his ideas.

But she also went beyond them. In this, surprisingly, she drew particularly on the mothering experience of her sex that she otherwise so shunned. Specifically she drew on her experience of helping to bring up the children of her life-long companion Dorothy Burlingham, and subsequently her experience, with Burlingham, of looking after children during the Second World War. The former experience led her to pioneer child analysis and ego psychology, the latter the modification of her father's account of child development to take account of its dependence on early mothering.

Her early life, however, was entirely dominated by her father. Her conception coincided with his discovery of psychoanalysis. That year he and his then mentor Josef Breuer described the talking cure and free association method developed particularly by Freud to treat the psychological conflicts of middle-class women in nursing their dying fathers, a destiny that later befell Anna. Freud also dated his discovery of the unconscious to four months before her birth.

Otherwise her birth on 3 December 1895 was inauspicious. Freud's practice was suffering from the reverberations of his intimate friend and colleague Wilhelm Fliess's botched surgery on one Emma Eckstein. Freud seemed disappointed by Anna's sex. 'If it had been a son I should have sent you the news by telegram,' he told Fliess. 'But as it is a little girl . . . you get the news later.'[1] Previously he had suffered premonitions of death, and within a year of her birth he announced that his sex life was at an end.

His wife, Martha, had borne the pregnancy ill. Unlike her older children – Mathilde, Martin, Oliver, Ernst, and Sophie – Anna was not breast-fed. And within months of her birth her mother went away on her first holiday without the children. Soon afterwards Martha's sister, Minna, moved in. Freud referred to them as the 'two mothers'. But Anna was less attached to them than to other maternal figures, beginning with Josefine, the nursemaid hired at her birth.

Unlike her mother, Josefine seemed to favour Anna over the others, to whom Anna felt she was a 'bore' and by whom she often felt 'left out', as on an occasion when they

> all went off in a boat and left me at home, either because the boat was too full or I was 'too little'. This time I did not complain and my father, who was watching the scene, praised me and comforted me. That made me so happy that nothing else mattered.[2]

Freud was endeared by such forbearance. Likening Anna to her brother Martin, he was also charmed by her masculine appetite and aggression. She first figures in psychoanalysis, in *The Interpretation of Dreams*, as a greedy toddler calling out in her sleep: 'Anna Fweud, stwawbewwwies, wild stwawbewwies, omblet, pudden!'[3] Another time he wrote enchantedly: 'Annerl complained that Mathilde had eaten all the apples, and demanded that someone slit open her belly (as in the fairy tale of the little goat).' 'Little Anna,' he added, 'is positively beautified by naughtiness.'[4]

Later he praised her 'intellectual interests', her dissatisfaction with 'purely feminine activity'. But he did not send her to schools that could prepare her for university entrance. Instead she went to the local Cottage Lyceum, which she later described as quite stultifying. Nonetheless she quickly gravitated to her father's work. She soon met all his leading followers, and begged to go with him and Jung on their 1909 visit to the USA.

Instead she was left at home, where her mother was more attached to Mathilde and Sophie. All three enjoyed smart clothes, handicrafts, and knitting – pastimes Freud later dismissed as motivated by women's desire to make 'concealment of [their] genital deficiency'.[5] Whatever his attitude, Anna struggled to gain a place in her mother's knitting circle. But she conceded the ground to Sophie as regards looks, men, and children. As a child, she later recalled, she wanted 'beautiful clothes and a number of children'. But she only fulfilled these wishes vicariously, through helping Sophie and others with their clothes and children. She herself felt 'shabby and inconspicuous'.[6]

Try as she might, she could not win Sophie's affection. Instead they quarrelled, so much so that Freud suggested, at the time of Sophie's wedding (in January 1913), that Anna stay away in Italy, where she had been sent after finishing school for a rest-cure because of weight loss and menstrual problems.

Bereft of both Sophie, who was now living in Martha's birthplace, Hamburg, and of Mathilde, who had married in 1909, Freud likened Anna, as he had previously likened her mother, to King Lear's faithful Cordelia. Lear's daughters, he wrote, represented

> the three forms taken by the figure of the mother in the course of a man's life – the mother herself, the beloved one who is chosen after her pattern, and lastly the Mother Earth who receives him once more.[7]

However ominous the maternal character Freud thus attributed to Anna, he clung to her. After working in a daycare centre for working-class children, and taking her first teacher's examination, she visited England in the summer of 1914. Before she left, Freud warned her against the attentions of Ernest Jones. But she was more fearful lest her father not miss her in her absence. And she obediently dismissed Jones's suit as geared more to Freud than to her. Instead, and like her father, she was more taken with Jones's sometime mistress, Loe Kann. It was to Loe that she attributed her safe return to Vienna after the outbreak of war. And it was of Loe she now dreamed.

In her work she seemingly stayed very much a child. She now taught in her old school, where her lack of height made her hardly distinguishable from her pupils. The war and its aftermath resulted in terrible poverty. With the 1919 dismemberment of the old Austro-Hungarian empire, its capital, Vienna, lost all its former glory. Previously the Emperor Franz-Josef had helped hold Viennese anti-semitism in check. Now he was dead. Freud had worried about his soldier sons in the war, when food shortages had even caused him to ask to be paid in potatoes for one of his papers. Anna had also worked extra hours for food and money. After the war she helped Bernfeld with orphaned and homeless Jewish children. In the previous summer of 1918 she had conducted a school party to Hungary, where she was taken under the motherly wing of Katá Levy.

But she remained still more tied to her father. During the war she had attended his Saturday evening lectures on psychoanalysis, where the sight of Felix Deutsch in his white coat had briefly made her think of becoming a doctor. But Freud dissuaded her. In autumn 1918, unsure what to do next, she became his analysand along with Katá Levy and Helene Deutsch – that year's Budapest Congress having ruled personal analysis a condition of becoming an analyst. Two years later, ostensibly on grounds of ill-health after her wartime TB, Anna abandoned teaching. Instead she did translation work for her father's psychoanalytic journals. And in 1920 she went with him to the Hague Congress, where he successfully put her off yet another suitor, Hans Lampl.

Freud was more encouraging of her friendships with older women. Disappointed by Loe Kann's rejection of his invitation to The Hague, and still fearful of losing Anna, he invited his old friend, Lou Andréas-Salomé, to keep her company at the end of 1921. Lou was the same age as Anna's mother. She had once been the intimate of Nietzche and Rilke. Now she became Anna's confidante.

Lou apparently supervised Anna's May 1922 qualifying paper for the Vienna Psychoanalytic Society. Analyst Max Eitingon had made this qualification a requirement of her attending that year's Berlin Congress as an analyst. Like her later talks, and in imitation of her father, she gave it without notes and used the occasion to reiterate his account of beating fantasies.

On the basis of his analysis of Anna and others, Freud had argued that such fantasies express the girl's sexual wish for the father. Often the girl disguises this wish from herself by imagining herself to be a boy, even though her beating fantasies involve a masochistic stance that Freud later equated with maternal femininity – with 'being castrated, or copulated with, or giving birth to a baby'.[8]

Years later Anna acknowledged her rivalry with her mother and Minna for her father. She dreamed, for instance, of going on a tortuous journey only to discover the two sisters already with Freud before her. In her 1922 talk, however, she made no mention of the mother in illustrating Freud's beating fantasies theory from her own experience as though it were that of one of her patients. In particular she described how as a very young child she used to get sexually excited by the idea, 'A boy is being beaten by a grown up.' Later she embroidered this monotonously repeated and guilt-ridden masturbatory formula into a medieval romance about a noble youth imprisoned in the sinister and violent castle of a knight, representing her father. The youth is threatened with all sorts of torture, including the rack. The main excitement, however, lay in the fact that, at the very moment of inflicting pain, the knight becomes friendly and generous: 'He nearly kills the youth through the long imprisonment, but just before it is too late the knight has him nursed back to health.'[9]

Anna herself transformed this father-centred story into an unpublished novel, *Heinrich Mühsam* (*Painstaking Henry*). Ironically, her colleague Jeanne de Groot (analysed by Freud in 1922) used Anna's beating fantasies paper to illustrate her thesis (based on de Groot's patients' experience of her as mother) that the girl's first love is the mother, not the father, as Freud and Anna then claimed. Beating fantasies like those described by Anna, wrote de Groot, are one means whereby girls turn away from the mother to the father by becoming masochistically subservient so as to make themselves more attractive to him.

Anna's paper certainly turned her further away from her mother. It qualified her as an analyst, a profession Martha Freud dismissed as 'a form of pornography'.[10] As Anna once put it, 'So far as psychoanalysis was concerned, my mother never cooperated.'[11] This included obstructing Anna's wish to move her study opposite Freud's. But Anna prevailed and she and her father shared the same waiting-room.

Her first patients were adults. Soon, however, she started treating children, having already had first-hand childcare experience in teaching and wartime rescue work, and in looking after her nephew Ernst, whom she even thought of adopting after his mother Sophie's sudden death in the influenza epidemic of early 1920.

Anna's involvement in Ernst's care in Hamburg, and her interest in working in Eitingon's newly established Berlin Clinic, promised to loosen her from her father. But this was not to be. In April 1923, just after she gave her first child analysis talk to the Vienna Society,[12] Freud consulted Felix Deutsch about a painful swelling on his palate. Dismissing Deutsch for not believing he was man enough to bear the diagnosis of cancer, Freud went on to see another doctor who, underestimating the seriousness of his condition, admitted him for outpatient surgery. Post-operatively Freud bled profusely and was only saved by a fellow-patient, a retarded dwarf, running for help.

Freud's narrow escape persuaded Anna she could never leave. Again and again she took her mother's place in accompanying her father on his many visits to Berlin for medical treatment over the next decade, and in fixing his various prostheses. She became his Antigone – Oedipus's faithful daughter – as her father more than once called her. She not only nursed him but also edited and became a major exponent of his work. This included major involvement in running the Vienna and International Psychoanalytic Societies.

The next Easter she also re-entered analysis with him. Perhaps this was the source of Freud's important essays on female sexuality, beginning with a 1925 article which Anna decided to read to that year's International Psychoanalytic Congress. In it Freud attributed the intense suppression in girls of masturbation – such as involved in Anna's beating fantasies – to narcissistic humiliation at not having a penis. The girl's penis envy, he argued in a now notorious passage, is then converted into a 'wish for a child: and with that purpose in view she takes her father as a love-object'.[13]

In a sense Freud colluded with this desire in Anna. Although he complained, 'I cannot free her from me, and nobody is helping me with it',[14] he now attached her ever more securely to himself. At the very moment, as the local paper noted, that Anna's erstwhile suitor Hans Lampl became engaged to Jeanne de Groot, Freud gave Anna a dog whom the two pampered like a child, much to Anna's mother's annoyance. It was only when Anna became involved with mothers more her own age that she began to break free of her father both personally and professionally. Only then did she no longer repeat his work, as she had in her beating fantasies paper, but go beyond it – first to pioneer child analysis.

2

Child analysis

> Children have become the main subject of psycho-analytic research and have thus replaced in importance the neurotics on which its studies began. (Sigmund Freud, 1925)[1]

In November 1924 Anna began treating fifteen-year-old Minna and soon became fast friends with her mother, Eva Rosenfeld. Within months she also became even closer friends with another mother, Dorothy Burlingham.

Dorothy was an heiress to the Tiffany jewellery fortune. Her own mother had died when Dorothy was twelve. Now in her thirties and separated from her mentally ill doctor husband, Robert, she had come from America with her four children – Bob, Mabbie, Tinky, and Mikey – to Vienna for help with ten-year-old asthmatic Bob's anxieties, 'childish perverse habits', stealing, and endless lying.

Anna began treating him in autumn 1925 and soon had all four children in therapy with her. By February 1926 she wrote:

> I think sometimes that I want not only to make them healthy but also, at the same time, to have them, or at least something of them, for myself . . . Towards the mother of the children it is not very different with me.[2]

Anna's involvement with the Burlinghams formed the basis of her first breakthrough in psychoanalysis. Since the early 1920s she had met regularly with Siegfried Bernfeld, Willi Hoffer and August Aichhorn in her home to discuss their work with children and delinquents. She had also given lectures on the subject to the Vienna Society. Now in her 1926 lectures, soon to become the basis of the first ever book on child analysis, she described her treatment of the Burlingham children and their friends the Sweetzers, whose father was unofficial US ambassador to the League of Nations in Geneva.

She used this experience implicitly to take issue with her father's technique, at least as regards treating children. But her much more explicit target was Melanie Klein's virtually unmodified use of Freud's method to analyse children, as described in her 1924 Würzburg Congress account of treating a six-year-old, Erna.

Against Klein, Anna insisted on the need for a preparatory stage in child analysis. Since, she said, children do not come because of their own suffering but because of the suffering they cause others, they have to be enticed into therapy.

Six-year-old Adelaide Sweetzer, for instance, was initially referred because of her parents' worries about her apparent intellectual backwardness and emotional withdrawal. She first came with eight-year-old Mabbie Burlingham, who was already in treatment with Anna 'because she cried so often and was angry with herself for doing so'. The next time Adelaide came alone. Was she coming for the same reason as Mabbie, Anna asked? No. 'I have a devil in me,' said Adelaide, 'can it be taken out?' Certainly, replied Anna, but it would be hard and disagreeable. 'If you tell me that this is the only way,' Adelaide concluded, 'then I shall do it that way.'[3]

Towards the end of a three-week trial period she urged Anna to get rid of her devil right away. But this was impossible. Treatment would take much longer. Sitting on the floor and pointing to a pattern in Anna's oriental rug, the little girl asked, 'Will it take as many days as there are red bits? Or even as the green bits?' No, treatment would take much longer – at least as many days, Anna indicated, as there were medallions on her rug. That said, her young patient helped persuade her parents to let therapy continue.

Anna went on to argue, quite unlike her father, that the analyst should not only analyse but should also meet some of the patient's demands at least initially to gain his or her cooperation. At first, for example, she followed the otherwise very rejecting and mistrustful Bob Burlingham's interests, whether in romance, pirate adventures, geography, or stamp-collecting. Then she made herself useful to him. This included repairing the damage he had done his relations at home. She returned money he had stolen and owned up for him to his parents about his misdeeds.

Meanwhile she crocheted and knitted clothes for another girl patient's dolls and teddies. Perhaps this was Mabbie, whose preparatory period Anna used to win her over against the Burlingham nanny, who threatened to sabotage her therapy.

Years later when Anna developed more confidence with children – Dorothy's included – she dispensed with this warm-up process. But she still sought to secure her child patients' affection. In the case of a particularly recalcitrant boy, she even suggested telling him that his imaginary friend needed treatment for which he would have to bring him.

As regards analysis proper, Anna used her father's method of dream interpretation. Mabbie, for instance, dreamed of helping Bob light the gas water heater. But it exploded, at which their nanny punished her by holding her in the fire so that she would burn up. Anna interpreted the dream in terms of masturbation guilt. Later Mabbie dreamed of a radiator with two different coloured bricks. The house was going to catch fire. Then someone – representing Anna and her soothing reassurance – came to take away the bricks with which Mabbie feared her masturbation might otherwise be punished.

Anna also supplemented her father's technique by analysing children's daydreams, just as she had her own as a teenager. Mabbie, tormented by competing with her brothers and sister, imagined dying and coming back to life as an animal or doll belonging to her nanny's previous charge – a supposedly particularly nice, good little girl. Mabbie wanted to be the girl's dear little baby, to be washed and liked best of all by her, even better than the doll the girl got the next Christmas.

As well as analysing children's daydreams, and unlike her father, Anna also analysed her patients' drawings. Mabbie's included a human-like monster, 'Bitey', with a protruding chin and a fearful set of teeth. Another time she drew a number of figures including herself as a sailor boy accompanying her father round the world. Above them all was her mother as a witch pulling out a giant's hair.

Anna's major difference from her father, however, concerned the use of free association and transference. She believed that children, unlike adults, are incapable of voluntary free association. The child analyst therefore has to make do, she said, with children's unintended associations. Adelaide, for instance, entirely rejected Anna's suggestion that her 'devil' represented her split off and denied anger with her mother. Indeed she protested she loved her. But then, as though fortuitously, she recalled a dream in which 'All my dolls were there and my rabbit as well. Then I went away and the rabbit began to cry most dreadfully.'[4] Now the source of her anger became clear. She felt her mother always went away just when she needed her most. She then recalled how abandoned she felt on holiday when her brother rejoined their parents in town, leaving her with the nursemaid who preferred her younger siblings.

Children's play, argued Anna against Klein, is not equivalent to free association. Indeed, she decried the equation of child analysis with play therapy as cause of its relegation to 'the domain of women'.[5] 'Providing sand and water,' she expostulated, wrongly seduces children into regression, while the use of toys for 'the child to make a so-called little world' is 'greatly overrated'. 'What is really important,' she stressed, 'is what the patient and analyst say and how they relate to each other.'[6]

She ridiculed as wild analysis Klein's interpretation of every aspect of the child's play as symbolic of sexual fantasies about the parents:

> If the child overturns a lamppost or a toy figure, she [Klein] interprets this action, e.g. as an aggressive impulse against the father; a deliberate collision between two cars as evidence of the child having observed sexual intercourse between the parents ... [But] The child who upsets a toy lamppost may have witnessed some such incident in the street the day before; the car collision may be reproducing a similar happening.[7]

All too often, Anna said, Klein neglected external reality in attending to the internal, psychic determination of children's play. This often led to over-hasty interpretation of unconscious material, resulting in children prematurely quitting therapy, so ready are they to act out rather than use free association to talk and think through their problems. Furthermore, since acting out is usually aggressive this can easily be exaggerated to the neglect of children's more positive transference feelings.

The whole issue of transference was one on which, beginning in 1927, Anna departed from her father's technique. He had argued that interpretation of patients' transference – particularly of their positive feelings towards the analyst – is crucial if the otherwise repressed and unconscious childhood source of their problems is to become conscious. By contrast, and addressing her criticism not against her father but against Klein, Anna rejected the latter's focus on transference. Only much later, and here she again implicitly dissented from her father's work, did she acknowledge that the patient's negative as well as positive transference feelings, if rightly interpreted, can help as well as hinder therapy. For the moment, however, she attended only to the obstructive effect of such feelings. Again she illustrated the point by reference to Adelaide and Mabbie.

One day, after Anna had visited the Burlingham home where Adelaide was staying, the latter imagined everyone hated both her and Anna. Another time she felt warned against Anna by an inner voice saying:

> Don't believe Anna F. She tells lies. She will not help you and will only make you worse. She will change your face too, so that you look uglier.[8]

Mabbie likewise felt warned against her. She imagined her nanny flying away overseas and Anna surrounded by dancing devils as if she were sending her nanny away so Mabbie would have no one to stop her masturbating and thereby becoming wicked.

Such fear of the analyst, Anna insisted against Klein, does not directly reflect the child's attitude to the mother. Indeed, she argued, the one relation may well invert the other. The better the child is attached to the mother the more hostile it will be towards the analyst and vice versa.

Children, she argued, do not develop the same transference fantasies about the analyst as adults, not least because the analyst is less of an unknown quantity in child analysis especially since, she. maintained, child analysts should indicate what they believe is right and wrong so as to educate as well as analyse the child.

Later, perhaps due to her Second World War childcare experience, Anna modified this view. But she still maintained that the transference is never full-blown in child analysis. Even if it were, she said, its existence could not be proved because of the child's lack of free association. Furthermore, she maintained, whatever the child's positive transference feelings they are often overshadowed by aggressive acting out.

In general Anna emphasized the difference between her own child analytic and her father's adult analytic technique stemming from the relative immaturity of the child's ego and superego internalization of its parents' prohibitions. Its good behaviour, she said, depends on their presence. The child cannot be relied upon to control the impulses set free by analysis. They accordingly have to be controlled either by the parents or by the analyst acting as the child's 'auxiliary ego'.

Adelaide, for example, found it a great relief to talk to Anna about her previous repressed anal fantasies. But she then began indulging them at home, telling such filthy jokes at table that the Burlinghams completely lost their appetite. Dorothy was at a loss what to do. So Anna revised her technique. She realized she had overestimated Adelaide's superego ability to keep at bay the impulses liberated by therapy. She therefore used her authority to control these impulses by telling Adelaide therapy would end if she did not confine her dirty talk to her sessions with her.

Unlike Anna, Klein implied that the child early represses its anti-social impulses in obedience to a severe internal superego version of its parents' discipline. But, asked Anna, if this were the case why does the child's behaviour change as soon as its parents' behaviour changes? An instance was a two-year-old whose fear of the dark, which Klein might have attributed to internalization of her mother's discipline, disappeared immediately the latter was relaxed specifically as regards toilet-training.[9] Child analysis (like mothering), Anna concluded, oscillates between freeing and restricting the child's impulses in the process of educating them.

This recipe for treatment was hardly radical. And Anna altogether rejected Klein's claim that child analysis could lead to discoveries about earliest pre-verbal development. Here she sided with her father's view that analysis is essentially a talking cure. Her Vienna–Prague–Berlin group, unlike the Kleinians, believed at least initially that children should not be analysed until they can talk. Anna also rejected Klein's radical claim that all children can benefit from analysis. Even where children can benefit from therapy, she warned, it cannot succeed without parental support.

Freud himself described his daughter's technique as 'reactionary' compared to that of Klein. But he staunchly defended her against Klein, and attributed Jones's support of the latter both to pique at Anna's 1914 rejection of him, and to his need to use Klein's work as substitute for his own lack of originality.

Jones in turn retaliated by obstructing the publication of Anna's book. It was not published in England until 1946. Elsewhere it was the first to transform into psychoanalytic form the technique of Hermine von Hug-Hellmuth, also a former elementary school teacher and Anna's only child therapist predecessor in the Vienna Society. Anna's use of her mothering experience in the Burlingham household to pioneer a child analytic technique distinctively different from her father's adult technique, with her continuing lectures and supervisions, made Vienna a world centre of child analysis. Her child analysis seminar involved many of psychoanalysis's founding mothers, including Grete Bibring, Marianne Kris, Jenny Waelder-Hall, Annie Reich, Berta and Steffi Bornstein, Margaret Mahler, Edith Sterba, Anny Katan, Edith Buxbaum and Jean Lampl-de Groot. Unlike Klein's method, Anna's dominated child analysis in the USA and continental Europe virtually to this day.

More immediately, her book's first publication was followed by the strengthening of an increasingly mother-centred life away from her father. That Easter Anna went on holiday for the first time with Dorothy Burlingham, who had now moved into a flat above the Freuds from which she had a direct telephone link installed between her and Anna's bedrooms.

Although Anna did not yet live with Dorothy – and she was much too much her father's daughter ever to have a sexual relationship with her – Freud now regarded the Burlingham household as Anna's home. She holidayed with the Burlinghams in Semmering, Berchtesgaden, and Grudisee. And in late 1930 she and Dorothy together bought a farm cottage, Hochroterd, for weekends and holidays in the Wienerwalk, about forty-five minutes by car from the Freud apartment in Vienna.

3

Ego psychology and adolescence

Life with the Burlinghams led to Anna's first independent educational experiment. Believing children in analysis should have a psychoanalytically informed upbringing, she, Dorothy, and Eva Rosenfeld set up a school in Eva's home for their children and Anna's virtual adoptee, Ernst Halberstadt, among others. It was staffed by Bob's tutor Peter Blos and Erik Erikson. The latter was also analysed by Anna, who occasionally irritated him by knitting through his sessions. But she disarmed his criticism by giving him a handmade sweater for his new-born son.[1] Meanwhile in the Rosenfeld school he and Blos adopted Anna's 'project method', which she had previously used on her school trip to Hungary in 1918 and which now informed her child analysis work in that she felt this too should begin with the child's own interests.

In 1929 she was invited to talk about psychoanalysis to people working in Vienna's working-class after-school centres. She told them of nursery school children's transfer of family conflicts on to their teachers. But she also warned against mistaking professional childcare for mothering, and criticized those who sought to compensate for lack of mothering through such work. An example was an eighteen-year-old governess who spoiled the least loved of her three pupils only to become envious of him – so much so that she quit her job immediately her care of this boy secured him the parental affection of which she herself felt starved as a child.[2]

As well as lecturing, Anna also became an editor in 1931 of the *Journal of Psychoanalytic Education* – forerunner of the post-war Anglo-American periodical, *Psychoanalytic Study of the Child*. The same year the psychoanalytic publishing house's assets collapsed in the wake of the June failure of Austria's main bank. Within a couple of years Hitler came to power. And in May 1933 Freud's books were burnt in Berlin for their 'soul-rending overrating of instinctual life'.[3] Next February saw the socialist uprising in Vienna in which Martin Deutsch was involved. This was followed by German-inspired agitation and the July 1934 Nazi assassination of Dollfuss.

Anna, however, was preoccupied with more domestic concerns. The Burlingham children were now teenagers. She drew on this experience in writing arguably her most important book, *The Ego and the Mechanisms of Defence*. It was first published in May 1936 as an eightieth birthday present for her father. It enormously expanded his theory of the Oedipus complex division of id, ego, and superego, and his account of the defences caused by anxiety. It also culminated in one of the first and most influential psychoanalytic accounts of adolescence, the groundwork of which lay in the book's early chapters on the ego's defences against the id and superego.

Anna's major innovation – one which earned her the contempt of later Freudians[4] – lay in the way she used her childcare experience to emphasize the adaptive as well as maladaptive effects of the ego's defences. This in sharp contrast to her father, whose radicalism arguably resided in his emphasis, from 1895 onwards, that such defences are always essentially pathological.

In the case of five-year-old Hans, Freud had focused on the neurotic, agoraphobic effects of Hans's defence of displacing his aggression against his father on to horses, which he now feared would attack him in the street. Later Anna drew attention to the potentially helpful effect of phobia in protecting children against trauma. True, Hans's phobia prevented him going out. But, she pointed out, it also enabled him to be with his father. She also drew attention to Hans's adaptive identification with his father's otherwise feared aggression by playing at being him as a biting horse. For the moment, at the 1929 Oxford Congress, she stressed the adaptive aspects of Hans's other defences, his imagining, for instance, in defence against envy of his mother and father, that he had 'a number of children whom he looked after and cleansed in the water-closet', and that a plumber took away his 'buttocks and penis with a pair of pincers, so as to give him larger and finer ones'.[5]

Freud had been only indirectly involved, through Hans's father, in Hans's treatment. Anna, by contrast, had much more direct childcare experience on which to base her claims about the adaptive function of the ego's defences. Just as she herself had adaptively used daydreams to fend off rivalry with her mother, she now described a seven-year-old patient's defence against fear of the father as of Freud – whom he described as 'also a sort of lion'[6] – by daydreaming he had a tame lion who accompanied him everywhere and would frighten others if they discovered it was real. Another boy managed similar fears by pretending to be a circus owner whose animals protected him against a marauding thief. Children's stories and rhymes, Anna pointed out, appeal to these self-same defences – like *Little Lord Fauntleroy* who 'tames' an otherwise grumpy old man, and the three-year-old in A. A. Milne's poem who imagines himself in turn as an explorer, a lion, and a sea captain – fantasies that teachers appeal to, she said, by starting natural history with the big and dangerous animals.

Critics, herself initially included, argue that by attending to the conscious ego, analysis loses sight of Freud's discovery of the underlying unconscious id determinants of the psyche. But, Anna insisted, it is necessary to pay attention to the ego to access the id unless, like Klein, one believes the unconscious can be directly accessed through play and free association. An example was a patient of Anna's whose underlying anxiety, which prevented her going to school, could be dealt with only by first addressing the girl's defensive contempt for such anxiety. This contempt originated in her father mocking her for giving way to her feelings – mockery the girl now experienced as also coming from Anna.

By attending to the ego, Anna later added, the scope of psychoanalysis is widened to include character analysis. Furthermore, she pointed out, analysis of the unconscious id to the neglect of the conscious ego or vice versa loses sight of psychoanalysis's main concern, namely the conflict of the one with the other.

Nevertheless and in keeping with her long-standing, down-to-earth approach – as a child she had always preferred true to fantasy stories – Anna focused more on the reality-based ego than on underlying fantasy that so enlivens our experience of the world. As a result her writing, while very clear, is often rather drearily matter-of-fact.

In her 1936 book she systematically listed and illustrated the adaptive and maladaptive effects of the ego's defences of repression, regression, reaction formation, isolation, undoing, projection, introjection, turning against the self, reversal, and sublimation. She also showed how these defences can occur together. An example was a residential childcare worker who dealt with her jealousy of her mother's repeated pregnancies by variously loving her mother while hating other women, by masochistically turning her hatred of her mother against herself, and by projecting it into others, thereby becoming fearful of them.

Contrary to her father, and on the basis of her childcare experience, Anna also stressed that, whereas the adult's defences are mobilized by fear of parental threats internalized within the superego, the child's defences are aroused by fear of the parents themselves. She also described two further defences, again on the basis of her mothering experience, namely 'altruistic surrender' and 'identification with the aggressor'.

Freud described projection of feelings and wishes into others as dysfunctional, as leading to paranoia. By contrast, Anna also stressed its adaptive, altruistic aspect as in Freud's lesbian case whose lesbianism he had attributed, among other things, to her having 'retired in favour of' her mother's craving for male attention.[7] Anna also described her own use of projection – the way she vicariously enjoyed mothering by looking after other women's children – a form of gratification she likened to the noble self-sacrifice of the hero of Edmond Rostand's *Cyrano de Bergerac*, which she so admired she learnt it by heart.

Anna is better remembered, however, for her account of a perhaps more typically male defence – identification with the aggressor. In this she may have drawn on the way her father dealt with the assaults of illness and surgery through which she so long nursed him in place of her mother. She certainly drew on her childcare experience: her analysis, for instance, of a seven-year-old who got over fear of ghosts by pretending to be the ghost she feared; and her later experience of looking after a little girl who urged her brother 'be a doggy and no doggy will bite you', just as the girl herself dealt with her fear of her mother by becoming sharp-tongued like her.[8] Another child similarly handled his fear of the dentist by identifying with the latter's assaults through sharpening, breaking, and resharpening the points of his pencils in Anna's consulting room. She was accordingly convinced, more against Klein than her father, of the relatively independent development of sex and aggression, the latter in her view being more often used in the service of the ego.

Anna's last major breakthrough in her 1936 book was its concluding account of adolescence. Against her father and his followers, and again on the basis of her childcare experience, she drew attention to the differences between adolescence and other stages of development. In particular she drew attention to the specific problems posed adolescents by pubertal increase in sex drive. Teenagers, she pointed out, alternate between self-indulgence and ascetism. They often refuse to accept any compromise between their conflicting drives. Or they adaptively transform instinctual and concrete thought into abstract 'formal operational' reasoning as described by Piaget. And, as in the socialist movement in which some of the Burlinghams were involved, she wrote, teenagers often forge new ideals in opposition to the norms of their parents.

Almost as an afterthought, Anna pointed out that adolescence involves not only ego defence against the instincts described by her father. It also revives earlier sexual attachment to the parents against which the adolescent defends by becoming infatuated and identifying – 'as if' style – with others as described by Helene Deutsch, or by retreat into self-love. As illustration Anna cited the case of a girl who withdrew socially to pre-empt being rejected and left alone by the boy she loved.

Later, largely as a result of her wartime childcare work alerting her to the maternal factors shaping instinctual development, Anna gave more attention to the interpersonal aspects of adolescence. In a still very influential US talk[9] she listed the following adolescent defences against infantile attachment to parents (and analysts): displacement of this attachment on to others and indulgence of 'family romances' whereby teenagers invent themselves aristocratic parents in place of their own; decreased superego internalization of the parents' authority resulting in anti-social behaviour, reduced internal conflict, and hence less motivation for, and greater acting out in psychoanalytic therapy; reversal of love of parents into hatred, self-hatred, and self-injury; emotional withdrawal from others into narcissistic self-love; and regression to infantile lack of boundary between self and other. *In extremis* this can involve anorexic defence against imagined emotional surrender to, and fusion with the mother.

Such defences, Anna insisted, are entirely normal and adaptive in adolescence. Mental illness occurs only when there is excessive or exclusive use of one or other defence. Otherwise adolescent turmoil, she maintained, is quite normal and inevitable – a conclusion that set the scene for today's debates about adolescent psychology.[10]

Her 1936 book also paved the way for the development of ego psychology – its attention to adolescent identity formation,[11] and to the adaptive and 'conflict free zone' of the ego, so named by Heinz Hartmann, with whom Anna did ward rounds in the Wagner-Jauregg Psychiatric Clinic in the early 1920s. Even Freud himself was persuaded by her book in changing his therapeutic focus from undoing the infantile defences of the ego to reviewing and making them more adaptive to current reality.

By 1937 current reality was becoming increasingly threatening. That March Freud wrote to Jones: 'There is probably no holding up the Nazi invasion . . . Mussolini seems now to be giving Germany a free hand.'[12] Anna's own concerns, however, continued to be more child- and mother-centred. In February 1937 she was involved in opening the Jackson day nursery for toddlers whose mothers, faced with their husband's unemployment, worked at best as charwomen. As well as having a charitable aim, the nursery also provided an opportunity for direct infant observation, thereby enabling Anna and her colleagues to go beyond her father's account of infant development solely through its reconstruction via adult analysis. It also led Anna to take issue with received paediatric opinion, specifically with New Zealand paediatrician Truby King's insistence on scheduling children's eating. Given free choice of food, she pointed out, the Jackson children were clearly able to schedule and balance what they ate for themselves without their pleasure in eating being deadened by an externally imposed regime.

But this childcare experiment soon came to an end. On 12 March 1938 Hitler invaded Vienna and the nursery was closed. The Gestapo visited the Freud home, where they were disarmed by Anna's mother's hospitality. Later Martha reproved them for messing up her laundry. Anna herself was taken for questioning, having first supplied herself with veronal in case of torture or internment. She narrowly escaped both by using family connections to make sure she was interviewed rather than left waiting in the corridor, from which she might well have been deported when the office closed at the end of the day.

Her narrow escape finally convinced Freud of the need to leave Austria. But first the Gestapo insisted he settle his debts. And the family had to get visas (Anna later compared their difficulties then with those of the 1970s Vietnamese refugees). Meanwhile Freud wrote an introduction to the French analyst Princess Marie Bonaparte's account of her dog Topsy. In it he drew on his attachment to the dogs Burlingham had given him.

With the help of Ernest Jones and the Princess, who now replaced the recently deceased Lou Andréas-Salomé in Anna's affections, and just days after Dorothy's long estranged husband's suicide, the Freuds left Vienna on 4 June for London. Others – including Hartmann and Kris – left for the USA, where Anna's lack of medical training precluded her working as an analyst despite her and her father's long campaign to gain international recognition of non-medical lay analysis. Nevertheless the States now became the centre of the ego psychology she had done so much to pioneer in Vienna. And a US charity funded her next major venture – the Hampstead war nurseries.

4

War nurseries

The Freud family now settled in Hampstead. Freud himself soon became gravely ill. Just after war was declared he died, on 23 September 1939. Anna's mother was bereft: 'My life has lost its sense and meaning.'[1] Anna herself, who had already given lectures to London teachers and child analysis seminars and talks to the British Psycho-Analytical Society, immediately went back to seeing patients. And within a year she and Dorothy began a childcare project that led Anna to pioneer a much more mother-centred approach to psychoanalysis than her father.

In 1941, the year of her Aunt Minna's death, when Dorothy first moved in with Anna, Anna became director of two nurseries in Hampstead and one near Dunmow in Essex for children from London's badly bombed and impoverished East End. She very much sympathized with the children's mothers' plight and never sought to take their place. Instead she continued to identify more as her father's child, even doing duty as Santa Claus at Christmas. Yet in running the nurseries she and Dorothy showed the same attention to domestic detail as Anna's mother. They recorded the friendliness of local tradesmen, nursery provisions and the lack of fresh fruit, ways of making do as rationing bit deep, infestations, infections, and childhood illnesses. In common with mothers in more usual settings, they also worried about the neighbours' complaints of the children's noise, and about the practical problems caused by the babies' increasing mobility. Anna also crocheted hammocks, like those the children slept in during air raids, for their dolls.

She and Dorothy very much recounted the war through the

children's eyes. Some assimilated it to oral ideas – 'The sirens are eating me up';[2] others to anal fantasies, telling off an air raid warning for being 'naughty . . . doing big job, high in the sky'.[3] For the older children the bombs aroused their own aggression and their only recently internalized controls against it. Hitler and his arsenal seemed to join forces with the ghosts and bogeymen, gypsies and robbers, chimney sweeps and dustmen, lions and tigers, earthquakes and thunderstorms that people children's peacetime defences against anti-social feeling.

For six-year-old Anne, however, an early 1943 air raid triggered uninhibited murderous thoughts: 'I want big guns and lots of bombs . . . I want them . . . to make a big hole in the wall and the house will be all open and I'll bleed and everybody will bleed.' She went on to recall her father's death in the 1941 Blitz. The superintendent, Ilse Hellmann, told her the fire-watchman (and poet) Stephen Spender would come, at which Anne sang: 'Spender, Spender, suspender, my mummy has got suspenders on her pink rubber belt.'[4]

More than anything it was the mother's presence or absence that shaped the children's response to war. Anna never saw the same distress the nursery children felt on separation from their mothers in children sleeping next to their mothers in the underground. For the former, she observed, 'conditions of air raid danger and underground sleeping . . . is the state of bliss to which they all desire to return'.[5]

The mother's response to war, not the bombing itself, determined the child's reaction. If the mother was calm, so was the child. The reverse happened if she were distraught, like five-year-old Jim's mother who 'never went to bed while the alarm lasted, stood at the door trembling, and insisted on the child not sleeping either'. He 'had to get dressed, to hold her hand and to stand next to her'.[6] He became anxious like her and wet the bed. During renewed bombing eighteen months later he became very pale, trembled, and asked the nursery staff, 'Where are all the children?' just as his mother asked herself in the earlier raids what had become of her soldier sons.[7]

Similarly four-year-old Bertie rushed around 'aimlessly to

the far corners of the nursery in a curious rabbitlike manner'[8] just as his mother frantically searched for his father after his death in the autumn 1940 Blitz. At the time she took Bertie with her to look for her husband – to the police and even to the morgue – Bertie comforting her the while. He himself was later hospitalized with tonsillitis, at which his mother went mad. Thinking he too was dead, she rushed around looking for him just as Bertie now agitatedly ran around the nursery.

But it was wartime children's distress at maternal separation –which they resented much more than separation from their fathers – that most revolutionized psychoanalysis. At the time it led Anna vehemently to criticize the government's failure to notice this distress in evacuating children away from their mothers.

Often children's response was quite heartbreaking. Two-year-old Maggie, for instance, came to Anna's nursery so that her mother could take up munitions work. Initially Maggie was delighted with her new surroundings. Soon, however, she completely broke down, cried incessantly, and could not be comforted. Then for two weeks she clung to one teacher after another. Another two-year-old, Derrick, was also relatively happy at first. But when his mother visited he alternately scolded and clung to her, and demanded that she baby his toy dog. He had tantrums in her absence whenever the dog got knocked, so much did he transfer on to it his bereft feelings about losing her.

Particularly distressing was sudden separation. Two-year-old Dell, brought by her mother lest she catch TB from the grandmother with whom she slept, responded with frenzied searching half an hour after her mother left. She then became promiscuously attached to one member of staff after another. Three-year-old Billie, by contrast, did not make a fuss because his mother had told him she would only visit if he did not cry. Instead of crying he monotonously repeated: 'My mother will put on my overcoat and take me home again . . . she will zip up the zipper, she will put on my pixie hat.'[9] Later he repeated this formula under his breath, then enacted it till all that was left was a 'compulsive tic'.

The children's distress was much less lamentable where maternal separation was more planned and gradual. A couple of months before her expected confinement, two-year-old Hilda's mother accustomed her to the nursery by first bringing her as a day child. Similarly the mother of three-year-old Paul, whose delicate health prevented him going on sleeping beside her in Baker Street underground station, kept him company till he got used to the nursery.

Children often coped with separation by remembering their mother with a piece of clothing, doll, or toy she had given them. Anna and Dorothy accordingly deplored foster mothers and nurseries restricting children's access to such things. They were very important to three-year-old Bob, who clung to particular clothes whenever separation from his mother felt particularly unbearable – to his shoes when he first arrived in the nursery, to an overcoat when his mother could not visit for several weeks, and then to a hat when the November 1941 scarlet fever quarantine of the Essex nursery prevented her visiting. Others used dolls to keep their absent mothers in mind. Five-year-old Rosette carried a collection of tiny toys from her mother which she showed to everyone, saying 'my very own', while four-year-old Georgie wanted all his toys wrapped up like the parcels that remained his only link with his mother, who was hospitalized with TB.

Maternal separation, Anna and Dorothy noted, is made all the worse by children experiencing it as rejection, punishment, or effect of their bad, Oedipal feelings. To compensate, children stress their love and idealize the mother in her absence. Her visits are therefore bound to be disappointing, especially given the increasing division with time between the child's loyalty to family and nursery. This is only made worse where nurseries fail to welcome mothers. Anna and Dorothy accordingly did everything, petrol rationing permitting, to facilitate parental visits. These often had a carnival atmosphere – like a wedding party, as one mother described a fruit-picking expedition to the Essex nursery. Wherever possible Anna and Dorothy employed the mothers in the nurseries. But they also sympathized with the plight of visiting fathers faced with the nurseries' appropriation, in mothering their children, of their traditional family-based authority.

Having so long neglected mothering, Anna now publicly stressed its importance. The child's first relation to its mother, she emphasized in an October 1941 talk,[10] patterns all its subsequent relationships. Unlike her father, she drew attention to the dependence of instinctual development on the mother – her absence resulting in regression from emotional to physical attachment, to primitive aggression and temper tantrums, and to loss of bladder and bowel control. Two-year-old Bobby, for instance, whose father was a soldier in India, and who was dry both night and day when he arrived at the nursery, soon became enuretic when his expectant mother was no longer able to visit every day. He also soiled himself when she stopped visiting because of her imminent confinement. Similarly two-year-old Tony began wetting and soiling after being evacuated because of his mother's hospitalization with TB.

Tony's case also illustrates another effect of Anna's wartime childcare work – her use of this experience to emphasize the need to organize residential care along what later came to be adopted as a 'family grouping' or 'key worker' system. Tony was initially no trouble when he arrived, aged nearly three, at the Essex nursery. Indeed he seemed devoid of all feeling. He only became obviously emotional, alternately screaming for and at his nurse Mary, when he became ill. Gradually, as he became more securely attached to Mary, he became more even-tempered. Nevertheless he could still be very clinging, as when he became upset after a visiting soldier turned out not to be his father as he expected.

The freeing from repression of Tony's emotion and capacity to be comforted as a result of his attachment to Mary, and other similar experiences, led Anna to introduce family grouping in spring 1942. To minimize the children's otherwise fraught attachments to individual staff, the children were now divided into groups of about four, each group being assigned to a nursery 'mother'.

At first there was pandemonium. The insecurity bred in the children by maternal separation resulted in their becoming intensely attached to their new nursery mother. They wept every time she left the room, and were aggressively jealous of each other. Three-year-old Bridget, for instance, insisted 'my Miss Freud very own'.[11] Within a couple of weeks, however, their frenzy gave way to quieter, more stable and comforting attachment. At the same time the children's toilet training and speech progressed by leaps and bounds.

These advantages, argued Anna and Dorothy, outweigh the unhappiness caused children by separation from the key worker when either she or the child leaves the nursery. Although this was cited as a reason for not developing children's ties to residential staff and foster parents, Anna and Dorothy's family grouping system was so successful that it was incorporated into post-war British childcare legislation.[12]

Meanwhile they stressed the need to prepare children for reunion with parents, and criticized the government's failure to consider children's attachments to their substitute carers with what they took to be its blanket ruling that evacuated children be returned home immediately they reached school age. Their own charges' return was prepared by social worker (and conscientious objector) James Robertson prior to the nurseries' closure in summer 1945.

Anna now became involved in a project that convinced her still more of the importance of mothering to children's development.[13] Soon after the war she directed a Sussex home, Bulldogs Bank, for six Vienna- and Berlin-born Jewish toddlers, who had all lost their mothers early in their lives. They had spent their first two years in a motherless children's ward in Thereinstadt concentration camp, and had then been sent first to a castle in Czechoslovakia, then to Windermere, and finally to Sussex in autumn 1945.

For want of mothering, the children had become intensely attached to each other. But this did not prevent them being very aggressive both to grown-ups and to themselves – including biting, spitting, and endless head-banging. They engaged in constant and compulsive autoerotic activity – especially Paul who endlessly sucked and masturbated. They were also very retarded in other respects. Toilet training, which had taken a long time to establish in Thereinstadt, deteriorated on their arrival in Sussex. They were also very backward in play, thinking, general knowledge, and speech.

The implication seemed obvious. Children's development and therapy depends not so much on instinctual repression, as Freud implied, but on their attachments to adults. These offset and mitigate with love children's otherwise naked destructive and anti-social tendencies.[14] Hence, concluded Anna and Dorothy,[15] the delinquency observed by Anna's close friend and admirer, August Aichhorn, in teenagers with a history of childhood institutionalization. Hence too their lack of self-esteem due to having no mother to be proud of them as extensions of herself.

Anna's own mother hardly seemed proud of her in this way. In Hampstead she decried Anna's dress and work as she had in Vienna. Some escape was afforded by Anna and Dorothy buying a country home in Walberswick, Suffolk, in 1946. Here they holidayed with Dorothy's children. Here too Anna rode and drove a tractor.

Her mother died in November 1951. This seemingly prompted one of Anna's most moving essays, 'About losing and being lost'.[16] In it, and drawing on Winnicott's account of the child's use of a piece of cloth, or 'transitional object' to manage maternal separation, Anna pointed out that the child often clings to toys as though, like itself in losing its mother, the toy also felt hurt and discarded. Alternatively, and implicitly taking issue with her father's view that absent-mindedness serves unconscious wishes, she suggested children lose things out of identification with the mother's seeming neglect and loss of narcissistic interest in them. So too with the bereaved, who, displacing on to the dead their own feelings of being deserted and neglected, seek both to discard the dead and to follow and console them in their imagined desolation. In the self-same way, Anna later recalled, a three-year-old war nursery boy wanted to phone and console his mother on the assumption she missed him as much as he missed her, just as analytic patients want their analysts to think of them when they are away.[17] For the moment, however, another aspect of mothering preoccupied her, that involved in childhood illness.

5

Paediatrics

> The Englishman ... does not want to be upset, to be reminded that there are personal tragedies ... he refuses to be put off his golf. (Winnicott on paediatrics)[1]

One of the immediate effects of projects like Anna's wartime nurseries was a shift of childcare policy towards supporting children in their own families or, failing that, in foster families rather than sending them away to residential nurseries or children's homes. It also led to changes in paediatric care. Anna's war nursery social worker, James Robertson, now a researcher with John Bowlby, sought to convince doctors, despite their scepticism, of the ill-effects of hospitalizing children away from their mothers. He illustrated this point by making a film of a two-year-old, Laura's, mounting unhappiness and regression on being separated from her mother for umbilical hernia surgery. The trauma of such events, Anna later wrote, is due to their overwhelming the child's own ego resources. The mother's presence is usually necessary as a protective shield or buffer against the child thus being overwhelmed by internal and external stress, illness and medicine included.

Robertson's films eventually persuaded doctors of the need to enable mothers to stay with their children in hospital – just as Paul's mother stayed with him to help him get used to the war nursery (see p. 171 above). Since children experience maternal separation as rejection, made all the more bewildering when the child's anxieties are heightened by illness, Anna suggested that mothers be encouraged to introduce the child to hospital, stay with it through medical procedures, and help in its physical care.

An example was Joyce Robertson's accompanying their four-year-old daughter Jean through tonsillectomy, and helping her keep external reality in mind while also understanding the internal, psychological forces unleashed by surgery. These included Jean's initial denial of anxiety, subsequent fear of loss of consciousness during the operation, followed by a sense of her mother as both cause and protection against post-operative pain. Here, for once, Anna[2] likened the mother's role to that of her own as child analyst in helping the child deal with the internal feelings mobilized by external reality. But, she stressed, mothers are better placed than childcare workers to understand the child's psychological response to illness, since it is not fragmented for them by professional divisions of labour.

The distress of children, like war nursery Bobby (see p. 172), on being separated from their mothers because of the latters' hospital confinement also led to changes in this aspect of childcare. Again largely as a result of the Robertsons' films – particularly of seventeen-month-old John's almost autistic withdrawal, as Anna put it, in a residential nursery while his mother was in hospital – alternative short-term foster care was introduced to cover such contingencies.

Anna's own contribution to changes in hospital care stemmed from her mothering experience – her wartime child-care work, nursing her father, whose throat cancer often prevented him eating, attending to Dorothy through her long illness with TB, and from her own experience of pneumonia just after the war. Her own illness prompted dreams of mothering – 'I have a baby. Someone throws it (for reasons unknown) on to the ground from above, again and again' – and thoughts of childcare – 'People forget to consider how much a child [like an ill adult] must suffer from the fact that it needs so much help.'[3]

In the first of several psychoanalytic lectures to paediatricians,[4] she pointed out that her child patients' parents often attributed the origin of their children's neurotic difficulties to bodily illness. Indeed, she observed, illness often provokes neurotic conflict – about operations, about being dependently nursed, and about restrictions of diet and mobility, the latter often being unnecessarily severe.

The child's response to illness, like that of the war nursery children to the stress of bombing, is crucially affected by the mother's response, both actual and imagined. Quoting Klein approvingly, Anna suggested that children can unconsciously experience medical treatment – surgery included – as though it involved the mother getting back at them for bad behaviour towards her.

The mother's own behaviour can also cause problems – resentment and distrust, for instance, if the mother camouflages bad medicine. At thirteen Anna had similarly felt bitter at her mother concealing from her the fact that she had to have her appendix removed. Other problems, she suggested,[5] arise from the mother forcing her sick child to eat even though it has lost its appetite and from the mother's resistance to giving treatment. An example was the mother of eight-year-old Ann. She hated getting Ann to do painful exercises for her arthritis, so much was their relation founded on Ann's belief that her mother could remove her pain.[6] Other complications are posed by the mother's distress at her child's illness, like war nursery Bertie's mother's response to his tonsillectomy (see p. 170 above), or mothers' depression at having a blind child, or at the medical procedures involved in handicap generally.

Five-year-old Shirley's mother, for instance, felt she herself was being punished by the hospital putting Shirley (who had Legg-Perthes disease) in a restraining vest to prevent her getting out of bed when her leg had to be kept in traction. Nevertheless – as Anna's student Thesi Bergmann points out – children often find it easier to cope with illness with such visible orthopaedic effects than with less obvious conditions like cardiac disease.

Anna also pointed out the individual differences between children in their response to maternal and hospital care. Some give in, others resent the mother's anxiety about their sick body in which she treats it as though it were her own. And while some vehemently reject and rebel against hospital care, others – particularly deprived children – welcome the regressive dependence it affords, like ten-year-old polio victim Harriet, who had been in foster care since she was a baby. Yet others become increasingly demanding, like war nursery Tony when he was sick (see p. 172 above). Or they become resigned, obediently submissive, or emotionally withdrawn like the war nursery children, who, deprived of their mothers, hypochondriacally nursed themselves. One forlorn boy, for instance, wore his sweater and overcoat even in hot weather lest he catch cold. Another with diarrhoea and vomiting nursed himself with the words 'I my darling'.[7]

Doctors, Anna[8] told London's Royal College of Physicians, need to be aware not only of the psychological causes of illness but also of its psychological effects. In particular she described resistance to the potential anal and phallic excitement – depending on the child's age and sex – involved in suppositories and injections. Paediatricians, she argued, need to recognize that psychological unlike bodily development involves both progress and temporary or permanent regression to earlier (oral, anal, or phallic) fixations as effect of parental and/or medical intervention.

Just as Anna earlier showed that children's response to war cannot be read off from external reality, so too she pointed out that the psychological severity of children's response to illness is not necessarily proportional to its physical severity. All too often doctors and others recognize the seriousness of the child's anxiety only when they are seriously ill or have to undergo major medical treatment. But, Anna noted,[9] minor medical events and short-term illness can provoke just as intense anxiety, so readily does illness and its treatment, like Hitler's bombs, trigger the frightening internal figures that people children's conscience.

Bergmann's book *Children in the Hospital*, which Anna introduced, provides many illustrative examples. Eight-year-old Ernest and nine-year-old Ruth assimilated their rheumatic fever to guilt about masturbation. Four-year-old Cindy thought she had been hospitalized for being the 'bad girl' her father told her she was. She panicked every time a doctor came near, pleading that she would always be good if only they would do nothing to her. By contrast ten-year-old Elizabeth feared having blood taken lest it reveal her to be 'bad', as her dead, Indian, alcoholic father had been described.

Others manage their illness with more encouraging fantasies: ten-year-old Donna coped with spinal TB by imagining herself to be a fairy princess who would only regain her true form through undergoing a series of ordeals; nine-year-old Dave laughed off the guilt his illness provoked by describing its onset in mock judicial terms: 'I was charged with having polio . . . my sentence was life imprisonment in a wheel chair'.[10]

Yet others cope by displacing their worries on to something minor: five-year-old Joel was far more ashamed of having a bandage round his head for earache than of having extension weights to treat his much more long-term Legg-Perthes disease; ten-year-old Leah phoned to check that her alarm clock was still ticking while she had heart surgery.

Such idiosyncratic and subjective response to illness can easily cut children off from the breezy realism of medical staff. Anna accordingly recommended that hospital therapists, like Bergmann, be appointed both to acquaint staff with children's emotional response to illness and to help children grasp its objective, medical reality. This advice has now been adopted by many major children's hospitals.

Certainly, Anna[11] acknowledged, medical adoption of psychoanalytic insight had not been helped by psychoanalysts' obscure jargon. But doctors, for their part, wrongly tend to treat the body as entirely separate from the mind, just as teachers divorce thought from feeling, and just as family lawyers divide financial and moral from emotional considerations in child custody cases. This one-sidedness, Anna maintained, can only be overcome through day-to-day involvement with children and babies in whom such divisions of internal and external, psyche and soma, are absent. For in the infant every

> frustration, impatience, rage, or anxiety . . . finds expression in disturbances of sleep, feeding, or elimination; [and] every physical upset . . . leads to changes of mood, diffuse excitation, and anxiety reactions.[12]

Again and again Anna urged the need for an all-round practical as well as theoretical core training in work with children of all ages, normal as well as abnormal, for all those working professionally with children – whether in medicine, education, law, or social welfare. Only then would childcare workers be alerted to the interaction of fantasy and reality, mind and body, cognition and emotion, security and morality, from earliest infancy onwards.

6

Developmental assessment

In 1941 Anna initiated just such an all-round approach to childcare training, paying particular attention to mothering, for her war nurseries staff. Their programme included lectures on physical health and illness, cognitive and emotional development, household management (budgeting, cooking, sewing), gymnastics, and Montessori education. In turn it inspired Anna's post-war Hampstead child therapy course, first started in 1947.

Five years later, just a couple of months after her mother's death in 1951, Anna also began the Hampstead Clinic. It included child analysis, sometimes involving simultaneous analysis of mother and child; a well-baby clinic providing mothers with medical-psychological counselling; a kindergarten catering mainly for children from poor, deprived, and increasingly from immigrant, particularly Jamaican, backgrounds; a special unit for blind children and their mothers; and a research unit in which Anna developed the Hampstead diagnostic profile, and Dorothy instituted a system of indexing observations of children first developed in their pre-war Vienna and wartime Hampstead nurseries.

This last initiative provided a 'collective psychoanalytic memory'[1] of clinical examples of transference, acting out, reactions to interpretation and the ending of therapy, and so on. It thereby went beyond previous psychoanalysis in subjecting it to systematic research through pooling individual case material on, for instance, 'child heroes', and the effects of immigration and maternal separation.[2]

Anna's diagnostic profile also went well beyond her father's work. It assessed children not in terms of Freud's adult psychiatric categories but in terms of maturational processes. Her war nursery experience also persuaded Anna that child development cannot be adequately characterized in terms of a unilinear instinctual sequence – oral, anal, and phallic. It also persuaded her that, in attributing their difficulties to specific traumatic events of infancy, adult analytic patients often mistakenly telescope, in retrospect, several different childhood upsets.

Nor – as the lack of psychosis, mental deficiency, or delinquency in the motherless Bulldogs Bank children indicated – is pathology always caused by the mother as increasingly proposed by psychoanalysts in the post-war years. The 'rejecting mother', Anna emphasized, is no more the sole cause of childhood ills than an imagined 'castrating father'.[3] Indeed, she pointed out, all children inevitably experience the mother as rejecting, whatever her actual behaviour, given the unavoidable frustration involved in the impatience and insatiability of infantile desire.[4]

In place of unicausal theory, she insisted on the need to adopt a multi-faceted approach to child assessment sensitive to the many distinct 'developmental lines' constituting psychological growth. Her detractors, however, castigated this approach as a piecemeal 'potpourri'.[5]

That was in France. From 1949, however, Anna's main forum was the USA. Child development was the subject of her first major US lecture.[6] It commemorated her father's 1909 Clark lectures, and marked the first of many honorary degrees which, perhaps out of regret at never having had a university education, Anna displayed prominently on the walls of her Hampstead home.

She included material from this and other mainly US-based lectures and talks in her last monograph, *Normality and Pathology in Childhood*. Here she implicitly took issue with her father's tendency to treat child and adult psychology as one and the same. Identifying less with parents than with their children – indeed the clinic children often mistook her for one of themselves, so small did she become in old age – Anna emphasized the differences between child and adult experience. Just as children's experience of the war was affected by the maternal issues it raised for them, so too her clinic patients experienced trauma in their own rather than in adult terms. An extreme example was a girl for whom the crushing blow of witnessing her mother's murder by her father was not his violence but her mother's screaming at her to go away.[7] Another instance was a thirteen-year-old whose school failure seemed due less to having been sexually abused by her father, as adults might think, than to guilt at his imprisonment.[8]

Similarly, and less traumatically, while mothers may experience their work as forcing them to leave their children, the child can experience their departure as desertion and rejection. Likewise, if the mother is ill and therefore cannot play with her child, it may well experience this as due to her being cross, not ill.[9] Anna also pointed out[10] that children often understand what the mother tells them about sex in terms of their own oral and anal preoccupations rather than in terms of adult genitality as she understands it.

Children, and here Anna adopted her father's theoretical framework, often experience events in subjective 'primary process' rather than the objective 'secondary process' terms of adults. In particular, she emphasized, children's experience of time, as evidenced by the war nursery children's response to maternal separation, is governed more by id pressure of the instincts than by the ego's appreciation of clock or calendar.

Development, she believed, essentially involves the gradual mastery of id by ego, 'the education, or perhaps better, the socialization of the drives'.[11] In her view this depends crucially on the presence of the mother for whose sake the child first controls its instincts[12] – an aspect of psychological development recognized by Deutsch in her brief article about her son Martin but neglected by both Freud and Anna in their pre-war accounts of child development.

Now, however, like fellow-analyst John Bowlby, Anna[13] insisted that the mother's presence is as important psychologically as vitamins to the child's physical development. But she also took issue with Bowlby.[14] On the basis of her wartime childcare experience, she argued that initially the baby is attached to the mother only by 'stomach love' in so far as she meets its physical needs. Only after several months does the child become emotionally as well as physically attached to the mother. Nor, she said, is this attachment purely instinctual, as Bowlby suggested. It is also imbued with subjective desire and fantasy.

With the growth of emotional attachment infants become much more demanding of the mother – like war nursery Derrick (see p. 170 above). They now protest vehemently at separation from her. The war nursery toddlers, for instance, were much more upset by maternal separation than the babies. Similarly, Anna wrote, while babies' sleep disturbance is physiological, that of toddlers is mother-related. Furthermore, mothers and children vary considerably in their capacity to deal with such disturbance. Some war nursery children became increasingly distracted, while the panic of others was relieved only by the nurse coming to mother them. This in turn informs advice given parents by those working in association with the Anna Freud Clinic today.[15]

Initially, Anna noted, again on the basis of her wartime childcare experience, children are unable to keep their mother in mind through her absence. Later, towards the end of the first year, they develop 'object constancy' and a stable image of mothering despite its ups and downs. Like war nursery Tony, children then begin to recognize the needs of the mother or mother-figure, and are more able to share her with others and tolerate her absence. In this Anna anticipated those, including Michael Rutter, who criticize Bowlby for neglecting the effect of age on children's response to maternal separation.

Increasing independence from the mother constitutes one developmental line. It includes progress from initial failure to distinguish self from mother towards recognition of separateness. At first, Anna observed, the child treats parts of the mother's body – just as the war nursery children treated parts of their nurses' bodies – as though they are bits of themselves. Twenty-one-month-old Rose, for instance, sucked her thumb, then put her hand in the nurse's mouth as though it were her own and fell asleep. Another evening she tried to push the corner of blanket, which she gripped while thumb-sucking, into the nurse's mouth, again as though it were her own, as she slept.

A separate developmental line, wrote Anna, involves eating and potty training. In her analysis of Bob Burlingham she had pointed out his early sense of being refused by his mother when she went off with his father, so that he likewise refused food from her. Generalizing from such experience, Anna pointed out that children and mothers equate food and mothering, not least because of breast-feeding. The war nursery children, accordingly, often ate better away from the mother if they had conflicts with her. These can include problems with aggression, which Anna claimed can later cause food fads, vegetarianism, and anorexia.

She also drew attention to the place of mothering in toilet training. An example[16] was a two-year-old patient who reacted to maternal separation – caused by his mother's illness and then by her depression – by calling his faeces out of his body as if for company when he felt abandoned by her. Maternal factors – and here Anna again drew on her war nursery experience – are also involved in children's initial enjoyment in playing and messing with their food, and in later indulging in dirty play and talk.

This, she noted, then gives way to telling others off for making a mess, as the war nursery children rebuked the air raid warnings. Older toddlers become squeamish about food resembling faeces. They need the mother's help not to become obsessionally fastidious, to transform their anal pleasure instead into, say, sand and water play. In general Anna argued the need to redirect rather than repress or allow free rein to the instincts as advocated by strict- and liberal-minded educationalists respectively.

In drawing attention to the dependence of oral and anal development on children internalizing the mother's child-rearing, Anna moved away from her father's emphasis on superego internalization of patriarchal authority as the main basis of socialization. Indeed, she came to refer to the mother as the 'first legislator'.[17] She likened the mother's role to that of the child analyst as 'auxiliary ego'.[18] If such mothering is absent, she wrote, the child internalizes an imagined parental figure who then personifies the child's every longing and defence. Three-year-old war nursery Bob, for instance, said his father (whom he never knew) approved of his bad behaviour. So it was all right. Later he felt this figure disliked him being naughty. And later still he idealized him as able to put anything right that went wrong.

In detailing the developmental line towards internalizing the parent as a real figure, Anna also described the line from neglect to care of the body. This care, she pointed out, is often prematurely developed in the maternally deprived, like the mournful war nursery children described above (see p. 178).

Speech development, she observed, also depends on the mother's presence. The motherless Bulldogs Bank children were still very retarded in their speech at four. By contrast, Anna noted, the Hampstead war nursery children's speech improved when reunited with their mothers, only to regress on renewed separation. She thereby anticipated by several decades non-analytic psychology's recognition of the place of mothering in speech acquisition.

Other developmental lines – first described by Anna and Dorothy in their war nurseries book, *Infants without Families* – include progress from attack to defence, from lack of consideration to sympathetic identification with others, from egocentrism including subjective investment of 'transitional objects' to companionate play, and from pleasure-oriented play to reality-based work.

Children, Anna pointed out, vary in their progress along these different developmental lines. It depends on the mother's attitude and on the balance of the child's own forward- and backward-looking impulses. The latter dominate when the child is tired, ill, or distressed. Its ability to balance the developmental lines' constitutional, environmental, and intrapsychic determinants also depends on these factors being within 'expectable' limits.[19] Again this normative approach has earned her much scorn from psychoanalysis's self-styled radicals.

For her part Anna upbraided analysts for ignoring diagnostic assessment issues. But she acknowledged that it is less easy to distinguish different developmental lines in adults where assessment instead tends to be in terms of the degree to which neurotic suffering impedes love and work. By contrast, she insisted, children's behaviour must be assessed for its age-appropriateness, for imbalances between the different developmental lines, and for the degree to which symptoms involve transient or permanent disruption of id, ego, and superego development.

In a few cases such assessment is possible at the first interview. An example, Anna told a Philadelphia audience,[20] was a twelve-year-old Greek boy who became phobic of school and going out after his house was burgled. His account at first assessment of his fear of his sister being raped, of mail van robberies, and of himself being a kind of mail van in carrying letters from his uncle to his father, she said, soon revealed fear of becoming the passive victim of sexual assault as source of his school phobia. More often, Anna insisted in criticizing non-analytic psychiatry, children's symptoms and initial interviews do not unambiguously indicate the underlying cause of their problems, not least because unlike adults', children's symptoms do not permeate their whole character.

Returning to her pre-war development of ego psychology, she also drew attention to the adaptive as well as the maladaptive aspects of symptoms. But she now understood these in maternal terms as a protective shield against trauma, just as the mother acts as a buffer against the infant's initially precarious ego being overwhelmed by internal and external events.

Illustrative of the adaptive function of symptoms was her London school inspector friend John Hill's son. As a two-year-old he became obsessed with plumbing. This, wrote Anna, involved both fixation and sublimation of his anal impulses – sublimation in so far as he grew up to become a successful physicist. Another, older boy's scientific interest – this time in wasp stings – was mobilized, she said, by phallic anxiety which served to keep him in contact with reality, from which he was in danger of becoming psychotically divorced.[21]

While Freud traced all pathology to unconscious-conscious

and id-ego-superego conflict, Anna maintained that there are also conflicts within the id between love and hate, and between masculinity and femininity. The latter conflict was central in her analysis of Bob Burlingham, in her own life, and, she claimed[22] in the lives of several male homosexuals whose treatment she recounted just after the war. She also stressed the conflictful effect of maternal separation.

Her resulting diagnostic profile organized assessment information – gathered before, during, and after treatment – in terms of instinctual development (of aggression as well as sex); social development as regards mothering and schooling; and external, internal, and internalized conflicts. Internalized conflict, she insisted, is distinct from the pathological effects of what analyst Michael Balint termed a 'basic fault' in the child's earliest mothering occurring before the psyche becomes differentiated into id, ego, and superego.

Only where conflict between these mental agencies threatens to become ossified as in 'infantile neurosis', she argued, is psychoanalytic treatment warranted. Treatment then involves making conscious the ego and superego's unconscious resistance to the id. Consciousness and its control over the id is thereby extended. Even so, and disagreeing implicitly with Freud and explicitly with the Kleinians, she argued that untreated infantile neurosis does not necessarily lead to adult neurosis. Nor does child analysis prevent subsequent breakdown.

Like her father, she argued that the success of therapy depends on the strength of the ego. But, she added, this also depends on the child's tolerance of frustration, sublimation, mastery of anxiety, and drive to complete development. Again going beyond her father, she maintained that successful treatment also depends on the degree to which the child's symptoms are anchored in the mother. Some mothers, she said, keep the child enmeshed with them. Others collude with its voyeurism through their own exhibitionism.[23] Another mother, by contrast, needed her child to remain orally dependent on her to reassure her that he did not reject her like her husband and parents.[24] Sometimes, however, the mother's difficulties are more practical. Indeed, in one case Anna asked whether it was not more a matter of the mother needing a housekeeper than of the child needing analysis. Certainly she increasingly insisted that analysis is not appropriate where the child's problems are practical or related to early mothering difficulties.

For the moment, however, she was more concerned to secure international psychoanalytic recognition of her child analytic training programme. Both her course and others in England and the USA provided a model of full-time training, including infant observation and attention to normality as well as pathology, which she believed should also inform adult training which she criticized for its increasing rigidity.[25] To plead this cause to the International Psychoanalytic Congress she returned to Vienna for the first time in July 1971. But her mission failed. Infant observation, however, soon became a standard part of adult analytic training.

Anna herself stopped analysing children in 1949. But she continued to the end as a training analyst (still knitting through sessions), supervisor, and consultant to her clinic's activities. She remained in London, as in Austria, a childish 'slight figure in a pinafore dress with voluminous ankle-length skirt'. This attire, as her clinic's medical director Clifford Yorke says, was 'habitual, self-made with considerable skill, and timeless'.[26] Indeed, it was hand-sewn because, as she explained, it would be impractical to use a sewing-machine while seeing patients.

7

Child custody

If Anna's pioneering extension of her father's work in developing child analysis, ego psychology, and developmental psychology derived from identification with children that in women so often involves mothering, so too did it inform her last major extension of psychoanalysis – into the field of law.

Through Marianne Kris, who had taken over direction of the Yale Child Study Center after her husband's death in 1957, and in connection with lectures related to her 1965 book, *Normality and Pathology in Childhood*, Anna met Jay Katz and Joseph Goldstein. Both were involved in psychoanalysis, and in family law at Yale. They invited her to contribute to their seminars. These resulted in books that have enormously influenced recent childcare policy both here and in the USA.

This work's beginning coincided with Marianne Kris's endowing Anna's clinic with money left her by her analysand Marilyn Monroe. The clinic's work with Yale focused very much on issues of disrupted mothering like that suffered by Monroe. Fostered from birth till she was seven, then taken to live with her mother who was soon hospitalized as insane, Monroe was briefly fostered by an English and then by a New Orleans couple before being placed, aged eight, in an orphanage because her mother would not release her for adoption. She stayed there for nearly two years. Then she was fostered with two different families before settling first with a friend of her mother, then with the friend's aunt, before finally being married off when she was just sixteen.

Anna's Yale seminars drew on her wartime experience of similar cases of interrupted mothering in commenting on cases described by Goldstein and Katz in their 1965 textbook, *The*

Family and the Law. These included a divorcing couple's dispute about their children's custody; care proceedings in the case of a fifteen-year-old whose mother had become psychotic; and a two-year-old removed from foster care for adoption.[1]

In each case Anna recounted the issues involved from the child's viewpoint. This perspective, not the adults' needs, she insisted, should be paramount in determining childcare decisions. In particular she stressed the child's need for stimulation, continuity, and mutual affection. An example[2] was seven-year-old Mark, whose father, a TV personality, fought his parents-in-law for Mark's custody even though they had looked after him since he was five when his mother and sister were killed in an accident. The crucial issue in such cases, Anna emphasized, is the child's attachments, not the warring adults' needs – Tony's father's need to boost his public image, for instance, and his grandparents' wish to replace their daughter.

Previously psychoanalysts had only been involved with the law in cases of pleas of diminished responsibility. Now Anna took psychoanalysis into the arena of family law, particularly through her contribution to *Beyond the Best Interests of the Child* and *Before the Best Interests of the Child*. Both books were based on discussions with Goldstein and Solnit in the USA, in England, and in Baltimore, County Cork, where Anna and Dorothy bought a second country home in 1967 – the same year Anna was awarded a CBE.

The first book begins with Anna's conclusions from her war nursery work, namely the child's emotional and developmental need for 'unbroken continuity of affectionate and stimulating relationships'.[3] It also stressed the difference between children's and adults' needs and experience of time and moving house, and the determination of children's, unlike adults', attachments by physical closeness rather than biological relatedness.

Above all, Anna and her co-authors emphasized that the child needs to be with a 'psychological parent' – not necessarily the biological parent – whom the child wants and by whom it feels wanted. They therefore recommended that in cases of disputed custody the child should be placed with the person who is, or is most likely to become, through continuity of care, the child's psychological parent. This, they said, means finalizing custody decisions as soon as they are made, minimizing loyalty conflict by assigning custody to only one parent, recognizing and funding 'common law adoptions' (reflected in England's 'custodianship' provision), and speeding up childcare decisions to take account of the child's limited capacity to brook delay or keep parental figures in mind through their absence. This had been particularly obvious in the war nursery children's response to maternal separation.

The authors roundly criticized placement decisions based more on the needs of adults than on those of children. Examples included an English boy and an American girl, both placed at birth in temporary foster care because neither the US nor the UK legal and welfare systems would curtail the mother's right to delay deciding whether to release her child for permanent adoption. Anna and her Yale colleagues, by contrast, recommended speedy adoption of newborns with minimal appeal time so as to increase the child's chance of securing psychological parenting, thereby respecting its need to be wanted and cared for without disruption or discontinuity.

Using as a guideline Anna's observations on the internal and instinctual rather than the external determinants of the child's sense of time, they argued that a crucial issue in child placement is whether the time the mother spends with the child – whatever her intentions, beliefs, and difficulties in visiting – is sufficient to secure and maintain the child's psychological attachment.

Perhaps drawing on Anna's own persistent refusal to see herself in the role of mother, and her criticism of those who equate professional childcare with mothering, the authors sought to puncture the omnipotent fantasy of legal and state welfare workers of being able to provide perfect mothering, of providing for the child's 'best interests' (a notion that replaced nineteenth-century legislation's neglect of the child's needs in automatically assigning its custody to the father). Anna and her colleagues insisted on a more realistic approach. The law, they said, should rest content with the limited aim of finding 'the least detrimental alternative' which, having due regard to the uncertainties of prediction, maximize the child's 'opportunity for being wanted and for maintaining on a continuous basis a relationship with at least one adult who is or will become a psychological parent'.[4]

Childcare decisions, they stressed, should be governed by realistic assessment of whether psychological parenting – however limited – has been established or broken down, and by whether it can be better established elsewhere. The burden of proof in cases of disputed custody, they argued, is for the parties involved to establish *both* that the child is unwanted in its present or envisaged placement *and* that this placement is not the least detrimental available. Furthermore, since there is no necessary identity between the mother's (or substitute mother's) needs and those of the child, the latter should be represented by an independent party – a recommendation adopted in Britain's *guardian ad litem* provision.

Otherwise they advised minimal state intervention in family life particularly because of its insecure-making effect. Such intervention thereby undermines the chances of stable attachment and psychological parenting being established and maintained.

Anna herself was no stranger to custody battles. Before the war she was involved in Dorothy's battles with her estranged husband and his leading New York lawyer father over her children's custody. The second oldest, Mabbie, whose care informed Anna's first child analysis extension of her father's work, continued into middle age to feel torn between Anna and her mother, and between her husband, her grown children and her New York analyst Marianne Kris. In July 1974 she took a fatal overdose.

That year saw growing pressure in England to place child custody on a firmer basis. This followed the tragic death in January 1973 of seven-year-old Maria Colwell at the hands of her stepfather, a few months after her return to his and her mother's care after living with her aunt since she was a baby. In Anna's view[5] the case was yet another example of the law wrongly favouring biological over psychological ties.

Pressure from such 'tug-of-love' cases and from the tendency of children, in the absence of firm custody decisions, to 'drift' in care led in England to the 1975 Children Act. In many ways it reflected Anna's insistence (on what is now known as 'permanency planning') both in her 1973 and in her later 1979 books with Goldstein and Solnit. The latter devoted considerable space to the Colwell case.

But its main stress was on minimizing state interference in family life. Such interference, its authors argued, is warranted only in divorce involving disputed custody, or where the parents themselves want to end their parental rights. Not that the child might not for ever feel unwanted in such cases. An example, they pointed out, was Agatha Christie (Anna being an avid detective story reader), whose widowed mother gave over her care to her sister just as, many years later, after the death of Maria Colwell's father, his widow fostered the infant Maria with her sister.

State intervention, argued the Hampstead and Yale writers, was justified, and indeed necessary, to put such arrangements on a permanent and formal footing. Arguing on the basis of Anna's war nursery experience that babies hold their absent mothers in mind for a shorter time than older children, they also recommended that the child's parental attachment should be presumed to have lapsed and been overtaken by attachment to those with whom it now lives if this placement began when the child was under three and has lasted a year, or if the placement began when the child was over three and has lasted two years. Perhaps this blanket ruling did less than justice to individual differences in the internal as well as the external factors governing children's attachments.[6] After all, Marilyn Monroe remained most attached to her mother through the first seven years of her life, even though she saw her only intermittently.

In other cases, Anna and her colleagues maintained, state intervention is warranted only if there is evidence of serious physical abuse, or if the parents have died or disappeared, or been hospitalized or imprisoned – say for sexual abuse. As regards illness, they recommended intervention only if the mother's mental health endangers the child's life – as in the case of a woman who, in a fit of depression, sought to kill herself and her two young children – or where the child is ill and the mother fails to provide adequately for its medical care. Even then, they argued, courts should intervene only if this jeopardizes the child's life, and if medical treatment could result in a life worth living.

They entirely opposed state intervention – even in case of sexual abuse[7] – if it can offer no better care than the child is already receiving. This conclusion is particularly relevant given calls, following the recent Cleveland Inquiry (chaired by a judge who has also worked with the Anna Freud Clinic), to weaken the 'permanency principle'[8] provision of England's 1975 Act, not least because its implementation so often disregards Anna and her colleagues' 'least detrimental alternative' caveat.

As for emotional abuse, the authors of *Before the Best Interests of the Child* argued that the diagnosis is too vague to justify the disruption of psychological attachment involved in care proceedings. As examples of such unwarranted intervention they cited the case of a baby taken into care because her hippie mother's childcare was zany and unconventional; a three-year-old's removal from his mother merely because his putative father objected to her life with a black man in a black neighbourhood; and the case of six children removed from their parents simply because they looked unruly and unkempt.

If the Yale and Hampstead authors' first book identified with the child and its needs and feelings against those of the parent, their second book stressed the rights of parents. They totally opposed the tendency of courts and social workers to indulge 'rescue fantasies' of stepping into the parents' shoes to protect their children. This conclusion was in keeping with Anna's long-held conviction through her early teaching experience, child analysis, and nursery work that professional childcare workers and analysts cannot, and should not, take the place of the mother. She returned to this subject in her final work.

8

Against mothering psychoanalysis

With her sister Mathilde's death in early 1978 Anna became Freud's only surviving child. Nor was she well herself. From that year on she was regularly hospitalized for treatment of anaemia. And, after seeing the elderly Helene Deutsch's deterioration, she had no wish to live into her nineties.

Her work was now coming to an end. In it she returned to a theme that had long preoccupied her – the shift in psychoanalysis, to which she had herself contributed through her wartime childcare experience, from a father-centred to a mother-centred focus. She now deplored this shift as one-sided, and as diluting Freud's emphasis on the conflict of individual with society with attention instead to 'every individual's longing for perfect unity with the mother'.[1]

Perhaps drawing on her own dread of such unity, she countered its sentimentalization by pointing out the fears involved. She suggested, on the basis of her war nurseries experience, that these fears contribute to the sleeping difficulties of babies. These, she wrote, are due not only to separation from the mother, as her father had written, but to fear of sleep bringing about ego dissolution akin to psychic fusion with the mother. In her post-war work she had also dwelt on fear of such fusion as it occurs in homosexuality. She argued[2] that the passive homosexual seeks to avoid the apparent fusion with the mother involved in feminine passivity by identifying with his seemingly lost masculinity in his lover.

Unlike her father, and perhaps largely because of her childcare experience, Anna recognized that psychoanalysis lends itself to evoking – through the patient's transference to the analyst – early mothering, or its lack. Examples from her own practice included an adolescent girl who, as an infant, had been smuggled out of a Polish ghetto and handed from one person to another. She had never formed any stable identification. Now analysis seemed to promise the mothering she had never had.[3] Similarly maternally deprived post-war children also look to analysis to provide the mothering they feel they never had, like seven-year-old Frank, whose mother left the family when he was three.[4] An adult example was a man for whom analysis likewise revived early mothering, which he sought to escape by going to sleep in his sessions with Anna, as he likewise avoided intimacy with his wife.[5]

But, however much analysis revives early mothering, insisted Anna[6] in discussing Winnicott's work, the therapist's task is not to give in to this wish. Instead the analyst's task is to interpret and make it conscious. Where analysis revives an early sense of fusion with the mother the analyst's task is not to collude by mothering the patient but to interpret this illusion to bring about differentiation. Examples included two young women, both of whom merged in fantasy with their mothers' friends. One became hopelessly promiscuous and alcoholic in imitation of the good-for-nothings her mother frequented. The other became an artist like the painters for whom her mother neglected her. Both cases, Anna argued,[7] needed the analyst not to mother them but to foster ego differentiation and development through first undoing the patients' spurious sense of fusion with the mother, her lovers, and friends.

In a New York lecture in which she cited the work of Lampl-de Groot – now a frequent visitor since her husband's 1958 death in a car accident – Anna[8] maintained that analysis proper can get going only once there is ego differentiation. Psychoanalytic technique originated, and was most effective in dealing, with the conflicts of id, ego, and superego. It cannot succeed, she claimed, in the absence of such intra-psychic differentiation which, like her father, she saw as the product of the Oedipus complex. Such differentiation is lacking in children and adults who, like pre-Oedipal babies, treat the analyst like the mother as one with themselves. At its extreme this can involve psychotic collapse of the separation of self and other, of inner and outer worlds. Examples included a schoolboy who treated a sunflower as one with the frightening phallic properties with which he subjectively imbued it, and another schoolboy who reduced his relations with his peers to memorizing their names and addresses.[9]

The difficulties posed child analysis by children's inability to free associate, Anna argued,[10] are nothing to those involved in treating children and adults who lack any clear demarcation of id, ego, and superego. She likened such therapy to bringing up babies. Both optimally involve internalizing reliable, need-satisfying external figures.

Knowledge of earliest infancy, she argued, had been increased by the findings of child analysis and by the regression involved in adult analysis. Analysts had thereby come to recognize that the Oedipus complex was not the starting point, as her father had initially implied, but the endpoint of a long period of mothering and pre-Oedipal development.

But this does not mean that psychoanalysis can successfully treat the pre-Oedipal disorders its method has thus revealed. In such cases, she maintained, it is necessary to separate psychoanalytic discovery from the practice with which it had previously been unified. She roundly criticized those who, on the basis of psychoanalytic findings about earliest infancy, sought to extend her father's method to treat psychotic and maternal 'deficiency illnesses'[11] by seeking to mother and make good the defects of early mothering apparently causing these conditions in the first place.

She repeatedly insisted that this is not analysis. Such treatment, she said, neglects dynamic and structural factors. It wrongly dispenses with the therapeutic alliance her father recognized as necessary to successful treatment. The proper role of the analyst, she asserted, is neither to mother the patient nor to provide a 'corrective emotional experience'.[12] Instead the analyst should enable the patient to become conscious of, so as to resolve, the conflict of id and ego through analysing the transference resistance in which it results.

Indeed it is quite unrealistic for the analyst to hope to

mother the patient. Anna doubted whether the transference ever exactly replicates earliest mothering. The two are quite different from each other, not least because of the frustrations involved in analysis. Analysts like André Green and Donald Winnicott, she implied, indulge an omnipotent fantasy in supposing themselves able to make good the defects of women's mothering through acting as 'analyst-mother'.[13] Furthermore, she argued, in appropriating this function they bring psychoanalysis into disrepute by promising more than it can deliver, thereby rendering it endless.

Analysis, she maintained, was designed to treat internal and internalized conflict, not conflicts due essentially to external causes. In this she agreed with other analysts. She disagreed with them only in so far as they claimed that analysis can make good the internal effects of early maternal failure. At best, she said, analysis can provide 'supportive intervention' in the early years to correct glaring developmental discrepancies,[14] and can alleviate some of the after-effects of early maternal lack. The latter includes failure by the mother to act as ego or 'protective shield' to prevent the child suffering the 'cumulative trauma', so named by Pakistani analyst Masud Khan, of being overwhelmed by internal and external events.

Anna also entirely rejected the replacement by Klein and others of free association to dreams by focus on the transference as sole business of psychoanalysis. Indeed, she suspected that the transference is often artificially manufactured by the analyst constantly harping on it. Patients are thereby encouraged, she noted, not to remember and work through their experience, as her father had recommended, but emotionally to relive and act it out in relation to the therapist. Analysis had thereby wrongly shifted attention, in her view, from unearthing repressed past childhood sexual experience to dealing solely with the patient's present relations with the analyst. In the process aggression had been emphasized at the expense of sex, so annoyed does the patient rightly become with the analyst treating everything – real and imagined alike – as transference phenomena.

She also implicitly disagreed with the increasing tendency of therapists to focus on the non-verbal aspects of the patient's transference and the counter-transference feelings evoked in the analyst as in the mother by her pre-verbal infant. Drawing on her observations of the difficulties posed the war nursery toddlers in not being able to master problems by putting them into words, she insisted that analysis is quintessentially about helping people deal with painful feelings through verbalizing them.

Even her long-time ego psychology co-worker, Chicago analyst Heinz Kohut, seemed to be abandoning her, with his increasing emphasis on the analyst not so much verbalizing as empathizing with the patient's experience. 'What will happen to psychoanalysis in the future?' she asked in November 1978 of Kohut's defection, 'and where will its backbone be when our generation is gone?'[15]

The next November saw the death of Dorothy Burlingham, the mother for whom Anna had long been psychologically the twin whom Dorothy, the younger sister of twins, had craved since childhood. Anna tried to comfort herself by wearing Dorothy's jumpers. She also got a puppy she called after a chow Dorothy had given her father in pre-war Vienna. Anna had always been a swimmer and horseback rider. But now she too became ill – with heart trouble, and in March 1981 she had a stroke.

Shamed by her now shaky knitting, Anna auctioned off her earlier handiwork. Instead of knitting she drowsed, while a former analysand from Yale read her detective stories, as did her niece – Martin's daughter Sophie – who now adopted Anna as a mother. Anna, however, rejected this role to the end. She had never written of mother-daughter relations, she wrote to US feminist Nancy Friday, who asked her views on the subject, because she knew nothing about them. Instead she continued to identify as she had throughout her life as her father's child. Shrunken in her last weeks to schoolgirl size, she asked Manna Friedman, the clinic's first nursery school teacher and now her main nurse, to put her father's overcoat around her as she was pushed in a wheelchair to Hampstead Heath.

But, however enshrouded by her father, her death on 8 October 1982 left a legacy of child analysis, ego psychology, and psychoanalytic observations on paediatrics, developmental assessment, and childcare policy that was derived mainly from her experience of looking after children, which, however much she rejected the equation, is generally equated with mothering.

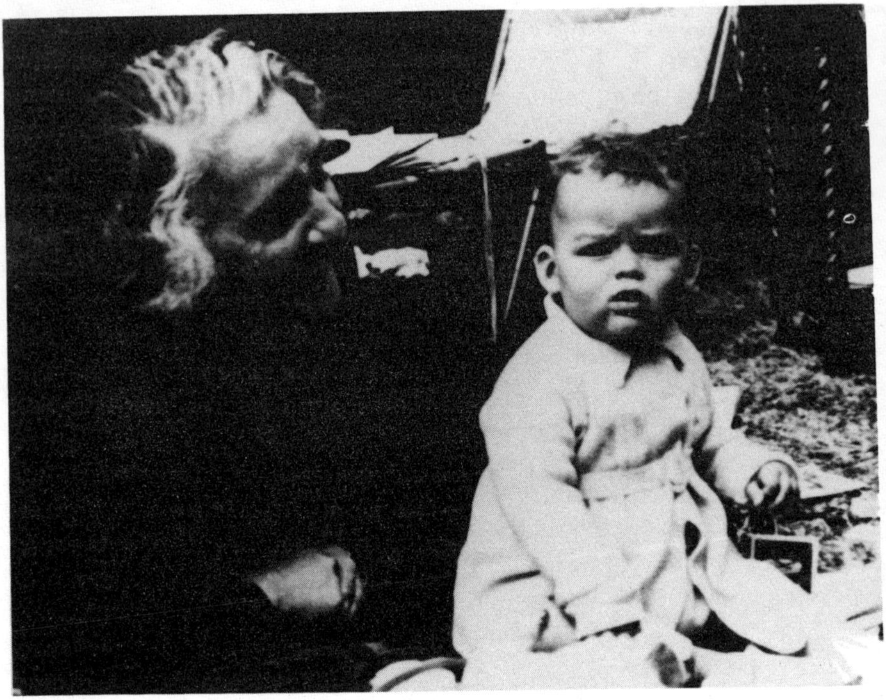

Melanie Klein with her grandson Michael, 1938

V

MELANIE KLEIN

1

Early mothering

While Anna Freud shunned mothering, Melanie Klein embraced it both for good and for ill. She thereby brought about a revolution in psychoanalysis, from concern with patriarchal taming of the child's 'lawless' instincts – as Anna[1] put it – to an understanding of instincts as always related to others, in the first place to the mother as loved and hated. Increasingly she demonstrated these relations – not the instincts shorn of relations to others – to constitute the stuff of mental life.

Melanie's Galician father, Moriz Reizes, was also something of a radical. In his youth he had rebelled against his family's rigid Jewish orthodoxy by becoming not a rabbi but a doctor, and by divorcing the wife of his first, arranged, marriage. He was working in Burgenland – some seventy miles from Vienna – and was already middle-aged when he first met Melanie's mother Libussa Deutsch, then in her mid-twenties, in Vienna, where the couple settled after the birth of their first three children.

Emilie was six, Emmanuel five, and Sidonie four when Melanie was born on 30 March 1882. It was to her mother and her enlightened Jewish Slovak family rather than to her father and his relatives, who still wore the ritual kaftan, that Melanie most warmed. Her mother, she later recalled, was one of the great standbys and examples of her life. She remembered her as an outstanding beauty, an acknowledged 'lady', and much more alive and understanding than Moriz. Most of all she admired her mother's interest in art, and her family's thirst for knowledge and dedication to learning.

Not that she did not also respect her father's education, particularly his teaching himself many different languages including Hebrew. But she felt he was already stuck in his ways – an old fifty – when she was born, and that he was almost entirely ineffectual with his various menial jobs as music-hall doctor and dental assistant. Nor was the situation made any easier by his father's arrival to live with them after being thrown out on the street by Moriz's sister.

It was Libussa and her family, Melanie felt, who most held her childhood home together. While Libussa ran a shop selling plants and reptiles (despite detesting them), her brother Hermann financed the family's move – when Melanie was five – from a relatively impoverished flat into a much more luxurious and impressive apartment where Moriz now set up as a dentist. The family later also bought a house in Dornbach.

Although dutiful to her husband, Libussa seemed to have little time for him. Melanie could never remember them going out alone together. Even her conception seemed fortuitous – at least according to what her mother gave her to understand. Nor did Libussa breast-feed Melanie, as she had her other children. Instead she was farmed out to a wet-nurse. Not that Libussa, unlike Moriz, and the later family governesses did not also favour her. To Melanie's distress, however, her father made no secret of his preference for Emilie who, together with Emmanuel, teased her for her ignorance. But the eight-year-old Sidonie came to Melanie's rescue and taught her reading and arithmetic during her long illness with glandular TB, from which Sidonie died when Melanie was only four.

This may well have contributed to Melanie's life-long tendency to depression. But she was also very forthright, never shy, and immensely self-confident from her first day in school, where she proved extremely ambitious, got many distinctions, and learnt 'all the things that a girl of good family was expected to know'.[2] Perhaps her self-assurance was fuelled by the pride of her favourite uncle Hermann and her mother in her beauty, as in Emmanuel's creativity, and by the latter's approval of her literary efforts, beginning with a patriotic poem she wrote when she was nine.

Later, as a medical and then an arts student, Emmanuel introduced her to the cultural life of *fin-de-siècle* Vienna. Many of his friends, Melanie later recalled, fast fell in love with her, as did her second cousin Arthur Klein, recently graduated in chemical engineering from Zürich. He soon proposed and Melanie accepted, even though she was only seventeen and felt they were ill-suited. It also put paid to her plans to study medicine, for which she had specially transferred to a school that could prepare her for university entrance. Perhaps she was swayed by her brother's high opinion of Arthur, and more particularly by Arthur's fine job prospects. Her own family's finances were again in a parlous state thanks, it seemed, to Moriz's incompetence, which Melanie attributed to senility. Then, in April 1900, he died, shortly after Melanie's informal engagement to Arthur.

With Moriz's death her 'indefatigable' mother, as she described her, made plans to make over his dental practice to Emilie's prospective husband, Leo Pick. To make room, Libussa packed Melanie off to Arthur's parents in Rosenberg (now Ruzomberok), while Arthur continued his training in Italy and America. Meanwhile Emmanuel, who had long suffered heart disease after having rheumatic fever when he was twelve, decided to make the best of his few remaining years by devoting himself to writing and travelling. Nor was Libussa keen to have either child home – Emilie's pregnancy, she told them, made it too inconvenient.

In Emmanuel's absence both his mother and Melanie beseeched him to confide in them. Libussa assured him that her mother-love for him was much more enduring than any love Melanie could give. But it was the latter he most adored. To her he recounted his affairs, hinting that her fiancé was likewise unfaithful; his writing plans, including a libretto and revisions of Melanie's creative writing; and his lack of money to fund ever more distant southern travels, get his shoes mended, or pay off his gambling debts and medical and dental expenses. As a child he had had an embattled intellectual relationship with his father. Now he became increasingly world-weary and envious of Melanie as a beautiful young girl with all her life before her.

No wonder he was envious. Despite Arthur's repeated postponement of their marriage, Melanie apparently remained supremely self-confident. Arthur's sister Jolan, she wrote to Emmanuel, unhesitatingly admired and recognized her, Melanie's, superiority. Meanwhile she regaled Libussa with accounts of parties at which she shone as 'the prettiest of all', and of the pride of her prospective parents-in-law in her education and good looks.

Meanwhile Emmanuel became increasingly ill and peevish with the news of Arthur's return in September 1902 and Melanie's imminent marriage. On the night of 1 December 1902, some time after writing complaining of the brevity of her last note to him, Emmanuel died of heart failure in a hotel in Genoa which he had just checked into on a projected trip south to Sicily.

Melanie had been very close to him, enamoured of him even, as a genius and the best friend she ever had. Years later she wrote that her mother never got over his death. But it seems more likely Melanie never did. Still grieving his loss, she married Arthur the day after her twenty-first birthday. She found her wedding night repulsive. 'Does it therefore have to be like this,' she complained, 'that motherhood begins with disgust?'[3] She was indeed soon pregnant – and nauseous. Her mother wrote full of advice about what to eat and how to behave, with hopes that the child would be 'less nervous' than Melanie, whom she compared unfavourably with Emilie and her supposedly completely cheerful pregnancy.

Melanie was indeed unhappy. But she found some solace in editing Emmanuel's papers and persuading the literary historian Georg Brandes to write a preface to their publication as a book. When her daughter Melitta was born, on 19 January 1904, she also tried her best to throw herself into motherhood and interest in her child, whom she breast-fed for seven months.

Her mother meanwhile wrote, as ever, of her financial worries. This gave way to complaints that the Kleins had not invited her to join them on their first holiday alone after Melitta's birth. Emilie also felt neglected when Libussa left her to look after Melitta in Rosenberg while the Kleins vacationed in Italy and Abbazia (a resort in Yugoslavia).

In 1907, following a pregnancy filled with depression at feeling trapped in a hopeless marriage, Melanie gave birth to her second child, Hans, on 2 March. Nor was her mood lifted by Arthur's work taking them, a few weeks later, to Krappitz, a small town in Upper Silesia (now Poland), which she found even drearier than Rosenberg had become for her with her sister-in-law Jolan's departure, following her marriage, to Budapest. But Arthur's new job paid well. He could therefore settle his mother-in-law's long outstanding debt to her brother. This done, she was able to give up the shop and move in with them. Melanie found this a great comfort – her mother seemed so much more companionable and compatible with her than Arthur.

In later life she remembered her mother as quiet and retiring as a result of Emmanuel's death. But she also seems to have been very intrusive. Concerned at her daughter's evident domestic unhappiness, Libussa encouraged her to spend lots of time away visiting Budapest, Rosenberg, and Abbazia. Meanwhile she took over Melanie's place in the Klein household. She wrote telling her how well her husband and children were getting on without her, acted as intermediary for Arthur's and Melanie's messages to each other, and even assumed her daughter's clothes and name. Furthermore she told Melanie whom to see, and what to do and wear – advice Melanie seemed positively to welcome, at least in retrospect. Less comforting, perhaps, was Libussa's also indicating that Arthur was too busy with foreign trips to see her. This must have fuelled Melanie's long conviction of his infidelity to her. But even when he wanted to see her, her mother interfered. She told them both it was bad for their health to meet. Meanwhile she got Melanie – then on a trip to Rosenberg with Melitta – to inveigh on her behalf against Emilie's supposed adultery and extravagance. She even went so far as to dictate the letter Melanie should write.

Melanie herself was now so depressed that she went into a sanatorium in Switzerland the next May 1909 for a couple of months. Arthur was due for transfer to yet another small Silesian town – Hermanetz. But this was more than Melanie could bear. Arthur therefore negotiated a move to Budapest – then a thriving cultural centre and home both to Jolan and to her sister-in-law, Klara Vágó.

The move, supervised by Libussa while Klara stayed with Melanie in Hermanetz, certainly seemed an improvement. Arthur was now director of several factories, and Melanie became much more in charge in getting her mother to look after the children while she went away with Klara, as she often had before. Possibly her growing confidence was also due to the treatment she was now getting for her nerves. In 1912, or shortly after, she began analysis with Sandor Ferenczi.

Meanwhile her mother had seemingly been chastened by the ill-effects of her management of, and intrusiveness into, her other daughter, Emilie's, life. The latter's infidelity and extravagance turned out to be nothing but an invention of her husband's morbid jealousy and compulsive gambling, exacerbated by his unhappiness in the dental practice in which Libussa had installed him.

Libussa herself now became increasingly wretched during Melanie's third pregnancy. Erich was born on 1 July 1914 – on the eve of the First World War. Unlike Melanie's other children but like herself, he was wet-nursed. Soon her analyst and husband would be called up to serve in the Austro-Hungarian army. Meanwhile Libussa, worried about her other son-in-law, stationed in Helene Deutsch's birthplace Przemysl, fell ill. She was X-rayed. Melanie always remembered her mother feeling icy cold in the surgery, and her own overwhelming grief as afterwards they climbed the hill to their home, Melanie trailing behind Arthur and her mother, on whom she still so much depended for advice – this time about Erich's impossibly difficult wet-nurse. The doctor had assured them that Libussa's illness was nothing serious. But she completely lost her appetite. Three weeks later she died, on 6 November 1914, leaving Melanie full of guilt and regrets, but most of all full of gratitude for her mother's unstinting concern for her and serenity at the end.

2

Analyst mother

In old age Klein dated her first reading of Freud's *On Dreams* and the start of her analysis with Ferenczi to the year of her mother's death. Her treatment may well also have been taken up with the depression she had so long suffered in mothering her own children. It also saw the start of her turning this experience to creative effect. She now wrote a number of stories and poems dwelling on a mother's ties to her children and her sexual longing for someone other than her husband. Much more enduring, however, was her now using her mothering experience to found the child analytic technique from which all her subsequent developments of psychoanalysis stemmed.

Ferenczi had himself advocated child analysis in a 1913 talk about a woman patient's five-year-old son and his phobia of cocks, which he attributed to the boy's projection into these animals of the hatred he felt for his father. He now encouraged Melanie to analyse children – this eventually resulted in the overthrow of the father-centred account of neurosis he had adopted from Freud. For the moment, however, Melanie's first forays into child analysis – beginning with analysing her own children – simply supplemented Freud's account of the Oedipus complex with an account of its cognitive ramifications in which she drew on the then increasing stress on women's educational function in mothering.

Her first psychoanalytic publication and 1919 Congress paper, which earned her membership of the Hungarian Psychoanalytic Society, dwelt particularly on her analysis of Erich. Initially slow, Erich's development was followed by rapid progress when he was four. He then began asking lots of questions:

'How is a person made?' 'What is a papa needed for?' and, more seldom, 'What is a mamma needed for?'[1] To all of which Melanie explained the child's growth inside the mother's body. Thus enlightened, Erich went on to ask how dogs and chickens are born, how babies are fed inside the mother, how the sun and rain are made, and the part of God in all this. This led in turn to discovery of his mother's disbelief against his father's belief in God.

Still troubled by the father's part in his creation, he went on to ask about sexual difference. Had he and his father never been girls like his mother and sister? 'When I am a mamma,' he mused. Another day he put his father's walking stick between his legs, saying 'Look papa what a great big wiwi I have.'[2] Why, he wondered, did his mother not have a penis too, since she crapped like him. It was as though he equated the two – penis and shit.

By openly answering all such queries, wrote Klein, she fostered rather than repressed his curiosity about other things as well: about money, the war, and food shortages; about the difference between wanting and getting, wishes and reality. Not that he gave up wishing he and his parents were all-powerful: he still asked his mother to cook spinach into potatoes.

Mindful perhaps of her own mother's love of knowledge, Klein concluded by stressing the importance of meeting and encouraging the child's curiosity, or 'epistemophilia'. Otherwise he risks becoming the sort of person who, despite a wealth of ideas, cannot pursue any in depth, or who, like her own father, becomes immersed in one area of study while remaining completely oblivious to everyday practical reality. Alternatively the child is liable to become prey to ready-made ideas and religious authority in flight from the difficulties of thinking about and investigating the world for itself.

Klein's own world now suffered a major upheaval. The ending of the war and the defeat of the Austro-Hungarian Empire was followed by Bolshevik revolution in Hungary, led by Bela Kun. Ferenczi was now made the first ever university professor of psychoanalysis. But the revolution was short-lived.

Violently anti-semitic counter-revolution supervened. Arthur Klein, who had been invalided back from the war in 1916, lost his job and in autumn 1919 went to work in Sweden. Meanwhile Melanie and the children returned to Arthur's father and mother, whom Melanie particularly liked, in Rosenberg, which had now become part of Czechoslovakia.

Bereft of Klara Vágó and other Budapest friends and colleagues, Melanie kept up her interest in psychoanalysis by continuing the child 'upbringing with analytic features'[3] she had begun in Budapest. She now addressed not only her children's direct questions but also their anxieties stemming from unconscious worries.

Erich had recently become much more clinging, and had lost interest in stories and in playing with or without other children. He was increasingly silent apart from monotonously repeated questions: 'What is the door made of?' 'What is the bed made of?' 'How is wood made?' 'How is glass made?' 'How is the chair made?' 'Where do stones, where does water come from?' and so on.[4]

Perhaps his worries stemmed from the anti-semitism he had suffered from other children in Budapest, from the move to Rosenberg, and from loss of his father. Klein, however, attributed them to unconscious preoccupation with his father's place in his origin. Perhaps she was right. Addressing, rather than sidestepping, as she had before, what she took to be this his leading anxiety – this later becoming a hallmark of her analytic technique – she directly addressed his so far barely voiced question about his father, whereupon his gloom lifted.

She took the opportunity of his asking which plants grow from seeds to explain human fertilization. Thereupon Erich recalled other children telling him a cock is needed for a hen to lay an egg. He was now amused by the story of the woman whose husband no sooner wished a sausage on the end of her nose than it grew there. This in turn unleashed a wealth of fantasies, including one of two cows walking together – one then jumping on the back and riding the other.

Erich now played more. But he was still bothered by the idea of children growing in the mother's tummy. He wanted to look inside her to 'see whether there isn't a child in there', adding 'I would like to know everything in the world',[5] including seeing his mother's poohs inside her as though he thought babies, like shit, are made from food.

Again Klein addressed his leading anxiety. She explained that babies are made from 'something that papa makes and the egg that is inside mamma'. Erich was now all ears. 'If papa puts his wiwi into mamma's wiwi and makes seed there,' she went on, 'then the seed runs in deeper into her body and when it meets with one of the little eggs that are inside mamma, then that little egg begins to grow and it becomes a child.' Erich's enthusiasm knew no bounds: 'I would so much like to see how a child is made inside like that,' he said. But that was impossible. Well then, he 'would like to do it to mamma' when he was older or, if that meant excluding his father, he could do it with him.[6]

Now his previous worries were replaced by lively Oedipal fantasies in which he variously joined forces with, or fought, his father – represented by a toy motor, king, or soldier entering his mother as an electric car, beautiful house, or garden. But he once more became fearful following Klein's absence at the 1920 Hague Congress. There she met Karl Abraham, who encouraged her to settle in Berlin which, with the recent defeat of Austria, now rivalled Vienna as the main centre of psychoanalysis.

Following her return, Erich's anger came more to the fore. But it was split off and directed not so much towards her as at cows, which he treated as though they had a penis in that he said as he pissed, 'The cow is letting down milk into the pot.'[7] Again his mother found his mood lightened as a result of her analysing his anxiety, this time that associated with his hated image of the cow-mother with penis. His playfulness, sociability, and cheerful chattiness now returned, including repeated games of journeying under the bedclothes, into her tummy as he once told her.

Klein concluded that addressing the child's unconscious anxiety is crucial to its well-being – cognitive as well as emotional. In the absence of such enlightenment, she wrote, her other son Hans had early become socially aloof, while her daughter Melitta lost her initially keen intelligence and curiosity through never asking or being told about sex.

However outrageous Klein's analysis of her own children – despite men since Darwin having done much the same in furthering their science – it laid the basis of her psychoanalytic play technique and its attention to the symbolism of children's play. Ferenczi had already noted children's tendency to symbolize themselves in their surroundings. Klein now provided direct evidence of this from her own mothering. In particular she drew attention to the way all three of her children experienced school in terms of personal family matters.

Seventeen-year-old Melitta, for instance, 'did not like the letter "i", it was a silly jumping boy who always laughed'. By contrast the letter 'a' was 'serious and dignified, it impressed her and her associations led to a clear father-image whose name also began with an "a"'.[8] Thirteen-year-old Hans also thought of his father in relation to school. He wanted his master, when he was leaning back against the desk, to fall down and hurt himself just as he wanted an injury to befall his father. Meanwhile six-year-old Erich thought of the number '1' as a gentleman who lives in a hot country. Hence his lack of clothes.

All this can enliven schooling, says Klein, provided the child is able to surmount any Oedipal and castration anxiety involved. This proved no problem for Melitta, for instance, in adding identical numbers, which she enjoyed. But she was at a loss adding non-identical numbers, so much did it evoke anxiety about sexual difference. She also had difficulty thinking through algebraic equations with two unknowns because of inhibition about thinking about her parents' sexual intercourse. Meanwhile Hans hated school games. They evoked a masturbation fantasy of playing with little girls whose breasts he caressed as they played football together. That would have been all right, Klein wrote,[9] had his fantasy not also evoked fear of castration due to an early operation on his penis, and his father's punitiveness.

Klein not only spelled out possible educational effects of the castration complex. She also emphasized, through analysing a tic of Hans's, the way hysterical symptoms symbolize not so much body parts, as Freud had claimed (he suggested, for instance, that Anna O's hysterically paralysed arm symbolized an erect penis), as relations with others – 'object relations'.[10] Hans's tic was three-fold: a feeling of depression in the back of his neck; an urge to throw his head back and move it sideways; lastly he pressed his head down as deep as possible. The whole movement, his mother claimed, recalled the time before Hans was six when he shared his parents' bedroom and wanted to be in on their sexual intercourse. With the tic's first two movements he identified with her seeming passivity in relation to his father, while with the last movement he identified with his father's active drilling into her.

However far-fetched this analysis, it marked a major step away from the individual instinct theory of Freud towards a psychoanalytic theory and practice much more attuned to relational issues. But its generalization depended on Klein analysing children other than her own, which she began to do following her move with Erich to Berlin in January 1921, leaving Melitta in Rosenberg and Hans in a boarding school in the Tatra Mountains.

She also continued analysing Erich, this time his fear of going to school, and inhibitions regarding geography and other subjects. These were linked to a game in which he made a tiny dog slide over her body, imagining the while her breasts as mountains, her genital area as a great river. Suddenly, however, the dog was stopped in its tracks by toy figures who accused it of damaging their master's motor. The whole scenario ended in quarrelling and fighting. Through interpreting the anxiety expressed in such fantasies, claimed Klein,[11] Erich's school difficulties – including difficulties in writing linked to thoughts of the letters fighting each other – were resolved.

Her other analysands now included children of her colleagues in the Berlin Psychoanalytic Society, of which she became an associate member in 1922. This and her mothering experience of analysing her own children led her to go well beyond the work of the first child analyst, Hermine von Hug-

Hellmuth, in advocating both analysis of very young children and the extension of Freud's depth treatment, essentially unmodified, to children's therapy.

Contrary to warnings against going too deep in child analysis, she insisted[12] on addressing the child's leading anxiety and its unconscious roots. For as she had learnt from analysing Erich, this brings children much more relief than dealing only with their superficial worries and concerns. She also emphasized, again as with Erich, interpreting both children's conversation and make-believe play, the latter being essentially no different in her view from the dreams and free associations used by Freud to access the unconscious.

Just as she interpreted her own children's behaviour in terms of their relation to her, so too she insisted on interpreting other children's therapy material in terms of their relation to her as mother – a focus on transference much valued by many of today's Kleinian analysands.[13] Moreover, and this she discovered particularly from working with children other than her own, it is important to address the patient's negative as well as positive feelings towards the therapist as mother – the negative transference having previously been regarded as a mere hindrance to therapy. By contrast, she found that unless such feelings are confronted it is often impossible to get analysis going at all.

An example was two-year-old Rita, referred for treatment because of night terrors, animal phobias, obsessionality, and depression, for which Klein treated her, as she had her own children, in the child's home. Initially Rita was completely silent. But she became less frightened on going outside. Only by linking her fear of being alone indoors with Klein to Rita's fear lest a bad mother-like woman attack her when she was alone at night could Rita bear to return to the nursery and further analysis.

To overcome children's resistance to transferring on to her the full force of their feelings towards their parents, Klein began seeing children away from their own homes in her house in Dahlem, where she now lived again with Arthur. Soon she also provided each patient with their own set of toys. This began after she treated a seven-year-old truant who had remained withdrawn in therapy until Klein fetched her some of her children's toys. Thereupon the little girl began playing with two toys, representing herself and a little boy, between whom there seemed to be something secret. Other toys seemed to interfere and were therefore discarded. Meanwhile the activity of the two main figures led to disaster – falling and collisions – with mounting anxiety which Klein interpreted as effect of the play between them involving something sexual, which the girl was frightened of being found out by her teacher. Hence her distrust of school, her mother, and Klein. Through thus interpreting her toy play, as she had her own children's play, Klein helped restore the little girl's interest and pleasure in school.

Klein now made a point of providing each child patient with their own drawer of toys – little wooden men and women, carts, carriages, motor-cars, trains, animals, bricks and houses – as well as water, beakers, spoons, paper, scissors, pencils, and paints. Sometimes things got broken, and water and paint splashed about. But Klein insisted, contrary to Anna Freud, on allowing children thus to express their aggression provided the analyst interpret why, at this particular point in their relationship, the child is being aggressive, this forestalling actual physical attacks on the analyst.

Thereby equipped with a technique she had evolved from analysing her own children, Klein went on to describe the discoveries to which it gave rise, particularly regarding children's very early internalization of their relations with others – far earlier than Freud had recognized in his account of the Oedipus complex reconstructed from the analysis of adults.

3

Early object relations

> Freud acquainted us with the child in the adult, and Klein with the infant in the child. (Hanna Segal)[1]

Reunited in 1923 with all three of her children and her husband in Berlin, Klein became immersed in analysing children and even a few adults. Her work, Abraham enthused to Freud, provided 'amazing insights into an infantile instinctual life'.[2] In particular he seemed to have had in mind her treatment of three-year-old Peter, whose case she described at the 1924 Salzburg Congress, where Ernest Jones was also impressed with her work.

Peter's difficulties, she claimed, began with witnessing his parents' intercourse when he was eighteen months old. In his very first session he apparently represented what he had thus seen and his feelings about it by putting some toy carriages and cars first behind each other and then side by side. Then he knocked two toy horses together, adding: 'And now they are going to sleep.' Then he buried them with bricks, saying: 'Now they're quite dead.' Another time he represented himself and his brother by two pencils on a sponge and shouted at them in his father's voice as he had wanted to attack his parents: 'You're not to go about together all the time and do piggish things.'[3]

It seemed that Peter had already internalized a harsh super-ego version of his father inside himself. But Klein soon found that the child first internalizes and identifies not with the father, as Freud had claimed, but with the mother. An example was four-year-old Ruth. Initially she was so frightened of seeing Klein that her older stepsister had to accompany her. One day Ruth rummaged through her sister's bag and shut it tight 'so that nothing should fall out'. She had done the same with her sister's purse. Then she drew a tumbler with round balls inside and a lid on top 'to prevent the ball from rolling out', as though she also wanted to keep her mother's babies safely shut up inside, so upset had she been at her younger sister's birth. Another time she played at feeding the dolls jugfuls of milk only to cry out at Klein when she put a wet sponge by one of them, 'No, she mustn't have the big sponge, that's not for children, that's for grown-ups!' as if she could not bear what her grown-up mother enjoyed, the sponge seemingly representing her father's big penis.[4] This, and other aspects of her play, maintained Klein, revealed that Ruth's envy of the seeming contents of her mother's body – penis, babies, and so on – made her want to harm and rob her. This in turn had led to fear of her mother's retaliation now internalized as a vengeful superego figure inside. Hence her terror of Klein in therapy.

Through children's experience of her as mother in therapy, Klein discovered that such internal figures are first formed as a result of the oral and anal frustrations of weaning and potty training – well before the phallic stage described by Freud as source of patriarchal superego formation.

Indicative, in her view, of the anal aspects of the early maternal superego was three-year-old Trude.[5] In her therapy she repeatedly pretended it was night and that she and Klein were asleep. She would then come over to Klein and threaten her, saying she wanted to hit her in the stomach, take out her poohs, and make her poor. Then she hid terrified behind the sofa, covered herself up, sucked her fingers, and wet herself. She thereby re-enacted, it turned out, every detail of the way, when she was not quite two, she used to run into her parents' bedroom at night as though wanting to rob her pregnant mother of her babies and kill her – just as she now attacked Klein and wanted to rob her of her poohs. But this in turn gave rise to fear lest her mother likewise attack her. It was, says Klein, Trude's internalization of this anally attacking image of her mother, formed out of Oedipal rivalry with her for her father, that now plagued her and caused the night terrors that brought her to therapy.

Oral aspects of the early superego included the fear of another patient, two-year-old Rita, lest something come through the window at night and bite her just as she had earlier wanted to attack her mother when she was pregnant with her baby brother. The vengeful, biting, maternal figure she had thereby internalized now prevented her playing with her doll lest she attack it as she had wanted to attack her brother.

Klein described these processes in April 1924. That month also saw the marriage of her medical student daughter to a friend of Freud's, Walter Schmideberg. This apparently brought to an end Melanie and Arthur's brief reconciliation, the stresses of which had led Melanie to seek treatment with Karl Abraham. Leaving Arthur, she now moved with Erich to the same hotel as Helene Deutsch.

That autumn Deutsch talked about menopause at the Würzburg Congress. At the same Congress Klein gave her most important account to date of the child's early internalization of its relations with the mother – oral, anal, and phallic – as illustrated by the case of an only child, six-year-old Erna, referred for obsessive head-banging, rocking, thumb-sucking, and compulsive masturbation. Her mother felt drained, swallowed up by her. No wonder. Erna even tried to bite off Klein's nose at her first session.

Her symptoms dated from a holiday when she was two, shared her parents' bedroom and, as she later told her grandmother, 'Daddy got into bed with Mummy and wiggle-woggled with her.'[6] In sessions with Klein she repeatedly re-enacted this scene in her play. Sometimes she cast Klein as the mother who she felt endlessly tormented and excluded her from the pleasures – oral, anal, and phallic – she seemingly enjoyed with her father, leaving Erna feeling bitterly left out and envious. At other times Erna ousted Klein from this imagined orgy and subjected her to the same ill-treatment she felt she had suffered from her mother.

She tried to persuade Klein to take into her mouth and suck an engine with gilded lamps – 'all red and burning' – as though she thought her mother did that with her father's penis. Then she took the mother's place and sucked the lamps herself, just as she sucked her thumb. Other times she would play at 'wurling' fish with a policeman-father, Klein having to be the excluded mother who retaliates by secretly trying to get the fish from the couple. Such scenes alternated with ones in which Erna would pretend to dirty herself, and get Klein as mother to scold her, whereupon Erna would attack her by vomiting up her bad food.

Erna sought to keep at bay with her obsessions the intense feelings of exclusion, deprivation, envy, and rage evoked by her mother's apparent oral, anal, and phallic enjoyment of her father. Hence the attacks she imagined making on Klein in therapy. But she also feared lest her mother likewise attack her. This was expressed in an image of a flea that was all 'black and yellow mixed', like a piece of shit, that Erna imagined came out of Klein's body and forced itself into her.

By interpreting such fantasies, claimed Klein, Erna began to distinguish more clearly between her internal image of her mother (as fearsome and attacking) and her actual relation with her. The result was a less harsh maternal superego, as evident from her play now becoming more warmly maternal and tender. This in turn mitigated her previously unalloyed feelings of deprivation by, and envy of, her mother. She therefore no longer felt so pressed to stave off these feelings with obsessional, auto-erotic activity.

Whatever the success of Erna's therapy – Abraham said it showed that 'the future of psycho-analysis lies in play technique'[7] – its extremely primitive and aggressive material, including Erna's fantasy of revenging herself on her mother by making her and her father into 'mincemeat' and 'eye-salad', was hardly the stuff to reassure Klein's colleagues, made particularly nervous of child analysis by von Hug-Hellmuth's murder the previous month. Klein had already suffered from Berlin analysts as the only non-academic and one of the only child analysts in their Society. They found her 'feeble-minded about theory',[8] and her nursery talk embarrassing and ridiculous. Now, with von Hug-Hellmuth's death, it seemed that child analysis was positively dangerous. Nor were Vienna Society analysts, to whom Klein gave a talk that December, any more sympathetic.

The British Psycho-Analytical Society – in keeping with England's more empiricist tradition, and long-standing snobbish preference for the gifted amateur over the technically qualified professional – proved much friendlier to child and lay analysis. Its members had for some years been interested in child analysis. And in 1924, following lively discussion of Nina Searl's talk on the subject, James Strachey asked his wife Alix, also in analysis with Abraham, to send him notes of Klein's Vienna talk, with which he regaled the Society in January 1925.

Cheered by this, Melanie pressed Alix to engineer an invitation for her to give a course of lectures in London, having so far singularly failed to get such an invitation from the Berlin Society. Alix agreed and prepared her with lessons in English. Much more enjoyable to Melanie, however, were their outings to parties and the opera, Alix finding Melanie 'frightfully excited & determined to have a thousand adventures', indeed sometimes too much so, as when she chattered through Mozart's *Cosi fan Tutte*.[9]

For her British Society lectures – given in July 1925 to packed meetings in Adrian Stephen's drawing-room – Klein kitted herself out, as was to become her custom, with a special hat. Alix warned her husband it was like 'an overblown tea-rose with a slightly rouge'd core'.[10] But the excitement of these lectures was followed by a bleak return to Berlin. That spring Klein had begun an affair with a much younger married man, a travel journalist by the name of Kloetzel whom she had met at a dancing class. Now he wrote that he had fallen in love with another woman. Klein was terribly hurt but promised to leave him alone. Anyway she planned to return to England. Her marriage was over, and in May 1925 her analysis had ended with Abraham's sudden illness that month. Now she had nobody to keep her Berlin Society detractors in check. That Christmas Abraham died, and within weeks Klein accepted Ernest Jones's invitation to analyse his children in London.

1926 saw the opening of the London Clinic for Psychoanalysis. Klein arrived that September, living first in a flat in the Temple, and then in a maisonette near the Institute of Psychoanalysis in Gloucester Place. Her practice soon included not only Jones's children and wife but also six other patients. She soon decided to settle permanently in England – 'her second motherland'.[11] And with Erich's arrival at the end of the year she moved to a house in Notting Hill, from which he went to St Paul's School.

Meanwhile Anna Freud canvassed her quite different approach to child analysis in Vienna and Berlin. Indeed, she rejected the very basis of Klein's claims regarding the child's early internalization of its relation with the mother – namely their supposed transference of this relation on to her. In a special 1927 British Society symposium convened to answer Anna's charges, Klein[12] insisted that children do indeed transfer their internalization of early mothering into therapy. As evidence she cited the fact that interpretation of children's play in these terms diminishes their anxiety and is indeed often essential to get analysis under way – as in the case of Rita (see p. 217 above).

The intensity of children's transference feelings, Klein maintained, is evidence of the early disjunction between the parents' actual behaviour and the internal images formed out of the child's primitive oral, anal, and phallic response to it. Four-year-old Gerald, for instance, had never been overtly punished or threatened by his parents, but nonetheless imagined being eaten up, cut to pieces, and castrated – these expectations being transferred on to Klein, who figured in his play both as an idealized mother who could fulfil his every wish and as a malevolent witch.

Such fearsome images of the mother, Klein claimed, people children's nightmares and are the stuff of the early superego. All too often it impedes cognitive and emotional development in so far as this internal superego figure is formed out of belief that play, creativity, and curiosity amount to aggressive intrusion into the mother's body, thereby risking vengeful counter-attack – a fantasy Klein had first discovered through analysing

Erich. Therapy, she argued, should therefore aim to mitigate the harshness of the early superego by interpreting the child's play expression of it. Analysis certainly should not increase its severity. Yet that was precisely what Anna Freud's method did in fostering children's positive feelings towards her as analyst, as though negative feelings could not be borne and were something to feel guilty about. Anna, she went on, also fuelled the child's superego anxiety by curbing the child's instincts through acting as the child's 'auxiliary ego'.

Having thus disposed of Anna's technique, Klein now turned to spelling out her findings about sexual development from her own very different method of child analysis.

4

Sex, art, and reparation

Klein's discovery of the child's early internalization of its first relation with the mother led to a major revision and expansion of Freud's account of female and male sexuality. The result was also an important shift in psychoanalytic perspectives on art, now understood as stemming not from sublimation of instinct but from wish to repair relations with others, in the first place with the mother.

Drawing on her child patients' experience of her as mother, Klein indicated – this time at the July 1927 Innsbruck Congress – the oral and anal envy of the mother elicited by the frustrations of weaning and toilet training.[1] At first, she said, the child vents its rage by wanting to bite, devour, cut up, and rob the mother, just as it felt robbed of milk and faeces by her. But this gives rise to dread of being similarly attacked by her. The child's resulting orally and anally attacking image of the mother, claimed Klein, forms the basis of the superego, of a common 'femininity phase' in boys as well as girls.

But here the paths of the two sexes diverge. The boy's penetrative impulses, she argued, lead him genitally to desire his otherwise orally and anally hated mother. The dread of her to which these earlier impulses give rise is the source, she claimed, of the boy's subsequent dread of the father as castrator described by Freud. Hence the boy's fear of Oedipal and genital rivalry with the father for the mother. He may avoid such rivalry by retreat to pre-genital impulses – including those of robbing and destroying the faeces, babies, and father's penis imagined as orally and anally incorporated within the mother in sex. But in thus wanting to destroy his father inside the mother the boy fears the parents' joint vengeance, this giving rise to an avenging image of the parental couple attacking him within. Both this, and the boy's envy of his mother's childbearing, determine later sexuality – men feeling warmth or contempt for their sexual partners depending on the success with which they negotiated early ambivalent identification with the mother and subsequent Oedipal rivalry and identification with the father.

Meanwhile, claimed Klein, the oral and anal deprivation of weaning and toilet training, together with the receptive aims of the vagina, lead girls to abandon the mother for the father. This move is also fuelled by hatred of the mother for seemingly incorporating the father's penis within her in sex. It is the girl's resulting sense of deprivation by the mother, said Klein, that launches her into heterosexuality. She looks to good and loving sexual relations, in the first place with the father, as means of mitigating the hatred involved in early mothering. But the transference of this hatred into sex can inhibit and sour women's sexual pleasure or lead to frigidity, as can guilt at seemingly abandoning the mother in sex.

Such feelings are all the more intense, maintained Klein, since girls lack the external genitals whereby to reassure themselves that the mother's feared revenge on their attacks on her sexuality has not taken place. Hence women's lesser confidence in their femininity and capacity for childbearing, compared to men's much more sure pride in their phallic masculinity.

Not that boys do not also fear castration. But such fears in either sex, Klein argued, are not the source of conscience as Freud claimed in his account of the patriarchal superego. Genuine concern for others, she maintained, can hardly stem from such a punitive source. Rather it results from the child's internalization of an 'indulgent' image of the mother formed out of the loving genitality that succeeds the more savage impulses of orality and anality.

Klein's 1927 Innsbruck talk in which she first advanced these ideas was followed by her election, a few weeks later, to the British Psycho-Analytical Society. The next year her daughter, Melitta, joined her in London. Here she worked on her medical thesis before returning in 1929 to Berlin. Previously she had been analysed by Max Eitingon. Now she began a training analysis with Karen Horney.

Back in England Ernest Jones staunchly defended Klein's work to Freud. But, apart from approving her account of the disjunction between the parents' behaviour and the child's superego version of it, Freud rejected Klein's claims regarding the early Oedipus complex and its maternal roots. No wonder he remained hostile to Klein. Not only had she seemingly set the British Society against his daughter's work. She also questioned his account of creativity. Both he and Anna attributed art to sublimation of individual instinct. Not so Klein. She explained it as reflecting our relations with others, in the first place with the mother.

In a British Society talk in May 1929 she illustrated this theme by reference to Ravel's opera, *L'enfant et les sortilèges*, and the work of artist Ruth Kjär. First the opera. It opens with a little boy in high dudgeon at having to do his homework. He would much rather go to the park, pull the cat's tail, and scold everyone, particularly his mother. She now enters and asks if he has finished, at which he puts out his tongue only to be rebuked: 'You shall have dry bread and no sugar in your tea.'[2] Faced with such oral deprivation, as Klein puts it, the boy flies into a rage. He attacks the tea things, the pets, the fire, and the pendulum inside a grandfather clock, just as the Oedipal child, Klein wrote, seeks to attack its mother's body and the father's penis inside. Then the things he attacks come to life. A wild rumpus starts (not unlike that depicted in Maurice Sendak's *Where the Wild Things Are*). The boy takes refuge in the park. Yet this too is filled with dread – with animals fighting and biting him. They personify his image of the mother, says Klein, attacking him as he wanted to attack her. A squirrel falls to the ground beside him. The boy picks it up and binds its injured paw. Instantly his world becomes more friendly – the once fearsome animals now look on appreciatively at his kindness, and he is restored to his mother.

Klein went on to illustrate a similar development in girls – from attack to loving restoration – through an account of

Kjär's life and work. Beautiful, rich, and independent, Kjär also suffered occasional bouts of depression in which she felt unbearably empty. This was matched by the emptiness left by the space on her wall when her brother-in-law removed one of his paintings. This made her feel more desolate than ever until she decided to fill the space with a picture of her own.

Mindful of her girl patients' fear of emptiness and being alone at night – the mother then not being around to reassure them that their imagined attacks on her have not entirely done away with her – Klein suggested that Kjär's painting was an attempt to make good the emptiness and damage seemingly done by such attacks. Hence her pictures of a black woman, her sister, an old woman all wrinkled and worn, ending with a portrait of her mother – magnificent, imperious, and challenging.

Klein thereby inaugurated a new trend in art and literary criticism focusing on the maternal and reparative aspects of creativity.[3] More immediately, her 1929 essay was followed by her daughter's arrival in England, where she lived with Klein and became involved in the British Psycho-Analytical Society, to which she gave talks along the lines of her mother's work. Klein's work was also given official blessing in 1930 by the Society agreeing rules for training in child analysis that Klein had done so much to pioneer. In 1931 she took on her first trainee analysand, Canadian Clifford Scott, and was soon analysing another trainee, American-born David Slight. As well as analysing both men in London and on holiday in Germany and France, she also supervised their first child analysis cases and perhaps thought of them in developing her 1932 account of male and female sexuality.

As before, she maintained[4] that the child's first sexual impulses – oral, anal, and genital – are directed towards the mother's body and its supposed contents. This results in fear of the mother's counter-attack with consequent early repression of knowledge of the vagina, and later avoidance of sex. Alternatively we look to sex as a means of allaying our otherwise hated and vengeful image of vagina and penis formed out of Oedipal envy of the mother, and of the father imagined as incorporated within her. Sex can also reassure women, Klein added, that their insides have not been damaged by the mother in revenge for their attacking her insides for seemingly withholding and keeping to herself everything they desire.

Klein went on to emphasize children's guilt about such attacks, and the way both children and adults, like Kjär, seek to make good the damage seemingly done in attacking the mother. Girls' drawings and writing in therapy, she argued, are an attempt to staunch this guilt by replenishing the mother represented by the paper on which they work. Similarly children fill up boxes or draw houses representing the mother replete with tree and flowers (as penis and babies). Older girls likewise draw and sew dolls and dolls' dresses or books to restore the mother, while boys build toy houses and villages, even placing a toy man to control the traffic and prevent any damage from cars running into each other, pedestrians, or houses.

This, however, alternates with fear lest the analyst as mother damage what they have made. Little girls, Klein reported, often wrap up their creations and put them away with suspicious looks at her as though she might spoil or replace them with bad things. On the other hand they also seek to reassure themselves – through doll play – that their creativity has not been spoilt, that they have not been robbed by the mother of their capacity to have children and look after them. In thus identifying with the mother, said Klein, girls also reassure themselves of not being abandoned by her. Furthermore, she argued, through schoolwork the child seeks to reassure itself that it has the inner capacity to make good any harm done the loved mother by envy and hatred of her. Similar motives, she said, impel the search of adults for sexual approval and sex, and women's childbearing, breast-feeding, and caring activity generally. Where all goes well such activity serves to convince us of our capacity to make good any harm done to self or others by the hatred and envy first felt toward the mother.[5]

Illustrative of the sense of the mother as damaged was a thirty-five-year-old homosexual's experience of Klein's street and house as nothing but a sea of dirt. Klein herself seemed as disgusting as he found her charlady and his mother, who he felt could no more clean up her messy-seeming insides than the charlady Klein's house. Other times, when he felt particularly destructively envious of his mother and father, he hated Klein and feared for his own insides. This was expressed in hypochondriacal anxiety as though the hated and attacked parental couple were likewise attacking him from within.

But what happens when all confidence in restoring the effects of such damage is lost? Then, said Klein, depression can set in, as in five-year-old John. After sticking together a box and filling it up as though to make restitution for the damage he felt he had done his mother, he angrily threw a tantrum, despairing that all his efforts were in vain. Another example was a middle-aged American who sadistically tormented his older half-brother as a child. Later he sought to make amends by nursing his brother when he became ill. But his brother died. The patient thereby lost all belief in his reparative capacity. His resulting depression was expressed in anxiety for both Klein's and his mother's well-being.

With this case Klein concluded her first book. It was celebrated by leading members of the British Society. Edward Glover pronounced it 'a landmark in analytic literature worthy to rank with some of Freud's own classical contributions'.[6] He and his wife, the Joneses, Rivières, and Stracheys, as well as Erich, Melitta and her newly arrived husband, Walter Schmideberg, attended a party in its honour in November 1932. Within months, however, this happy union fell apart. Klein used the experience to consolidate the object relations account of depression she had begun to formulate on the basis of her 1920s' and early 1930s' patients' experience of her as mother.

5

Depression and loss

By the end of 1932 Melitta had left her mother to live with her husband near the Institute of Psychoanalysis, where she was elected a member in October 1933. This followed a paper in which, for the first time, she implicitly criticized her mother's work by emphasizing the influence of the mother's own behaviour as well as that of the child on its development. Criticism, however, soon turned into vituperative attack. She stormed at Klein for neglecting the father in her work, and for depriving her of patients. The latter was a sensitive issue given the competition for work resulting from the arrival of analysts from Hitler's Germany, among them Paula Heimann, who, as recently dramatized in the London play *Mrs Klein*, went into analysis with Klein in January 1935.

Melanie's loss of Melitta was compounded by loss of Hans, who had become an engineer like his father. In April 1934 Hans died while climbing in the Tatra Mountains. It might have been an accident. Melitta, however, attributed his death to suicide. But most of all she complained of her mother's intrusiveness into her life both personally and professionally. Meanwhile Klein, who had moved to St John's Wood, was too distressed by Hans's death to attend either his funeral (in Budapest) or professional meetings. Instead she threw herself into work on a talk about depression for that summer's Lucerne Congress.

In it[1] she formulated for the first time her theory of 'the depressive position'. Previously she had held that children only internalize good and loving images of others with the onset of genitality. Now she insisted that such internalization begins at birth. She thereby virtually abandoned Freud's theory of instincts as arising independently of those to whom they are directed. Instead of viewing development in terms of self-generating oral, anal, and genital stages, she now viewed it as shaped from the beginning by internalization of our relations with others, understood in terms of love and hate and shifting states of mind – paranoid, depressive, and manic – to which she said such internalization gives rise.

At first, Klein argued, the baby's whole interest is focused on the mother's breast. In so far as this is hated, she said, adopting her own version of Freud's 1920 theory of the death instinct, the baby also incorporates it, in fantasy, as a hated, attacking object inside itself. To ward off this image, and here Klein approvingly cited her daughter's work, the baby conjures up an ideally loved picture of the breast free of all frustration and hate.

With repeated reassurance of the mother's love, however, such splitting of love from hate diminishes. The baby can begin to bear experiencing her as hated as well as loved. It thereby experiences both the mother and itself as more whole. This unity is founded not, as Freud claimed, on narcissistic bringing together of oral, anal, and genital instincts but on identification with all the infant's conflicting feelings towards the mother combined.

Integration, however, brings about 'depressive position' anxiety lest in attacking the hated mother the baby thereby lose the loved mother. For the two are now recognized as one and the same. This anxiety, wrote Klein, culminates in the losses of weaning, and is overcome only through the child's growing confidence, stemming from internalization of good and loving mothering, that it has sufficient inner goodness effectively to make good any damage done the mother by hatred and frustration.

Freud attributed self-reproach in depression to hatred of others internalized in imagination within the self. Klein now attributed it to love of others and despair at feeling unable to restore the harm done by hatred to them. Sometimes, however, such despair is so unbearable that we retreat from it to persecutory anxiety. Hypochondriacal concern for the self is sometimes used in this way to stave off worry about others.

Other times hypochondria gives way to concern for others, as in the case of a patient who imagined a tapeworm or cancer eating through his body as though Klein, of whom he then felt very suspicious, were attacking him from inside. This was superseded by depressive anxiety lest Klein be damaged by his seeming cancer, just as he had always worried about his mother's health.

This maternal viewpoint on depression in turn shed light on a question left unanswered by Freud. If, as he claimed, depression is rooted in self-love and attachment to others only in so far as they reflect the self, then why does it ever eventuate in suicide – the very antithesis of self-love? The answer, Klein suggested, is that depression does not stem from self-love but from concern for others. Suicide in such cases involves a last-ditch attempt to preserve those one loves within the self by destroying the bad.

This perspective, bred of her mothering experience, also resulted in Klein going beyond Freud's individual instinct account of mania in depression. Helene Deutsch, she pointed out, had begun this process by indicating that mania involves denial of external loss. Klein now added that it also involves denial of internal loss and dependence on others. This is then replaced by disparagement, contempt, and hyperactive attempts omnipotently to control them. Yet this can fuel the very guilt it seeks to quench.

An example was a man who dreamed he was in an open-topped railway carriage with his parents end to end in bed. The patient the while pissed for his father into a cylindrical object which reminded him of old-fashioned gas-lights and dilapidated houses. He then dreamed he heard something sizzling in a pan as though it were being fried alive. Previously he complained that Klein threatened to hit him with the lighted end of her match the way she struck it to light her cigarette. Then he bemoaned feeling bunged up with a cold.

His dreams, it seemed, represented attacks on his parents – pissing on them, frying them – and the sense of desolation and persecution to which such attacks give rise. Hence his dilapidated houses association and fear lest Klein burn him just as he burnt others in his dream. But his dreams also expressed manic control over others in defence against feeling dependent and controlled by them. He travels in an open not a closed carriage. Rather than depend on others, he manages everything for them, even peeing for his father, and controls his parents inside himself, represented by their being inside a carriage, in his dream. Yet this exacerbates the very anxiety it seeks to allay. For his attacked and controlled parents now seem to attack him from within like the thick phlegm of his cold.

Klein concluded by insisting that this mixture of paranoia, depression, and mania is a regular feature of infancy. This 'infantile depressive position', she implied, is even more central to development than the Oedipus complex described by Freud. No wonder her 1934 Lucerne talk intensified divisions in the British Psycho-Analytical Society. Edward Glover now joined Melitta, who was in analysis with him, in attacking Klein while Melitta, still mindful of her brother's apparent suicide, insisted against her that such self-destruction is due not to love but to deep disappointment in the mother. In February 1936 she went on scathingly to attack the idealization her mother supposedly fostered in her patients. Others, however, were drawn to Klein by her account of depression, among them Anna Freud's close friend, Eva Rosenfeld. She now went into analysis with Klein, Freud describing her defection as a matter of choosing 'who is better, father or mother'.[2]

His 1956 eightieth birthday celebration saw a spirited exchange on this issue. Joan Rivière reiterated Klein's mother-based account of depression, while Robert Waelder remained sceptical whether babies are capable of the complex mental processes Klein attributed to them. She and Rivière were now charged with plagiarism by Melitta. Even Jones seemed to be deserting her. He gave much more attention to Anna Freud's 1936 book than to her and Rivière's book *Love, Hate, and Reparation*.

In July 1937 Klein underwent gall bladder surgery, after which she stayed with her younger son Erich and his wife, Judy, then pregnant with their first child, Michael. Meanwhile Klein's childless daughter Melitta continued to berate her with yet another talk about suicide in May 1938 when Freud's staunchest supporters began arriving from Vienna.

Undaunted, Klein went on developing her mother-centred account of depression in a talk to the 1938 Paris Congress. She began with yet another puzzle left by Freud. If, as he claimed, depression is rooted in self-love, then why is the work of detaching love from others with their loss and narcissistically withdrawing it into the self so painful? The answer, Klein suggested, is that grief involves recognizing both external and internal loss. Loss does not so much initiate internalization of the other as Freud claimed. Rather it painfully disrupts internalization processes begun in relation to the mother in infancy.

In this, Klein now also drew attention to the triumph involved in loss, and to the way this thwarts attempts to recognize, work through, and repair its damaging effects, save through ever more futile manic and obsessional attempts at reparation. A case in point was her reaction to Hans's death. At first she sorted out his things – keeping the good, throwing out what she did not want as though to keep him entirely good inside. But she felt no grief. Instead she dreamed it was not him but her mother's son who had died. Next she dreamed she was flying with her son, who then drowned. She herself escaped to safety. These triumphed-over dream figures – mother, brother, and son – now peopled her inner world. It only became repopulated with less damaged figures as she began to take comfort in looking at nicely situated houses in the country. She thereby regained a sense of also having good things inside herself, of being able to make good her loss. She could therefore fully acknowledge it. Therewith her grief came out in full; indeed, she abandoned herself to it. She let go her previous manic control over memories of her mother and others. They accordingly became more available and alive as sources of comfort. Nevertheless some persecutory feeling remained, as when, some weeks after Hans's death, she went for a walk with Paula Heimann only to feel overwhelmed by passers-by and by a café into which they retreated, as though only her home were safe.

Such paranoia, Klein pointed out, can also be used to ward off grief. An example was a middle-aged American who, the night before his mother died, dreamed they were either side of a dangerous bull from whom he fled, leaving his mother unprotected. This reminded him of shooting buffalo to eat, and thoughts of their being an endangered species needing protection. At the next session he arrived hating Klein as though she were one with his internal dream image of his mother mixed up with a dangerous bull-father. Only when Klein drew attention to the counterpart of this image – his reparative concern for buffalo, for instance – did he tell her of his mother's death, and of how sick he felt on getting the news. His hatred of Klein now turned to sorrow, but was revived after his mother's funeral when he complained that Klein's treatment was disintegrating him, just as his attacked mother in his bull dream seemingly disintegrated him from within. It turned out that he had long cultivated such negative images to ward off all depressive concern and fear of his mother's loss. Only as he achieved increasing confidence in his reparative capacity could he acknowledge his love and longing for her with fond talk of 'my dear old parents'.[3] This image now replaced the attacked and attacking image that so stymied his past relations with them.

In general, Klein concluded, persecutory and manic defences against loss can be undone and reparation set in motion only by reinstalling, or in the case of abnormal grief installing as it were for the first time, a securely established image of mothering as loved and good. She thereby completed her theory of the depressive position – a theory ranked equal by Winnicott, her son Erich's analyst, with Freud's discovery of the Oedipus complex. The latter she now viewed as effect, not cause, of the child's first internalization of relations with others. Her resulting concept of 'internal objects' led to the near tearing apart of the British Society in the war.

6

War

1939 began well enough, with a dinner celebrating the British Society's twenty-fifth anniversary at which Virginia Woolf felt Klein to be 'a woman of character & force some submerged . . . like an undertow; menacing'.[1] But Klein already feared that the Society she had so long dominated would be destroyed by the Freuds' arrival, for which she blamed Ernest Jones. Open battle, however, started only with England's declaration of war and Jones's retreat to the country, leaving the society to the newly arrived émigrés and an Emergency Committee run by Edward Glover and Sylvia Payne.

Klein herself stayed with her friend and colleague Susan Isaacs in Cambridge. The next May her sister Emilie died in London. Klein, however, seemed more preoccupied with the British Society Training Committee's recent attacks on her work: Anna Freud described it as a substitute for psychoanalysis; while Glover implied it was too controversial to be taught to students. This quasi-religious fight, as Strachey dubbed it, was soon overtaken by England's 'phoney war' turning into full-scale bombing. Klein accordingly moved in July 1940, at the invitation of the parents of one of her child patients, Dick, to Pitlochry in Scotland. Meanwhile in London her house was bombed that October, and Glover published a book obliquely criticizing her as a 'self-aggrandizing, tyrannical and selfish' mother who wrongly neglected the influence of such external factors on psychological development.[2]

Except for a brief visit in December, however, Klein remained absent from the British Society. Her Pitlochry practice now included Dick, his brother, and two doctors – Fieldman and Matthew. On 28 April 1941 she also began analysing a ten-year-old, Richard. His case history details the therapeutic implications of her depressive position theory. In doing so it marvellously conveys the to and fro movement between one mood and another characteristic of the child's earliest relation to the mother, quite differently from Freud's case histories with their unidirectional penetration into earlier and earlier supposed stages of instinctual development. Moreover, and much more than in her previous work, Klein focused on the good and loved aspects of mothering. So much so that Freudians complained her method threatened to 'imprison both patient and analyst in a matriarch world'.[3]

At referral Richard suffered a host of anxieties, including such intense fear of other children that he had been unable to attend school since he was eight. Now his home had been bombed. This and the war's other reverberations dominated his therapy, in which he exhibited the whole gamut of fears and defences – paranoid, depressive, and manic – characteristic, according to Klein, of the depressive position.

From his very first session he worried lest Klein, as an Austrian like Hitler, contain him as it were as an attacking figure inside. But he also felt he contained this combined, attacking, and mixed up Hitler–Klein figure inside himself, just as the boundaries of different countries had become mixed up by the war, as he indicated on a wall map in the Girl Guides hut in which he saw Klein.

Sometimes he relished such damage. It was such fun, he recalled, seeing a sledging couple fall with the man's nose getting all bloodied. And he drew pictures of himself as a German U-Boat attacking the British, representing Klein and his parents. Or he would goose-step around the room as though he had Hitler within.

At other times, particularly when Klein went to London for ten days in June 1941, he worried lest she be attacked by Hitler's bombs as he wanted to attack her for leaving him. Another day, when his session had to take place in Klein's lodgings, he became uneasy about what her fellow 'grumpy' lodger might do to her, just as he sometimes attacked her in sessions, even wanting to bite into a parcel addressed to her grandson.

Such attacks evoked persecutory anxiety lest he be similarly attacked. Hence his fear of other children, even of the maids at the hotel (where he stayed weekdays to see Klein), as though they might poison him. Perhaps they were foreigners like Hitler and Klein, he mused, the then intense national fear of invasion feeding his own personal fear of being invaded by hostile forces.

Sometimes, especially when his mother was ill, he worried lest his attacks had drained and turned his mother and Klein bad. Perhaps his water play had exhausted Klein and thereby robbed her other patients. She seemed so lonely and overworked. Why else did he never see her at the cinema? Then he would feel as if this desolate figure were inside him. His stomach felt thin and small. Another time his teeth seemed to be decaying. Then, referring as it were to Klein, he lamented: 'Poor playroom – it will soon be in ruins.'[4]

Occasionally the playroom, representing variously himself and Klein, felt so awful he took her into the garden to keep her safe outside. Such division of good from bad also figured in his drawing two loops of a railway line – one reminding him of 'dear' Mrs Klein of whom he was so fond, the other of the 'impudent old fish cadger' cook at the hotel.

Through coming to know about and understand such splitting, Richard gradually became more genuinely concerned for Klein and his mother, to whom he sent a drawing. His confidence in his reparative capacity increased. He cleaned Klein's room, and told her he was also doing his bit for his country – putting money in National Savings, and planting seeds. Digging for England indeed. And in one of his last sessions he sought to restore Klein by switching on the electric fire to keep her good and warm.

Previously he had despaired of his capacity for such restitution, as in a game he played with toy battleships representing the recent blowing-up of HMS *Hood*, from which the sailors could not be saved. His depression at being unable to make good the havoc wrought by war and his own attacks on others, represented by the maternal figure of Klein, seemed to be one reason he had given up playing the piano.

Sometimes he defended against such depression with manic denial or retreat into paranoid fear for himself, particularly after his father's sudden heart attack midway through his treatment. He now disparaged Klein. She was no longer the kind 'light-blue Mummy' of his drawings, especially since she had not been able to give him change for a shilling. He marched up and down – shouting and stamping. Then he picked his nose. But he feared his 'nose-pick' might harm him. Another time, turning his back on concern for Klein after attacking her by vehemently hammering the floor of her room, he manically wrapped himself up in a Union Jack and triumphantly sang the National Anthem.

By interpreting such defences in the light of her depressive position theory, Klein enabled Richard gradually to overcome his sense of their relation as attacked and attacking. He became calmer and more trusting and hopeful of their relation's helpfulness. Her room seemed cosier. The light-blue mother figure of his drawings increased in size. It was less often divided off from more negative maternal images. And he began to recall good early memories alongside the dangers of war. He also sought to keep Klein as a good maternal figure inside by having her help tie his shoelaces, thinking of becoming an analyst like her, and taking her photo.

He thereby felt more confident of being able to withstand and restore any damage resulting from rivalry with others. His Oedipus complex could therefore come out in full force. Klein[5] used his case to demonstrate that the working through of the depressive position in relation to the mother is a precondition of Oedipal rivalry with the father as described by Freud.

For Richard this included competition with the confectioner from whom he saw Klein get her cigarettes; willing the ironmonger to leave off talking across the street from her room; worrying about a frail old professor in a German film; and questions about Mr Klein. Richard also became sensitive to any suggestion that he was not as much a man as his father. He hated it when, in front of Klein, the tobacconist sent him to the back of the queue; when the bus conductress shouted 'Half fares stand up'; and when his mother did not want him to swim.

But his confidence grew as he more and more internalized his relation with Klein as good and helpful. As a result he could bear feeling lonely – in the cinema for instance. No more did he feel unbearably intruded upon by workmen coming into their therapy room. Nor did he feel so frightened of other children. Indeed, he now felt able to start school. Not that he did not also feel empty and sorry, with renewed manic and persecutory feelings, at losing Klein – feelings he was now hopeful of dealing with by keeping her inside, thinking about nice women, and touching her several times in his last session.

No sooner did his treatment end, in August 1941, than Klein returned to London and battle over control of the British Society. She and her now very few stalwart followers were increasingly pressurized to defend their deviance from Freudian orthodoxy. Skirmishes about administration and training – in which Klein was regularly accused of unwarranted domination over trainees – were followed by a series of 'Controversial Discussions' through 1943 and early 1944.

First Isaacs defended Klein's concept of 'unconscious phantasy' as a natural development of Freud's account of dreams. Klein had simply indicated how fantasy representation of relations with others permeates our whole mental life (not just the superego) from earliest infancy onwards. Many agreed that babies early internalize an image of the mother to tide them over her absence. But several objected to Klein's emphasis on the hostile aspects of such internalization, in contrast to Freud's initial emphasis on the unconscious as pure wish fulfilment unsullied by fear or hatred.

Next the Edinburgh-based analyst W. R. D. Fairbairn insisted that infants primarily seek not pleasure, but relations with others. Whereas Freud focused on repression of past pleasure into the unconscious, Fairbairn and the Kleinians attended to here-and-now internalization and projection of mothering and other relations, as though conscious and unconscious thought differed only in terms of spatial location – inside or out – rather than in terms of history and structure.[6] A perhaps apocryphal story tells how through it all an air-raid raged outside, with Winnicott having to warn the assembled company to withdraw.

The following meeting was introduced by Anna Freud, who defended her father's claim that the infant is initially completely self-centred – mothering being entirely secondary to instinct gratification. But, as critics pointed out, her own war nursery experience showed that babies also early internalize an image of the mother. Why else are they so disturbed at being handled by someone else?

The implications for therapy of such internalization were now detailed by Paula Heimann, who, with Isaacs, then went on to contrast Freud's attribution of symptoms to repressed sexuality with Klein's attribution of them to splitting of love and hate. The Controversial Discussions were concluded by Klein reiterating her theory of the early depressive position with illustrations from direct infant observation.[7] Meanwhile Anna Freud, who failed to attend this or any of the other later discussions, rejected the main basis of Klein's claims – her assumption that patients project on to the therapist their internalization of the mother from the start of therapy. Adopting her father's historical perspective, she insisted that the transference only develops gradually over time and should never be the sole focus of therapy.

Debate now shifted to training. Glover, who had long sought to oust the Kleinians as a group, was outraged by a January 1944 suggestion that teaching cover Klein's controversial ideas. He resigned, complaining that the Society was hopelessly 'woman ridden'. Oh for the days, he grieved, when Jones was 'First in Command'. Michael Balint likewise attributed the Society's recent dissensions to loss of its previous 'patriarchal organization'.[8]

Certainly disagreement persisted under the leadership of Sylvia Payne. Glover and Melitta quit the Society, the latter for New York while her husband went to live with the poet H. D.'s lesbian lover, Bryher, in Switzerland. Meanwhile Melanie spent the summer with her daughter-in-law and grandchildren, Michael and Diana (born in September 1942).

The war's ending saw the beginning of the end of London's psychoanalytic battle. Anna Freud proposed a scheme of training which was soon broadly accepted and was finally agreed in November 1946. One course was to be taught as before, another along her lines. With this 'ladies agreement' the British Society prevented the fragmentation suffered by the New York Society in reaction to Horney's dissension from Freudian orthodoxy. The British Society instead ended up housing under one roof three distinct groups – Kleinian, Anna Freudian, and a Middle Group whose members' only common ground arguably consisted in their independence from the other two groups. Meanwhile Klein turned her attention to mental splitting – her account subsequently being applied to the kinds of organizational splitting that had plagued the British Society during the war.[9]

7

Schizoid mechanisms

Klein had long been interested in splitting and schizoid mechanisms. She had regularly drawn attention to the way children and adults seek to sort out contradictory experience by splitting and keeping apart the good and the bad.[1] She had also worked with manifestly schizophrenic and autistic patients, beginning with Dick, whom she first treated when he was four.

Initially Dick hardly played, spoke or felt anything. He seemed totally indifferent to the presence or absence of his mother, and left his nanny without a backward glance for his first session with Klein, where he ran aimlessly about without any of the interest or anxiety usual for his age.

As a baby he had nearly died of starvation, so apathetic was he in breast-feeding by his mother and then by a wet-nurse. Neither seemed to show him any affection, unlike another nurse and his grandmother, who increasingly looked after him when he was two. With their help he became toilet trained and learned a few words. But he still only ate pap.

It was as though he could not bear to be interested in food or anything else, as if such interest necessarily involved fearful frustration and attack. Instead he shut off all such fear and interest in his surroundings. He thereby lost the very impulse that leads children to play and speak. His only interest was in trains and stations, door-handles and doors, in so far as they represented the anxiety he wanted to avert – the fearful wish to re-enter his mother's body like going into a room or a station.

However far-fetched this equation – indeed it is psychotic – some corroboration was provided by Dick's response to interpretations in terms of it. To make contact with this otherwise very withdrawn little boy, Klein took up two trains, calling one 'Daddy' and the other 'Dick', whereupon Dick took up the latter and rolled it to the window, saying 'Station', to which Klein responded, 'The station is Mummy: Dick is going into Mummy.' Dick then re-enacted the scenario she described by running into the dark space between the outer and inner doors of her room. This at last made him openly anxious. He asked for his nurse. This same sequence was repeated in subsequent sessions in which, moved by Klein's maternally based comments, his play and feelings gradually became freed from their previous stultifying inhibition.

First he tried to scratch a toy coal-cart. He then threw it into a drawer and covered it with other toys. Later still he put it and the drawer's other contents into Klein's lap, as though to restore to his mother the things he had wanted to damage in her, lamenting the while, 'Poor Mrs Klein.' Stirred into life by such concern, Dick's speech also developed, and with it growing attachment to Klein and his mother.[2]

Freud had claimed that it was impossible to treat such patients psychoanalytically because their withdrawal prevents any transference. By contrast Klein's mothering experience – dating from observation of her own children's intellectual inhibition related to fear of exploring her body – had alerted her, as with Dick, to the possibility that such fear can be transferred into analysis. By articulating this otherwise unvoiced and scarcely symbolized anxiety in autistics like Dick, she found she could mobilize both this anxiety and the speech necessary to its analysis.

Klein continued to treat Dick through the war and became increasingly impatient to develop her ideas about schizoid mechanisms, especially after Fairbairn's 1944 publication on the subject. His work was the starting point of her December 1946 talk in which, for the first time, she identified a distinct 'paranoid-schizoid position'. Like Fairbairn, she maintained that schizoid disorders are rooted in earliest infancy. Unlike him, she insisted that the newborn baby internalizes loved as well as hated images of the mother. Nor does this reflect only the mother's behaviour. It also reflects the baby's prior impulses towards her of love and hate.

At first, she argued, the baby resolves the conflict between these feelings by splitting. Freud had described the splitting of the mind into conscious and unconscious, and into id, ego, and superego. By contrast Klein described splits resulting not from the social and patriarchal repression of sex but from destructiveness related to earliest mothering.

Initially, she implied, such splitting is a passive process of unintegration. This, not sexual repression, she argued, is the primary source of anxiety.[3] The baby fears falling to pieces – annihilation – and feels as though this threat came from the mother, a feeling akin perhaps to the paranoia infusing drug-, drink-, or dementia-related confusion. In adults a paranoid picture of the world can hold together, albeit very damagingly, otherwise chaotic feelings. In babies, by contrast, it only increases fear of fragmentation – later equated with madness. Babies, claimed Klein, accordingly actively seek to get rid of such feeling by splitting it off and evacuating it into the mother. She is now experienced as the locus of disintegration, as when a baby whose feed is unavoidably delayed becomes so torn apart by crying that it cannot feed, so much has the breast seemingly become fragmented and bad with the baby's previous mounting frustration.[4]

In such circumstances the baby feels it takes into itself a breast shattered into bits and pieces. This adds to its sense of dispersal, which is only allayed, Klein maintained, through the baby taking in the loved breast as whole and complete, as in the integrative experience of being held physically and emotionally in sucking at the breast, looking at the mother's face the while.

To ward off contrary, frustrating experience and the 'paranoid-schizoid' anxiety to which it gives rise, the baby seeks to do away with such negative experience. Instead it idealizes the breast as though it were free of all frustration, as a veritable inexhaustible cornucopia of pleasure. But the destructiveness involved in thus disposing of the mother's bad aspects leads to attempts 'to suck dry, bite up, scoop out and rob' the mother's body of all goodness,[5] even to expel dangerous substances into her – initially body products (sick, piss, and shit) – just as Klein's 1920s child patients imagined doing to her.

This involves identifying with others in terms of the things and parts of the self projected in fantasy into them. Such 'projective identification' involves omnipotent control over others and its obverse – claustrophobic fear of being trapped inside others. It also evokes fear of being likewise intruded into by others, just as Erna feared Klein as mother might intrude poisonous excrement into her – a fantasy akin to the schizophrenic symptom of believing others are actually putting thoughts into one's head, taking them out, or broadcasting them. Fear of such intrusion both conscious and unconscious – of which her mother and Klein were often guilty (Klein even supervised Marion Milner's analysis of her grandson, Michael) – can also result in self-preserving schizoid withdrawal.

Projective identification can also involve putting good things and parts of the self into others – first the mother, as when the baby puts its food into her mouth. This fosters good relations with others. But, if carried to omnipotent excess, it can paradoxically result in feeling depleted and empty, over-dependent on others, and devoid of the capacity for love.

Similar processes occur when the idealized other is internalized but not assimilated to the self. Assimilation and integration come about, claimed Klein, only through repeated good experience. This has the effect of countering the splitting that *in extremis* can cause mental subnormality or schizophrenia.

But the very process that counteracts such splitting – namely experiencing the mother as loved and whole – evokes depressive fear of her loss. Sometimes, as we have seen, this proves so unbearable that the child or adult is thrown back on to more primitive defences. An example was a nine-year-old boy who no sooner felt sad at being unable to express affection for his mother than he retreated to paranoid-schizoid destructiveness. Taking his beloved watch out of his pocket, he stamped it into little pieces.[6]

Other instances included a manic-depressive patient full of self-reproach, tears streaming down her cheeks, who split off and remained entirely numb to the depression her behaviour betrayed. She likewise split off all feeling towards Klein and remained entirely impassive to her comments, as in dream images of herself as blind or entirely buttoned up.

Such splitting clearly makes it difficult to reach people in schizoid states of mind. But this, Klein argued, is no reason to abandon analysis of such conditions, as Freud had, since interpretation of splitting in terms of the patients' relation to the analyst and mother restores contact and the emotion necessary to analysis and integration.

How different from Freud's account of schizophrenia in the case of one Judge Schreber, in which Freud dwelt on the patient's sense of fragmentation in relation to the authority of his father, doctor, and God. Drawing on Freud's account of the collapse of symbolic processes in schizophrenia, today's self-styled 'true' Freudians attribute this collapse to disavowal of sexual difference and the castrating power of the father which they say first divides self and other, things and words. Such disavowal, they argue, rules out the possibility of psychoanalytic 'talking cure' for schizophrenics.[7]

While they thus close off the possibility of treating schizophrenia psychoanalytically, Klein's mother-based theory has opened up this condition to psychoanalytic therapy. Some non-Kleinians argue the need to modify psychoanalytic technique in such cases. They advocate in effect that the analyst should become 'the good enough mother' the schizophrenic seemingly lacked in infancy. By contrast Klein argued that psychoanalytic technique can be used essentially unmodified in treating schizophrenics, that as in treating neurotics, therapy in their case can be effected through interpreting rather than confounding and colluding with the patient's transference to the analyst as mother.

Others soon adopted Klein's approach, including her analysand Rosenfeld in a paper to the British Society in March 1947, the year in which Klein's third grandchild, Hazel, was born. Rosenfeld and another of her analysands – Hanna Segal – also gave Kleinian-based accounts of schizophrenia at the 1949 Zürich Congress. Klein's own paper to this Congress,[8] however, was about the ending of therapy not, as Freud described it, in terms of patients' working through their transference relation to him as father-figure, but in terms of working through the paranoid-schizoid and depressive anxieties and defences first felt towards the mother and re-evoked by the loss involved in therapy ending.

Meanwhile Klein's own daughter remained lost to her. They were never reconciled, even though they saw each other at this and other Congresses. The Zürich Congress also marked the beginning of a rift between Klein and Paula Heimann, who had increasingly replaced Melitta in Klein's affections. In particular Klein rejected Heimann's Zürich Congress claims about the therapeutic value of 'counter-transference' feelings stirred up in the analyst by the patient. Freud regarded such feelings as an obstacle to therapy calling for further treatment of the analyst. Klein agreed. By contrast Heimann argued that the counter-transference also includes feelings unconsciously communicated by the patient. As such it is a means of knowing about and understanding the patient's experience and state of mind.

Winnicott had already suggested as much in a February 1947 talk stressing the need for analysts to be aware of the hatred evoked in them by patients. Nowhere is this more crucial, he argued, than in treating psychotics. For they need the analyst to recognize rather than act out such feeling, just as the baby needs the mother to acknowledge and bear the hatred it evokes in her. Only by experiencing another tolerating hatred without retaliating or expelling it can psychotics likewise begin to tolerate knowing about their own hatred without recourse to splitting, projection, and acting out.

This theme was in turn developed by Klein's analysand, Wilfred Bion. He argued that, rather than re-projecting feelings evoked by patients, analysts should instead 'contain' and bear with such feelings just as ideally the mother takes in, contains, responds with appropriate anxiety, digests, thinks about, and thereby detoxifies uncomfortable states of mind induced in her by her child. If she is capable of such 'reverie' – rather than denying, refusing to be moved, collapsing, or becoming hostile in face of the infant's distress – the mother enables the infant gradually to know, think about, and bear such feelings in itself rather than disown and split them off.

In this Bion drew on Klein's concept of projective identification, particularly on the individual and group analysts' sometimes alien feeling of being induced to play a part in the patients' fantasy.[9] Klein herself was sceptical of this use of her concept of projective identification. She told students who talked in this way that if, for example, they felt confused, this was their own not the patient's doing.[10] Her interest in projective identification – now a central concept in psychoanalysis's increasingly interpersonal orientation – was only in the person doing the projecting, not in the person into whom the projection is made.

In 1953 – having broken with Winnicott because he did not sufficiently relate his theory of 'transitional objects' to her theory of 'internal objects', and with Heimann because the latter could not endure Klein's demands on her during her house-move to West Hampstead – Klein[11] began work on her most extensive account of projective identification, which she illustrated by reference to Julian Green's 1947 novel, *If I Were You*.

The book's main character, Fabian Especal, is a petty official whose dreary life seems devoid of all love, mother love included. Only by entering others' bodies, Fabian believes (like the schizophrenic convinced of being Napoleon), can he enjoy the relatively much greater seeming richness of their lives. He magically secures this wish through a pact with the devil. His first victim, appropriately enough, given his sense of maternal deprivation, is a waiter – one who feeds. This theme continues when, imprisoned inside the body of a poor and inadequate student, Fabian reaches out for a baker-woman's rolls, bites into them, thinking longingly of her breasts, only enviously to discover she loves another just as his mother did. With this attention to envy Klein inaugurated her last major work.

8

Envy and gratitude

In 1955 Klein gave a talk about envy and gratitude at that year's Geneva Congress. It marked the culmination of her transformation of psychoanalysis. Children's experience of her as a mother figure had long convinced her of their inability to bear recognizing that the mother has things they want but lack. It convinced her of children's early impulse enviously to spoil and destroy everything living in the mother, so much does it excite its opposite – namely death-dealing destruction. In 1924 Klein had described Erna's envious attack on her mother for apparently gratifying her father at her expense, even feeding him a marvellous concoction of whipped cream while Erna had to make do with semolina. In retaliation she had toy figures – variously representing Klein and her mother – enjoy themselves only to be attacked by herself in the guise of another figure, who variously bit, robbed, killed, and even roasted them alive.

More generally, Klein now claimed,[1] the child seeks both enviously to spoil good things in the mother, and greedily to expropriate and devour and destroy them within itself. Such greed and envy, she insisted, begins not with envy of the father's penis as symbol of self-esteem and maternal lack as Freud had claimed. Rather it begins with envy of the seeming plenitude of the feeding mother – her breast – albeit such envy is often defensively split off and denied.

It nevertheless remains to obstruct the child's development of a secure inner world. In so far as it cannot bear wanting what the mother has to give, the child enviously rubbishes her. It thereby fails to recognize, enjoy, feel grateful for, or internalize their relation as loved and loving. This, in turn, results in relations with others being similarly devalued. One patient, for instance, envied Klein's supposed relation with another man. He then went on to console himself that her private life was probably very dreary and dull. But this made his own relation with her also seem worthless, thus impeding its internalization as helpful and therapeutic.

Klein attributed such envious spoiling to childhood inability to bear knowing that the mother has anything good inside her, to the workings of the death instinct that seeks to destroy whatever is good and life-giving. Klein thereby arrived at a new understanding of what Freud called 'the negative therapeutic reaction' – the process whereby patients no sooner experience therapy as useful than they devalue it as useless.

As indicated in previous chapters, Freud believed this reaction to be due to unconscious fear lest being helped by therapy involve submission and castration by the analyst, just as the child construes the mother's submission to the father in sex. Women, he argued, likewise feel therapy is useless in so far as they feel that nothing short of the analyst fulfilling their childhood wish for the father's penis can help.

By contrast, Klein[2] traced such negative reactions to therapy to defence against envy first felt towards the mother. An example was a patient who, after two missed sessions, arrived complaining that no one looked after her when she was ill just as nobody came when she wanted to be looked after as a baby, and just as nobody in her previous night's dream served her in a restaurant. Instead she had had to queue up for food behind a woman reminiscent of Klein, who took a couple of cakes, feeding herself as it were at the patient's expense just as her mother had done. Only through interpretation and acknowledgement of her resulting envy could she experience the session not as uncaring, as she had complained of others at the beginning, but as helpful and satisfying. This in turn enabled her to recover and feel grateful for happy early mothering experiences that she had previously destructively denied and forgotten.

Just as envy of what the mother has to give leads to her goodness being denied and devalued, so too patients can likewise destroy all hope of getting better through therapy by enviously disparaging it. A case in point was a patient who dreamt of Klein as an apathetic, contemptible, and useless cow-like woman, the patient looking down on her from a magic carpet while Klein – the cow – munched an endless strip of blanket as though the dreamer were making her eat her words as woolly and worthless. Through interpreting this otherwise split off envious spoiling and the depression it involved, the patient began to be able to take in therapy as whole and helpful rather than hopelessly spoilt and useless.

Klein also described possibly her own envy of her mother as revealed in a dream of herself alone in a railway carriage with another woman. The latter had her back to her and would have fallen out of the door of the compartment had the dreamer not grasped her belt. This endangered woman in turn called to mind the dreamer's envy of a dress her mother wore, particularly the way it showed the shape of her breasts.

But it is not only women who envy the mother. So too do men, as Horney had long ago pointed out. Klein now illustrated this by reference both to a man who dreamed of putting her papers in his pipe and smoking them, and to a patient who dreamed he was carrying a woman's laundry basket. In it was a beautiful baby dressed in green like the covers of Klein's books. The baby was also damaged by a fish-hook. This represented the patient's envious destruction of Klein and her work, just as he wanted to deprive his mother of her babies, so little could he bear his envy of the fact that she, unlike him, could have babies. Next he dreamed of Klein as an old, tired, and very worn-out looking pike, destroyed as it were by his previous dream's envy.

Envy of woman as mother, Klein suggested, was the source of his homosexuality – a perspective quite different from that of Freud, who attributed this sexual preference to avoidance of confrontation with woman's phallic lack and its implication that the father could likewise, as it were, deprive the boy of his penis, in which Freud claimed so much of male individuality is invested.

Defences against envy, Klein went on, include self-devaluation. But this breeds yet more envy. Or we try to suppress envy by instead eliciting it in others only to feel persecuted by them. At other times envy is warded off through indifference or withdrawal from others – a character trait likewise described by Horney. The only effective means of countering envy, Klein claimed, is through acknowledging and making good its damaging effects, thereby increasing our capacity to enjoy relations with others, both past and present, as no longer hopelessly spoilt but restored as whole and good.

Klein returned to this theme both in a December 1958 talk emphasizing the paradox that envy involves attacking what is loved, and in perhaps her most accessible account of her work – a May 1959 talk to Manchester sociologists about ways in which adulthood revives early wishes greedily to empty the mother of everything good and enviously to spoil everything inside her.[3] Such feelings, she pointed out, readily obstruct our capacity to enjoy the creativity and achievements of our peers and those younger than ourselves – an incapacity Klein herself evinced in wanting to better others, including Helene Deutsch.

Many today adopt her account of envy, among them Carolyn Steedman. She describes the envy bred by the reality of working-class poverty and its embittering effect on mother–daughter relations, and the way this is exacerbated by the internal processes of envy described by Klein. Feminist therapist Marie Maguire suggests that envy informs these relations irrespective of class. Daughters, she suggests, often fear acknowledging their difference from the mother because of the sense of emptiness and consequent envy it arouses in themselves or her. Similarly, US poet and counsellor Kim Chernin understands women's eating disorders as an attempt to both punish and atone to the mother for enviously draining her in feeding from her in the process of growing up – a fantasy made all the more real by the actual depletion of women in mothering given its social devaluation.

Others, however, balk, as did many of Klein's colleagues, at such stress on envy and the death instinct. Winnicott was appalled by her 1955 paper. If envy as described by Klein occurs in infancy, he protested, it is the mother's not the baby's doing – an effect of her tantalizing the child. Heimann likewise rejected Klein's account of envy.

Klein now asked Heimann to withdraw from the Melanie Klein Trust, established in 1955 to perpetuate her work. She likewise dropped others who disagreed with her – among them former analysands Rickman and Scott. No wonder she was regarded as a powerful figure. Some deplored her 'adamantine dogmatism', and 'overweening self-righteousness'.[4] Others idealized her as 'the most impressive human being I have known'.[5] Often they were surprised that she was not as physically big as the force of her personality led them to expect.

The result, either way, was considerable loneliness. Although she went abroad with her grandson, who later, like Helene Deutsch's son, became an atomic scientist, her last holidays were spent alone in Norway and Switzerland. Loneliness was the subject of her last 1959 Copenhagen Congress paper,[6] in which she dwelt on longing for understanding by the mother all too often spoilt by envy and distrust.

An example was a man whose loneliness was linked to a dream of a girl playing with a lioness, representing Klein and her cat. The dream girl enticed the lioness to jump through a hoop to its death down a precipice the other side. In his dream Klein's patient thereby sought to destroy Klein as in the past he had sought to destroy his mother, so little could he bear wanting to have what she had – femininity. But in enviously seeking to destroy her he lost the sense of good mothering that could enrich and fill his otherwise empty and forlorn inner world.

Klein herself was not entirely lonely. Far from it. She continued working to the end. She had stopped analysing children in the late 1940s, but was still analysing trainees – Hyatt Williams, Clare Winnicott, and Donald Meltzer. And she also continued supervising students' child analytic work. Nor was it all seriousness. Colleagues recall her chuckling infectiously even at scientific meetings.[7] 'She was like a jolly, nice granny,' Anna Freudian analyst Ilse Hellman recalls, albeit she also felt she was a 'poor old lady' in being so bereft of her daughter and also of one of her sons.[8] Neither was mothering all. She entertained, went to parties, music, and theatre.

This was the subject of her last writing – a piece about Aeschylus's *Oresteia* in which Klein returned to her very earliest insights about the infant's envy and consequent dread of the mother, this time as personified in Electra's sense of deprivation by her mother whom she hates, and in the Furies urging vengeance on Orestes' matricide.[9]

In a sense the paper marks the distance Klein had taken psychoanalysis from its beginnings in Freud's father-centred account of Sophocles' *Oedipus Rex*, now interpreted in terms of maternal envy by today's Kleinians.[10] That summer she was taken ill in Switzerland, from where she was shipped home by her former analysand Esther Bick. In hospital she was operated on for cancer, worked with Elliott Jaques on the proofs of Richard's case history, and broke her hip falling out of bed as a result of the same obstinacy that had secured the survival of her pioneering ideas against Freudian orthodoxy. She died on 22 September 1960. Her renowned pianist friend Rosalyn Tureck played Bach at her funeral. The same day her daughter, to whom she had left her jewellery, gave a lecture in London wearing red boots.

It was precisely because Klein refused to turn her back on such antagonism, as well as love, in mother–child relations that she took psychoanalysis so far from its previous patriarchal, individualistic focus. In the process, as shown above, she enormously extended the scope of Freud's theory and therapy to include analytic understanding and treatment not only of neurosis but also of depressive and schizoid states of mind in children and adults. She thereby drew attention to the place in culture generally of early mothering and the splitting, envy, loss, depression, and reparation therein involved.

VI

CONCLUSION
Forgetting the father?

Women analysts' use of their own and their patients' mothering experience has indeed advanced psychoanalysis a long way from its patriarchal beginnings. Helene Deutsch, as we have seen, used this experience to pioneer the first extensive psychoanalytic account of women's psychology and current psychoanalytic interest in narcissism in men as well as women. Karen Horney used it to indicate the envy of women's mothering that Freud had so singularly neglected, while also beginning psychoanalytic interest in the effects of sexual inequality and abuse on gender development and character analysis. Anna Freud likewise used the maternal experience of her sex, even though she turned her back both on it and on feminism,[1] to develop child analysis, ego psychology, and the applications of psychoanalysis to developmental psychology, paediatrics, the law and social welfare. Lastly Melanie Klein drew on her mothering immensely to forward child and adult psychoanalytic treatment of schizoid splitting and depression.

In the process all four women attended much more than Freud to the influence of interpersonal factors, specifically mothering, in shaping human psychology: Deutsch to the influence of identification with others; Horney to the influence of sex discrimination and social factors generally; Anna Freud to the ill effects of maternal separation and loss; and Klein to the formation of the psyche through internalization and projection of our relations with others. This interpersonal focus has in turn been built on by today's psychoanalysts both in England and the USA.

To very varying degrees all four women also indicated, unlike Freud, the place of identification with the mother in psychological development. None more so than Klein. Deutsch, Horney, and Anna Freud assumed that such identification simply mirrors the mother's behaviour – whether hated as in the case of Deutsch's own mother, panicked or self-assured in face of bombing in the case of Anna's war nursery children, or as given by biology as Horney assumed. By contrast Klein viewed mother–child identification as characterized first and foremost by the child's prior impulses of love and hate whatever the mother's actual behaviour.

In this Klein arguably attended to inner factors to the neglect of the external factors that Deutsch, Horney, and Anna Freud addressed somewhat to the neglect of inner fantasy. Subsequent analysts, influenced by these women's work, have sought to right this balance, in particular paediatrician and analyst Donald Winnicott, whose work in a sense marks the apotheosis of mothering psychoanalysis. He argued, as already shown, that just as the infant identifies with the mother, so too does the mother identify with her child. This, he said, is ensured by the 'primary maternal preoccupation' he believed to be brought about by pregnancy. Such identification is essential, he claims, if the 'good enough' mother is to anticipate and meet the baby's needs as they arise. She thereby brings external and internal reality into accord with each other without reducing one to the other. Instead each is enriched – the child's inner world by details of outer reality, while its perception of the latter is enlivened by inner fantasy and imagination.

But mother–child identification, thus described by Winnicott, raises a major problem already latent in the work of Deutsch, Horney, Anna Freud and Klein. A central issue in Freud's theory and therapy concerns the adaptation, without undue repression, of individual instinct and desire to social and patriarchal pressure. By contrast, a more central issue for mothering psychoanalysis concerns the individuation of self from other, in the first place from the mother.

In a sense this posed no problem for Deutsch, Horney, Anna Freud and Klein. In so far as they followed Freud, both Deutsch and Anna believed individuality to be assured, at least in nascent form, by instincts operating prior to any relations of identification with mother or others. Similarly, although Horney eventually rejected Freud's instinct theory, she too believed individuality to be innate however warped it might subsequently become as a result of social and parental selfishness and abuse. Klein likewise assumed innate awareness of self distinct from other. How else could the baby incorporate and expel, internalize and project experience inside and outside itself as she believed to happen from the very beginning of life?

'Separation/individuation' of infant from mother, as US analyst Margaret Mahler terms it, poses much more of a problem to these women analysts' successors to the extent that they believe the baby to be initially psychologically, as well as biologically, fused with the mother. Deutsch, Horney, Anna Freud and Klein implied that such fusion and identification is a later development and that the infant separates from psychic identity with the mother – particularly to the extent that this fusion is hated and feared – through flight to the father.

By contrast Mahler and Winnicott attribute such separation to the work of mother and child alone. Mahler assumes an inherent tendency towards independence in the child that depends for its coming into being on the mother's affirmation and approval.[2] Winnicott argues that psychic separation of infant from mother results from the latter gradually failing absolutely to meet the baby's needs as they arise. She thereby 'disillusions' the baby of the omnipotent fantasy of having the whole world – represented by her – at its beck and call. This also involves exploding the infant's illusion of oneness with the mother and its surroundings generally. To tide it over such dawning separation, Winnicott adds, the toddler often infuses an external 'transitional' object – a much thumbed and handled piece of cloth or blanket, say – with its internal sense of being one with the mother. Such things are therefore particularly important to the child when separated from the mother as at bedtime.

Winnicott likened analysis to early mothering. Drawing on the discoveries of Klein and others regarding the importance of mothering to psychological development, and quite unlike Freud, he and many other analysts today almost wallow in being experienced in maternal terms by their patients. Winnicott himself viewed the analyst's task as akin to that of the good enough mother – as one of both anticipating and meeting individual need, thus fuelling the analysand's illusion that the analyst's interpretation, like the mother's care, were self-created, and then gradually facilitating awareness of separation through gradual failure of adaptation. The analytic session thereby serves as an object transitional between subjective fantasy and objective reality, between sameness and difference as first experienced, according to Winnicott, in early mothering. No wonder he has been regarded as the quintessential matriarch – 'Madonna' even[3] – of modern analysis.

This epithet is all the more apposite since – despite qualifying mothering and its analytic counterpart as only needing to be 'good enough', and quite contrary to psychoanalysis's founding mothers – Winnicott idealized mothering as though it alone brings about the infant's psychological birth as separate and distinct from the mother and others. He thereby completely ignored the place of the father as documented not only by Freud – in the case of Little Hans, for instance – but also to varying degrees by Deutsch, Horney, Anna Freud, and Klein.

Such valorization of women's mothering, as indicated at the beginning of this book, has not surprisingly been much welcomed by many feminists and feminist therapists as an antidote to Freud's father-centredness that seemingly both reflects and reinforces the patriarchalism and sexism of society generally. It also speaks to the omnipotent illusion of oceanic oneness with the mother which, as Freud himself pointed out, we often conjure up as source of hallucinatory gratification in times of stress. Deutsch likewise drew attention to the seductiveness of the parthenogenetic fantasy of recreating ourselves free of dependence on others outside ourselves. And Klein and her daughter also drew attention to anxiety-motivated flight to an idealized image of mothering – such retreat to mother nature, according to Christopher Lasch, also informs the more illusory appeal of today's Green Movement.

But as well as fuelling a sense of omnipotence, the illusion of oneness with the mother can also involve a paralysing sense of ineffectiveness. As Deutsch and Anna Freud observed on the basis of their own experience, return to early childhood illusion of psychological fusion with the mother can undermine all positive sense of self. Because of their shared sex with the mother, some have argued, women are particularly liable to feel constrained and inhibited in their individuality by continuing sense of being enmeshed with the mother, and the mother's image of them, whether hated or loved.[4]

An extreme example perhaps was Susan – a patient of British psychoanalyst Marion Milner. Susan's mother gave her to believe that they were everything to each other – that Susan was the moon of her delight, indeed the whole world. She dismissed Susan's father as merely the lodger, as though he had had no part in her conception either physical or psychological. It was as though Susan was entirely self-created out of an all-encompassing, mother–child matrix. Hence, hypothesizes Milner, her acquiescence in an elderly neighbour's repeated exhibitionism. At least the sight of his penis reassured her that some potency, represented by the phallus, lay outside her and her mother's otherwise all-inclusive terrifying and guilt-inducing power.

However frightening or gratifying the illusion of mother–child self-sufficiency, it is, in a sense, fostered by Klein's work in so far as – starting with her analysis of her son Erich – she increasingly tended to ignore the place of the father in biological and psychological generation, as though the mother and, by identification, the child, in fact as well as fantasy, contained everything the latter desires – milk, faeces, and penis too. But this illusion is even more fostered, despite the long voiced reservations of Anna Freud, by the developments in psychoanalysis to which Klein's work as well as that of Deutsch and Horney gave rise. Specifically it is fostered to the extent that modern psychoanalysis allies the analyst–analysand dyad to that of mother and infant at the expense of neglecting both relationships' wider social and patriarchal determinants.

Such neglect is not surprising given the apparent immunity of both from social and patriarchal influence, neither being much in evidence in consulting room or nursery. Indeed, fathers are often absent from the latter through work or parental separation and divorce, as in the Horney and Klein households. Observation of babies in their own homes – now a standard part of analytic training introduced by Klein's analysand Esther Bick – is accordingly in effect mother–infant observation. This in turn directs trainees' clinical practice and attention towards a maternal focus, thus increasing the concentration of psychoanalysis on pre-symbolic and pre-verbal maternal transference and countertransference sometimes to the neglect of the 'talking cure' aspects of psychoanalytic therapy emphasized by Freud.

Patients' psychological ills thereby often come to be attributed to defects of early mothering, as reflected in the therapy relationship even in cases of obvious patriarchal, social, and sexual abuse. Yet despite the physical absence of the father and wider society from early mothering, both decidedly determine our psychological being both for good and ill. Indeed, as indicated in preceding chapters, patriarchal factors determined the vehemence or otherwise with which Horney and Klein, and Deutsch and Anna Freud, used their mothering experience to take issue with Freud's work. These factors also affected the reception of their work by their psychoanalytic colleagues to the extent that Horney was thrown out of orthodox psychoanalysis and Klein very nearly suffered the same fate.

The influence of the father in his absence also clearly shaped each woman's attitude to the others. Just as she idolized her father as a child, so too Deutsch idolized Freud and was extremely respectful of his daughter. Into old age she reserved only for special occasions a cardigan Anna had knitted her. And she even refused to help her own biographer when his work upset Anna.

By contrast, Horney, true to her childhood experience of siding with her mother against her father, was contemptuous of such adulation, particularly of Deutsch's seeming reiteration of Freud's account of female masochism. On the other hand she felt considerable solidarity with Klein, particularly in 1920s

Berlin when both used their maternal experience to draw attention to the envy of mothering so ignored by Freud.

Meanwhile his daughter Anna, who had always been rivalrous for his affection with her older sister Sophie, felt similarly rivalrous with Helene Deutsch, especially when they were both in analysis with Freud. More notoriously, Anna could never stomach Klein's appropriation of her father's work. Ironically, Klein likewise suffered similar childhood longing to be as much loved by her father as her older sister Emilie, and into old age was determined to better Deutsch and Anna Freud as Freud's most worthy successor.

Yet their legacy's subsequent development ignores such patriarchal influences and the very sexual inequality and difference – specifically the social equation of women with mothering – that so crucially shaped all four women's pioneering development of psychoanalysis. Irrespective of their sex, US psychoanalysts today often experience themselves in essentially maternal terms and attend to self-psychology and narcissistic personality disorders to the neglect of issues raised by the sex of analyst and analysand, as though sexual identity had nothing to do with self and narcissistic integrity. Similarly with modern British psychoanalysis; not for nothing its sex-neutral characterization as 'object relations theory'.

Little surprise, therefore, that feminists such as Juliet Mitchell, concerned to draw attention to – in order to undo – the social and psychological ill-effects of sexism and patriarchy have urged a 'return' to Freud in the manner indicated by French psychoanalyst Jacques Lacan. Specifically they urge a return to Freud's theoretical and clinical attention to the way conscious and unconscious mental life is shaped by patriarchal authority and sexual difference through the Oedipus and castration complex.

This is where we came in. But we have to go beyond this return. Lacanian feminism's account of patriarchy remains entirely formal and devoid of detailed historical, social, or clinical specificity. Both as theory and therapy it fails to indicate how such details shape and are shaped by individual consciousness in the ways described by Deutsch and Horney –

particularly in their accounts of women's psychology – and by Anna Freud and Klein in their analysis of adults' and children's reactions to war and peace.

Furthermore, although Freud rightly attended to the patriarchal determinants of human psychology, he failed to attend to its maternal and interpersonal determinants so well addressed therapeutically by Deutsch, Horney, Anna Freud and Klein. Their more even-handed attention to the influence of both maternal and patriarchal factors is therefore a better starting point for going beyond Freud's work and current psychoanalysis – and their single-minded focus either on patriarchy or mothering – towards a practice more attuned to the variety of factors that have to be addressed and overcome in order to secure a world that more nearly meets our needs, both inner and outer. Above all, their lives and work illustrate the intriguing but unnerving intersection of historical process and change with theory, therapy and individual biography.

Notes

PART I: INTRODUCTION

1. For further elaboration of the fundamental concepts of psychoanalysis see the extremely useful dictionary of J. Laplanche and J. B. Pontalis, *The Language of Psycho-Analysis*, London, Hogarth, 1973.
2. S. Freud, letter of 15 October 1897, *Standard Edition of the Complete Psychological Works of Sigmund Freud*, Vol. 1, London, Hogarth, 1966, p. 265.
3. S. Freud, letter of 31 May 1897, ibid., p. 254.
4. S. Freud, 'Analysis of a phobia in a five-year-old boy' (1909), ibid., Vol. 10, pp. 7–8.
5. S. Freud, 'The psychogenesis of a case of homosexuality in a woman' (1920), ibid., Vol. 18, p. 169.
6. S. Freud, 'Some psychical consequences of the anatomical distinction between the sexes' (1925), ibid., Vol. 19, p. 258.
7. Diary entry for 9 March 1933 in HD, *Tribute to Freud*, Manchester, Carcanet, 1985.
8. W. R. Bion, *The Long Week-End*, London, Free Association Books, 1982, pp. 9, 12.
9. E. Showalter, *The Female Malady*, London, Virago, 1987, pp. 249–50.

PART II: HELENE DEUTSCH
Chapter 1: Socialist rebel

1. S. Gordon, 'Helene Deutsch and the legacy of Freud', *New York Times Magazine*, 30 July 1978, p. 23.

2. H. Deutsch, *Confrontations with Myself*, New York, Norton, 1973, p. 62.
3. ibid., p. 54.
4. H. Deutsch, 'On the pathological lie' (1921), *Journal of the American Academy of Psychoanalysis*, 10 (1982), pp. 369–86.
5. H. Deutsch, *Confrontations with Myself*, p. 44.
6. ibid., p. 65.
7. ibid., p. 85.
8. S. Gordon, op. cit., p. 23.
9. H. Deutsch, *Confrontations with Myself*, p. 99.
10. ibid., p. 104.

Chapter 2: Madness and mothering

1. P. Roazen, *Helene Deutsch*, New York, Meridian, 1985, p. 124.
2. H. Deutsch, *Confrontations with Myself*, New York, Norton, 1973, p. 114.
3. H. Deutsch, 'Two cases of induced insanity' (1918), *International Journal of Psycho-Analysis*, 62 (1981), pp. 145–50.
4. H. Deutsch, 'A case that throws light on the mechanism of regression in schizophrenia' (1919), *Psychoanalytic Review*, 72(1) (1985), pp. 1–8.
5. For a recent critique of Chodorow on this point see C. Steedman, *Landscape for a Good Woman*, London, Virago, 1986.
6. H. Deutsch, *The Psychology of Women, Vol. 2: Motherhood*, New York, Grune & Stratton, 1945, pp. 146, 147.
7. A. Roiphe, 'What women psychoanalysts say about women's liberation', *New York Times Magazine*, 13 February 1972, pp. 12–13, 63–6, 68, 70.
8. H. Deutsch, 'A two-year-old boy's first love comes to grief' (1919), *Neuroses and Character Types*, New York, International Universities Press, 1965.
9. H. Deutsch, 'On the psychology of suspicion', *International Journal of Psycho-Analysis*, 1 (1920), p. 135.
10. P. Roazen, *Helene Deutsch*, p. 178.

11. H. Deutsch, 'On the pathological lie' (1921), *Journal of the American Academy of Psychoanalysis*, 10 (1982), pp. 369–86.
12. H. Deutsch, short communication, *International Journal of Psycho-Analysis*, 3 (1921), p. 135.
13. A. Kardiner, quoted by P. Roazen, *Helene Deutsch*, p. 246.
14. H. Deutsch, *Confrontations with Myself*, p. 142.
15. M. Grotjahn, 'Gleanings from Grotjahn', *Bulletin of the Southern Californian Psychoanalytic Institute and Society* (Winter 1986), p. 40.
16. H. Deutsch, *Confrontations with Myself*, p. 141.

Chapter 3: Female sexuality

1. H. Deutsch, 'A contribution to the psychology of sport' (1923), *International Journal of Psycho-Analysis*, 7 (1926), pp. 223–7.
2. H. Deutsch, 'The psychology of women in relation to the functions of reproduction' (1924), in R. Fliess, *The Psychoanalytic Reader*, London, Hogarth, 1950.
3. H. Deutsch, *Confrontations with Myself*, New York, Norton, 1973, p. 148.
4. See e.g. A. Rich, *Of Woman Born*, New York, Bantam, 1976; A. Oakley, *Women Confined*, Oxford, Martin Robertson, 1980.
5. H. Deutsch, 'The psychology of women', in R. Fliess, *The Psychoanalytic Reader*, p. 172.
6. K. Horney, 'Review of Deutsch 1925', *International Journal of Psycho-Analysis*, 7 (1926), pp. 92–100.
7. H. Deutsch, 'On satisfaction, happiness and ecstasy', *International Journal of Psycho-Analysis*, 70 (1927), pp. 715–23.
8. H. Deutsch, *Confrontations with Myself*, p. 136.
9. P. Meisel and W. Kendrick, *Bloomsbury/Freud: The Letters of James and Alix Strachey 1924–1925*, London, Chatto & Windus, 1986, p. 87.
10. H. Deutsch, 'The menopause' (1925), *International Journal of Psycho-Analysis*, 65 (1984), pp. 56–62.
11. S. Freud, *New Introductory Lectures on Psycho-Analysis* (1933), *Standard Edition of the Complete Psychological Works of Sigmund Freud*, Vol. 22, London, Hogarth, 1966, pp. 134–5.

12. H. Deutsch, 'George Sand: A woman's destiny?' (1928), *International Review of Psycho-Analysis*, 9 (1982), pp. 445–60. For a recent feminist argument along similar lines see e.g. A. Berger, 'Let's go to the fountain: on George Sand and writing', in S. Sellers, *Writing Differences*, Milton Keynes, Open University Press, 1988.
13. H. Deutsch, 'On the genesis of the "family" romance' (1928), *Internationale Zeitschrift für Psychoanalyse*, 16, pp. 249–53.
14. H. Deutsch, 'The significance of masochism in the mental life of women' (1930), in R. Fliess, *The Psychoanalytic Reader*, p. 199.
15. ibid., p. 201.
16. H. Deutsch, 'Motherhood and sexuality' (1933), *Neuroses and Character Types*, New York, International Universities Press, 1965.
17. J. Simpson, 'A woman envoy from Freud', *New York Herald Tribune*, 3 August 1930, pp. 9, 20–21.

Chapter. 4: Mothering and neurosis

1. H. Deutsch, *Psychoanalysis of the Neuroses* (1930), in *Neuroses and Character Types*, New York, International Universities Press, 1965, pp. 16–17.
2. ibid., p. 19.
3. ibid., p. 23.
4. H. Deutsch, 'Psychoanalytic therapy in the light of follow-up' (1959) in *Neuroses and Character Types*, pp. 347, 349.
5. G. Rochlin, 'Tribute to Helene Deutsch', *American Imago*, 40 (1) (1983), p. 18.
6. H. Deutsch, *Neuroses and Character Types*, p. 108.
7. ibid., p. 112.
8. ibid., p. 149.

Chapter 5: Lesbianism, loss, and 'as if' identity

1. H. Deutsch, 'Homosexuality in Women' (1932), in *Neuroses and Character Types*, New York, International Universities Press, 1965, p. 179.

2. H. Deutsch, 'The psychology of manic-depressive states' (1933), in ibid., p. 216.
3. H. Deutsch, 'The psychological type: "as if"', reprinted as 'Some forms of emotional disturbance and their relationship to schizophrenia' (1934), in ibid., p. 267.
4. ibid., p. 279.
5. ibid.
6. Martin Deutsch interview.
7. H. Deutsch, 'Don Quixote and Quixotism' (1934), in *Neuroses and Character Types*.
8. Martin Deutsch interview.
9. H. Deutsch, 'Control analysis', *Contemporary Psychoanalysis*, 19 (1935), pp. 59–67.
10. Quoted by B. Bandler, 'Tribute to Helene Deutsch', *American Imago*, 40(1) (1983), p. 12.
11. Quoted in P. Roazen, 'Obituary: Helene Deutsch', *International Journal of Psycho-Analysis*, 63 (1982), pp. 491–2.
12. Quoted in P. Roazen, *Helene Deutsch*, New York, Meridian, 1985, p. 284.
13. H. Deutsch, 'Absence of grief' (1937), in *Neuroses and Character Types*.
14. H. Deutsch, 'A discussion of certain forms of resistance' (1939), in ibid.
15. H. Deutsch, 'Freud and his pupils', *Psychoanalytic Quarterly*, 9 (1940), pp. 184–94.
16. H. Deutsch, letter of 16 August 1948 to Betty Cobb, Helene Deutsch Archive, Schlesinger Library, Radcliffe College, Cambridge, Mass.
17. Quoted in P. Roazen, *Helene Deutsch*, p. 298.
18. In e.g. R. M. Kaufman and M. Heiman, *Evolution of Psychosomatic Concepts*, London, Hogarth, 1965.
19. H. Deutsch, 'Anorexia nervosa' (1941), *Bulletin of the Menninger Clinic*, 45 (1981), pp. 499–511.
20. H. Deutsch, 'Some psychoanalytic observations on surgery' (1942), in *Neuroses and Character Types*, p. 294.
21. Quoted in P. Roazen, *Helene Deutsch*, p. 298.
22. H. Deutsch, *Confrontations with Myself*, New York, Norton, 1973, p. 69.

23. Quoted in P. Roazen, *Helene Deutsch*, p. 303.

Chapter 6: Women's psychology – youth

1. Quoted in P. Roazen, *Helene Deutsch*, p. 294.
2. H. Deutsch, *The Psychology of Women, Vol. 1: Girlhood*, New York, Grune & Stratton, 1944, p. 233.
3. ibid., p. 275.

Chapter 7: Women's psychology – motherhood

1. H. Deutsch, 'Occult processes occurring during psychoanalysis' (1926), in G. Devereux, *Psychoanalysis and the Occult*, New York, International Universities Press, 1953.
2. H. Deutsch, *The Psychology of Women, Vol. 2: Motherhood*, New York, Grune & Stratton, 1945, p. 320.
3. ibid., p. 377.
4. See e.g. S. de Beauvoir, *The Second Sex* (1949), Harmondsworth, Penguin, 1972; G. Greer, *The Female Eunuch*, London, McGibbon & Kee, 1970; K. Millett, *Sexual Politics*, New York, Avon Books, 1970.
5. M. Brierley, 'Critical review (of Deutsch 1944–45)', *International Journal of Psycho-Analysis* (1948), pp. 251–4.

Chapter 8: Narcissism – male and maternal

1. H. Deutsch, 'The pyschiatric component in gynecology' (1950); 'Psychoanalytic therapy in the light of follow-up' (1959); 'Frigidity in women' (1960); 'Acting out in the transference' (1963), in *Neuroses and Character Types*, New York, International Universities Press, 1965.
2. H. Deutsch, 'The impostor' (1955), ibid.
3. H. Deutsch, '*Lord Jim* and depression' (1959), ibid.
4. J. Conrad, *Lord Jim* (1900), Harmondsworth, Penguin, 1949, p. 148.
5. H. Deutsch, 'Some clinical considerations of the ego ideal' (1964), *Journal of the American Psychoanalytic Association*, 12 (3), pp. 512–16.
6. H. Deutsch, 'Posttraumatic amnesias and their adaptive function'

(1966), in R. M. Lewenstein, *Psychoanalysis*, New York, International Universities Press, 1966.

7. H. Deutsch, *Selected Problems of Adolescence*, New York, International Universities Press, 1967.
8. H. Deutsch, *A Psychoanalytic Study of the Myth of Dionysus and Apollo*, New York, International Universities Press, 1969.
9. S. Freud, 'Some psychical consequences of the anatomical distinction between the sexes' (1925), *Standard Edition of the Complete Psychological Works of Sigmund Freud*, Vol. 19, London, Hogarth, 1966, p. 257.
10. S. Freud, 'Why war?' (1933), ibid., Vol. 22.
11. H. Deutsch, 'A note on Rosa Luxemburg and Angelika Balabanoff', *American Imago*, 40 (1) (1970), pp. 29–33.
12. A Roiphe, 'What women psychoanalysts say about women's liberation', *New York Times Magazine*, 13 February 1972, p. 65.
13. P. Roazen, 'Helene Deutsch, M.D.' in L. Dickstein and C. Nadelson, *Women Physicians in Leadership Roles*, Washington DC, American Psychiatric Press, 1986, p. 58.
14. H. Deutsch, *Confrontations with Myself*, New York, Norton, 1973, p. 131.
15. Gifford interview.

PART III: KAREN HORNEY
Chapter 1: Adored mother

1. K. Horney, *The Adolescent Diaries of Karen Horney*, 1980, pp. 28, 42.
2. ibid., p. 36.
3. ibid., p. 71.
4. ibid., pp. 171–2, 180.
5. ibid., p. 185.
6. S. Quinn, *A Mind of Her Own: The Life of Karen Horney*, New York, Summit Books, 1987, p. 125.
7. In 1917 Deutsch published an article on the neurological ill-effects of coal-dust on miners' brains. See P. Roazen, *Helene Deutsch*, New York, Meridian, 1985, p. 130.

8. K. Horney, *Adolescent Diaries*, p. 238.
9. ibid., p. 251.
10. ibid., pp. 260, 262.
11. ibid., p. 268.
12. T. Maeder, *Children of Psychiatrists and Other Psychotherapists*, New York, Harper & Row, 1989, p. 216.

Chapter 2: Innate femininity

1. K. Abraham, 'Manifestations of the female castration complex' (1920), in *Selected Papers*, London, Hogarth, 1968, p. 340.
2. Eckardt, in E. H. Baruch and L. J. Serrano, *Women Analyze Women*, in New York, New York University Press, 1988.
3. K. Horney, 'On the genesis of the castration complex in women' (1922), in *Feminine Psychology*, New York, Norton, 1967, p. 38.
4. ibid., p. 43.
5. J. L. Rubins, *Karen Horney*, London, Weidenfeld & Nicolson, 1987, p. 73.
6. K. Horney, 'Review of Deutsch' (1926), *International Journal of Psycho-Analysis*, 7 (1926), pp. 92–100.
7. K. Horney, 'The flight from womanhood' (1926), in *Feminine Psychology*, pp. 60, 68.
8. ibid., p. 65.
9. K. Horney, 'Inhibited femininity' (1926), in *Feminine Psychology*.
10. K. Horney, 'Discussion of lay analysis', *International Journal of Psycho-Analysis*, 8 (1927), pp. 255–9.
11. K. Horney, 'The problem of the monogamous ideal' (1927), in *Feminine Psychology*.
12. K. Horney, 'The distrust between the sexes' (1930), in *Feminine Psychology*.
13. K. Horney, 'Premenstrual tension' (1931), in *Feminine Psychology*, p. 106.
14. K. Horney, 'The denial of the vagina' (1932), in *Feminine Psychology*, pp. 154, 155.
15. For a recent feminist version of this argument see e.g. H. G. Lerner, *Women in Therapy*, Northvale NJ, Jason Aronson, 1988.

16. K. Horney, 'Problems of marriage' (1932), *Feminine Psychology*, p. 129.

Chapter 3: Womb envy

1. Quoted in S. Quinn, *A Life of Her Own: The Life of Karen Horney*, New York, Summit Books, 1987, p. 216.
2. K. Horney, 'The flight from womanhood' (1926), *Feminine Psychology*, New York, Norton, 1967, pp. 60–61.
3. K. Horney, 'The distrust between the sexes' (1930), *Feminine Psychology*, p. 114.
4. S. Freud, 'Female sexuality' (1931), *Standard Edition of the Complete Psychological Works of Sigmund Freud*, Vol. 21, London, Hogarth, 1966, p. 230.
5. e.g. H. R. Hays, *The Dangerous Sex*, New York, Putnams, 1964.
6. K. Horney, 'Problems of marriage' (1932), *Feminine Psychology*, p. 127.
7. K. Horney, 'The dread of woman' (1932), ibid., p. 137.
8. ibid., p. 142.
9. ibid., pp. 143–4.
10. M. Grotjahn in J. L. Rubins, *Karen Horney*, London, Weidenfeld & Nicolson, 1987, p. 138.

Chapter 4: Transition

1. K. Horney, *New Ways in Psychoanalysis*, New York, Norton, 1939, pp. 12–13.
2. K. Horney, 'Culture and aggression' (1931), *American Journal of Psychoanalysis*, 20 (1960), pp. 130–38.
3. K. Horney, 'On Rank's *Modern Education*', *Psychoanalytic Quarterly*, 1 (1932), pp. 349–50.
4. K. Horney, 'Psychogenic factors in functional female disorders' (1933), *Feminine Psychology*, New York, Norton, 1967, p. 169.
5. K. Horney, 'Maternal conflicts' (1934), *Feminine Psychology*.
6. K. Horney, 'The overvaluation of love' (1935), *Feminine Psychology*, p. 199. Horney's account of women's overvaluation of love has recently been taken up in a feminist context by M. Westkott, *The Feminist Legacy of Karen Horney*, New Haven, Yale University Press, 1986.

7. K. Horney, 'Personality changes in female adolescents' (1935), *Feminine Psychology*.
8. Quoted in S. Quinn, *A Life of Her Own: The Life of Karen Horney*, New York, Summit Books, 1987, p. 268.
9. K. Horney, 'The problem of feminine masochism' (1935), *Feminine Psychology*.
10. F. Alexander, *The Western Mind in Transition*, New York, Random House, 1960, p. 109.
11. K. Horney, 'Conceptions and misconceptions of the analytic method', *Journal of Nervous and Mental Diseases*, 81 (1935), pp. 399–410, 404.
12. K. Horney, 'Certain reservations on the concept of psychic bisexuality', *International Journal of Psycho-Analysis*, 16 (1935), pp. 510–11.
13. Katie Kelman, quoted by S. Quinn, op. cit., p. 285.

Chapter 5: Maternal culturalism

1. K. Horney, 'Restricted applications of psychoanalysis to social work', *The Family*, 15 (1934), pp. 169–73.
2. K. Horney, 'Maternal conflicts' (1934), *Feminine Psychology*, New York, Norton, 1967.
3. K. Horney, 'The problem of the negative therapeutic reaction', *Psychoanalytic Quarterly*, 5 (1936), pp. 29–44.
4. K. Horney, 'The neurotic need for love' (1937), *Feminine Psychology*, p. 254.
5. K. Horney, *The Neurotic Personality of Our Time*, New York, Norton, 1937, pp. 96–9.
6. ibid., p. 133.
7. ibid., p. 164.
8. ibid., p. 218.
9. ibid., p. 248.
10. K. Horney, 'Can you take a stand?', *Journal of Adult Education*, 11 (1939), p. 129, quoted by J. L. Rubins, *Karen Horney*, London, Weidenfeld & Nicolson, 1987, p. 233.
11. See e.g. H. Marcuse, *Eros and Civilization*, Boston, Beacon Press, 1955.

Chapter 6: Psychoanalytic exile

1. K. Horney, *New Ways in Psychoanalysis*, New York, Norton, 1939, pp. 140, 144.
2. ibid., p. 181.
3. Quoted in J. L. Rubins, *Karen Horney*, London, Weidenfeld & Nicolson, 1987, p. 235.
4. Quoted in S. Quinn, *A Mind of Her Own: The Life of Karen Horney*, New York, Summit Books, 1987, p. 335.

Chapter 7: Self-analysis

1. Norman Kelman, quoted by S. Quinn, *A Mind of Her Own: The Life of Karen Horney*, New York, Summit Books, 1987, p. 376.
2. K. Horney, *Self-Analysis*, New York, Norton, 1942, pp. 44, 45, 46.
3. ibid., p. 121.
4. Ingram interview.
5. Quoted in S. Quinn, op.cit., p. 383.

Chapter 8: From mothering to self-realization

1. S. Freud, *Studies on Hysteria* (1895), *Standard Edition of the Complete Psychological Works of Sigmund Freud*, Vol. 2, London, Hogarth, 1966, p. 305.
2. K. Horney, *Neurosis and Human Growth*, New York, 1950, p. 20.
3. ibid., p. 53.
4. ibid., p. 222.
5. ibid., p. 353.
6. See e.g. J. Lacan, *Écrits*, London, Tavistock, 1977.
7. Eckardt in E. H. Baruch and L. J. Serrano, *Women Analyze Women*, New York, New York University Press, 1988, p. 294.

PART IV: ANNA FREUD

Chapter 1: Father's child

1. S. Freud, *The Origins of Psycho-Analysis*, New York, Basic Books, 1954, p. 136.
2. Gardiner in B. Litowitz, *Anna Freud Remembered*, Chicago, Erickson Institute, 1983, p. 5.

3. S. Freud, *The Interpretation of Dreams* (1900), *Standard Edition of the Complete Psychological Works of Sigmund Freud*, Vol. 4, London, Hogarth, 1966, p. 130.
4. S. Freud, letters to Fliess of 23 February 1897 and 3 July 1899.
5. S. Freud, *New Introductory Lectures on Psychoanalysis* (1933), *Standard Edition*, Vol. 22, p. 132.
6. A. Freud, *The Ego and the Mechanisms of Defence (The Writings of Anna Freud, Vol. 2)*, London, Hogarth, 1936, p. 124.
7. S. Freud, 'The theme of the three caskets' (1913), *Standard Edition*, Vol. 12, p. 301.
8. S. Freud, 'The economic problem of masochism' (1924), ibid., Vol. 19, p. 162.
9. A. Freud, 'Beating fantasies and daydreams' (1922), *Introduction to Psychoanalysis (The Writings of Anna Freud, Vol. 1)*, London, Hogarth, 1974, p. 146.
10. Laforgue in H. M. Ruitenbeek, *Freud as We Knew Him*, Detroit, Wayne State University Press, 1973, p. 342.
11. Quoted in E. Young-Bruehl, *Anna Freud*, New York, Summit Books, 1988, p. 30.
12. A. Freud, 'A hysterical symptom in a child of two years and three months' (1923), *Introduction to Psychoanalysis.*
13. S. Freud, 'Some psychical consequences of the anatomical distinction between the sexes' (1925), *Standard Edition*, Vol. 19.
14. Letter to Lou Andréas-Salomé of 10 May 1925, quoted in P. Gay, *Freud: A Life for Our Time*, New York, Norton, 1988, p. 441.

Chapter 2: Child analysis

1. S. Freud, Introduction to Aichhorn's *Wayward Youth* (1925), *Standard Edition of the Complete Psychological Works of Sigmund Freud*, Vol. 19, London, Hogarth, 1966, p. 273.
2. Quoted in E. Young-Bruehl, *Anna Freud*, New York, Summit Books, 1988, p. 133.
3. A. Freud, *Introduction to the Technique of Child Analysis* (1927), *Introduction to Psychoanalysis (The Writings of Anna Freud, Vol 1)* London, Hogarth, 1974, pp. 8–9.
4. ibid., p. 33.

5. A. Freud, 'Fears, anxieties, and phobic phenomena' (1977), *Psychoanalytic Psychology of Normal Development (The Writings of Anna Freud, Vol. 8)*, London, Hogarth, 1982, p. 193.
6. J. Sandler, H. Kennedy and R. L. Tyson, *The Technique of Child Psychoanalysis: Discussions with Anna Freud*, London, Hogarth, 1980, pp. 126–7.
7. A. Freud, *Introduction to the Technique of Child Analysis*, pp. 37–8.
8. ibid., p. 43.
9. A. Freud, 'The theory of child analysis' (1928), *Introduction to Psychoanalysis*.

Chapter 3: Ego psychology and adolescence

1. Erikson in B. Litowitz, *Anna Freud Remembered*, Chicago, Erickson Institute, 1983. Anna was not the only analyst to do needlework while seeing patients. So too did Princess Marie Bonaparte. Whether seeing patients indoors or out, she lay on a chaise-longue behind their couch and crocheted. See C. Bertin, *Marie Bonaparte*, New York, Harcourt Brace Jovanovich, 1982.
2. A. Freud, 'Four lectures on psychoanalysis for teachers and parents' (1930), *Introduction to Psychoanalysis (The Writings of Anna Freud, Vol. 1)*, London, Hogarth, 1974.
3. U. H. Peters, *Anna Freud*, London, Weidenfeld & Nicolson, 1985, p. 126.
4. e.g. J. Lacan, *Écrits*, London, Tavistock, 1977.
5. A. Freud,*The Ego and the Mechanisms of Defence (The Writings of Anna Freud, Vol. 2)*, London, Hogarth, 1936, p. 73.
6. J. Sandler, *The Mechanisms of Defence*, New York, International Universities Press (with A. Freud), 1985, p. 329.
7. S. Freud, 'The psychogenesis of a case of female homosexuality' (1920), *Standard Edition of the Complete Psychological Works of Sigmund Freud*, Vol. 18, London, Hogarth, 1966, p. 158.
8. J. Sandler, op.cit., p. 389.
9. A. Freud, 'Adolescence' (1958), *Research at the Hampstead Child Therapy Clinic and Other Papers (The Writings of Anna Freud, Vol. 5)*, London, Hogarth, 1969.
10. See e.g. M. Rutter, 'Adolescent turmoil: fact or fiction?', *Journal of Child Psychology and Psychiatry*, 17 (1976), pp. 35–57.

11. See e.g. E. Erikson, *Identity: Youth and Crisis*, New York, Norton, 1968; P. Blos, *On Adolescence*, New York, Free Press, 1962.
12. Quoted in E. Young-Bruehl, *Anna Freud*, New York, Summit Books, p. 202.

Chapter 4: War nurseries

1. Quoted in E. Young-Bruehl, *Anna Freud*, New York, Summit Books, p. 240.
2. A. Freud, *Infants without Families (1944) (The Writings of Anna Freud, Vol. 3)*, London, Hogarth, 1973, p. 278.
3. ibid., p. 415.
4. ibid., pp. 333–4.
5. ibid., p. 178.
6. ibid., pp. 170–71.
7. ibid., p. 280.
8. ibid., p. 66.
9 ibid., p. 20.
10. A. Freud, 'The need of the small child to be mothered' (1941), in *Infants without Families*.
11. A. Freud, *Infants without Families*, p. 442.
12. See e.g. J. Packman, *The Child's Generation: Child Care Policy in Britain*, Oxford, Blackwell, 1981.
13. A. Freud, 'An experiment in group upbringing' (1951), *Indications for Child Analysis and Other Essays (The Writings of Anna Freud, Vol. 4)*, London, Hogarth, 1968.
14. See e.g. A. Freud, 'Notes on aggression' (1949), ibid.
15. A. Freud and D. Burlingham, 'The case for and against residential nurseries' (1944), *Infants without Familes*. For more recent first-hand accounts of wartime evacuation experiences see e.g. B. Wicks, *No Time to Wave Goodbye*, London, Bloomsbury, 1988, and R. Inglis, *The Children's War*, London, Collins, 1989.
16. A. Freud, 'About losing and being lost' (1967), *Indications for Child Analysis*.
17. J. Sandler, H. Kennedy and R. L. Tyson, *The Technique of Child Psychoanalysis: Discussions with Anna Freud*, London, Hogarth, 1980.

Notes to Part IV: Anna Freud

Chapter 5: Paediatrics

1. D. W. Winnicott (1938) quoted in A. Phillips, *Winnicott*, London, Fontana, 1988, p. 48.
2. A. Freud, 'Comments on Joyce Robertson, A mother's observations on the tonsillectomy of her four-year-old daughter' (1956), *Indications for Child Analysis and Other Essays (The Writings of Anna Freud, Vol. 4)*, London, Hogarth, 1968.
3. Quoted in E. Young-Bruehl, *Anna Freud*, New York, Summit Books, p. 284.
4. A. Freud, 'The role of bodily illness in the mental life of children' (1952), *Indications for Child Analysis*.
5. A. Freud, 'The psychoanalytic study of infantile feeding disturbances' (1946), *Indications for Child Analysis*.
6. Unless otherwise indicated, this and other examples in this section come from T. Bergmann, *Children in the Hospital*, New York, International Universities Press, 1965.
7. A. Freud, 'The role of bodily illness' (1952), p. 278 n.
8. A. Freud, 'Answering paediatricians' questions' (1961), *Research at the Hampstead Child Therapy Clinic and Other Papers (The Writings of Anna Freud, Vol. 5)*, London, Hogarth, 1969.
9. A. Freud, Foreword and Conclusion to T. Bergmann, op. cit., in *Research at the Hampstead Clinic*.
10. T. Bergmann, op. cit., p. 96.
11. A. Freud, 'Psychoanalytic knowledge and its application to children's services' (1969), *Research at the Hampstead Clinic*.
12. A. Freud, 'On the interaction between paediatrics and child psychology' (1975), *Psychoanalytic Psychology of Normal Development (The Writings of Anna Freud, Vol. 8)*, London, Hogarth, 1982.

Chapter 6: Developmental assessment

1. A. Freud, Preface to J. Bolland and J. Sandler, *The Hampstead Psychoanalytic Index* (1965), *Research at the Hampstead Child Therapy Clinic and Other Papers (The Writings of Anna Freud, Vol. 5)*, London, Hogarth, 1969, p. 484.
2. A. Freud, 'Research projects of the Hampstead Child Therapy

Clinic' (1969) and 'Services for underprivileged children' (1969), *Research at the Hampstead Clinic.*

3. A. Freud, 'Psychoanalysis and education' (1954), *Indications for Child Analysis and Other Essays (The Writings of Anna Freud, Vol. 4)*, London, Hogarth, 1968, p. 321.
4. e.g. A. Freud, 'The concept of the rejecting mother' (1955), ibid.
5. F. Roustang, *Dire Mastery: Discipleship from Freud to Lacan*, Baltimore, Johns Hopkins University Press, 1982, p. 12.
6. A. Freud, 'The contribution of psychoanalysis to genetic psychology' (1951), *Indications for Child Analysis.*
7. A. Freud, 'Child observation and prediction of development' (1958), *Research at the Hampstead Clinic.*
8. A. Freud, 'Comments on psychic trauma' (1967), ibid.
9. A. Freud, 'The emotional and social development of young children' (1962), ibid.
10. A. Freud, 'Clinical problems of young children' (1962), ibid.
11. Quoted by Piers in B. Litowitz, *Anna Freud Remembered*, Chicago, Erickson Institute, 1983, p. 32.
12. A. Freud, 'Instinctual drives and their bearing on human behaviour' (1953), *Indications for Child Analysis.*
13. A. Freud, 'Freedom from want in early education' (1946), ibid.
14. A. Freud, 'Discussion of John Bowlby' (1960), *Research at the Hampstead Clinic.*
15. See e.g. D. Daws, *Through the Night – Helping Parents and Sleepless Infants*, London, Free Association Books, 1988.
16. A. Freud, 'Problems of infantile neurosis' (1954), *Indications for Child Analysis.*
17. A. Freud, 'A discussion with René Spitz' (1967), *Problems of Psychoanalytic Technique and Therapy (The Writings of Anna Freud, Vol. 7)*, London, Hogarth, 1971, p. 31.
18. A. Freud, 'Psychoanalytic knowledge applied to the rearing of children' (1969), *Research at the Hampstead Clinic*, p. 278.
19. A. Freud, 'The principal task of child analysis' (1978), *Psychoanalytic Psychology of Normal Development (The Writings of Anna Freud, Vol. 8)*, London, Hogarth, 1982, p. 105.
20. A. Freud, 'Diagnosis and assessment of childhood disturbances' (1974), ibid.

21. A. Freud, 'Child observation and prediction of development' (1958), *Research at the Hampstead Clinic.*
22. A. Freud, 'Studies in passivity' (1968), *Indications for Child Analysis.*
23. See e.g. A. Freud, Introduction to K. Levy, 'Simultaneous analysis of a mother and her daughter' (1960), *Research at the Hampstead Clinic*; 'Indications and contraindications for child analysis' (1968), *Problems of Psychoanalytic Technique and Therapy.*
24. A. Freud, 'Problems of infantile neurosis' (1954), *Indications for Child Analysis.*
25. A. Freud, 'Child analysis as a subspecialty of psychoanalysis' (1971), ibid.
26. C. Yorke, 'Anna Freud', BBC Radio 3, 11 February 1987.

Chapter 7: Child custody

1. A. Freud, 'Three contributions to a seminar of family law' (1965), *Research at the Hampstead Child Therapy Clinic and Other Papers (The Writings of Anna Freud, Vol. 5)*, London, Hogarth, 1969.
2. A. Freud, 'Painter v. Bannister' (1971), *Problems of Psychoanalytic Technique and Therapy (The Writings of Anna Freud, Vol. 7)*, London, Hogarth, 1971.
3. A. Freud, J. Goldstein and A. Solnit, *Beyond the Best Interests of the Child*, New York, Macmillan, 1973, p. 6.
4. ibid., p. 53.
5. A. Freud, 'Children possessed' (1975), *Psychoanalytic Psychology of Normal Development (The Writings of Anna Freud, Vol. 8)*, London, Hogarth, 1982.
6. See e.g. M. Rustin, 'Post-Kleinian psychoanalysis and the post-modern', *New Left Review*, 173 (January/February 1989), pp. 102–28. Recent social work critiques include e.g. S. Millham et al., *Lost in Care*, London, 1986.
7. But see A. Freud in M. P. Beezley and H. C. Kempe, *Sexually Abused Children and Their Families*, Oxford, Pergamon, 1981.
8. For current social work discussions of this principle see e.g. A. N. Maluccio, *Permanency Planning for Children*, London, Tavistock, 1986; J. Thoburn, A. Murdoch and A. O'Brien, *Permanence in Child Care*, Oxford, Blackwell, 1986.

Notes to Part IV: Anna Freud

Chapter 8: Against mothering psychoanalysis

1. Quoted in E. Young-Bruehl, *Anna Freud*, New York, Summit Books, 1988, p. 457.
2. A. Freud, 'Studies in passivity', *Indications for Child Analysis and Other Essays (The Writings of Anna Freud, Vol. 4)*, London, Hogarth, 1968.
3. A. Freud, 'The widening scope of indications for psychoanalysis' (1954), ibid.
4. J. Sandler, H. Kennedy and R. L. Tyson, *The Technique of Child Psychoanalysis: Discussions with Anna Freud*, London, Hogarth, 1980, p. 110.
5. A. Freud, 'Problems of technique in adult analysis' (1954), *Indications for Child Analysis*.
6. A. Freud, 'The theory of the parent–infant relationship' (1962), *Research at the Hampstead Child Therapy Clinic (The Writings of Anna Freud, Vol. 5)*, London, Hogarth, 1969.
7. A. Freud, 'Problems of technique in adult analysis', *Indications for Child Analysis*.
8. A. Freud, 'Difficulties in the path of psychoanalysis' (1969), *Problems of Psychoanalytic Technique and Therapy (The Writings of Anna Freud, Vol. 7)*, London, Hogarth, 1971.
9. A. Freud, 'The assessment of borderline cases' (1969), *Research at the Hampstead Clinic*.
10. A. Freud, 'Beyond the infantile neurosis', *Psychoanalytic Psychology of Normal Development (The Writings of Anna Freud, Vol. 8)*, London, Hogarth, 1982.
11. A. Freud, 'Problems of termination in child analysis', *Problems of Psychoanalytic Technique and Therapy*, p. 19.
12. e.g. A. Freud, 'Indications and contraindications for child analysis' (1968), ibid., p. 119.
13. A. Freud, 'Changes in psychoanalytic practice and experience' (1976), *Psychoanalytic Psychology of Normal Development*, p. 184.
14. A. Freud, 'Mental health in terms of internal harmony and disharmony', ibid., p. 118.
15. Quoted in E. Young-Bruehl, op. cit., p. 440.

PART V: MELANIE KLEIN
Chapter 1: Early mothering

1. A. Freud, 'Address to the Yale Law School', *Problems of Psychoanalytic Technique and Therapy (The Writings of Anna Freud, Vol. 7)*, London, Hogarth, 1971, p. 259.
2. Quoted in P. Grosskurth, *Melanie Klein*, London, Hodder & Stoughton, 1986, p. 14.
3. ibid., pp. 40–41.

Chapter 2: Analyst mother

1. M. Klein, 'The development of a child' (1921), *Love, Guilt and Reparation (The Writings of Melanie Klein, Vol. 1)*, 1975, p. 3, n. 1.
2. ibid., p. 9.
3. ibid., p. 44.
4. ibid., p. 28.
5. ibid., p. 33.
6. ibid., pp. 33–4.
7. ibid., p. 43.
8. M. Klein, 'The role of the school in the libidinal development of the child' (1923), ibid., p. 66.
9. M. Klein, 'Early analysis' (1923), *Love, Guilt and Reparation.*
10. M. Klein, 'A contribution to the psychogenesis of tics' (1925), ibid., p. 121.
11. M. Klein, 'Early analysis', *Love, Guilt and Reparation.*
12. The following account of Klein's technique is based on M. Klein, *The Psycho-Analysis of Children* (1932) *(The Writings of Melanie Klein, Vol. 2)*, London, Hogarth, 1975, and 'The psycho-analytic play technique' (1955), *Envy and Gratitude and Other Essays (The Writings of Melanie Klein, Vol. 3)*, London, Hogarth, 1975.
13. See e.g. N. Herman, *My Kleinian Home*, London, Quartet Books, 1985.

Chapter 3: Early object relations

1. H. Segal, 'Kleinian analysis', in J. Miller, *States of Mind*, London, BBC, 1983, p. 254.

2. Quoted in P. Grosskurth, *Melanie Klein*, London, Hodder & Stoughton, 1986, p. 106.
3. M. Klein, *The Psycho-Analysis of Children* (1932) (*The Writings of Melanie Klein, Vol. 2*), London, Hogarth, 1975, pp. 17, 23.
4. ibid., pp. 26–8.
5. M. Klein, 'The psychological principles of early analysis' (1926), *Love, Guilt and Reparation*. (*The Writings of Melanie Klein, Vol. 1*), London, Hogarth, 1975; and *The Psycho-Analysis of Children*.
6. M. Klein, *The Psycho-Analysis of Children*, p. 49, n. 2.
7. ibid., p. xi.
8. P. Meisel and W. Kendrick, *Bloomsbury/Freud: The Letters of James and Alix Strachey 1924–1925*, London, Chatto & Windus, 1986, p. 180.
9. ibid., pp. 193, 194.
10. ibid., p. 279.
11. Autobiography, Melanie Klein Archive, Wellcome Institute for the History of Medicine, London.
12. M. Klein, 'Symposium on child-analysis' (1927), *Love, Guilt and Reparation*.

Chapter 4: Sex, art and reparation

1. M. Klein, 'Early stages of the Oedipus complex' (1928), *Love, Guilt and Reparation (The Writings of Melanie Klein, Vol. 1)*, London, Hogarth, 1975.
2. M. Klein, 'Infantile anxiety situations reflected in a work of art and in the creative impulse' (1929), ibid., p. 210.
3. See e.g. A. D. Stokes, *Painting and the Inner World*, London, Tavistock, 1963; P. Fuller, *Images of God*, London, Chatto & Windus, 1985; C. F. Alford, *Melanie Klein and Critical Social Theory*, New Haven, Yale University Press, 1989; H. Segal, *The Work of Hanna Segal*, New York, Jason Aronson, 1981.
4. M. Klein, *The Psycho-Analysis of Children* (1932) (*The Writings of Melanie Klein, Vol. 2*), London, Hogarth, 1975.
5. Klein's account of envy in mother–daughter relations has in turn been taken up in recent feminist-inspired discussions of childbirth. See e.g. D. Birksted-Breen, 'The experience of having a baby', *Free*

Associations, 4 (1986), pp. 22–35; J. Sayers, 'Childbirth: Patriarchal and maternal influences', *Journal of Reproductive and Infant Psychology*, 7 (1989), pp. 15–24.

6. Quoted in P. Grosskurth, *Melanie Klein*, London, Hodder & Stoughton, 1986 p. 195.

Chapter 5: Depression and loss

1. M. Klein, 'A contribution to the psychogenesis of manic-depressive states' (1935), *Love, Guilt and Reparation (The Writings of Melanie Klein, Vol. 1)*, London, Hogarth, 1975, p. 271.
2. Quoted in P. Grosskurth, *Melanie Klein*, London, Hodder & Stoughton, 1986, p. 242.
3. M. Klein, 'Mourning and its relation to manic-depressive states' (1940), *Love, Guilt and Reparation*, p. 368.

Chapter 6: War

1. Quoted in P. Grosskurth, *Melanie Klein*, London, Hodder & Stoughton, 1986, p. 237.
2. E. Glover, *The Investigation of the Technique of Psycho-Analysis*, London, Baillière, Tindall & Cox, 1940, p. 139.
3. J. Padel, 'No man's formula', *Bulletin of the European Psychoanalytic Federation*, 8 (1977), p. 13.
4. M. Klein, *Narrative of a Child Analysis* (1961) *(The Writings of Melanie Klein, Vol. 4)*, London, Hogarth, 1975, p. 441.
5. M. Klein, 'The Oedipus complex in the light of early anxieties' (1945), *Love, Guilt and Reparation (The Writings of Melanie Klein, Vol. 1)*, London, Hogarth, 1975.
6. See e.g. J. Laplanche and J.-B. Pontalis, 'Fantasy and the origins of sexuality', *International Journal of Psycho-Analysis*, 49 (1968), pp. 1–18, and J. Mitchell, *The Selected Melanie Klein*, Harmondsworth, Penguin, 1986.
7. M. Klein, 'The emotional life and ego-development of the infant with special reference to the depressive position', British Psycho-Analytical Society, 1 March 1944, Melanie Klein Archive.
8. Quoted in P. Grosskurth, op. cit., pp. 343, 349.
9. See e.g. E. Jaques, 'Social systems as a defence against persecutory and depressive anxiety', in M. Klein, *New Directions in Psycho-*

Analysis, London, Hogarth (with P. Heimann and R. Money-Kyrle); I. Menzies, *The Dynamics of the Social*, 2 vols., London, Free Association Books, 1989.

Chapter 7: Schizoid mechanisms

1. e.g. M. Klein, *Love, Hate and Reparation*, London, Hogarth (with J. Rivière), 1937.
2. M. Klein, 'The importance of symbol-formation in the development of the ego' (1930), *Love, Guilt and Reparation (The Writings of Melanie Klein, Vol. 1)*, London, Hogarth, 1975, p. 227.
3. M. Klein, 'On the theory of anxiety and guilt' (1948), *Envy and Gratitude and Other Essays (The Writings of Melanie Klein, Vol. 3)*, London, Hogarth, 1975. See also M. Klein, 'The emotional life and ego-development of the infant with special reference to the depressive position', British Psycho-Analytical Society, 1 March 1944, Melanie Klein Archive.
4. M. Klein, 'On observing the behaviour of young infants' (1952), *Envy and Gratitude*. For recent Klein-based accounts of infant observation see e.g. L. Miller, M. and M. Rustin and J. Shuttleworth, *Closely Observed Infants*, London, Duckworth, 1989.
5. M. Klein, 'Notes on some schizoid mechanisms' (1946), *Envy and Gratitude*, p. 8.
6. M. Klein, 'A note on depression in the schizophrenic' (1960), ibid.
7. See e.g. J. Lacan, *Écrits*, London, Tavistock, 1977, and S. Mitchell and J. Rose, 'Feminine sexuality', *m/f*, 8 (1983), pp. 3–16. For an opposite view see e.g. H. Segal, *The World of Hanna Segal*, New York, Jason Aronson, 1981.
8. M. Klein, 'On the criteria for the termination of a psycho-analysis' (1950), *Envy and Gratitude*.
9. W. R. Bion, 'Group dynamics', in M. Klein, *New Directions in Psycho-Analysis*, London, Hogarth, 1955 (with P. Heimann and R. Money-Kyrle), and, for a more recent account, see e.g. E. G. Debbane, F. L. de Carufel, J. P. Bienvenu and W. E. Piper, 'Structures in interpretations', *Journal of Group Psychotherapy*, 36 (1986), pp. 517–32.
10. E. Bott Spillius, 'Some developments from the work of Melanie Klein', *International Journal of Psycho-Analysis*, 64 (1983), pp. 321–2.

11. M. Klein, 'On identification' (1955), *Envy and Gratitude.*

Chapter 8: Envy and gratitude

1. See e.g. M. Klein, 'Some theoretical conclusions regarding the emotional life of the infant' (1952), *Envy and Gratitude and Other Essays (The Writings of Melanie Klein, Vol. 3)*, London, Hogarth, 1975.
2. Unless otherwise indicated, this and other examples in this section come from M. Klein, *Envy and Gratitude.*
3. M. Klein, 'Our adult world and its roots in infancy' (1959), *Envy and Gratitude.*
4. R. D. Laing and John Bowlby respectively, quoted by P. Grosskurth, *Melanie Klein*, London, Hodder & Stoughton, 1986, pp. 446, 405.
5. R. Wollheim, 'Melanie Klein', *The Spectator*, 30 September 1960, p. 469.
6. M. Klein, 'On the sense of loneliness' (1963), *Envy and Gratitude.*
7. T. Main, 'Melanie Klein', *British Journal of Medical Psychology*, 34 (1961), pp. 163–6.
8. Quoted in P. Grosskurth, op. cit., p. 437, and personal communication.
9. M. Klein, 'Some reflections on *The Oresteia*' (1963), *Envy and Gratitude.*
10. See e.g. J. Steiner, 'Turning a blind eye', *International Review of Psycho-Analysis*, 12 (1985), pp. 161–72.

PART VI: CONCLUSION

1. See e.g. A. Freud, 'A study guide to Freud's writings' (1982), *Psychoanalytic Psychology of Normal Development (The Writings of Anna Freud, Vol. 8)*, London, Hogarth, 1982. But see also E. Young-Bruehl, 'Anna Freud for feminists', in *Mind and the Body*, London, Routledge, 1989.
2. For a feminist discussion of this point, see J. Benjamin, 'The Oedipal riddle', in J. P. Diggins and M. E. Kahn, *The Problem of Authority in America*, Philadelphia, Temple University Press, 1981.

3. Katherine Whitehorn, quoted by P. Grosskurth, *Melanie Klein*, London, Hodder & Stoughton, 1986, p. 233.
4. See e.g. S. Palazzoli, *Self-Starvation*, London, Human Context Books, 1974; S. Ernst, 'Can a daughter be a woman?', in S. Ernst and M. Maguire, *Living with the Sphinx*, London, Women's Press, 1987.

Bibliography

Abraham, K., 'Manifestations of the female castration complex' (1920), in *Selected Papers*, London, Hogarth, 1968.

Balint, M., *The Basic Fault*, London, Tavistock, 1968.

Baruch, E. H., and Serrano, L. J., *Women Analyze Women*, New York, New York University Press, 1988.

Bergmann, T., *Children in the Hospital*, New York, International Universities Press, 1965.

Bernheimer, C., and Kahane, C., *In Dora's Case*, London, Virago, 1985.

Bertin, C., *Marie Bonaparte*, New York, Harcourt Brace Jovanovich, 1982.

Bion, W. R., *Seven Servants*, New York, Jason Aronson, 1977.

Blos, P., *On Adolescence*, New York, Free Press, 1962.

Bott Spillius, E., *Melanie Klein Today*, 2 vols., London, Routledge, 1988.

Bowlby, J., *Maternal Care and Mental Health*, Geneva, WHO, 1951.

Bowlby, J., *A Secure Base*, London, Routledge, 1989.

Burlingham, M. J., *The Last Tiffany*, New York, Atheneum, 1989.

Chaplin, J., *Feminist Counselling in Action*, London, Sage, 1989.

Chasseguet-Smirgel, J., *Female Sexuality* (1964), London, Virago, 1981.

Chasseguet-Smirgel, J., 'Loss of reality in perversions', *Journal of the American Psychoanalytic Association*, 29, (1981), pp. 511–34.

Chernin, K., *The Hungry Self*, London, Virago, 1985.

Chodorow, N., *The Reproduction of Mothering*, Berkeley, University of California Press, 1978.

Clare, G., *Last Waltz in Vienna*, London, Macmillan, 1980.

Coles, R., 'Karen Horney's flight from orthodoxy', in J. Strouse, *Women and Analysis*, New York, Dell, 1974.

Dana, M., 'Boundaries: One way mirror to the self', in M. Lawrence, *Fed Up and Hungry*, London, Women's Press, 1987.

De Beauvoir, S., *The Second Sex* (1949), Harmondsworth, Penguin, 1972.

Deutsch, H., Zür *Psychoanalyse der weiblichen Sexualfunktionen*, Vienna, Internationaler psychoanalytischer Verlag, 1925.

Deutsch, H., *Psychoanalysis of the Neuroses* (1930), in H. Deutsch, *Neuroses and Character Types*, New York, International Universities Press, 1965.

Deutsch, H., *The Psychology of Women, Vol. 1: Girlhood*, New York, Grune & Stratton, 1944.

Deutsch, H., *The Psychology of Women, Vol. 2: Motherhood*, New York, Grune & Stratton, 1945.

Deutsch, H., *Neuroses and Character Types*, New York, International Universities Press, 1965.

Deutsch, H., *Selected Problems of Adolescence*, New York, International Universities Press, 1967.

Deutsch, H., *A Psychoanalytic Study of the Myth of Dionysus and Apollo*, New York, International Universities Press, 1969.

Deutsch, H., *Confrontations with Myself*, New York, Norton, 1973.

Dyer, R., *Her Father's Daughter: The Work of Anna Freud*, New York, Jason Aronson, 1983.

Eichenbaum, L., and Orbach, S., 'Separation and intimacy', in S. Ernst and M. Maguire, *Living with the Sphinx*, London, Women's Press, 1987.

Erikson, E., *Identity: Youth and Crisis*, New York, Norton, 1968.

Ernst, S., 'Can a daughter be a woman?' in S. Ernst and M. Maguire, *Living with the Sphinx*, London, Women's Press, 1987.

Ettinger, E., *Rosa Luxemburg*, London, Harrap, 1987.

Fairbairn, W. R. D., *Psychoanalytic Studies of the Personality*, London, Tavistock, 1952.

Ferenczi, S., 'A little chanticleer' (1913), in *Contributions to Psycho-Analysis*, London, Maresfield Reprints, 1954.

Freud, A., *Introduction to the Technique of Child Analysis* (1927), in A. Freud *Introduction to Psychoanalysis (The Writings of Anna Freud, Vol. I)*, London, Hogarth, 1974.

Freud, A., *The Writing of Anna Freud*, Vols. 1–8, London, Hogarth:

Vol. 1: *The Introduction to Psychoanalysis* (1927), 1974.

Vol. 2: *The Ego and the Mechanisms of Defence*, 1936.

Vol. 3: *Infants Without Families* (1944), 1968.

Vol. 4: *Indications for Child Analysis and Other Essays* (1945–56), 1968.

Vol. 5: *Research at the Hampstead Child Therapy Clinic and Other Papers* (1956–65), 1969.
Vol. 6: *Normality and Pathology in Childhood*, 1965.
Vol. 7: *Problems of Psychoanalytic Technique and Therapy* (1966–70), 1971.
Vol. 8: *Psychoanalytic Psychology of Normal Development* (1970–80), 1982.

Freud, A., *Beyond the Best Interests of the Child*, New York, Macmillan (with J. Goldstein and A. Solnit), 1973.

Freud, A., *Before the Best Interests of the Child*, New York, Macmillan (with J. Goldstein and R. Solnit), 1979.

Freud, S., *The Origins of Psycho-Analysis*, New York, Basic Books, 1954.

Freud, S., *The Standard Edition of the Complete Psychological Works*, 24 vols., London, Hogarth, 1966.

Freud, Sophie, *My Three Mothers and Other Passions*, New York, New York University Press, 1988.

Fromm, E., *The Fear of Freedom*, London, Routledge, 1941.

Gay, P., *Freud: A Life for Our Time*, New York, Norton, 1988.

Gifford, S., 'Tribute to Helene Deutsch', *American Imago*, 40 (1) 1983, pp. 3–10.

Grosskurth, P., *Melanie Klein*, London, Hodder & Stoughton, 1986.

Guiles, F. L., *Norma Jean: The Life and Death of Marilyn Monroe*, London, Collins, 1984.

Guntrip, H., 'My experience of analysis with Fairbairn and Winnicott', *International Review of Psycho-Analysis*, 2 (1975), pp. 145–56.

Heimann, P., 'On counter-transference', *International Journal of Psycho-Analysis*, 31 (1950), pp. 81–4.

Hinshelwood, R., *A Dictionary of Kleinian Thought*, London, Free Association Books, 1989.

Horney, K., *The Neurotic Personality of Our Time*, New York, Norton, 1937.

Horney, K., *New Ways in Psychoanalysis*, New York, Norton, 1939.

Horney, K., *Self-Analysis*, New York, Norton, 1942.

Horney, K., *Our Inner Conflicts*, New York, Norton, 1945.

Horney, K., *Neurosis and Human Growth*, New York, Norton, 1950.

Horney, K., *Feminine Psychology*, New York, Norton, 1967.

Horney, K., *The Adolescent Diaries of Karen Horney*, New York, Basic Books, 1980.

Hug-Hellmuth, H., *A Young Girl's Diary*, (1919) (ed. D. Gunn and P. Guyomard), London, Unwin Hyman, 1990.

Irigaray, L., *This Sex Which Is Not One* (1977), Ithaca, Cornell University Press, 1985.
Jones, E., *Papers on Psychoanalysis*, Boston, Beacon Press, 1927.
Kardiner, A., *My Analysis with Freud*, New York, Norton, 1977.
Keller, E. F., 'Feminism and science', *Signs*, 7(3) (1983), pp. 589–602.
Khan, M., 'Clinical aspects of the schizoid personality', *International Journal of Psycho-Analysis*, 41 (1960), pp. 430–37.
Khan, M., 'Cumulative trauma' (1963), in G. Kohon, *The British School of Psychoanalysis*, London, Free Association Books, 1986.
Klein, M., *The Writings of Melanie Klein*, Vols. 1–4, London, Hogarth, 1975:
Vol. 1: *Love, Guilt and Reparation* (1921–45).
Vol. 2: *The Psycho-Analysis of Children* (1932).
Vol. 3: *Envy and Gratitude and Other Essays* (1946–63).
Vol. 4: *Narrative of a Child Analysis* (1961).
Klein, M., *Love, Hate and Reparation*, London, Hogarth (with J. Rivière), 1937.
Klein, M., *Developments in Psycho-Analysis* (with P. Heimann, S. Isaacs, and J. Rivière), 1952.
Klein, M., *New Directions in Psycho-Analysis*, London, Hogarth (with P. Heimann and R. Money-Kyrle), 1955.
Kohut, H., *The Restoration of the Self*, New York, International Universities Press, 1977.
Lacan, J., *Écrits*, London, Tavistock, 1977.
Lampl-de Groot, J., 'The evolution of the Oedipus complex in women' (1927), in R. Fliess, *The Psychoanalytic Reader*, London, Hogarth, 1950.
Laplanche, J., and Pontalis, J.-B., *The Language of Psycho-Analysis*, London, Hogarth, 1973.
Lasch, C., *The Minimal Self*, London, Pan, 1984.
Maeder, T., *Children of Psychiatrists and Other Psychotherapists*, New York, Harper & Row, 1989.
Maguire, M., 'Casting the evil eye', in S. Ernst and M. Maguire, *Living with the Sphinx*, London, Women's Press, 1987.
Mahler, M., Pine, E., and Bergman, A., *The Psychological Birth of the Human Infant*, New York, Basic Books, 1975.
Marcuse, H., *Eros and Civilization*, Boston, Beacon Press, 1955.
Meisel, P., and Kendrick, W., *Bloomsbury/Freud: The Letters of James and Alix Strachey 1924–1925*, London, Chatto & Windus, 1986.
Miller, A., *For Your Own Good* (1980), London, Virago, 1987.
Miller, A., *Thou Shalt Not Be Aware* (1981), London, Pluto Press, 1985.

Milner, M., *An Experiment in Leisure* (1937), London, Virago, 1986.
Milner, M., *The Hands of the Living God* (1969), London, Virago, 1988.
Milner, M., *Eternity's Sunrise*, London, Virago, 1987.
Mitchell, J., *Psychoanalysis and Feminism*, Harmondsworth, Penguin, 1974.
Mitchell, J., *Women: The Longest Revolution*, London, Virago, 1984.
Mitchell, J., *The Selected Melanie Klein*, Harmondsworth, Penguin, 1986.
Olivier, C., *Jocasta's Children*, London, Routledge, 1989.
Peters, U. H., *Anna Freud*, London, Weidenfeld & Nicolson, 1985.
Phillips, A., *Winnicott*, London, Fontana, 1988.
Quinn, S., *A Mind of Her Own: The Life of Karen Horney*, New York, Summit Books, 1987.
Reich, W., *The Mass Psychology of Fascism* (1933), New York, Farrar Straus & Giroux, 1970.
Rich, A., *Of Woman Born*, New York, Bantam, 1976.
Roazen, P., *Helene Deutsch*, New York, Meridian, 1985.
Robertson, J. and J., *Separation and the Very Young*, London, Free Association Books, 1990.
Rosenfeld, H., *Psychotic States*, London, Hogarth, 1965.
Rubins, J. L., *Karen Horney*, London, Weidenfeld & Nicolson, 1987.
Rutter, M., *Maternal Deprivation Reassessed*, Harmondsworth, Penguin, 1981.
Sandler, J., *The Mechanisms of Defence*, New York, International Universities Press (with A. Freud), 1985.
Sandler, J., Kennedy, H., and Tyson, R. L., *The Technique of Child Psychoanalysis: Discussions with Anna Freud*, London, Hogarth, 1980.
Schmideberg, M., 'A contribution to the history of the psycho-analytic movement in Britain', *British Journal of Psychiatry*, 118, (1971), pp. 61–8.
Segal, H., *Introduction to the Work of Melanie Klein*, London, Hogarth, 1973.
Segal, H., *Klein*, Glasgow, Fontana, 1979.
Segal, H., *The Work of Hanna Segal*, New York, Jason Aronson, 1981.
Showalter, E., *The Female Malady*, London, Virago, 1987.
Steedman, C., *Landscape for a Good Woman*, London, Virago, 1986.
Thorburn, J., Murdoch, A., and O'Brien, A., *Permanence in Child Care*, Oxford, Blackwell, 1986.

Thompson, N., 'Early women psychoanalysts', *International Review of Psycho-Analysis*, 14, (1987), pp. 391–407.

Thompson, N., 'Helene Deutsch', *Psychoanalytic Quarterly*, 56(2) (1987), pp. 317–53.

Webster, B. S., 'Helene Deutsch', *Signs*, 10(3) (1985), pp. 553–71.

Westkott, M., *The Feminist Legacy of Karen Horney*, New Haven, Yale University Press, 1986.

Winnicott, D. W., *Collected Papers*, London, Tavistock, 1958.

Winnicott, D. W., *Playing and Reality* (1971), Harmondsworth, Penguin, 1974.

Winnicott, D. W., *The Maturational Processes and the Facilitating Environment*, London, Hogarth, 1972.

Wydenbruck, N., *My Two Worlds*, London, Longmans, Green & Co., 1956.

Young-Bruehl, E., *Anna Freud*, New York, Summit Books, 1988.

Zweig, S., *The World of Yesterday*, London, Cassell, 1943.

Index